Grand Cru

Grand Cru

A NOVEL

Sandra Lee Stuart

A Lyle Stuart Book
Published by Carol Communications

A Lyle Stuart Book
Published by Carol Communications

Editorial Offices
600 Madison Avenue
New York, NY 10022

Sales & Distribution Offices
120 Enterprise Avenue
Secaucus, NJ 07094

In Canada: Musson Book Company
A division of General Publishing Co. Limited
Don Mills, Ontario

Manufactured in the United States of America

Library of Congress Cataloging-in-Publication Data

Stuart, Sandra Lee.
    Grand cru : a novel / Sandra Lee Stuart.
      p.   cm.
    ISBN 0-8184-0431-0 : $18.95
    I. Title.
  PS3569.T825G74   1989
  813'.54--dc 19   89-30315
                                            CIP

Grand Cru

Prologue

Wraiths of mist swirled up from the water's dark surface, embraced one another, and moved to shore.

The ground there hadn't lost the warmth from yesterday's sun, the heat being husbanded by tiny pebbles laid down thousands of years before when ice sheets gouged their way across the earth. The warmth fought the mist, trying to push it back to the river. Still the tendrils crawled forward, wrapping whatever they met in a filmy shroud. The mist covered the boat's landing, slowly enveloped fences, the footbridge, and veiled vegetation.

Suddenly a melancholy note rang out, long and high, immediately followed by others, strung in a cadence of supplication. The first voice was soon joined by new ones, coming from somewhere above the mist on the hill.

As the day became lighter, one could see faint outlines of the singers as they plodded slowly downward. There were two lines of men, women, and children being led by a priest, heavy-set with robes sent flowing as his arms waved from side to side in mechanical blessing.

He chanted in a language foreign to his flock, making it all the more sacred by its incomprehensibility. It was enough that they knew they were asking for bountiful fields and good crops. They prayed to their god as men and women of the soil throughout the ages had prayed. Like their forebears they believed their appeal, if heartfelt and strong, said with appropriate fervor, would reach the deity and cause him, her, or it to smile on and favor them.

The mist muffled their song so that it barely carried to the squat, oddly shaped man standing above them on the hill. It didn't matter because he wasn't listening. He didn't have time. All the praying in the world wouldn't produce a fine harvest if he didn't do his job well, and at that moment he was worried.

i

Jacques Mazet stared at the fields around him as if the mist was not there. There was no need to actually see the straight rows of vines with his eyes. He knew where each was, he knew each gnarl and curl of the branches, when they had been planted, the state of their health, how much fruit each had borne the year before and the year before that and as long back as he could remember, which was when he was five years old and his father, Gaston Mazet, had taken him out for his first harvest.

Even then Jacques, a tiny, little gnome with an overly large head, long arms, and short legs, had worked diligently and tirelessly. His mother had cried the first night he returned from the fields. His small hands had been bloodied from the vines. After bathing them in warm water and tenderly wrapping them in soft cloth, she had spoon-fed Jacques his dinner. Later, after she had tucked him in, Jacques heard her speaking angrily to his father, berating him for putting his son to work so young. The boy had never heard his mother speak in such a manner to his father before. Nonetheless, the next morning, Gaston Mazet had led Jacques to the fields and the boy was glad.

When he was older, the other boys, jealous that Jacques could fill as many panniers as most men, had teased and taunted him. Of course he could pick so much, they had said, because he didn't have to bend down as far as a normal person. Those little stumps he called legs kept him close to the ground, and his monkey arms hung down as far as the vines.

Those boys, now men, no longer taunted Mazet, for the gnome had become maître de chai, the master of the cellar and field, and his former tormenters were now obliged to report to him for work and orders. Most would admit that Mazet deserved his position. He worked harder and knew more than anyone, except, perhaps, the count's son. That was to be expected, for they had both learned from Gaston Mazet and he from his father and he from his. The Mazet men were as much of these fields and land as the owners, the Saint-Savins, themselves.

Today Jacques Mazet was worried. Grapes must be picked at the exact right moment. A decision had to be made. Wait too long and it was disaster. Pick too early and it was worse. The fruit had not reached the precise sweetness when it would get no sweeter and perfection was attained. The exact right moment. And it hadn't come yet. Mazet was sure of that.

He bent to pluck a grape from its vine. Rolling it between his fingers, he felt its texture, gauged its weight, and then bit gently through its skin. Juice gushed into his mouth.

Neighboring maîtres had all started harvesting, and despite himself he was worried. Perhaps this year he had made a mistake and waited too long. No, he couldn't be wrong. The sweetness on his tongue told him that. It also told him that one or two more days of coaxing sun would be needed to draw the grapes to their peak. He hoped that the count's son, the young Saint-Savin, would return in time to confirm his decision. As different as the two were in appearance, family, education, they were one in the fields and cellars. It was good when the young Saint-Savin was there working with Mazet. But if he didn't return in time, Mazet would make the decision himself, and the count, as always, would concur.

In the distance the last note of the chant died softly and forlornly, and the lines broke up. The women, herding their broods of children, trudged back to their tiny huts, to begin the cooking, cleaning, and the rest of the day's drudgery. The men headed downhill, to the inn near the dock. There they would have their customary morning glass of wine.

The sun was coming up. Reluctantly and sullenly the mist drew back to the river. Day had dawned.

Book One

Chapter One

September, 1851

Persistent beams of sun pushed through closed shutters, dappling the long, narrow room. The paunchy, balding man behind the bar, Jean-Gabriel Bellay, would have preferred to open the slats and let in a rush of cheering light, but he could sense that the men seated around the scarred wooden tables didn't want to be reminded that the day was getting on and they were doing nothing.

Their morning glass of wine had become two, three, and, for some, more. Hours earlier, wives had thrown away the breakfasts they had hurried back up the hill to prepare. Now the women were wondering if there was any point bothering with lunch.

Seldom were there more than one or two people in the bar at late morning. Men usually came in before work for a glass of rough, bracing red wine, rouge, as it was called for short. Some dropped in just before lunch for another glass. After the evening meal was the busiest time for Bellay. Then the bar was filled with men drinking, playing cards, and being as convivial as their work-exhausted bodies allowed.

Today the rhythm was off. Tension sapped the men. They sought the shadows.

One of the men muttered something and low self-conscious laughter followed. Bellay automatically reached for an uncorked bottle.

"Jean-Gabriel, if you please, a little more wine."

"Of course, Pierre. Here. Pour yourself."

It had been like this all morning. The men were uneasy with their indolence, too embarrassed to acknowledge it by asking straight out for more. Each request had to be preceded by a small joke, along the lines of making room in the cellar for what was to come—once they started working.

Who can blame them for being troubled? thought Bellay, squinting through the gloom at the hunched and huddled outlines. They work all year long for this moment and the damned moment does not come. I wish Jacques Mazet would ring the bell and get on with it. This waiting would drive anyone crazy.

Of course, as far as Bellay was concerned, they were all a little crazy to begin with. He was the only one in the room who hadn't been born within a two-mile radius of where they were sitting. Everyone else had spent their entire life here, all doing the same things at the same time. Wanting the same things and getting the same things, a life of predetermined aspirations and predestined paths.

They were Bordelaise. More precisely, they were Medocain. From their few miles and a few miles more running north and south in a narrow strip along the Gironde estuary came the finest wine in the world. No one could tell them differently and few would try. These Bordelaise were winemen. There was much pride to being one. There were also many fears. Fear of hail, fear of wind, fear of frost and heat, of too much rain in May and not enough sun in August, fear of picking too soon or not soon enough, fear of pest, fear of mildew, fear of misjudgment in blending or in fermenting. And then there was fear that the grape would mysteriously turn to vinegar or that there wouldn't be enough tannin or there would be too much.

Worry followed worry throughout the year until finally the maître de chai ordered the château's bell rung, the bell that waited in the tower next to the château until it was time to signal the events of great magnitude, births, marriages, deaths, and harvests. When its commanding, powerful notes rang out, every able-bodied man, most of the women, and many of the children fanned out through the fields to take the grapes from their vines. It needed to be done quickly and relentlessly in order to beat the autumn rains, which could come at any time and destroy the crop. With harvesting done, the grapes pressed and their juices fermenting in the enormous oak vats, the cycle began anew and with it came another year of fears.

Bellay always listened carefully when the men spoke of their work, yet he could never understand their dedication. If he questioned them, he invariably got the same response.

"How can you expect to understand?" he would be asked. "You're Parisian. You know crowded streets and carriages and people shoving each other to get a cafe table. We're speaking of land and grape and wine. You have to be born to them to understand."

Bellay supposed they were right. It would never make sense to him. Not one of them owned so much as a clod of earth himself. Nor were they likely to ever taste the best of what they sweated so hard to produce. They were little more than hired hands, living at the beck and whim of the owners of the vineyard, the Saint-Savins of du Clocher.

Still it didn't matter to the men in the bar that they owned nothing. Du Clocher made them something and gave them their niche in a society that pigeon-holed everyone.

At least, thought Bellay, what I work for is mine.

True, his Bar du Port du Clocher wasn't much if one compared it to the elegant hotel in Paris where he had worked for many years. Bellay's establishment had a bar on the first floor which could hold about twenty customers with a bit of squeezing. There was a cramped kitchen, wedged under a staircase where Bellay's servant girl cleaned and cooked. Upstairs were four bedrooms, one of which Bellay used.

Bellay had worked many years at that Parisian hotel, starting as a pot scrubber in the kitchen and ending up at the concierge's desk where gratuities had been generous. He had saved all that was possible, foregoing marriage because of the expense.

When a distant relative died, the widow offered to sell Jean-Gabriel the bar in the Medoc at a reasonable price. The businessman in him said, "Take it," despite it meaning he would be stuck out in the country far from his exciting Paris. Still, what was excitement compared to a man being his own master? Now if he wanted a little pleasure, he could choose his own time to pat the nicely rounded rear end of his servant girl and herd her up to his accommodating bed. And being the master, it was amazing what that girl could be ordered to do and would not refuse.

But things were too busy at the moment in his fine establishment for him to be distracting himself with thoughts of getting under the girl's skirt. It was indeed a fine establishment, without question, and it was Bellay who made it so. Clean with fair prices, good food, better wine, and a judicious generosity when it came to granting credit. His regulars were for the most part local vineyard workers who lived in the small cottages provided them and those who lived in the nearby village of St. Julien, down the main road from du Clocher.

His other customers were usually connected with the wine business in one way or another. They came from Bordeaux city, twenty-five miles down the Gironde, near where the Dordogne and Garonne rivers met. Many came by boat and landed at the stone pier jutting into the water a hundred yards from the inn.

These were not the important wine brokers, of course. The important gentlemen were entertained at the grand châteaux. Bellay hosted the humbler merchants, who scoured the district for what they could find. Employees of the major wine merchants who were sent to check on the firms' investments also stayed at his hotel. These employees did their investigating and then returned to the vast warehouse caves on the Quai de Chartons in Bordeaux with their findings. There were enough of these guests to insure Bellay a comfortable living.

There were certainly no complaints about his bar or his inn. Even some from the château itself came down the hill. Granted, the count Edouard Saint-Savin had never been inside, but from what Bellay had heard, the count wouldn't deign to sip from anything less than the finest Baccarat crystal. His son, Guy, on the other hand, came often, whenever he was home from the capital. And if he had any friends with him, he brought them along. Once he had even brought his younger sister, Solange. What a beautiful woman that one would be! For a second, Bellay allowed himself the pleasure of wondering what it would be like to have something as lovely as that in his bed instead of the little cow who was outside scrubbing chamberpots.

He dismissed the thought out of loyalty to Guy, with whom he had spent many hours talking of Paris, a pastime which made the innkeeper a little less lonely for his native city. All of which reminded Bellay of something he had been meaning to ask all morning. "Is the young master expected for the harvest? Is that why Mazet is holding up the picking?"

It took quite a while for the raucous laughter to subside. Finally one of the men who lived in a château cottage sputtered, "Dear god, Jean-Gabriel, will you never learn anything about wine? Jacques

Mazet wouldn't hold up the harvest for the pope's blessing if the grapes were ready to be picked."

"All right, then, so he's not waiting for Guy. Answer my other question. Is Guy expected? Will he be coming home? Wouldn't this be the first time he's missed a harvest?"

That was true and the realization almost sobered the men. What would a harvest be without the young master working with them? He had started picking when he was a boy. Everyone considered him good luck. No other son of a château owner in Bordeaux had ever been known to do such a thing. And even when the crop wasn't good, it was believed that without their talisman, the catastrophe would have been worse.

A little unpleasant man, Paul Ricard, piped up, "Marie from the château told my wife she heard Count Edouard reading a letter to Solange from Guy the other day."

Ricard, usually so pointedly ignored, relished the attention that was immediately focused on him and continued with great pomposity. "Well, Marie says that the young master says right now business in the National Assembly is very complicated. You know, with Louis-Napoleon wanting to be president of the republic for a second term. In my opinion, he's not half the man his uncle, Napoleon Bonaparte, was, but who could be? There was a real Frenchman, all right."

His audience showed with their surly "Be on with it, fool" and similar comments that they had little interest in Ricard's opinion on politics, so he returned to his subject.

"Well, according to Master Guy, strange things are happening right now. And he might have to stay in Paris to write a speech for that deputy he works for. I always say that it's extremely important work for one so young as Master Guy, him only twenty-two and all. To be an aide, that's very important, specially when it's to such an important member of the Assembly."

"Ricard," someone said menacingly, "we all know what Guy does and who he does it for, so get on with the letter."

Ricard shot a reproachful look at the disrespectful interrupter before continuing. "As I was saying, the young master may have important, very important matters to ... to ... now what was that word he used? ... 'attend' to and may not be coming home. His deputy doesn't know. The count doesn't know. And *I* don't know."

Ricard had stood up from his chair during the middle of his speech and now sat down, for once quite pleased with his drab, droning wife for having such a well-placed and loose-tongued confidante as Marie.

If Ricard had expected some kind of appreciation for imparting this morsel of information, he didn't get it.

"Ricard, you wouldn't know your prick from your big toe," was the closest he got to thanks.

It was well past noon and time for the men to go home to lunch and snarl at their wives. They would wait for the château bell there. They filed out. Ricard, seeing he would get no further mileage from his news, left as well.

Only one customer remained. That wasn't surprising, for on any given day he could be found in the same chair in the same dark corner. Even when Bellay threw open the shutters and the sunshine eagerly invaded the room, the man was still in shadow.

He hadn't said a word all morning. Which wasn't unusual either. He rarely talked to the other workers and Bellay doubted he had a single friend.

What a sour bastard he is, the innkeeper thought. It would be nice to toss him out on his ugly face. But his money is as good as anyone's and he certainly spends it here.

Bellay was about to ask if lunch should be served when the man finally spoke. "They're all assholes, you know, trusting that piece of manure, Jacques. Jacques shouldn't have been made maître. It should have been me. I was the oldest. But no, my old fart of a father makes that toad Jacques the maître. Well, they'll all get what they deserve now. That dwarf has waited too long this time. The grapes'll be too ripe this time, and he'll end up with fermented piss. It'll serve them all right."

Bellay was accustomed to such diatribes from Claude Mazet, and he paid little attention to them. There was one point, however, with which he agreed. Traditionally the position of maître did go to the eldest. Gaston Mazet, acting wisely from what Bellay understood, had ignored tradition and given the job to Jacques, who was supposed to have a real gift, an inner sense of what was right in the vineyard and in the cellar where juice became wine. Jacques also had an even hand with the workers and was liked and respected. Claude, on the other hand, was a bully and would have relished smothering his subordinates with his venom. There were no two ways about it.

As it was, Claude spent most of his time in the bar—he seldom worked and sullenly accepted money from his mother, who, of course, received it for Jacques now that Gaston was dead. Bellay heard that, once in a while, Claude wasn't above intimidating some poor girl into spreading her legs for him by threatening to have her family thrown off the vineyard. Bellay had come across his servant girl trying to clean up one of Mazet's "conquests." The poor little thing, a mess of torn clothes, bruises, and blood, hadn't been more than thirteen. She was terrified that Mazet would want her again.

Bellay glanced at his customer with disgust. Innkeeping had some disadvantages. He quickly averted his face to the window so Mazet wouldn't notice his expression. Bellay enjoyed his view of the water and the long sliver of island halfway between the shores. The big sailing ships that came up from Bordeaux city on their way to the Atlantic had to use great care to steer around that island where the current was notoriously treacherous. Bellay loved to watch the big ships as they maneuvered up the estuary, their august and proud prows beating back the water.

Such a beauty could be seen on the Gironde just then. Bellay watched it as Mazet droned on. It took the innkeeper a while to realize the ship was dropping anchor. Ships that size didn't stop at the port du Clocher which was only, in truth, a small stone jetty. They were loaded in Bordeaux and tried to make open water as fast as possible.

"Mazet, will you look at that. One of the tall ships, here."

Mazet didn't share Bellay's excitement. "Probably some asshole captain who woke up from his nap thinking he was already in London."

"Really, Mazet, come look. Now they're putting a rowboat over the side. What does it mean?"

"Who cares. I want my lunch."

Reluctantly Bellay left the window to tell his girl to bring out the plates of steaming sausage, boiled potatoes, and tiny sweet carrots. While he was at it, he reached down her bodice, got a hold of a nipple, and rolled it between his fingers. It hardened immediately. He hoped there was no business that afternoon. He was ready for her.

Reluctantly he withdrew his hand and went out to the front steps to watch the rowboat pulling up to the lichen-covered pier. He could see two sailors and a passenger. The smaller of the sailors started to get out, but the passenger waved him off. With no seeming effort, the latter was out of the boat and on the pier.

The small sailor held up an elaborately embroidered satchel. The passenger didn't notice. He was transfixed by the graceful building on the hill above.

Bellay didn't need to see the man's face to know who it was. The concentrated gaze, the self-assured posture, the brown hair glinting copper in the sun.

"Guy. It's Guy. He's home in time."

Chapter Two

The young sailor—he liked to think of himself as a sailor although actually he was a lowly cabin boy—was getting impatient.

"Hey, mate," he called up from the rowboat and then quickly amended that to "Hey, sir," when the other sailor kicked him on the shin in reminder of the comportment lessons he'd received since signing on board.

"Please, sir, ain't you ever going to take your friggin' bag?"

The months of gray, tense Paris were being washed away from Guy by the soaring, sun-bleached majesty of du Clocher. Seen from the river, the château stretched with composure and authority toward clouds and sky. Its single-storied center was balanced by two towers at either end, its white stone punctuated by fourteen tall, multi-paned windows. Along its length a grand terrace ran, from which stone steps wended their way to a garden below, a garden both formal and comfortable, a verdant sanctum where a young woman might wish to accept an ardent proposal or a wicked proposition and where many had.

"Aw, c'mon, sir," the cabin boy yelled again, "I ain't going to get my duties done at this rate, and I'm sure to have the tar beaten out of me."

The boy's twang and surprising English idiom brought Guy's attention back to the pier. The boy's last phrase was new to Guy, still he had no trouble understanding it. He spoke English fluently and with no accent. His English nanny had seen to that.

"I am so sorry." Guy smiled with such warmth that the boy quite forgot his impending problems.

Guy addressed the other sailor. "Please give Captain Wethersby my thanks once again and remind him to visit du Clocher the next time he anchors in Bordeaux. With a little notice, I'll make a special trip from Paris to entertain him."

9

"Yes, sir, I'll be sure to tell him that."

Guy waved a quick farewell and was about to leave when he called out again to the older sailor. "There is one other thing. Please don't punish this fine lad because of my dawdling."

"Don't worry about that, sir. This little weasel don't need no help at all when it comes to getting into hot water. No, if he gets a whack from the cat-o'-nine-tails, it'll be all his own doing."

As the boat pulled away, the cabin boy whispered, "Ain't these Frenchies queer ones? I mean that fellow was nice and all. I could even understand what he was saying. But did you see the way he was looking at that house? Like it was a naked lady or something."

The older man paused from his rowing long enough to swat the boy's ears. "Now, you listen here," he said sternly. "That there was a gentleman, a real gentleman who's some kind of duke or count or least he will be when his pa croaks. And he's a friend, a very good friend, of the captain's. So if you don't want swimming lessons in the middle of the Atlantic, keep your jabbery little tongue from wagging so much. And one other thing, just what do you know about naked ladies, anyway?"

Even after the gentle slapping of oars on water faded, Guy stood on the dock delighting in the beauty of the château. Despite its regal, imposing lines, to him du Clocher was welcoming and warm. It was his home and he could imagine no other. Just then a cloud passed overhead and the château was suddenly cold and harsh. Guy shivered.

Then he laughed at himself. What was he, some kind of super-stitious peasant? He had no time for such nonsense. And it was time to stop his dawdling. There was much to be done, and he knew the first item was to present himself to his father. Good manners and proper respect dictated that.

Good manners and propriety were all-important to his father. They were not, however, to Guy. The fields and the chai took precedence over etiquette on any day and in any season.

Edouard was unable to understand this attitude. To him, it was highly improper to search out workers, even the maître. They should be summoned to him. Guy had no patience for such rules. If something needed to be done, he did it. If someone needed to be talked to, he sought them out. If a task or undertaking was worth doing, to Guy it was worth doing with commitment, enthusiasm, concentration, imagination, and passion.

Guy did nothing by half measure. Edouard had no concept of what a full measure was.

Guy shrugged. He would get to his father and his protocol when he had time.

Just then Jean-Gabriel Bellay came running from the inn. "Guy! Guy! Welcome home! Wait, don't say anything. Give me a chance to stop panting." Bellay clutched his chest in mock pain. "Now explain to me, how you managed to turn a sailing ship into your personal ferryboat."

Guy threw his arm across the shorter man's shoulder in easy camaraderie. "I hate to disappoint you," he said, "but it took very little effort. Do you remember that American sea captain I brought to the inn once?"

"The one who looked like a giant bear?"

"Yes, I guess that beard does make him look a bit like a bear. I happened upon him in Bordeaux city and mentioned I was in a hurry to get home. By chance he was ready to sail and said something like 'It would be an honor to contribute to another great vintage at du Clocher.' How could I deny him that?"

The innkeeper shook his head. "Guy, I have never met anyone with so many friends so eager to help him out. What kind of magic do you work on them or perhaps that wonderful wine of yours has something to do with your charmed life?"

Bellay laughed at the absurdity of his own question. Guy Saint-Savin could have been a bootblack with no worldly possessions except for his polish, and he would still have had friends falling over themselves to help him. It was a matter of offering loyalty and receiving loyalty.

"Without question, it's the wine," Guy answered. "Which reminds me, have you seen Jacques Mazet today?"

"No. I've seen almost everyone else. I hope you're not planning to ring that bell today. I don't think anyone's up to picking. The men drank so much wine this morning, they might throw away the grapes and keep the leaves. Claude Mazet's inside, though, if you'd like a tête-à-tête with him," Bellay added mischievously.

"Spare me. It would be a happy day for du Clocher if that particular Mazet took his grumblings elsewhere."

"And why should he do that?" Bellay snorted. "Between what his mother and brother give him, he can be a man of leisure here and sit on his fat rear end all day."

Guy agreed with the innkeeper but chose not to comment further.

He'd made a resolution recently to be more judicious and politic in what he said instead of impatiently blurting out whatever was on his mind. Guy had gotten himself in trouble by speaking out impetuously, not to mention acting without thought. To cut off further conversation, Guy promised to come down that evening for a glass of wine—although he could imagine the cold stare he'd received from his father for doing so—and fill in Bellay on the news of Paris.

As Guy walked up the dusty road, he glanced at the sun. It was well past noon. The hill faced east. As the sun worked its way across the sky, Jacques Mazet worked his way up the hill. By then, Guy calculated he would be two-thirds to the top.

Guy went only a few feet when the road forked. For a second he hesitated. If he went left, where the road became a narrow lane that curved under a leafy bower of tall trees, over a moss-covered stone bridge, through a small field of grape vines and finally ending at a wall of thick hedges which sheltered the château's garden, Guy could present himself to his father and perhaps avoid his father's disapproval. Guy went right. His father was very disapproving these days anyway. One more transgression would hardly make a difference.

This fork ran past fields laid out in precise rows of gnarled, twisting, bending, and looping old vines. At harvest time these knurly old soldiers were hidden by vibrant clusters of grapes and deep green leaves. Guy looked down each row until he spotted Mazet at the far end of one that was more than halfway up the hill, precisely where Guy had expected him to be.

Guy moved quickly down the row, taking care not to brush the grapes and bruise them. He hadn't realized how glad he was to be back and how anxious he was to see Jacques.

The maître was eight years older than Guy, but in many respects they had been treated as contemporaries throughout their childhood. Guy was only six when he started tagging along with Jacques and Gaston. The old maître had taught them both about the cellars and fields. If the younger boy didn't understand, he'd never ask Gaston for an explanation, fearing the maître might realize how young he was and send him back to his nanny.

Instead Guy waited until he was alone with Jacques and he would ask, "Remember what maître said about too much 'chaptalization' being for the lazy or the scoundrel?" The words sounded so strange in his little-boy voice.

"Yes, I remember," Jacques would answer.

"Well, I bet *you* don't really know what that chaptalization is. You tell me what you think it is, and I'll tell you if you're right."

Although this ploy did not fool Jacques, he would not embarrass his younger friend by calling his bluff. Instead he answered in his slow, careful way, "Chaptalization is when sugar is added before the grapes ferment so there will be enough alcohol in the wine later."

Guy would scrunch his lips, make his eyes squinty, and nod wisely. "Very good, Jacques. Very good. That is right. You did know what it meant."

"I'm at your service," Guy was saying. "Reporting for duty."

Jacques didn't look up. Instead he continued to frown at the vine in his hand. Guy stopped smiling when he saw what Mazet was holding. Still he tried to mask his concern by making light of it. "So what have you been up to, maître? Letting the grapes stay on the vine so long that noble rot sets in? Have we given up clarets for sauternes?"

Guy could usually make Mazet smile, but not this time.

"Nothing noble here," the maître said. The vine he was holding should have been covered with full, ripe fruit. Instead, the grapes had taken on an unnaturally deep color, had split, and dried up. The vine's leaves were curled and dropping off. The fruit on the adjacent vine was covered with sickly white spots. All this destruction from a small mushroom growth that had a liking for young leaves and young grapes.

"This mildew," Guy said, "weren't some of the vines affected by it last year? But wait, wasn't that over there?" Guy pointed at a lower field. "My god," he whispered, "has the odium spread so much?"

"It's bad," was all Mazet would say.

They began walking the fields together, occasionally bending to examine a diseased plant, other times picking a healthy grape to squeeze and gauge its stickiness or taste for sweetness. In this way they worked their way up the hill for an hour.

At the top Mazet finally spoke. "Well?"

"Tomorrow. We wait until tomorrow."

"Yes. I think so, too. The other châteaux have already been picking for days. I think they'll regret that in the bottle."

Guy smiled. At least there was some good news. "All the better for us," he said. "Now come, Jacques. Jean-Gabriel's bound to have something delicious left in the kitchen. Let's have lunch there. Knowing you, you haven't bothered to eat yet."

"Thank you, no. I have to check the fermenting vats." Mazet was already walking toward the chai.

"And how many times have you checked them since last month? What could have changed since yesterday morning or whenever it was that you last looked at them?"

Mazet didn't answer nor did he stop. Guy fell into step behind him. It was time for the young Saint-Savin to go to the château and pay his respects, what little he had, to his father.

Chapter Three

From sharp autumn sunlight to cool dark sanctuary.

Guy's eyes were still adjusting to the hallway's shadow when he heard an urgent, familiar whistle. It always came at moments of grave crises. The governess insisting on Saturday afternoon lessons. Edouard ordering dress fittings in Bordeaux. Loneliness getting the upper hand. Then that insistent, sad sound came searching out Guy.

Solange.

When she was little, Guy's sister, often from the shelter of a corner or closet, would send out her signal, anxious yet sure that whatever her problem, her big brother would remedy it. And if he couldn't make it disappear, he would at least soften the blow.

"Okay, little girl, come out from wherever you are."

Guy could now see the hallway that bisected the château. It created the feeling of two houses, and it was not unknown in the history of the château for spouses to take up residence on opposite sides of the hallway and live amicably separate existences.

Solange had wedged herself into a small alcove behind a mahogany pedestal displaying a Louis XIV vase of impressive detail. On her brother's command, she wriggled out.

"All right, baby sister, unburden yourself and tell me about the terrible peril you're in now. Pirates invading your boudoir? Don't want to eat your asparagus? Skinned your knee again?"

Solange cocked her head at the precise angle and in the same way she'd been doing since she was a toddler, jutting out her chin, and planting her feet in preparation for any onslaught or argument. While this pose was so familiar, Solange herself had changed dramatically since the last time Guy had seen her, more than a year before. He was startled that in so little time the fifteen-year-old girl had become a sixteen-year-old woman.

15

"This is serious," Solange said with determination. "I can't go back to that terrible school. I'm not learning anything worth knowing. The lessons have no value for me, and I hate the other girls. All they want to do is prattle on about next year's balls, and which young man is the most eligible catch with the most land and the best title and the greatest fortune ... it's just too silly."

Guy tried to look properly concerned when he asked, "Doesn't my sister, who doesn't look so little anymore, like dressing up and fussing with her hair and flirting with all the young beaux who buzz around her?"

While Guy's question was lighthearted and teasing, Solange's reply couldn't have been more earnest.

"I hate it, Guy! I hate it! It's so stupid the way those girls put on airs. They only care about marrying some fat-faced lord and ... " She paused to emphasize that the worst was yet to come, "... and they don't even know a Meursault from a Margaux. They drink ... sherry."

Guy stifled a laugh with great difficulty, not wanting to offend his so-earnest sister. "That is a terrible indictment," he managed to say. "But what would you have me do? Go to Jolly Old England and give lessons in appreciating Bordeaux wines, what ho and all that?"

Solange shook her head. She knew what she wanted done and she would not be swayed from her goal. "Tell father I'm not going back," she said. "Tell him I can't go back. Tell him."

"And how am I supposed to tell father anything?" Guy was no longer bantering. "We're barely speaking to each other as it is. Listen, I'm sorry, but I think you'll have much better luck if you tell him yourself. He doesn't deny you anything."

Solange looked stricken with a soul-consuming dismay. "I can't. I just can't. You know how I hate to make him unhappy. If he says he wants me to do something, I do it. I went to school in England even though I didn't want to. But you stand up to him. You could persuade him."

"Oh fine," Guy snorted with mock injury. "Let me take the pain of his iciness, but not you. Fine loyal sister you are."

"No, no, that's not what I want. It's just that he really will listen to you. Besides, father needs me here. You know how isolated and alone he is. And ... and I could help Jacques while you're in Paris."

Guy was well aware that his current standing with his father was at the lowest it had ever been and therefore he was probably not the best champion for Solange's cause. Still, she had asked for his help and, despite his protests, that was all that was needed for him to try.

"All right, sweet sister. I was on my way to see him anyway. I shall broach your subject."

"Promise?"

"Promise."

"You won't forget?"

"Solange, you know perfectly well that between us promises are never forgotten and never broken."

Chapter Four

It was three o'clock and Count Edouard Simon Armand Saint-Savin was just finishing his lunch.

He had begun it an hour and a half earlier with a small filet of lotte, delicately embellished with tarragon sauce and accompanied by a '47 Château Carbonnieux, an especially distinguished year for a white Graves.

A meal for the count was never a matter of merely quelling hunger and providing nourishment for his body. Rather, it was a ceremony, a rite, to be planned and orchestrated down to the smallest detail.

First there was a morning conference with the cook. What had been good at market? What was ready to be picked in the garden? Had there been anything interesting in the fishermen's nets that day?

After the lengthy consultation and the menu decided for both lunch and dinner, he pondered the merits of various wines and vintages with the dishes he had chosen.

Next a servant girl was told which of the forty-some sets of china, silver, and crystal should be set out and which linen, candelabras, flowers, and finger bowls should be used.

It was a truly arduous process. In most such households the lady of the château would have turned the tasks over to a well-trained and entrusted butler or housekeeper. Edouard would not have considered doing so. These matters were not merely details to him. They were important elements of his existence, and decisions concerning them could not be treated lightly or delegated.

It didn't matter to him if he was dining alone or having a formal dinner for twenty. The food, wine, setting, and service had to meet his exacting standards. It had been a proud moment in his life when he was assured that Queen Amelie herself, wife of the then King Louis-Philippe, was unable to surpass the sumptousness and perfection of his table.

The count had been dining alone quite often in the last year. Both his children were away, and he had entertained less frequently. For the latter, he felt quite derelict.

Entertaining was not an occasion for pleasure. It was a duty, a way of further enhancing the reputation of du Clocher among the wealthy and influential, maintaining good relationships with the important wine merchants, cultivating those in power, those who might someday be in power, and those who had been in power and could return. Edouard lived by the creed that it was best to be gracious to all and offend none.

For all this elegant dining and absorption with food and wine, the count was thin and bony. In truth he ate very little. If a whole rack of lamb was prepared for his dinner, he took only a small sliver. He never had more than a glass or two from any bottle, and was appalled at the prospect of drinking wine left over from a previous meal (making his household staff the envy of the other châteaux since his cook and butler and sometimes even the servant girls finished off what was left).

While there was no question the count fully appreciated the excellence of the food he picked at and the wonderful wines he sipped, he really didn't enjoy them.

Enjoyment, pleasure, fun were not particularly sought after by Edouard. What he desired was continuity, order, and tranquility. Emotion was messy. He couldn't abide surprises. And if it weren't for maintaining the name and reputation of his château, he would have had little to do with his fellow man.

By inclination and nature, Edouard was a man of many acquaintances but had only one friend, General Winston Sebastian Hopewell.

The general, robust and sanguine, had been with the British occupying force after the Napoleonic Wars. He had been so enchanted and fascinated by Bordeaux that, on his retirement, he purchased a small château there, not far from du Clocher, and had set to making wine and being accepted by his neighbors with the attention and zeal with which he had successfully led his troops.

General Hopewell—"Please call me 'Win,'" he had urged Edouard on their first meeting—was outgoing, ebullient and truly liked his fellow man, even the French. At first he had pressed his friendship on Edouard because of admiration for du Clocher, hoping for advice. In time, despite their divergent personalities and temperament, General Hopewell came to genuinely like his neighbor—although he would have been hard pressed to explain why—and through the enormous strength of his own good nature gradually broke through the count's reserve. In the end what finally won over Edouard completely was the general's adoration of Solange. For next to the château and its traditions, Edouard loved his daughter most.

Solange seemed a very different sort from her brother. Guy was the doer, the persistent inquirer, the initiator, a rambunctious, climb-anything, afraid-of-nothing whirligig dynamo. He frightened his father, who felt pale and insufficient next to him.

Solange was the observer, the student, the reader. She listened intently to her father and reverently followed her brother. Yet whatever Guy did, whatever he climbed, whatever challenge he took, Solange did also. She wasn't the initiator—with Guy around she had little opportunity to be one—but neither was she afraid. Like her brother, when she undertook a task, she followed it through with intensity. And when the need arose, Solange shocked everyone by taking charge. Once when she was ten and Guy sixteen, a worker got his hand caught in the grape crusher. All the adults were immobilized with horror as the heavy stone mangled the poor man's hand. It was Solange who began shouting orders, for the donkey to be stopped, for the grounding stone to be tipped, for what was left of the worker's hand to be gently extricated. She had him cleaned and wrapped and on his way to a doctor before it occurred to the adults it was a young girl giving out the orders.

Inside those solid stone walls of the château, Solange belonged to her father. When she was little, he would read to her as she sat on his lap, once in a while brushing back a strand of her flyaway chestnut hair with his lips. After dinner they would sit side by side, in good weather on the terrace, in bad in his study, while he had some more wine, often a Château d'Yquem sauterne or perhaps a grande champagne cognac. Sometimes they sat in silence, more often Edouard would talk about an upcoming dinner or he would lecture on the value of various wines.

When Solange finally fell asleep, he loathed to move her. Sitting on his terrace, feeling a soft touch of wind mixed with his daughter's gentle breath on his cheek and drinking a velvety wine, the count was satisfied.

As Solange got older, Edouard spent more and more time discussing wine with her, infusing her with awareness of their subtleties and strengths. It was important that she be knowledgeable. Frequently Guy sat in on these discourses, although he knew Edouard would have preferred to be alone with Solange. Guy could not allow his father that luxury. It was important he learned, as well, although, all other things being equal, Guy would have spent as little time with Edouard as possible. From an early age, Edouard had exasperated him. Usually Guy took refuge with Gaston Mazet.

It was different for Solange. She needed to please her father. She would often return to her room, late at night, and write down everything he had told her. While her obvious desire to learn pleased Edouard, it was her extremely fine palette that delighted him. He loved to show off her talent at his parties. He would have a guest choose a bottle of wine at random from the household cellar. It was opened, decanted, and poured in another room and then presented to the girl.

"Now my child," Edouard would say, "tell us the region, the wine, and its vintage."

Solange would solemnly accept the glass, glad for the opportunity to honor her father with her performance.

She would hold up the glass against a light background to study the wine's color. Next the glass went under her narrow, slightly upturned nose so that she could inhale deeply and strongly. The audience couldn't help smiling at her concentration, but she never noticed.

She took a healthy swig of wine and swirled it in her mouth. She drew air through her slightly parted lips so that vapors could rise from the back of her throat to her nose. Done, she spat the liquid into a silver bowl her father held for her. Only then did she speak and then only to Edouard.

"Father, it is from the Medoc, north of du Clocher. St. Estephe. The wine is deep-hued and deep-flavored. It is full and commanding, with less perfume than du Clocher. Quite fine, one of the better from St. Estephe. The vintage, it's fairly young with the harshness of youth. A year when rains came early and the grapes picked too soon. Château Montrose. 1845."

She was rarely wrong and then only in some detail.

Edouard hadn't wanted to send her away to school. It was General Hopewell who had pressed the idea one sparkling warm June day.

The two men were on the terrace following a superb lunch, highlighted by a cassolette of seafood and truffles to which the general had done more than justice. After several minutes of watching distant workers pulling weeds, the general plunged into what had been bothering him.

"You know, my dear host, it's time you did something about Solange."

Edouard whirled in his chair to look at the general, genuinely bewildered. "Something about Solange? Is there something wrong I don't know about?" he asked.

"Nothing wrong except the girl's almost fifteen and virtually a woman. Do you mean for her to spend the rest of life with you? Here?"

Edouard hadn't thought about it before. And if he had, he would have found that an acceptable future for his daughter.

General Hopewell didn't need to be told what his companion was thinking. "Listen to me," he said none too gently. "I'm your friend, and while I'm admittedly not the brightest of men, in this case I know what's best for you and for that angel of yours. She's a beautiful young thing and deserves to have some young fellow fall in love with her, wed her, and give you lots of grandchildren."

Edouard was uncomfortable even thinking of what it would mean for Solange to have children. "I certainly wouldn't stand in her way ..." he began to say.

"Standing in her way has little to do with it. Solange must meet people her own age and of her own station. She has no friends at all now that that peasant girl—what was her name?"

"Marie-Odile."

"Yes, now that Marie-Odile and her family are gone. Solange needs to enter society. She needs a life and a world beyond du Clocher. Beyond you, my friend."

Edouard didn't attempt to hide his bitterness. He had not liked what he saw of the outside world. It was sordid and without honor.

The general looked back at the workers in the field to give Edouard a chance to compose himself. It was that damned wife, the general thought. She's to blame for this model of misanthropy seated next to me. Edouard didn't speak of her. He never mentioned her, in fact, but other people did. In great detail and with great relish. From the gossip and what he knew of Edouard's temperament, the general felt he had a sound notion of what had transpired those many years before.

He looked back at Edouard and pressed on. "It needn't be the same for Solange, you know. Oh hell, you've got to let her discover for herself. Make her own mistakes, harvest her own happiness. It's not just me who feels this way. I've an ally, that old prune who calls herself Solange's governess."

Old prune! Edouard liked the description, but made himself sound properly scandalized by Hopewell's using it. "I suppose you mean

Miss Riddleysham," he said sounding more priggish than usual. She had been first Guy's governess then Solange's. She was precise, demanding, and kind. Edouard valued her unerring sense of etiquette and seemliness.

"Of course, I mean Miss Riddleysham," the general sputtered. "Can't stand her even if she agrees with me. Anyway, she says Solange is too damned—well, she didn't exactly say that—smart not to get more education. Said it would be a shame, waste, or some such nonsense. Also says the girl needs some refining, you know the finer points of society and comportment, points a man—you—can't give her. Well, she's right. You've got to let the girl go. It'd be damned selfish of you if you didn't."

Selfish. Edouard would not be selfish when it came to Solange. If his friend and Miss Riddleysham both counseled so, perhaps it was right to educate Solange further, to let her leave.

He agonized over the decision through June and into July. Finally one morning, without so much as a hint beforehand to Solange, Edouard announced that she was to leave for England as soon as the arrangements could be made. Within weeks she was enrolled at a fine finishing school, packed up, and shipped off, for once in her life protesting vehemently.

It wasn't surprising Edouard had chosen England. The Bordelaise and English had been traditionally and historically close. The very word "claret," another name for Bordeaux wine, came from a British bastardization of the French "clairet," meaning "clear." The primary market for Bordeaux was England, with fellow Frenchmen opting for wines of other regions. Napoleon Bonaparte, for one, had been a great drinker of Burgundy.

The Bordelaise weren't bothered by their countrymen's lack of appreciation, not as long as the British were eager to pay high prices for the best of the vineyards and the north countries were ready to snap up what was left over. Of course, there were those bothersome periods of political inconvenience, such as when the aforementioned Burgundy drinker, the Little Colonel, had brought on the continental blockade and no ships were allowed to cross the Channel. Bordelaise winegrowers suffered then.

Edouard deeply missed his daughter. She never questioned or censured him. She accepted the way he faced life by retreating from it. There was no need for posturing with her. In some ways she understood him better than he understood himself.

The count always left growing the grapes and producing the wine to his maître, contrary to du Clocher tradition. Previous counts had taken active participation. Edouard did not feel comfortable doing so. His father hadn't gotten around to training him before he took his unfortunate afterdinner swim halfway across the Gironde.

None of Count Paul's guests believed he would go through with his bet, certain that the mile between the château's terrace and the water's edge would be ample distance for the effects of the evening's wine to wear off and for the count to think better of his proposed undertaking.

But a bet was not a trifling matter to Count Paul. He had raced down to the pier shedding piece after piece of clothing as he went. He was quite naked by the time he streaked past the inn, scandalizing poor Beatrice, Jean-Gabriel Bellay's distant relative, who was taking some air on the porch after a strenuous day's work.

Paul threw himself into the water's iciness and with strong strokes set off to win his wager.

His guests reached the pier soon after him. They could make out his arms knifing through the water, one strong stroke after another. Then he disappeared. One second they could see him and the next he was gone. The currents around the island had grabbed him and sucked him under as if he had never been there.

Edouard was fifteen when he became Count Saint-Savin du Clocher and was totally unprepared for it. He was a boy of little confidence, having always been afraid of the exuberant father who had ignored him. Count Paul hadn't been intentionally neglectful. The very suggestion would have shocked him. The sorry fact was his son bored him.

On becoming count, it was extremely important to Edouard that he prove himself, that he show the world and his dead father that he could succeed with skill and finesse. And he might have done just that, for he had a great capacity for detail, if events hadn't intervened in the form of that English blockade of Europe that made it impossible to get wine from the caves of Bordeaux to the cellars of Britain.

Those first vintages under Edouard's leadership had been excellent. There were just no buyers. All the châteaux suffered. That didn't comfort the young count. It was his personal failure the wine of du Clocher was not being drunk. Of course, after the war, England could not get enough claret and bought all that was available. It was too late for Edouard. He was a failure and would no longer take an active role in the château management.

Instead he created a new function for the Count Saint-Savin. It would be for him to popularize Bordeaux in France, to make it a favorite of the nation's elite. So began Edouard's obsession with dinner parties and entertaining as a duty.

General Hopewell had once tried discouraging him.

"Can't see it myself," he had said. "All you get is a passel of freeloaders who eat your food, drink your wine, and soil your sheets. They never buy. They only take."

The observation fell on closed eyes and deaf ears. If Edouard lost the belief that entertaining influential people was essential in furthering the reputation of du Clocher, he would lose his reason for being. There would be no justification for Edouard Saint-Savin's existence. But try as he did, his efforts had only minimal success. The very nature of the Bordelaise wine trade precluded more.

At the time, wine was not sold directly by the individual châteaux. Instead, each vineyard had contracts with negociants, wine merchants. A short while after each harvest the fermenting juices were transferred to the caves, the storage areas, of these negociants, most of whom were clustered on the Quai des Chartons in Bordeaux city. There the negociants supervised the rest of the fermentation and did the blending, bottling, labeling, selling, and shipping.

Very little wine was kept by the château itself. Therefore, there was little for Edouard to sell. Most of what du Clocher produced was shipped by its Bordeaux negociant to foreign customers. And his balance sheet preferred the dependability of these buyers over the established fickleness of the Parisian haut monde.

Edouard sat in his mahogany-panelled library, a room panoplied on three walls with books from floor to ceiling, ponderous tomes of history, slim volumes of poetry, pedantic philosophies, fanciful novels, all representing Edouard's windows on the world.

From one of the shelves he had taken a frayed, old ledger and with the solemnity of ritual, he opened it and began reading—as he did every year at harvest time. The ledger contained the château's vintage records, starting with the first in 1728, going through the last, 1850. The records had been kept meticulously and at times poetically from the time that Frederic Saint-Savin had committed himself to the folly—for that was what it was considered by many of his friends— and joy of creating du Clocher.

Edouard loved these records and allowed himself the pleasure of reading them only once a year. Their evidence of continuity gave him comfort. Why he began this yearly ritual, he no longer remembered. But it had become important to him and he disliked being interrupted. It was therefore with petulant annoyance that he heard the door at the far end of the room opening. The servants knew they were not to interrupt him.

Without looking up, Edouard scolded, "If that is you, Lise, you have been here quite long enough to know that I am not to be disturbed."

The interloper did not reply.

"As long as you are here, go tell Marcel I wish him to decant a bottle of the '37. Bring it back with one of the diamond-cut crystals. Marcel will know which one."

There was no responding movement. Wretched girl must be a moron, Edouard thought. Then the intruder spoke and it was not Lise.

"If there is one thing I have always admired about you, Father, it is your ability to choose the perfect wine for the occasion. The '37 is an excellent choice with which to savor the past triumphs of du Clocher, having been such a triumph itself."

Chapter Five

Minutes passed. Edouard continued reading. Guy knew better than to say more. When his father was ready to acknowledge his presence, he would.

Sun shimmered through the fifteen-foot-high windows at Edouard's back. It caught dust particles floating in a fluttery, anxious dance. Guy watched them rise, shudder, fall, rise again. Once or twice his eyes strayed toward his father, but there was nothing to see there except the shadowed figure bent over the almost-feminine desk.

It was no use. Edouard could no longer concentrate on the words before him although they were so familiar he could virtually recite them from memory. Words about to be spoken, angry, recriminating, humiliating words that he had postponed saying and hearing were crowding out those on the page before him. His revered past would no longer protect him from the unpleasant present.

Edouard looked up. "We've had our defeats, too, Guy. They are recorded here as well. I can only hope another is not about to be added."

He closed the book, scaring off the dust particles in a furious scamper.

"Father, I have just spoken to Jacques about this disease in the vineyard," Guy said quickly hoping to postpone the topic he was sure Edouard would be raising.

"Yes, he's mentioned it to me also," Edouard responded as eager as his son to speak of neutral subjects. He didn't even reproach Guy for not coming immediately to the château, although he was well aware that he hadn't. "I understand from General Hopewell we've been quite lucky."

"How can losing one-third of our fields be considered 'lucky'?" Guy asked with a certain amount of exasperation.

"I only meant in comparison to our neighbors," Edouard answered stiffly. "I understand at Latour almost half the vines are affected."

Guy felt guilty for snapping at his father, but could only manage an "I suppose that is something," in response. As he invariably did while he was thinking, Guy began pacing. "If production is down everywhere," he said more for himself than for his father, "prices must rise, so we won't be badly hurt after all."

Here was an opening, the perfect opening with which Edouard could broach the subject he dreaded. Still he hesitated and then said instead, "I'm glad you are finally taking some interest in du Clocher instead of this political foolishness in Paris."

It was as much his father's manner as his words that goaded Guy. Edouard addressed so many things with that air of condescension, indifference, and quasi-boredom. As usual, Guy's response was one of vehemence. He had to fight ice with fire.

"For god's sake, Father," he snapped, "du Clocher has been, is, and always will be of first importance to me. It is as much my life as it is yours. But what I am doing in Paris is also important. The Second Republic is an experiment, an opportunity for France to learn from the excesses of the first one, so that we can forge something noble and lasting."

"Kindly keep your speeches for the rabble in the Assembly. You are very young and impetuous. I had hoped that as you matured, you would discover that politics are passing fancies. Republics, empires, reigns, they don't last. They are quickly history, footnotes. Those who really control France will always control France no matter what happens in Paris. Du Clocher is what it is today because the Saint-Savins have avoided politics. For generations we have been uninvolved. Wine is our concern, not who's taxing it. I've allowed you to amuse yourself with this dabbling only because I thought you would tire of it and come to your senses."

God! Guy thought. His father was a fool, a fool self-imprisoned inside the walls of the château with hardly any knowledge of what went on outside. Even the château's fields and caves were beyond his ken or consideration. Yet he felt suitable to lecture Guy on politics and the realities of the world.

Guy tried to remember his resolve to rein in his temper. He would not be goaded by his father. He would be rational and he would be controlled. It was difficult.

"There is no argument," Guy said softly, "that I am young, but I am not so young that I can't agree with some of what you said. I know that many, maybe most, Frenchmen are giving lip service to the Republic. That many are watching the Republic as if it were some sporting match—who is on top this week? Who's waiting on the side to take over? And they don't really care what the outcome is so long as they are not inconvenienced by it. If you and I are aware of this, then so is the esteemed president Louis-Napoleon. Being a man of great ambition, he is undoubtedly getting ready to capitalize on the fragility of the government and shape it into something more to his liking."

For all his pretense at being removed from politics, Edouard was aware of the nitty-gritty of Parisian intrigues. He'd have had to be deaf not to be since it seemed to be the primary topic of his guests' dinner conversations. "But Louis is the head of government," Edouard said, feigning ignorance. "Oh, I see, you're referring to his attempt to change your constitution."

There it was again, the condescending distancing. "Not just *my* constitution, Father, *yours* as well. He wants to change it so he can be president a second term. I know it sounds innocuous, yet many of us feel that it's his first step towards changing President Louis-Napoleon to King Louis-Napoleon, or who knows, maybe he wishes to emulate his late uncle and become Emperor Louis-Napoleon. That must not be allowed. And so I wrote in that speech Monsieur de Pary gave before ..."

"So you did *what*?!" Guy was momentarily taken aback by the edge in Edouard's voice. It almost made him feel defensive.

"Surely, you know," Guy said. "I authored a speech condemning any change in the constitution. Everyone else knows that and it was well-received in the Assembly."

"And how did Louis-Napoleon receive it? Did he stand up and applaud." Just as quickly as it had come, the acid left Edouard and languor returned. "Guy, your naivete is alarming. Can you really believe your republic will last? Sooner or later France will have its king again because deep in our hearts we Frenchmen are all monarchists. Does it really matter if it is King Louis-Napoleon or Charles the Tenth or Louis the Three-millionth? No. It does not. What matters, to us, is that du Clocher prospers."

He sighed. "Did you consider for one moment what antagonizing Louis-Napoleon would mean for du Clocher? Our family has survived these past 150 years because we never insulted anyone. Now you may have ruined it all by casting yourself against one of the most powerful men in France today."

Edouard wished Guy wasn't such a nuisance. Edouard hated scenes, but he knew that one was about to ensue that would make what had transpired so far just so much chit-chat. Edouard was going to have to be firm. The news about the speech had made that more clear than ever. Once long ago Edouard had tried to get someone else to leave Paris and return to du Clocher. He had failed then. This time, with his son, he would have to succeed. It would not be easy.

Edouard sighed again, then said, "Guy, you must spend no more time in Paris. You must come home at once. I will make amends for your latest indiscretion and perhaps no harm will come from it. I will have a dinner for Louis-Napoleon. That is it. And I will serve the '33."

A dinner! How was Guy ever to take his father seriously when his solution to the problems of state and country was a dinner? But at least Edouard had finally tipped his hand.

"So," Guy said, "this little political conversation, so unlike you, was merely leading up to still another request—or is it a demand this time?—that I come home. I'm not sure why you want me here, but be that as it may, I must again tell you that it is impossible for me to quit Paris just now. You've asked me to come home before. I've refused before and I refuse again."

Edouard turned his back to his son so that he could look out the window. Solange had entered the garden below him, and he watched as she arranged her skirt on the stone bench under an arbor. He wished she would look up. A glimpse of her lovely, unspoiled face would make him feel so much better. But she didn't. With great effort Edouard turned back to face his son.

"I'm afraid I must insist," he said quietly. "There can be no arguing. I cannot let you return to Paris."

"No, no. It's not 'cannot,' it's 'will not.' You don't want me there. So what are you going to do next? Cut off my allowance to force me back?"

The exchange had become even more unpleasant than Edouard had anticipated. He'd hoped to skirt the real issue and avoid telling Guy what he'd kept to himself for so long. Guy should have been told long ago, except Edouard hadn't been able to face the reality of what was happening himself. Now there could be no hiding behind vintage book notations. He would have to tell Guy all—or as much as he could bring himself to tell.

"Guy, if I were the kind of father who tried to rein in his son by pulling the purse strings, I would have done that long ago. I said 'cannot' because I meant 'cannot.' I am not threatening to cut off money because there is no money to cut off. The Saint-Savin fortune is gone. We are existing on the wine alone."

Guy stopped pacing, paralyzed by what he had heard. No, he couldn't have heard right. Maybe this was his father's idea of a perverse joke, or ...

"What are you saying? What do you mean there is no money left? What about all the Saint-Savin property? The jewels? The companies we own? Where are they?"

"Gone. Sold."

"For what? Where's the money from their sale? I don't understand."

Edouard cleared his throat. Guy was getting close to forbidden territory, territory that his father would never allow him to enter. "It's not for you to understand," Edouard said. "I am the Count Saint-Savin and as long as I am, I am not accountable to you. I've told you this only so you will realize it is truly time to give up your games in Paris and concentrate your attentions here. Of course, an apology from you to Louis is in order ..."

"Louis-Napoleon be damned. You must tell me what happened. Even if you squandered everything else, our profits from the wine these past few years must have amounted to a small fortune by itself. We've produced one excellent vintage after another and du Clocher has been selling at extraordinary prices."

Dear god, thought Edouard, would this conversation never end? He was exhausted. Even the most mundane conversation with his son fatigued him. The younger man's energy made him too aware of his own pallor. "Perhaps," Edouard said dryly, "if you had spent more time in St. Julien these past years, you might know a bit more about the economics of the vineyard."

Edouard had answered with enough sanctimony to set Guy pacing again. "I know all there is about the business of wine-making," Guy said. "Gaston Mazet was kind enough to explain it to me even if you didn't have the time to."

"Then I suppose he told you about the wine merchants and brokers."

"What's there to know? The merchants descend on the château after each harvest. They offer a price on the fermenting juice. A deal is struck and later the wine is transferred to the Quai des Chartons."

"All very correct, except for one difference in the case of du

Clocher. Having had such a good relationship with our broker Monsieur Cornelius Schroeder, I signed an exclusive contract with him."

This did not sound good to Guy. Edouard had never evidenced any business acumen in the past. "What kind of contract?" Guy asked warily.

"A contract, a ten-year contract."

"That said what?"

"Why that Monsieur Schroeder should have all of our wine, of course."

Edouard was certainly not the only vineyard owner to have such a contractual arrangement, although Guy had never heard of such a long one before. His next question was the crucial one and although he feared what the answer might be, he didn't hesitate asking it.

"At what price did you give him the wine? At the price of ten years ago?"

Edouard nodded.

The sheer stupidity of the contract was overwhelming. The price of wine in the last six years had risen spectacularly. Du Clocher had not been able to produce enough to meet the demand. And yet Edouard was selling it to Schroeder for a fraction of what he should have been receiving. It was unbelievable and ghastly.

"And how much longer does this contract have to run?"

"It has another two years."

"This harvest and next?"

"Yes."

It was robbery, out and out robbery, and Edouard a willing victim to it. This was insanity!

"Have you gone to Schroeder? Talked to him? I mean if you tell him it's only fair to renegotiate now ... "

Edouard interrupted his son, annoyed. "Fair? A contract is a gentleman's word. A gentleman does not go back on his word."

"A gentleman won't remain one very long when he's broke."

Edouard raised his eyebrows with disdain. There was no need to comment on such a ridiculous statement. On his part, Guy needed time to think, time to calm down. He needed to change the subject. It was that or explode.

"If we're truly destitute, then there should be no question of Solange returning to England."

Edouard hadn't thought of that, but, of course, Guy was right. So

something good was to come of all this turmoil. He had missed her
so.

"Yes," Edouard answered, almost happily. "Solange will have to
stay here—as will you."

"No, no, Father, there you are wrong. I am going back and I'll
make do somehow. Live frugally. Earn money from my writings.
Others do it. So will I."

There was a frightening awareness just then, hanging between
father and son, that at that moment ugly words and recriminations
could permanently damage whatever meager relationship they had.
What little love they had for each could be excised and destroyed
forever. Edouard again turned his back on his son.

When at last he spoke, it was with a flat finality. "I forbid it," he
said. "I forbid it. 'Others' are not Saint-Savins. 'Others' cannot blacken
the reputation of du Clocher by living some squalid, bohemian
existence on the Rive Gauche. We have a name and a reputation to
honor and respect. And you will do so."

The time for holding back had passed. Guy shouted so loud that
the cook and her helpers dropped their knives and whisks in the
kitchen. "And why didn't you think of your precious honor and
reputation when you squandered everything away, you damned old
fool! What is it? Do you have some tart you're showering presents on?
Have you taken up gambling? Oh, to hell with you and all your
perverse values!"

Guy grabbed a book, leatherbound and gold-embossed, from the
nearest shelf, and with all the strength and anger within him, he
flung it, and then stormed from the room.

The sound of a once-regal vase smashing on the floor caused
Edouard to turn around in time to see Guy slamming the door
behind him. Edouard walked over to the desolate fragments. Perhaps
it can be repaired, he thought, calmly. Edouard returned to the
window, but Solange was no longer in the garden.

There was a tentative knock at the door. It was the maid.

"Lise, tell Marcel to decant a bottle of the '37. Bring it back with
one of the diamond-cut crystals. Marcel will know which one."

Chapter Six

Guy took five long strides down the hallway then stopped. He was embarrassed by his outburst and regretted the display of temper. He had to be more controlled. It was childish the way at times he needed to smash something. Once he had severely hurt his hand by striking out angrily and in deep frustration at a wall.

He was determined to change. His friend, Jules, with whom he often discussed politics over a glass of red wine, had witnessed one outburst that had culminated in Guy hitting a fellow student during an argument over whether the Second Republic was a new system of society or merely a new system of government.

While Jules was quick to admit that the other student had presented his position in a particularly mocking and scurrilous manner, he chided Guy. "Your response can only suggest that your verbal arguments carried less force than your fists. While seeing Claude knocked flat on his fat posterior was high entertainment, in the end, you are the one who looks the fool."

Jules had been right. Guy knew that. He would gain no respect if he couldn't curb his outbursts. He especially hadn't wanted to give his father a reason for feeling superior.

His father! Damn that man. Was he telling the truth about the Saint-Savin fortune? The anger returned. Guy knew Solange was waiting for a report on her request, but he wasn't prepared to give her one, not then, not the way he was feeling.

Guy left the château through a side door, followed a path that paralleled the main road for a few hundred feet and then turned down towards the river.

It took him to a large tree of spreading branches. Near it was the graveyard of the Saint-Savin family. There were no grandiose monuments, only simply stones marking birth and death.

Guy knelt down at the oldest one, placed there to fix the remains of Frederic Saint-Savin, the founder of du Clocher. Guy ran his fingers over the letters chiseled in the stone so long before.

FREDERIC SAINT-SAVIN
1679-1760

Frederic Saint-Savin had been a merchant in Bordeaux city, acquiring a good measure of success at the beginning of the 18th century through hard work and an affability that earned him many contacts, even among the aristocracy. It was one of these, a duke, who encouraged Saint-Savin to invest all he could in something called the Company of the West, a great venture meant to exploit French holdings in the part of the New World known as Le Mississippi.

Saint-Savin, taking the counsel of his friend, bought a great deal of stock at a low price. Shortly afterwards, a nationwide madness set in. Everyone wanted to invest in the Company of the West. People went to any lengths to own stock. One incensed person even yelled "fire" to clear the lines at a brokerage house. The price of the shares soared beyond comprehension or reason.

It was at this point that Saint-Savin, on his own counsel, sold all his shares. It might have been a lucky guess, intuition, or an uneasy realization that the Company was doing nothing except selling stock. For whatever reason he did it, it was indeed fortunate Saint-Savin had chosen that time to sell. Not much later, the Company of the West ceased to exist. It collapsed, taking with it the fortunes and savings of thousands.

Jurist and author Montesquieu, surveying the devastation, wrote, "All those who were rich six months ago are now in the depths of poverty, and those who had not even bread to eat are now swollen with riches."

Although Saint-Savin had had quite a bit more than bread on his table before the collapse, there was no denying he was swollen with riches after. It was, therefore, to him that many of his once-wealthy acquaintances turned for loans. By making those loans, his fortune doubled and tripled through interest and the land he acquired after defaults. He was quickly becoming one of the wealthiest men in the area.

A casualty of the financial disaster was the very duke who had originally suggested that Saint-Savin buy into the Company of the West. The duke, however, was not among those who turned to the merchant for relief. Instead he sold off, piecemeal, what was left of his once-large holdings—family jewels, works of art, some of his land. What he didn't sell, he put up as collateral to the moneylenders. Nonetheless, he never had enough money and was soon borrowing to pay off interest.

In desperation, the duke turned to the gaming tables, hoping that the next turn of the card would restore his fortune. It never did. Finally, he, being a cousin of the young Louis XV, decided it was time he followed the custom of so many of the royal family and take refuge from his French creditors in the more hospitable climes of Holland.

Through it all, the duke had kept one piece of property as insurance. It was this he offered to sell to Saint-Savin. The duke needed money to set up his household in Holland. The property was 150 acres along the Gironde and up a hill, with an ancient belltower—clocher—watching over some ruins. Saint-Savin bought it unseen. It could have been a quagmire for all he cared. The duke, after all, had been at least partially responsible for his new wealth.

It was two years before the merchant actually visited his property. It had been an exhausting time for him. New venture piled on new venture. New lands to be managed, some to be sold, others bought. Money making money.

Luckily his two eldest sons, both in their twenties, helped with his business affairs. His youngest son, Charles, all of four years old, helped, too, by offering his father a relaxing diversion in this hectic period.

It was during the time of profits and tumult that Frederic Saint-Savin was made a member of the Bordeaux Parlement, a coveted position, since it meant his family would be given a title and become part of the nobility.

One day, a polished teak landau rolled away from Bordeaux city carrying Frederic, Charles, and a basket crammed with fried chicken, goat cheeses, fruits, and wine. Frederic was exhausted beyond measure. He wanted to get away from the rigors of the city and enjoy a day in the sun with his mischievous, amusing boy. Feeling he needed an excuse for his day of freedom, Saint-Savin set a course for the parcel of land he'd bought from his impoverished friend, the duke.

Who is to say what it was that captured Frederic Saint-Savin that day? He never did. It might have been the industrious workers toiling in the fields. Or the hypnotic flow of the Gironde. Or the sense of history and mystery that radiated from the belltower. It could have been the mantle of quiet security that warmed him as he surveyed his acres from the top of that hill as his son scampered around him. Or maybe it was merely the pleasantness of that sunny day.

Whatever the reason, Saint-Savin knew that this was to be, from then on, his home. He would build a castle for himself, his family, and those to follow.

And he would have a vineyard.

If his neighbors at Lafitte and Latour could grow grapes and make wine praised by all those fortunate enough to sample it, so would he. And his would be better, his would be the finest and the best.

With one visit, his life was taken over by du Clocher. He turned over more and more of his business duties to his capable and trustworthy sons, and turned more and more of his own attention to the château.

He designed and supervised its construction, chose the furnishings, laid out the gardens. When completed it was even finer than he had dreamed possible.

The château was both regal and elegant without being intimidating, commanding and memorable yet livable. It was exactly what Saint-Savin had hoped to achieve, and he would have been gratified to know that even some hundred years later, when the richest men in France had their châteaux designed by the most talented architects with no expense spared, none surpassed the beauty of Château du Clocher.

Nor would he have been less pleased that his wine was to be considered among the best of the Medoc. For Frederic Saint-Savin had also lent his talents to the creation of his vineyards. He had cultivated the friendships of his wine-growing neighbors. He listened, watched, learned. For his laborers, he sought out families who had worked the fields since the land had been drained a century before, for these were the men and women who understood the care of the grapes and the needs of the wine. He enticed the best of them to du Clocher.

Saint-Savin experimented with methods, both old and new, and it wasn't long before, in part thanks to the soil, the slant of the sun on the vines, the pebbles that reflected heat back upward at night, and a myriad of other things, the wine of Château du Clocher was being praised and fetching high prices in London.

Saint-Savin was a truly happy and contented man. As the years passed, there was one worry that nagged at him. What would happen to du Clocher after his death? His three sons, now all grown and prosperous men, enjoyed their visits to the château and they certainly appreciated the wine. Still they were essentially disinterested in making it. Frederic Saint-Savin would not have his du Clocher become a minor entry in an impersonal account book.

For years, there seemed to be no solution. But Saint-Savin had always been a lucky man and his luck held true, this time in the form of his youngest son's son, Philippe. From when he was very young, the boy begged to visit his grandfather so that he could follow him among the oak barrels, around the fermenting vats, watch the fouloir egrappoir in action as it crushed the grapes, and walk the fields.

It soon became apparent that Saint-Savin had found his solution in Philippe. Still the grandfather waited. Philippe's interest and devotion didn't waver. Finally Saint-Savin implemented a plan he had mulled over for years.

What he did was quite simple. Without informing anyone except his notaire, the type of lawyer who dealt with deeds, marriage contracts, and such, Saint-Savin transferred ownership of du Clocher to his grandson along with a sizable portion of the rest of his wealth so that the vineyard need not suffer during bad years.

Had he willed du Clocher to Philippe, the will might have been invalid under the primogeniture laws and the other heirs could have contested it, although Saint-Savin doubted they would. He had given his sons a good part of the profits from the properties they managed for him, and they in turn had reinvested wisely, creating new fortunes of their own. Still he did not want to leave anything to chance.

Shortly before his death, at eighty, just after Philippe turned eighteen, the arrangement was revealed.

Of course, at the time of his death in 1760, Frederic had no way of foreseeing the French Revolution, yet he couldn't have planned better for it even if he had. By giving the château outright to his grandson, he inadvertently kept it from being confiscated during the Reign of Terror.

For Philippe, who was Count Philippe by that time, had been too busy with wine to get involved in politics. He had treated his peasants well and had not, as other Medocain owners had done, cheated them. The terrors of the new order swept right by du Clocher. Count Philippe rode out the Revolution virtually untouched, though, naturally, sales fell off somewhat. His cousins were not so fortunate. One fled France and his property was taken. Had he been part owner of du Clocher through inheritance, the château would have gone also.

Another cousin killed his dueling opponent. He was exiled and his property went to the State as well. Still another had the distinction of paying court to Madame la Guillotine. Of all the cousins, the grandchildren of Frederic Saint-Savin, Philippe was least touched. Thus du Clocher stayed Saint-Savin instead of being confiscated for Citizen Worthy-and-Deserving.

The château passed from Philippe to his son Paul and from Paul, prematurely, to his son Edouard, the present count. Paul's was such a pointless death and with such bad timing. He had promised himself that he would soon get to the task of educating his son. The disinterested force of the Gironde kept him from winning his bet and keeping his promise. Of course, it also saved him from being further bored by his son.

"Boring" would have hardly been the word Guy would have used just then to describe his father. The word pounding through Guy's mind was "foolish." Edouard had been foolish to enter into such a contract with Cornelius Schroeder. Foolish and stupid.

A hint of breeze on his back released him from his troubled thoughts. It was Solange, anxious and expectant.

"You ran out of the house in such a hurry, but I knew you would come here. You always come here when you're upset. What did Father say? Do I have to go back?"

Guy looked at his sister pensively, wistfully. It would be nice to be sixteen and have returning to school as one's greatest worry.

"Solange, my love, was there something I was supposed to discuss with Father for you? It must have slipped my mind . . . no, no, wait, something is coming back to me. Ah yes."

"'Ah yes' what?" Solange could barely breathe from anxiety.

"'Ah yes' I remember, of course. But wait a second. Don't I deserve a little something, a reward, maybe, for bearding the dragon? Yes, no doubt about it. I should definitely get something."

What he got was a good solid kick on his shins which Solange planted before crying, "Guy Saint-Savin, you're being cruel and mean—and if you don't tell me what happened right now, I won't tell you the wonderful news I have."

He had to admit, to himself, that he wasn't being very nice prolonging her agony. "All right, my love. I shall tell you. Father agreed. You no longer need suffer the cruel indignities of living in awful old England ..."

"I don't have to go back?" Solange was fairly scampering around her brother on her tiptoes, clapping her hands with happiness, laughing and giggling and talking all at once. "Is that what you're saying? I don't have to go back? Oh Guy, do you think Father would open a bottle of champagne? To celebrate? I could drink the whole bottle myself! Now I have two things to celebrate."

By this time Guy had her safely ensconsed in his arms as a defense from her whirling-dervishness that was making him dizzy. "Hold on there," he said. "I want my payment. That piece of good news you promised me, is that, by any chance, the other reason for celebrating?"

It was now Solange's turn to smile mischievously. "All right, I'll confess. My news is more for me than it is for you."

"Fraud," Guy yelled as he lunged to tickle her in punishment.

"You'll like it, you'll like it, too," Solange giggled. "Let go of me and I'll show you."

They retraced Guy's path, but instead of going into the château, they crossed the road that went down to the Gironde, and went over to the neat row of eight cabins that housed the vineyard's workers.

All but one were identical, single-storied with three rooms and a small garden in back. All were well-maintained and carefully tended. Any worker slovenly at home, no matter how good in the fields, was soon dismissed.

The eighth cabin was set apart and was larger than the others. It was the home of the Mazet family, and at first Guy thought that was where Solange was taking him. Instead she went to the second from the main road, slipped through the space separating it from the next house, and went back to its garden.

There was someone there, a girl, no, a woman, who looked pleasantly familiar to Guy. She was wearing the simple cotton dress of a peasant. Her light-brown hair was pulled severely back revealing a strong-featured, evenly proportioned face, sprayed with a charming swath of freckles across the bridge of the nose. The freckles!

"Marie-Odile, you're back! What a wonderful sight," Guy shouted as he swung her into the air as if she were still the eight-year-old playmate of Solange's she had once been.

"She's come back. Isn't it wonderful," Solange cried, delighted her surprise was so well-received.

Feet back on the ground and trying to catch her breath, Marie-Odile managed to gasp, "Only for the picking, Solange, I told you, Jacques took me on for the harvest."

"But what of your family?" Guy wanted to know. "Are they no longer in St. Emilion?"

Marie-Odile's family had lived for many years at du Clocher. That second house from the end had been theirs. Marie had grown up with Solange. When she was thirteen, however, and Marie's mother pregnant with still another child, her father had done something out of character for a French peasant. He had looked for work elsewhere.

His family was too large and there was no way he was going to better his position at du Clocher. Jacques had petitioned for Edouard's assistance. By chance, the count had heard of a new vintner in St. Emilion—a rocky, hilly area on the other side of Bordeaux city—whose maître had died and who wasn't pleased with the new one he'd hired. Edouard recommended Marie's father.

Rarely did such a man as her father have the opportunity to leave his own village. One's lot in life was what you were born to and there was very little chance of improving it. Society was virtually static. But out of Marie's father's desperation was born a courage to fly in the face of society's rigidity. His gamble paid off. He got along well with his new employer, managed to overcome the resentment of the locals, and, for the most part, prospered.

The rest of his large family, except for Marie-Odile and his wife, adjusted well also; children rarely taking long to meet new friends anywhere. For his wife, though, home would always be du Clocher and family and friends would be in St. Julien. So she was quick to understand when Marie-Odile asked to return for du Clocher's harvest that year. Further, her mother understood that missing Solange was not the only reason for the request. There were several local boys, one in particular, who were pressing suit.

Marie's father favored the persistent young man and was about to sanction a marriage. Marie-Odile was panicked. She had no feeling for the boy other than distress at the thought of marrying him and being forced to stay in the hills of St. Emilion forever.

For this reason, Marie's father was against the visit to du Clocher, even if it were to be a paid one. It was only after Marie's mother promised she would encourage the wedding after her daughter came home that the father reluctantly agreed.

Marie-Odile had already sent word to Jacques and he was happy to hire on such an industrious, intelligent worker who would also give Solange such happiness.

Marie was not about to tell Guy any of her problems with the young men of St. Emilion. Instead she answered, "Father is prospering as maître. Mother has had two more babies, both girls. And I am here visiting Aunt Louise to help with the harvest."

"So you say," Guy said quite seriously, "but I can tell you were no longer able to hold down that swill they call wine in St. Emilion, and you had to return to where the grapes are truly blessed."

To her own surprise, Marie-Odile jumped to the defense of her new district. "St. Emilion is a fine wine with a wonderful bouquet. It might not have the body of a Medoc ..." She stopped, realizing suddenly that she was being teased. "You were kidding," she blushed.

"Of course, I was, you goose."

To be polite and also to give herself time to regain her dignity, Marie asked, "And how are you faring at du Clocher?"

For a few brief minutes Guy had been able to put aside the disaster that confronted him. Now, he abruptly turned to go. "I have an errand in Bordeaux. Something that must be taken care of immediately. If you'll excuse me."

The two women watched puzzled and concerned as Guy, with the hunched concentration of someone oblivious of everything except his mission, went off towards the stables.

"Did I say something to offend him?" Marie couldn't imagine what it might have been.

"I don't think so," Solange answered thoughtfully. "I think it may have something to do with a conversation he had with Father. Marie, I must go with Guy. Please forgive me for running off, but I'll have to hurry to catch him."

Chapter Seven

The carriage stopped in front of a massive gray building, absurdly adorned with carvings of strange faces and ugly flowers, very solid and very bourgeois.

It was one of the many somber and self-important buildings that crowded along the Quai des Chartons, the harborside street where the wine merchants of Bordeaux had their offices, cellars, and vaults. Without exception, wine merchants did their business on this quai, partially for convenience to the port and its ships and partially because of history.

While by and large winegrowers were French, traditionally the wine merchants were foreign—Scottish, English and Irish, Scandinavian, Dutch, and German. In an earlier time, when Bordeaux was still a walled city, foreigners were not allowed to live or do business within it. So the merchants clustered outside in the Chartons area, so named for a Carthusian monastery that had once followed the strict rules of the order there.

By the time Guy and Solange pulled up in front of 1908 Quai des Chartons, there were no longer walls around Bordeaux and the area was considered a vital part of the city.

Number 1908, however, was not the most vital part of the vital area. Cornelius Schroeder, owner of this building, had to rent part of his space to several other merchants who dealt mostly with tiny vineyards in St. Emilion. His own business wasn't enough to support his warehouse.

If Guy had been one to notice such things and had he visited some of the other Quai des Chartons establishments, he might have seen the tell-tale signs of a less-than-prosperous operation.

The entrance vestibule was drab, with no oriental rugs or elegant sconces. There were no chairs, upholstered or otherwise. And certainly no sign of anyone taking cloth to dust in a long, long while. Nor was there pretense of any kind of elegant reception. A visitor could see plainly through a rickety partition into a shabby room where two bent bookkeepers scratched at their ledgers.

"Pardon me," Guy called to them. "I wish to see Monsieur Schroeder at once. Please get him."

The two old men looked up, startled and squinting. Each waited for the other to take the initiative, until finally the one closest to the door capitulated.

"There must be a mistake," the bookkeeper quavered. "Monsieur Schroeder is never here at this time, on this day. He's ... he's ..." The bookkeeper knew very well where Cornelius Schroeder could be found every Monday and Wednesday at that hour. He was in the well-appointed apartment of Mademoiselle Elise Deschamps, a dainty blonde who had only recently decided that she could provide for the future much better with someone who was a tad more generous than her wine merchant. She hadn't yet shared this insight with Monsieur Schroeder, being a judicious young woman who thought it better to have a new kind sir lined up to pay the rent and overwhelm her with baubles before discarding the old one.

The bookkeeper was saved from his face reddening any further by the arrival of a precise young man coming in from a rear door.

"Monsieur Busscher," the bookkeeper gasped with relief. "This gentleman has asked for Monsieur Schroeder, and well, it's Wednesday and you know that Wednesdays ..." The man had flushed deep red again.

Busscher ignored the bookkeeper, who decided the wisest course was to return to his accounts immediately.

"I believe you are Guy Saint-Savin," Busscher said. "And the mademoiselle ..."

"My sister Solange," Guy interrupted. "Where is Monsieur Schroeder? I have business with him that cannot wait."

"I'm afraid it will have to, unless I can help you. The monsieur has a regular appointment today, and then he will be leaving for London, for the month. I'm sorry, there's really no way to see him before he returns. I do know he plans to personally supervise the tasting of this year's wine." Busscher spoke with the polite deference of someone comfortable with his place and function. The precision of his manner carried over to his French. It was grammatically perfect with only the slightest coloring of his native Dutch in the accent.

Busscher was not at all perturbed when Guy snapped, "Come to supervise? A thief counting his booty is more like it."

"I beg your pardon. Really, Monsieur Saint-Savin, if there is a problem, I may be able to help. I am his chief assistant."

"No, I must see Monsieur Schroeder." Guy stopped and really looked at Busscher for the first time. "Wait. Have we not met before?" he asked trying to focus his memory.

"I was wondering if you would remember." Busscher smiled slightly. He ushered the brother and sister out of the office and into the vestibule, away from the interested ears of the bookkeepers. "And I hope you won't, shall we say, betray me to Monsieur Schroeder, who takes a dim view of anything more radical than Louis VII."

That was enough of a clue for Guy to place him. Busscher had been at a meeting, almost three years earlier, where several young men had discussed the possibility of deposing King Louis-Philippe. Although all those present were very serious types, none of them took what was said very seriously and were shocked several weeks later when Louis-Philippe had been, indeed, deposed. As Guy remembered it, Busscher had said little and really was more an observer than a participant.

"Your French is greatly improved," Guy noted.

"If only it were better. I have fluency in the vocabulary of business, but I'm afraid, in the idiom of much else, I am sadly lacking. I must confess to you that I attended that, shall we say, soirée, really to hear French. I had only been here a short time and wished to hear French spoken by others than fishwives and wine buyers. I did find the evening very interesting, though, and quite admired your position."

Yes, Guy remembered, Busscher, in his halting French, had raised an interesting point which had served to strengthen Guy's argument. He was only too pleased to renew his acquaintance with the Dutchman.

"Come with us to the Cafe Lido and practice," he urged. "What do you think, Solange? If there's no confronting the good wine merchant, let's at least give his assistant some French lessons. Some good should come out of this fiasco today."

Solange could do little else but agree since she hadn't any idea where Guy had met Busscher before, what kind of appointment Schroeder could have that would have caused the bookkeeper such embarrassment, or even why Guy had been in such a furied rush to see Schroeder. And even if she had the answers to those questions, she wouldn't have turned down the chance to be grown-up and sophisticated by sipping wine in the Cafe Lido. She had never been allowed to do anything like that before.

The Lido was a distance away, in the old section of the city near the Grosse Cloche, the Big Clock. If Solange hadn't been with them, Guy would have suggested walking there. Bordeaux was a city of grand boulevards, lovely parks, amusing sidestreets, and beckoning alleyways. But Solange was now a young lady and young ladies did not go tromping through the streets of Bordeaux. So the three went by carriage.

The Lido was bright, large, bustling, really more of a brasserie with an extensive menu than a cafe. It was the meeting place of much of Bordeaux. At lunch, men of business met to discuss commerce. At twilight they brought their mistresses. Often, later, they returned with their wives for dinner or supper. At all hours of the day, at least at two or three of the tables, wine was sure to be the topic under discussion.

There was a large crowd when Guy and his party arrived, but they did find a large round table near the front windows. The waiter had just taken their order—a bottle of 1845 Margaux—when they were seen by Marcel Duvier, owner of Château Belgrave, one of the smaller vineyards in Lamarque, somewhat south of St. Julien.

Duvier, over the years, had dined many times at du Clocher, and although he was closer in age to the father, he felt more affinity for the son. He greeted the younger Saint-Savin affectionately.

With him was a portly man, his face mottled from years of over-indulgence, who was wearing too much of everything to be in good taste. Duvier introduced him as the new prefect, Monsieur Aristide Donnadieu.

"He was just arrived and I was sure the Lido would keep him from getting homesick for Paris."

Donnadieu waved his hand in supercilious dismissal. "Well, this is not the Grand Vefour, but I suppose it will do."

"But then again, Monsieur le préfet," Guy said coldly, "it is not trying to be the Grand Vefour. It is doing quite well as itself." Turning to Duvier, he added, "But the honorable prefect and I need no introduction. We have already met in Paris."

Donnadieu reached for recollection and was not at all happy with what he remembered.

Aristide Donnadieu, soon to be forty years old, had realized early in his career that he was an ambitious man. Coming from a bourgeois family of moderate means and having no powerful mentors, he went into politics hoping that he might find a political star on whom he could hitch his ambitions. Not surprisingly, the men of influence in King Louis-Philippe's court weren't interested in the hustling, hungry Parisian. They had sons of relatives and friends to support and advance. Donnadieu had to be content with running errands for a Bonapartist, long out of favor and with little likelihood of regaining it.

But the years and fate were kind to Donnadieu. More and more whispers and then rumblings carried the name of Louis-Napoleon. Then came the unexpected fall of Louis-Philippe, the rise of the Second Republic, and the resounding victory of Louis-Napoleon in the presidential election. Donnadieu rode into the chambers of power on the coattails of his once-lowly Bonapartist. True, at first his ambitions were not fully realized. He was still little more than flunky, still running errands. He knew that. He didn't want others to know that. So he tended to be harsh and overbearing with those he believed could not fight back.

Which had led to an incident with Guy. Guy had been standing with a group of young aides in the austere marbled halls of the National Assembly. Donnadieu without really knowing any of them but recognizing them for what they were, had approached and chosen Guy to receive his curt order to deliver a note to a debating member within the chamber.

"I am sorry, monsieur," Guy had answered politely, "I am waiting for deputy de Pary. I am afraid I cannot leave." The other aides began shuffling nervously. They had all been bullied by Donnadieu at one time or another.

"Young man," Donnadieu said harshly, sensing that his hard-earned position of authority was being threatened, "you don't seem to be bright enough to understand. This is a note from the president, from Louis-Napoleon. Take it immediately."

"*My* good man," Guy countered, "*you* don't seem to understand. I work for deputy de Pary. Not Louis-Napoleon. Furthermore, it is my understanding the president of the republic works for the citizens of France and not the other way around."

A few of the aides started applauding, but stopped quickly when Donnadieu spun to spot the offenders. He cast a withering glare at Guy after deciding further wordplay was not to his advantage and then stomped off, dignity not intact.

The same glare was again apparent in the Lido, much to the puzzlement of Duvier, Busscher, and Solange. Guy ignored it and blithely and perhaps somewhat injudiciously invited Duvier and Donnadieu to join them as no other tables were available. Duvier accepted automatically before the prefect could protest.

When everyone was seated, Guy inquired politely as to Donnadieu's reception in Bordeaux. "I suppose you're already being bombarded with requests for road repair, perhaps construction of a new fountain or two?"

Guy was mocking him, Donnadieu was sure of that. Still he refused to give this provincial pup the satisfaction of acknowledging that he knew.

Instead he sniffed, "Yes. It's rather tiresome. I'm being petitioned for new roads, parks, street lights, even tax relief. Tax relief? Don't people out here have any idea what it costs to run a government? I, of course, tell them to speak to my assistants. I don't have time for petty details."

"You call them petty?" Guy asked sharply. "Isn't that the function of the prefect, to deal with such 'details' as these? To see that the best possible steps are taken for the welfare of the city?"

"My heavens, Saint-Savin, you do like speeches, don't you?" Donnadieu drawled. "I understand you've been writing a lot of speeches lately. They aren't too pleasing to my dear friend Louis-Napoleon, the same friend, I might add, who appointed me prefect here. I didn't want to leave Paris for this backwater, but as a favor to Louis, I agreed. So I don't think you need to tell me what it is I should be doing. The president may work for the republic, but I work for the president, not you."

Louis-Napoleon would have been outraged to be characterized as Donnadieu's "friend." The appointment was made only because Louis had been assured that Donnadieu was a non-thinking lackey who would carry out orders without question.

Luckily, before Guy could respond, the waiter arrived with the wine. Then Busscher diplomatically asked Solange if she were attending school.

Solange was flattered to be addressed. "I've been a student at the Greenbrier School for Young Ladies outside of London, but I won't be going back this year."

"You Bordelaise," snorted a still-smarting Donnadieu, "so preoccupied with everything English."

"If, perhaps, the rest of France supported us by buying more of our wine, we wouldn't have this 'preoccupation' as you call it," Guy snapped.

Now it was Duvier's turn to jump in, as it became increasingly clear that the Margaux was not the prefect's first glass of wine and that he was at least a little drunk. "But why aren't you returning, Solange, my dear? Have you completed your course there?"

Before she had a chance to answer, Donnadieu insinuated himself again. "I don't take to this ridiculous notion of educating women. Why do they need to know anything about philosophy or literature? Let their mothers teach them all they need to know."

He was sitting next to Solange and now he leaned his alcohol-shiny face inches from hers and let his plump hand slide up and down her arm in clear indication that he desired to slide it elsewhere soon. "From what I've heard and seen of *your* mother, I would be very interested to sample what she has taught you. Or I wouldn't mind getting lessons from her myself, but the line outside her boudoir door is probably too long for me."

Her mother? Her mother was dead. What was he talking about? Guy wasn't sure either, and he didn't care. All he knew was that this leering pig was handling his sister and insulting her with his suggestive remarks. He stood, ready to toss his wine at the prefect's face. Busscher's restraining hand gave him enough time to remember his resolve to be less short-tempered. Still Donnadieu's behavior was too outrageous to let pass. There was honor at stake, his sister's and his.

In a voice loud enough to effectively quiet the cafe and alert those present that something worth gossiping about was in the offing, Guy said, "Monsieur, if it wouldn't be a waste of such a fine wine, this would now be dripping off your face. Remove your hands from my sister and retract what you said about our mother. Our mother, as everyone knows, has been dead for years. Take it back, or I'll take this discussion to a more suitable spot and force you to retract your words."

A few angry blotches were the only color on Donnadieu's suddenly pasty face. He was being called out by this provincial nobody. It was inexcusable. But he wasn't so drunk and angry that he couldn't see that the provincial nobody was in better shape than he and could undoubtedly best him with little difficulty. Donnadieu searched frantically for a withering riposte, his mouth flapping open and shut in anticipation of the appropriate sounds emerging. The wine he had been imbibing since midmorning drowned the desired retort, giving Duvier time to intercede. While the owner of Château Belgrave was appalled by the prefect's boorishness and secretly would have applauded Guy's teaching him some manners, Duvier was a practical man. By the stroke of a pen in Paris, Donnadieu had become a man of power and influence, someone with whom great diplomacy should be employed. It was time Duvier stepped in and let face be saved.

"One moment, Guy," he said smoothly, "I am sure Monsieur Donnadieu was not aware of Solange's youth and believed himself to be bantering with a more worldly woman who would laugh off his remarks. Paris is, after all, much less conservative than we. He meant no harm." Duvier thought it best not to even mention the mother. And Donnadieu thought it best to let his face be saved. He mumbled something about having confused someone with Solange's dead mother, apologized for any improprieties, and allowed himself to be escorted, weaving, out of the cafe.

Solange could not accept Donnadieu's ridiculous explanation and wanted desperately to ask Guy what the prefect had meant about their mother. She knew so little about her, only that her name had been Fabienne and that her father did not speak of her. When she was very young, Solange had created a whole history about her mother, very romantic and very tragic. She had never questioned Edouard about her. It had been the cook who had said she had died, and Solange did not want to add to her father's deep grieving by speaking of her mother.

Now this dreadful man had talked as if Fabienne were alive and he knew her. Before Solange could ask her questions, Busscher observed quietly, "Monsieur Guy, I think you have just made an enemy."

"I think you're right. And do you know what? I don't care."

Chapter Eight

A loud peal, so long awaited, rang out up and down the Gironde. Pickers who had been in the fields for several days at Ducru-Beaucaillou, Leoville-Barton, and as far away as Latour, stopped to listen. At last du Clocher would begin gathering its full heavy grapes from the vines.

Guy had slept at the Mazet house after returning from Bordeaux. He didn't want to see his father and waste time in the morning with a confrontation that would have kept him from the fields.

He and Jacques had waited only for the sun to creep far enough up for them to see. Then they followed the same route through the vines that Gaston Mazet had taken at every vintage. After just an hour Guy said, "I'll go to the belltower now."

Any of the house servants could have climbed those well-worn forty-six steps and pulled on that massive rope, but Guy insisted on doing it himself. There was an exhilaration in ending the long wait, in watching the sudden flurry of movement on all sides below him. Women, men, boys, and girls rushed from their houses. Workers hurried to get their panniers, those long, squat, handled baskets they carried into the fields where Mazet had said he wanted the harvesting to begin.

By the time Guy had heaved one last time on the bell rope and was hurrying down the steps, more than forty people were already mobilized in the fields.

By the time he had hurried across the back terrace and over to the fields himself, most of the pickers were among the vines, bending over to pluck the fruit and put it into their panniers.

Guy grapped a basket and a secateur, the curved-bladed tool used to cut the grapes from the vine, and looked for an empty row.

The day was warming up and insects had begun their drone. For the first fifteen minutes it felt good to be bending over the rich purple grapes. But only a novice didn't know that soon the pleasure of working in the sun would be overwhelmed by a piercing aching in the shoulders and back, an agonizing protest of leg muscles, and intense, mind-numbing fatigue. It wouldn't be until the third or fourth day that the body capitulated and stopped noticing the pain. Picking was arduous and tedious work.

Still, Guy loved it. He played games with himself. Work faster to get the pannier a quarter filled, half filled, filled, and tipped into the horse-drawn cart waiting to take the grapes to the chai where stems and leaves could be removed from the fruit. The cleaned grapes were put into the egrappoir to be crushed. Finally the juice was drained into fermenting vats which had been cleaned and scoured and for several days filled with water to swell the wood.

Guy would cut the grapes from the vine, fill the basket, tip it into the cart. Cut, fill, tip. Cut, fill, tip. Keep count of the baskets. Fill another. Finish a row. Move to the next. The morning wore on. Finally the cry of "Lunch" was heard and all work stopped.

Two tables had been carried out from the kitchen to an open field on top of the hill. Several great pots of cassoulet, that hearty mixture of bean, pork, chicken, and beef, threw off enticing, soothing aromas. Baskets of bread and enormous wheels of cheese were set out as well, and the pickers went at it all. Plates heaping, they found places to wearily sprawl, eat, and muster their strength for the afternoon's work.

Guy was invited to join several of the groups. He declined in favor of going over to Solange and Marie-Odile who had found a shady spot under a nearby tree. With a small groan he was unable to stifle, the heir to the château stiffly lowered himself onto the blanket Solange had carefully spread out.

"I'm sorry to admit that Paris life can soften anyone, even me. Bouts at the fencing salle and walking everywhere rather than pay for a wretched cab are not enough. My body hurts."

Solange bit the corner of her lip, not wanting to show her concern. "Perhaps you shouldn't go back into the fields this afternoon. There's no reason why you can't be in the chai, why you have to be picking. Father always says you're the only owner's son who works in the fields."

Guy sloshed his good, fresh bread into the cassoulet's sauce as all the workers did. "Since when have I ever been like the foppish sons of the other châteaux? Am I so pampered that I have to leave the fields after a few short hours? Besides, if I know you, you'll be supervising the pressing. So why shouldn't I do my share?"

Despite his dismissal of Solange's suggestion, Guy was actually much stiffer than he could remember ever being before. The thought of fleeing the harsh sun and the back-breaking labor was more appealing than he cared to admit. He had always picked and he was determined to continue. He didn't want to seem as if he were suddenly putting on airs in front of the workers. And especially, he wouldn't want Marie-Odile, who was studying him so closely as she nibbled on a piece of goat's cheese, to think poorly of him.

What was she thinking. Was there laughter in those large, dark eyes? Was she mocking him or sympathizing with him? Was she starting to smile? He liked her smile. He'd decided that yesterday. It filled her face and was without deception.

Suddenly the smile vanished. Over Guy's shoulder, Marie could see Claude Mazet. He was staring at her. She didn't like him. As a little girl she'd been frightened by the whispers of the women as they told terrible stories about him while they pared their vegetables.

Guy turned to see what had stolen the smile from Marie. Damn that Mazet, he thought. He was leering at the girl. Guy would have ordered him from the château then and there, but, of course, he couldn't. It would hurt Jacques and it would hurt Jacques's mother. Guy would rather put up with Claude than do that.

Knowing he was being observed, Claude insolently scratched his crotch before slouching over to the three. He stopped very close at Marie. Instinctively she pulled the front of her dress together to shield herself, and by doing so only further accented the curve of her breasts. Claude grinned, sucked a piece of chicken from between his teeth, and walked on.

The bell rang again, summoning the workers back to the fields. When it stopped, Marie said softly, "Please, don't bother with him, Guy. Please."

She looked very worried and that disturbed Guy even more. He wanted to offer her protection and make her feel safe. Instead he could only say, "All right," and then added with vehemence, "but if he does cause any trouble for you, let me know. Come now, let's get back to the picking. We'll see at the end of the day who's filled the most panniers."

Chapter Nine

The smudgy grays of twilight lingered, unwilling to give up the day. Picking continued well after the sun had disappeared over the hill.

When the bell rang, signalling the end of the day's labors, the workers had dragged themselves wearily to their cottages to sponge off the grime and sweat and to steal a few minutes of rest. Now they were returning to du Clocher with the high spirits of anticipation, weariness already forgotten. Laughter bounced off the shadows of the coming night as men, women, and children hurried to the château's garden.

Only twice a year were they invited there. On Christmas Eve to receive and give well-wishes for the holiday. And on the first night of the harvest.

Generally the workers were ill-at-ease in the garden, fearful of straying and stepping on a precious plant or blundering into some other unforgivable act. They came because it was expected, it was ritual, and when the ritual was over, a party celebrating the first day of harvest could begin.

A murmur of welcome arose when Edouard, Solange, and Guy appeared at the terrace balustrade.

As called for by tradition, Jacques Mazet stepped forward with a large bouquet of sprigs and flowers and grape bunches. "Monsieur le compte, for the mademoiselle, and we all pray for a bountiful harvest."

Mazet, being so short, was unable to reach high enough to hand Solange the bouquet. So, as always, he was lifted up by two of the other men while the workers tittered.

"My daughter accepts your token with pleasure. God willing, there shall be a good harvest."

54

A subdued cheer went up. The ceremony was over and the fun could begin. The workers left the garden as quickly as possible and headed back to the field where they had eaten lunch. The same two tables were there. One was now covered with kegs of wine, the other with mountains of cold roasted chicken, vegetables, patés, and fruits.

The more prudent went to the food table first, so that empty stomachs wouldn't be assaulted by wine. Most, however, went directly to the wine. No reason to postpone the festivities.

The field could be seen from the terrace. Edouard sat down with his aperitif. Solange and Guy watched from the balustrade. Suddenly he grabbed her hand.

"Come little sister, why should we be left out?" He pulled her toward the steps and freedom until he remembered his manners. "Sir, we'll be dining out this evening. Please start dinner without us."

Ordinarily Edouard would have protested that the raucous peasant doings were not the proper setting for Solange. But their going meant a reprieve from spending time with Guy. Except for the few minutes on the terrace, the two men had not seen each other all day. Besides, Edouard would be able to keep an eye on his daughter from where he was. He would send Marcel to fetch her shortly.

Brother and sister, both so slender and long-legged, were running by the time they reached the field, drawn to the music that was coming from near one of the bonfires.

"Solange, they're dancing. Let's join them," Guy yelled above the noise.

"I don't know how to dance like that," she protested. The sedate little bows and whirls she learned at the Greenbrier School for Young Ladies was not going to help here.

"Neither do I. We'll learn. Look, there's Marie. She must know how. Marie," he called happily, "come dance with us. We need you to teach us."

Marie-Odile loved the abandonment of the dancing and was glad she was asked to join. If nothing else, it would give her something to do. She had been wandering around and feeling very much the outsider. It was strange. She knew these people, they had been her people. Yet the time she had been in St. Emilion, when she had gone from short dresses to womanhood, had created a distance between her and them. The men, especially, didn't know how to treat her. They knew a cute little girl. Suddenly in her place, answering to her name, was a desirable woman. The older women saw her as competition for their daughters, and couldn't help treating her coolly. And then there was Claude Mazet. Every time Marie-Odile looked around, he was there, stalking her, watching her, his crude, nasty thoughts evident in his every move and expression.

Now all her concerns were being whirled away in the lively dance that went faster and faster until the entire circle collapsed.

When the fire had subsided in Guy's lungs, he offered to get some wine. Solange declined. "I'd better get back to Father. He won't be pleased if I stay much longer."

"Solange, really, you must stop worrying about always pleasing Father. You're practically grown up now. You must think for yourself and be yourself. Just because you're a female doesn't mean you have to be a weak soul. Isn't that right, Marie?"

Since he wasn't expecting an answer, Guy didn't wait for one. "Okay, okay. If you insist, Solange. I will escort you home. Only on the condition that Marie promises me the next dance."

Marie, quite pleased, nodded her assent. Guy was so unpredictable, she thought. He'd always been. And he had always been so much fun. She had had such a crush on him when she was a girl. Daring, adventurous Guy, who had found time to teach her how to read and lent her his favorite books. She and Solange had followed him everywhere. So wonderful and so above her station.

Marie drifted toward the wine table. She filled her cup and was about to sip from it when someone behind her, very close, half-whispered in her ear, "You dance real well with the muckety-mucks. You too good to do it with one of your own?"

She was so startled, she spilled most of the wine down the front of her dress. It was Claude. How had she missed him? Her fear became anger and she was determined not to show it.

"Monsieur Mazet, you know Guy has never held himself above anyone."

"It's all a lousy act. A politician he wants to be. Loved by all he wants to be. So Guy High-and-Mighty comes to practice on us. Well, he won't be loved by me. He's just another goddamned aristocrat. We should of killed them all in the Revolution when we had a chance." Claude moved closer to Marie. "You, on the other hand, you can be loved by me any time."

He smelled from stale wine and reeked of foul intentions. Marie backed away.

"Where you going, Marie? A Mazet not good enough for you? After a bigger prize? Here let me show you I got manners, just like any Saint-Savin. Let me wipe that wine off your dress for you."

Before she could react, Mazet grabbed her with one hand and began rubbing the other across her bodice. Her breasts were firm and high. He felt himself harden as her nipples tautened under his demanding pressure. He wanted this one.

"There now, that's better." He said hoarsely, propelling her toward the darkness. "Now you're showing what you want. Your tits are ready. What about the rest of you? That ready, too?"

When he loosened his hold slightly to force his hand down her dress, Marie acted. Delivering a sharp kick to his ankle, she wrenched away, and didn't stop running until she was behind the door in the relative safety of her aunt's cottage.

Guy looked for her when he returned. He asked several people if they had seen her. None had. He was disappointed. Very disappointed. There no longer seemed any point in staying. He didn't.

Chapter Ten

Two weeks and the weather held. No downpour or storm or hail to ruin the harvest.

The forty-three pickers had wielded their heavy shortbladed secateurs in constant snips and cuts, taking care not to bruise or break the fruit, taking care to keep leaves and twigs out of the baskets, taking care to work without pause in their race against Nature. As the sun came up each day, it brought with it the smells of the harvest—soil, sweet fruit, and sweat.

And so they toiled until row after row was shorn of its fruit and thick vines could be seen through the drooping but still-green leaves. In the weeks to follow, these leaves would slip into the gold and oranges of autumn until finally falling to the relative harshness of winter. Now they provided a mothering mantle over the vines.

Guy snipped one last bunch of grapes and then meticulously wiped his blades clean. He had finished his row and there were no more to start. He went to the chai to replace his tool and watch the last fruit being pressed.

A mule slowly turned a tall vertical screw, which in turn forced a thick wooden beam down onto the grapes. Around and around the animal went while more and more of the grapes were fed into the press.

Jacques was there watching, also.

"One more cart," he said. "And it's done."

"How did we do?"

"Lucky. Very lucky. The odium killed maybe a third, no more. Next year could be worse. It spreads, it spreads fast."

"Jacques, I'm so tired from the last two weeks that I can't think about anything further in the future than tonight. We'll talk tomorrow. There has to be some way to beat this damned blight. We'll find it."

Jacques nodded dubiously. "And tomorrow you'll be less tired than now? After Count Edouard's banquet in the château and the workers' to-do out here?"

Guy laughed. "You may have a point. Though, believe me, sheer boredom will be the most fatiguing thing about my father's grand affair. Be that as it may, I promise to be refreshed and ready to make plans and begin next year's work. Tomorrow. Early."

"Perhaps we should finish vatting this year's grape before we start next year."

"Of course, that, too. We'll do everything, anything. Just let me get to my hot bath so that I may gird myself for all those gentle men and gentle women who will be arriving soon. God, how I hate these affairs. A *bientôt.*"

Despite disparaging Edouard's dinner parties, Guy was looking forward to this particular one. There was a certain guest he wanted to meet. Baron Nathan Libermann, the much-gossiped-about, speculated-over, sought-after prodigal son of the most powerful banking family in Europe, which, of course, meant the whole world. By all accounts, he was extremely intelligent, iconoclastic, and very amusing. The stories bandied about Paris concerning Baron Nathan's parties and escapades—well, they sounded most interesting indeed.

"Monsieur Guy, if you please ... " The butler Marcel materialized as Guy entered the château. "The count wishes to speak with you."

Guy and Edouard had successfully avoided each other throughout the harvest without admitting to themselves that was their objective. Now, very much in need of a muscle-relaxing soak, Guy was quite willing to admit he didn't want to see his father.

"Marcel, tell him I'll join him as soon ... "

"Monsieur, I think you should come now. The count, he is ... he is insistent on talking with you immediately. Please, Monsieur Guy."

There was no point in causing trouble for the butler. The bath would wait.

Edouard had been busy during the vendage also. This dinner was the most important of the year, and his guest list reflected that. There were so many to impress, and he would not have Guy ruin the evening by antagonizing any of them. Ordinarily Edouard approached a subject warily, skirting and circling it, gradually closing in on it until whomever he was talking to would acquiesce to anything as long as Edouard got to the point. It was a tactic that often worked well, but Edouard didn't have the time this evening.

As soon as Guy had closed the door behind him, Edouard began. "I must insist you remove yourself from all politics, now, tonight."

"What's wrong, Father?" Guy asked. "Will you never give up? Why can't you try to understand? I'm not going to change my mind, even if we are practically destitute."

Edouard shook his head impatiently. "Now listen, young man, while we may no longer have the Saint-Savin fortune, we do have the Saint-Savin legacy. I believe that is far more important than money."

"Yes, yes," There was no hiding Guy's disparagement. "The Saint-Savin legacy—our good name, our sterling reputation, our impeccable place in society ..."

Edouard waved him silent. For once he knew he was in control, even if Guy didn't know that yet. "While we have all those, the legacy I refer to is du Clocher itself. I have been increasingly concerned over what will become of it in the event of my death."

"It might have been wiser if you had been more concerned with it during your lifetime."

"Please don't interrupt, Guy. As I was saying, it was fortuitous that since Frederic gave the château to Philippe, there has been only one heir each generation. First my father, then me."

Guy was impatient. He didn't realize his father wasn't skirting his topic as usual. This was his topic.

"So what are you leading to? That in this generation Solange and I both inherit? That is the law."

"True. That is the law. And according to it, du Clocher will be divided between you. And that in itself constitutes no threat to the château. It's when you marry and have children the problem arises. On your deaths, the estate will be divided among all your children, and then their children and so on until there is nothing left except tiny parcels owned by many different people. I will not have du Clocher so butchered. It must remain in one piece, whole, as it is."

"What do you intend to do, Father? Ask my pledge to throw myself into the Gironde when a convenient tidal 'bore' comes sweeping up from the Atlantic and drown myself before I have any issue? Or do you want Solange to plunge a dagger into the heart of all her children after the first?"

"If you choose not to take this discussion seriously, so be it. However, I will continue by informing you of what has been suggested by Baron Nathan Libermann ..."

"Baron Nathan?" Guy was genuinely surprised and didn't notice Edouard's frowning disapproval of his informality with the baron's name. "I had no idea you were good enough friends with him to solicit advice."

"We have met and he has taken an interest in du Clocher. Besides this problem of inheritance is a problem for all of Bordeaux. It is his counsel that we create a limited company in which the family members have stock. In that way, on my death, only the stock and not the vineyard will be divided."

My god, thought Guy, how clever. Baron Nathan certainly lives up to his reputation. He had come up, almost offhandedly, with an ingenious circumvention of the stringent inheritance law, which though it had abolished the inequity of primogeniture, had produced a swarm of its own problems. In Burgundy, the estates had already fallen prey to the carving knife of inheritance, leaving only minuscule plots to be tilled.

Guy frowned. While very interesting, this couldn't be all that Edouard had been so adamant about telling him. "How does this worthy scheme have any bearing on my staying in Paris?"

"It's quite simple, my son. After the baron made this suggestion, I gave it much thought. So what I am about to say, I do not say rashly or in anger ..."

"All right, Father. What is it you want to say?"

"Simply this." Edouard was so wrapped up with his announcement, he didn't even frown at Guy's ill manners. "I must put the good of du Clocher above all else. Since the lack of money does not daunt you, perhaps this will."

Edouard paused. Guy pressed his eyes shut in frustration. If he interrupted anymore, there would be further digressions. He waited.

At last Edouard continued with as much solemnity as God must have evidenced handing down the commandments to Moses. "Unless you promise to quit Paris and these foolish intrigues of yours, I will turn all stock over to Solange. There will be nothing for you to inherit, and du Clocher will be done with you forever."

He could and would do it. Guy saw that immediately. His father had finally come up with an effective, powerful weapon against him. For no matter how strongly he felt about the Second Republic and France, Guy felt more for du Clocher. To rob him of that was to rob him of himself.

Suddenly Guy was consumed with bitterness. It was unlike any anger or rage he had felt before. It was an intense, sickening hatred that plunged into his very marrow. He hated his father—and he hated himself for his feeling. At that moment, it was all he could do not to strike out and rip the smugness from his father's face.

On his part, Edouard was relieved when his son failed to respond.

Wanting to believe he had gained the upper hand at last, he pushed his advantage. "Furthermore, I have been made aware of your, shall we say, unpleasantness with Monsieur Donnadieu at the Lido. I was not told the nature of the argument nor do I want to know. What it was about doesn't really matter. What does is you've managed to antagonize the most important man in Bordeaux, someone who can as easily do things for us as against us. Now I will have to do my utmost to mollify him. That's why he will be here tonight. So that we, both of us, can make amends."

Edouard turned away from the expected protest. When none came, he went on, a little puzzled. Usually Guy would have made some impassioned speech, refusing to abide by his father's wishes. What was he thinking now, what was he planning?

Edouard continued, "So I order you to make amends. And whatever else you do, do not enter into any conversation of a controversial nature. And ... and that is what I order."

Again he waited for a response. Again there was none. It was with relief that Edouard heard the door close as his son left the room.

A fury had enveloped Guy, so complete and smothering that he saw nothing, heard nothing, and had no idea where he was going or where he was until he could go no further because he had reached the river's edge.

Smashing through his thoughts was how myopic, insular, narrow-minded his father was. Why couldn't Edouard see that what happened to France happened to du Clocher?

He picked up a handful of stones and began hurling them one at a time with all the force his anger could call forth until muscles in his arm and shoulder scorched with pain.

A hand gently closed over his.

It was Marie-Odile.

She said nothing. There was no need to, for her face was etched with concern. When Guy finally tried to speak, he choked on the words, and then, to his horror and frustration, he felt tears forming, tears he couldn't control or stop.

Marie gathered him to her and guided him down onto the ground next to her. They sat, with her cradling his head and stroking his hair.

"It will be all right," she crooned. "It will be all right."

Coming from the north, from the town of Paulliac, Baron Nathan Libermann had witnessed Guy's explosive exit.

There's a very upset young man, he thought to himself. This could be an intriguing evening after all.

It certainly was not starting out as such. It took a great deal of effort for Nathan to refocus his attention back to the discourse of the other occupant of the ornate leather and velvet-appointed carriage, his brother, the Baron Jerome Libermann.

While it might not have been something to admit in polite company, although Nathan occasionally did, the youngest Libermann was not overly fond of his brother, the esteemed head of the Banque Libermann, one of the five Libermann banks in Europe. Nathan found him boring, pompous, rapacious, self-absorbed, petty, and only put up with him as much as he did because from time to time Jerome's intrigues and obsessive exercise of power amused him.

" ... and, of course, the Banque of André and Lottier does not have the resources they would pretend to have. My people say they are down to a mere four million francs. Four million! So naturally when the time comes and Morny is looking for capital for Louis-Napoleon, the Banque Libermann will be the one they turn to, as always. Were we not there for the Little Emperor after Waterloo? As I have always tried to instruct you, whoever sits on the throne doesn't necessarily rule the country."

"Yes, dear brother," Nathan felt behooved once in a while to make a contribution to the conversation, "as Stendhal wrote, 'The bankers are the heart of the state. The bourgeoisie has replaced the fauborg St. Germain'—how the aristocracy loves that section of Paris—'and the bankers are the nobility of the bourgeois class.'"

"Well, I certainly agree with the fellow that the Libermanns are among the nobility, but I hardly like being classed with the shopkeepers and petit industrialists of the bourgeois generale. Their pretensions and meager stabs at culture are so pitiful. Who is this Stendhal person, anyway? I don't recall him being discussed at any of my dear Rachel's Sunday salons."

"He probably hasn't been, Jerome. Stendhal isn't fashionable, you see. He is merely the most insightful and keenest writers France has ever produced."

"If you think so highly of him, perhaps Rachel should include him on the guest list for her next salon."

"Rachel is much too fastidious to invite Stendhal, my most learned brother. He's been dead for two years. But enough of this fascinating talk. I'm sure Edouard Saint-Savin, or, at the very least, his butler, must be wondering why we have stopped in front of his very beautiful château and have not deigned to descend from your modest conveyance."

"I do hope I'm not seated next to Edouard tonight," Jerome muttered. "The man talks nothing but wine. No wonder Fabienne left him."

Chapter Eleven

If it were not for the physical similarities that belied the notion, there were many who could have believed Nathan was a foundling.

Nathan Aaron Libermann, however, was indeed the youngest of five sons of the immensely wealthy banking family, a family whose very name was synonomous with money, power, and tasteful opulence.

His father, Lionel Libermann, had entered the realm of high finance in a most modest fashion. He had begun his wage-earning life—at the age of eight—as a shoemaker's apprentice in the warren-like Jewish ghetto of Vienna. Being of a profoundly frugal nature and having the good sense to marry a woman who could stretch one scrawny chicken over several days' meals, Lionel was able to put away some of whatever he earned. After years of scrimping, he had a nice sum of money tucked into the crannies and niches of his small, cramped house. It was enough to begin lending to others less fortunate and less economical than he at healthy if not quite usurious interest rates—which made him extremely popular and well-thought-of, since usury was the common practice at the time.

Lionel was both shrewd and lucky and became good at weeding out the less-fortunates who weren't likely to repay the loans. Within a couple of years, his money-lending income far surpassed that from his cobbling. Still he never relinquished his awl and did some shoe-making for the rest of his life.

It was Lionel's destiny to prosper. The factor that eventually pushed him over the line from prosperity to incredible wealth came in the form of one Prince Frederic of Mecklenburg.

The prince had been impressed with stories of Lionel's monetary wizardry and took him on as financial agent, whisking him out of the ghetto and giving him the world. Whisking him out figuratively, that is. Lionel never moved his household. Instead he bought the rest of the block and combined those houses with his own into one large residence, but he never left that winding cobbled street for a more impressive address.

As his sons grew, Lionel strove to instill them with the respect and reverence he had for work and for the power of money. He trained, pushed, and nudged them. One by one, as he deemed them ready, he dispatched them to different parts of the world to establish Libermann banks—London, Paris, Milan, Rome.

All except Nathan. Nathan was the misfit. Lionel viewed him as his one failure and rued the waste. Of the five brothers, Nathan was clearly the brightest. He could have achieved anything if Lionel had been able to make him hungry for business, make him enjoy commerce, and take pleasure in the increase of capital.

Nathan was more interested in useless pastimes like art and literature, travel and exploration, and when he reached puberty, women. Not the plain, obedient young Jewish girls with well-connected fathers that the other sons married. No, Nathan sought out flamboyant, outrageous, unusual, fascinating, of any color, nationality, religion but always beautiful women.

It bewildered Lionel that the attraction was mutual. Starting from when Nathan's voice was changing, women were drawn to him and were as likely to be seducing him as he them.

It certainly had nothing to do with Nathan's looks. There was no handsome Casanova there. He was of medium height and had a tendency to carry too much weight above the belt. He had a large, almost out-of-proportioned head and an equally large nose. Add to this the full, fleshy lips, and Nathan was not going to be pursued by any artist to pose as Adonis.

Yet these features went almost unnoticed by women. What they remembered were his dark, deep-set, knowing eyes that caressed the object of his attention and told her he understood her and promised all she could desire. Even the most elderly grande dame could be made to blush at the promise of those eyes.

Nathan delivered on the unspoken promise. By his count when he was twenty—and after that he stopped counting—he had made love to at least one hundred women. He learned from each of them.

Nathan's success with the ladies and his refusal to succeed in the banking arena was an embarrassment for Lionel. Finally his wife prevailed on him to give Nathan a chance on his own, arguing that with freedom his son might find banking interesting. Lionel chose to send him as far off as possible that made fiscal sense. Brazil.

Nathan obliged by going. He had an intriguing two years exploring the Amazon, purchasing art relics, playing patron to several talented artists, financing a coup in Paraguay, and, of course, savoring a generous sample of one of Brazil's most precious natural resources—its women.

All this left little time for the Banque Libermann. At the end of two years, Lionel conceded defeat and called his son home.

To show his intense displeasure in the strongest way he could imagine, Lionel cut Nathan off financially. For a while after that, helped only by what funds his mother sent him secretly, Nathan lived a catch-as-catch-can existence on Paris's left bank. He painted and caroused, attended classes, juggled in the Gruse Circus (and had a particularly satisfying liaison with a trapeze artiste whose suppleness and double-joints brought some delightful and unusual nuances to their love-making). He tried writing, but gave it up, not for lack of talent but for lack of patience.

He met one extremely lovely Russian countess on the Côte d'Azur and followed her to the court of Czar Nicholas I. He had to quit the court quite suddenly several months later when he was found in a compromising position with a favorite of the Czar. Nicholas might have overlooked the indiscretion if Nathan and the favorite hadn't chosen the balcony rail overlooking a grand ball in progress at which to succumb to their passion.

It was during this period that Nathan got his only itch to make money. He neither cared for relying on the generosity of others nor liked curtailing his pastimes for lack of funds. The only solution, therefore, was to earn his own fortune.

So he sold some of his art collection and invested the proceeds in friendships. He had many different circles of friends. Artists and writers. Waiters and chefs. Shoemakers and singers. He invested in them all.

Reynard Bernard was one.

They had met when they were both regulars at a cafe in Montmartre. Nathan was soon to learn from firsthand experience that Reynard was a sublime chef. He could fashion culinary masterpieces out of the simplest ingredients. Present Reynard with a few leeks, a potato or two, and a piece of lamb, and the resulting stew was ambrosia. Offer him more elegant ingredients and kings would have abdicated for the creation.

Reynard was a sous-chef when Nathan met him and never likely to battle his way up through the complex and mean-spirited hierarchy of the kitchen. Nathan backed him in a restaurant which was to become legendary for its food, clientele—and the audacious actions of a resourceful and patriotic waiter. It was there that a Prussian officer demanded some coffee be served to him in a cup that had never touched French lips. The obliging waiter brought the expresso back in a chamber pot.

Nathan financed bookshops, bought property, had some racehorses, invested and reinvested. He demonstrated much the same cleverness and shrewdness as his father and within a few years had acquired his own considerable fortune.

After a while, his father, unaware of Nathan's business activity, took pity on his son and reinstated his allowance. Nathan accepted, not out of greed, but because he realized his father's imagined control over him through the purse strings was the only pleasure he got from the relationship.

It was also during this period of bohemianism and investment that Nathan and Louis-Napoleon became friends. In some ways it was to be expected. They had many of the same friends, were from respected backgrounds but slightly disreputable themselves, and enjoyed fine foods and many affairs—indeed, over the years some of the same women were to be their mistresses, sometimes at the same time and in the same beds, for neither man was possessive or shy.

And yet they were also very, very different. Louis was at the core a political being. His father had been king of Holland and his uncle, Napoleon I, the emperor of France. Louis viewed himself as the pretender to the French throne, though not many others agreed. He made two attempts to claim what he felt was his birthright. In reward for the second, he was imprisoned in the fortress at Ham, though it was hardly an overly oppressive incarceration. Nathan was among those who saw to that. Louis's six years at Ham included good food, excellent wine, an adequate library, and a delightful mistress.

There were some who believed that Louis-Napoleon's escape from Ham—he simply donned a workman's clothes and walked out with a building crew there making repairs—was financed by Nathan. That was never confirmed or proven. But if Nathan had provided the money for bribing the guards and fleeing France, it was not for any political motivation or any fervent belief in Bonapartism. It would have been only to help a friend. Nothing more; nothing less. And if Nathan kept track of the intrigues and schemes in the National Assembly, it was because so many of his friends and acquaintances—

not only Louis—were involved in them. Besides it was a diverting pastime trying to divine the machinations of his dear brother, Jerome.

If asked, Nathan, now nearing fifty, would have admitted that he enjoyed life. His one cause for regret, despite all the women he had known, was he had never been truly in love. He thought he had been once. He had felt deep passion, concern, joy, even commitment. Then she had left him to be Jerome's mistress. When she was gone, Nathan realized that they had never had friendship and what he had felt for her wasn't love, after all. Yet he regretted her loss as he regretted no other. He still did.

In no way did he resent Jerome's "triumph," because he understood his brother's needs and motivation and actually found the consequences funny. In the beginning Jerome had wanted the woman only because she was Nathan's. But after he had her, she had overwhelmed him and he lost control. He actually needed her, and in a way, that was Nathan's unsolicited revenge.

Chapter Twelve

The bell's peals once again soared high into the still-cloudless sky, signalling that for one more year, man had outraced and outworked the caprices of Nature. Harvest was done.

Cheers were heard from every part of du Clocher, from the kitchen to the chai and fields. In his library, Edouard looked up from the vintage book and allowed himself one small sigh of relief.

At the Hotel du Port, Jean-Gabriel Bellay poured a brandy, knocked it back, and closed up. This was one night when there would be no business, for if the first-night festivities were long and hardly sedate, tonight's revelry would be ten times more so. There would be only a few people tomorrow who would remember what they did the night before. And Bellay would not be one of them.

Perhaps that was best. Some things were better forgotten. As the festivities wore on, more and more of the men and women paired off—and not always with their spouses—to find spots to grope and grapple and sow the seeds for next spring's harvest of babies. If too much were remembered, certain proud fathers nine months hence might not be so proud.

On this night, all manner of food, prepared weeks in advance in the château's kitchen and at the more modest hearths of the workers, would be spread out. There would be not one circle of dancers, but many dotted over the fields, dancing to different tunes and tempos in a kaleidoscope of movement, color, and light. All fine entertainment for the considerably more subdued guests of the château.

As twilight softened the harshness of day, these guests had begun to arrive, carefully alighting from trap and carriage and well-groomed steed. The Libermanns. General Hopewell. Madame and Monsieur d'Estournel, of Cos d'Estournel, with its chais of such fanciful Chinese style that many visitors mistook it for a palace.

Next to arrive had been the Marquis de las Marismas—Monsieur d'Aguado—a retired banker who had bought Château Margaux several years earlier. Some contended that the First Empire building of Margaux with its colonnaded portico was lovelier than even du Clocher.

Mademoiselle Hue of Château Lacombes, a highly regarded wine, came in a flustered rush, sure as always that she was late, constantly brushing out an imagined crease in a gown of billowing silk.

In contrast was the serene Vicomtesse Lavaur who was helped from her carriage by her brother, Baron de Pichon. The vicomtesse had never allowed anything or anyone in her eighty-three years to prod her faster than her accustomed majestic pace and assumed that she was never late, but rather the other party was early. She paused for a moment to welcome the next guest, Baron Poyferre, as if du Clocher were hers, before allowing her brother to escort her inside. It had only been in the last few years that the vicomtesse had even acknowledged the baron's existence, although they had often attended the same functions. His vineyard had once been part of the enormous Leoville estate that had been broken up during the Revolution. The grande dame had been a monarchist from birth and would remain such until death. Anyone who had benefitted even in the slightest or most tangential way from the Revolution took a long time to be forgiven.

The next guest, Aime Vanlergerghe, still had not been rewarded the vicomtesse's approval. She looked down upon him as a parvenu since his father had been a mere grain merchant. Of course, his father had been the grain merchant who supplied the armies of Napoleon I, making him one of the wealthiest men in France, but that mattered little to the vicomtesse. However, should it prove as rumored that Vanlergerghe was now the owner of Lafitte, then she would have to be at least civil to him. The grain-merchant's son was followed by a few other neighbors, several guests from the capital, and Monsieur Donnadieu.

Donnadieu had deliberated long over whether he should turn down Edouard's invitation as a rebuff to Guy. When he saw that Jerome Libermann was present, he was delighted he hadn't. Libermann could advance the prefect's career and therefore was someone Donnadieu wished to impress and was already trying to do so when Guy joined the guests in the front drawing room.

"Being prefect is an impossible task, you know," Donnadieu was saying. "Many of the locals resent you because you're not from the

region. Paris gets suspicious if you seem too much an advocate of the
region at the expense of the nation."

"Yes, yes," General Hopewell bellowed good-naturedly, "job needing great tact, great diplomacy. Something I never had myself. Don't
envy you at all. No, no, not at all."

Donnadieu acknowledged the interruption with a dismissive nod.
It was his birthright to detest the English, but one could never tell.
This might be an important Englishman and therefore should not be
ignored completely.

"Bordeaux need not worry. I have something far more important
than tact and diplomacy. I have influence, a great deal of influence in
Paris. Where it counts."

Nathan looked over to his brother with raised eyebrows, but
Jerome merely shrugged. Let the ass posture if he wanted. Nathan
and Jerome both knew that the braggadocio Donnadieu was in truth
an insignificant functionary being rewarded for years of groveling.
Louis-Napoleon had needed such men as Donnadieu after he had
purged members of the opposing party from the ranks of the prefects.

"As someone who knows Paris politics, Monsieur Donnadieu,"
Baron de Pichon, the timid and pale younger brother of the
vicomtesse, ventured, "do you think that Louis will persuade the
Assembly to change the constitution?"

"Running for a second term isn't what's worrying Louis," broke in
the always direct and forceful Marquis de las Marismas. "Wringing
more money from the Assembly is what's bothering him. Six hundred
thousand francs a year for his expenses wasn't enough. Another six
hundred thousand still didn't do it. I hear he's knocking on doors all
over Paris looking for money. Wish I was still in banking. Love to be
able to look into his eyes and tell him that the president of the United
States makes do with the equivalent of 125 thousand francs."

"Marquis, really," sniffed the vicomtesse, "how can you mention
France and the United States in the same breath? France is one of the
Great Powers. The United States is backward, uncivilized, insignificant, and shall always remain so. Louis-Napoleon has the good sense
to know France has its reputation and prestige to uphold, and that
can't be done by being miserly and cheap. What would the rest of
Europe think?"

"I don't know what the rest of Europe would think, but what I think
is the prestige of France could be well-maintained without lavish
balls for three thousand people," the marquis retorted.

Madame d'Estournel had been talking with Guy, but now she

turned to Donnadieu's circle. She was an elegant woman, who had once been considered one of the great beauties of Paris. More than her long-passed youth, she missed the capital and its gossip.

"I understand," she was happy to have a tidbit to contribute, "that Louis's, shall we say, companion, that Englishwoman, Miss Howard, has kindly helped him out financially. I understand it's close to a million francs. For the daughter of a shoemaker, she's done remarkably well, wouldn't you say?"

"I've had the pleasure of meeting her," the Marquis de las Marismas said. "She's charming and lovely and it is easy to see why she's done well. I, for one, do not object to her aiding Louis in his frivolity. It's all the others we need to worry about. He's gone begging to foreign leaders, like that butcher in Spain, Narvaez. Louis should be working to depose that monster, not cozying up to him for loans."

Donnadieu was getting very uncomfortable as the conversation became, to his mind, more and more anti-Bonaparte. It would not do for it to get back that the prefect had taken part in such criticism. He needed to make his loyalty unquestionably clear.

"Messieurs, mesdames, please," he whined, "I can assure you, assure you, that money is not utmost in the president's mind, but rather his greatest concern is being allowed to serve the Republic and the country further. It is appalling that the Assembly, because of its quibbling and self-interest, would deprive France of such a remarkable leader as Louis-Napoleon, someone who in such a short time has accomplished so much."

Although Guy had decided to acquiesce to his father's demand that he steer away from controversy that night, he had to speak up.

"Oh yes, he's done so much, such as allowing General Oudinot to break a truce and slaughter a thousand Italian freedom fighters outside of Rome?"

Donnadieu glared at Guy. "General Oudinot was trying to restore Rome to the Pope, to whom it belongs. France, as the Catholic Church's oldest daughter, had the responsibility to do so. And besides those thousand 'freedom fighters,' as you call them, were nothing more than rabble-rousing anarchists out to destroy civilization. Perhaps that is where your sympathies lie?"

Monsieur d'Estournel was appalled. "Oh really, you shouldn't suggest such a thing."

Edouard had moved over to the group when he saw that Guy had joined it. On hearing Donnadieu's belligerent question, he quickly motioned to the butler to announce dinner. Edouard then turned to the formidable vicomtesse. "My dear lady," he said, "please take my arm. And Guy, if you will escort Madame d'Estournel," thereby diplomatically ending the conversation.

The dining room was across the entrance hall from where the guests had been sipping aperitifs. Nathan and Jerome were among the last to leave for it.

As they stepped into the hall, Jerome was asking, "The young Saint-Savin, didn't I see him rushing out...?"

Something made him stop, a movement, an apparition from dreams at the top of the stairs.

It was Solange, wearing a gown of delicate cream chantilly, beaded at the collar. The sconces behind her cast her chestnut hair into a deep red, ethereal shimmer while shadowing her face.

Her pause was one an accomplished actress would have envied. All eyes went to her and all attention was riveted on her. In fact, it was done completely without artifice. She had stopped only to be sure that her feet wouldn't get tangled in her long dress.

"My god," Jerome sputtered. "It can't be her. Not here."

Then Solange moved down the stairs, and Jerome saw it was indeed not whom he had, for that instant, imagined it was.

"She must be the daughter," Nathan said quietly. Just then General Hopewell, who had been right behind the brothers, roared, "Solange, my lovely girl, shame on you. You've been back for days and did you come over to visit me? Come down right now and make amends."

Eager to comply, Solange started to hurry down the steps only to suddenly remember all the dreary lessons in comportment she had suffered through at the English finishing school. She slowed down abruptly, too abruptly, and her shoe got caught in the hem of her dress. She pitched down the last two steps.

Solange probably would have landed face down on the oriental runner if Nathan hadn't had excellent reflexes honed by hours of fencing. He moved quickly, caught her, and found himself looking straight into—for she was as tall, if not taller, than he—the lightest green, most crystalline eyes he had ever seen. He would have looked longer, but Hopewell's beefy hand grabbed his shoulder.

"Come, come. You'll have to get in line, monsieur le baron. This young lady is spoken for. I've had my claim in for years. Now you come here, Solange, give me a hug, and let me escort you in to dinner. There's a good girl. Have you turned sixteen yet? How much longer does an old man like me have to wait to marry you?"

Solange bestowed a shy smile of thanks on Nathan before she was hurried off.

Nathan stared after her until his brother interrupted his thoughts. "It is quite extraordinary, isn't it? So much alike, although I don't think this one will ever be the true beauty Fabienne was. Features aren't... aren't what? Delicate enough. And the hair is darker, too. No one's could match the fire of Fabienne's. It is so like her temperament, wouldn't you say?"

When Nathan failed to reply, Jerome snickered wickedly, "My god, Nathan, you're smitten. A mere child has rendered you speechless. Why I'd wager she still wears her little girl frocks during the day."

"I am far too experienced," Nathan answered stiffly, "to be 'smitten,' as you put it. However, I can admire a thing of beauty, and I have just seen something very beautiful. Come! We're wasting time. By all accounts, this dinner should be quite magnificent."

Through the first two courses, the dinner was a great triumph for Edouard. Although he did fret when Nathan, who was being uncharacteristically quiet and remote, hadn't commented immediately on the sea-urchin soufflé, a luxurious airy mélange of sauce and fish and truffles served in individual urchin shells. Edouard feared that perhaps the cook or butler had somehow ruined the baron's dish.

Naturally he was relieved when Nathan finally said, "Absolutely extraordinary, Edouard, just extraordinary. But serving something so exquisite is very dangerous."

"Why is that, baron?" Edouard asked.

"Now you must worry that Jerome will try and steal your cook away."

Jerome, who had been thinking of doing just that, indignantly denied it.

"Edouard." It was General Hopewell. "I have a complaint. It's cruel to serve a man something so wonderful as this and give him such a tiny portion."

At that very moment the butler with two serving women swirled in, all bearing more soufflés.

"You see, General," Edouard was pleased to explain, "sea urchins are small so the size of the soufflé is dictated by that. If you were to be served two at once, the second soufflé would have fallen before you were ready for it."

The soufflés were followed by an equally well-received crawfish tails au gratin.

The remainder of the dinner would have been equally triumphal had it not been for Donnadieu.

The prefect was not terribly good-looking or well-educated, and was certainly not witty or ingratiating. Nor on this particular evening was he very comfortable. The other people at the table, with the exception of Mademoiselle Hue in her perpetual state of flurries, were so self-assured, had so much in common, and discussed things of which Donnadieu had little knowledge.

As the dinner progressed and Donnadieu's wine glass was continually refilled, his alienation and resentment increased. It was not that he was totally gauche, that he didn't know which fork to use with which course. His bourgeois mother had pounded good manners into him. But these people... well, they spoke a different language with foreign nuances and Donnadieu suffered from being excluded.

It did not help his mood to be sitting across from Guy, who had the chiseled good looks and easy charm that Donnadieu envied. It rankled the prefect that he might be compared with Guy. He wished to show these people he was as good as the pampered son of du Clocher, but no opportunity presented itself at first.

Finally there was a lull in the conversation while the rack of lamb was being carved. None could deny that the prefect had some expertise in politics, so Donnadieu decided to steer the discussion back to that, an area where he could excel.

"Has anyone," he asked, "read Romieu's new book, *The Red of 1852*? Quite an interesting study, and certainly gives sound support for keeping a strong leader such as Louis-Napoleon at the head of government—if only to keep the socialists at bay."

Donnadieu hadn't actually read the book himself, but had heard enough about it that he was confident he could sound as if he had.

Monsieur d'Estournel fairly spit his wine out at the mention of socialists. "I have read it. Everyone should. Why that Romieu knows what he's talking about. Those Reds, if they take power, they're planning hideous massacres, heinous slaughters. No one will be safe if they win the Assembly next year."

Nathan couldn't help laughing. "You know, I do believe we as a nation are waiting for the elections of 1852 much as the people in the Tenth Century waited for the year 1000, thinking it would mean the end of the world."

"Well, it would be the end of the world for us," d'Estournel came back. "Get rid of this republic and find us a strong dictator, I say. Get us another Bonaparte and save the country from anarchy."

Although Guy himself was not sure which label should be put on his own politics— "socialist" would not have been the appropriate one—still d'Estournel's condemnation needed to be addressed.

"Monsieur, I'm not sure why you are so strongly opposed to the socialists. Some of their demands, if studied without prejudice, are just. Free state education, a ten-hour working day, abolishment of usury, benefits for the unemployed. In the long run these will help our nation."

"And in the short run they will bankrupt it," d'Estournel said angrily. "You can't have the workers demanding fewer working hours and more benefits. Where's this money to come from?"

Donnadieu saw his chance to jump in while Guy was on the defensive. "My, my Monsieur Guy"—he deliberately used the proper name as if he were addressing a child—"you are sounding decidedly socialist. And what do you say to their call for public ownership of land? Are you prepared to give up your land to a bunch of unwashed peasants? Do your convictions go that far?"

Nathan was liking Donnadieu less and less and Guy more and more and thought it was time he should intercede. "Really, Monsieur le préfet," he said, "I hardly think Monsieur Saint-Savin has shown himself to be anything but fair. He merely pointed out that some of what the socialists want can hardly be considered heinous. Louis himself has backed universal suffrage, for example."

"I still say we should have a dictatorship, or better yet, an emperor," d'Estournel said.

"My goodness my," fluttered Mademoiselle Hue, "there need be no talk of Louis-Napoleon ever becoming emperor. No, no, never."

"And why is that?" Nathan asked politely and, out of kindness, quickly so that no one else would have time to say something derogatory to the mademoiselle.

"Hadn't you heard? When Louis's dear mother, Queen Hortense, was alive she went to a Negress clairvoyante to find out what the future would bring her son. And the Negress said a great nation would choose him for its leader. 'You mean he will be emperor?' Hortense asked. 'No,' said the clairvoyante, 'he will never be emperor.' So you see," giggled Mademoiselle Hue, who rarely had the floor for so long, "no need to talk of an Emperor Louis-Napoleon."

"That sounds authoritative enough for me," said Nathan.

"Perhaps he won't be emperor," Donnadieu shot back, "but there are some, such as our young Guy here, who would not allow him to be president."

It was only the heat of his father's glare that kept Guy's anger in check. Donnadieu was so obviously trying to provoke him. However, everyone present could tell that despite Guy's efforts, an eruption was near.

"It is hardly me alone, monsieur," Guy responded, his words grating across clenched teeth. "It is the constitution which allows only one term. And in its wisdom, the Assembly has declined to change it."

"The Assembly?" Donnadieu sneered. "Don't talk to me about the Assembly. It runs on emotion not reason. Any fool who rants impassionately can sway the Assembly."

"Are you referring to the speech I wrote, by any chance, monsieur? In which case are you, by any chance, referring to me as a fool?" Guy spoke with the cold blade-sharp tone that usually preceded a calling out to duel. He rose halfway in his chair, ready to do just that, but this time it was Nathan Libermann not Harry Busscher who was sitting next to him and who tugged on his shirt sleeve, without the others seeing it, and brought Guy back to reason. While Nathan cared little about the life expectancy of Donnadieu, he found himself caring about the distress he saw in Solange's eyes.

"I happened to have heard the speech," he said. "I was in the Assembly with Louis that day. Very clear. Very reasoned. Personally, I would like nothing better than to see Louis finished with office. He's been far too busy with politics to pursue some of the finer things in life with me. And speaking of the finer things..."

Nathan paused and with a theatrical flourish took a healthy sip of wine.

"...this is a truly excellent vintage, Edouard. Would you have an extra case or two from your cellar that I might purchase? And, you Jerome, wouldn't you like some as well?"

The conversation safely turned to wine, vintages, and conjecture over who had the greatest cellar in France. Solange again smiled her gratitude at Nathan.

The remainder of the dinner was a trial by restraint for Guy. Not the excellence of the duck à le rouennaise, the cheeses ripened as he loved them, nor the bombe glacée could gentle his temper. He would have liked to have foregone them completely, but leaving the table would have marked him as a sulking child. He caught Solange staring

at him, near tears. He smiled to reassure her. It must not have
worked for she immediately averted her gaze to her lap and would not
look up again.

At last the torture was over. Guests moved to the veranda and
drawing room for cognac, depending on how much the slight nip in
the air affected them. Nathan lingered until only he and Guy were
left in the dining room.

"A small bit of advice," he said quietly. "Ignore the grand prefect
and all like him. He is an imbecile with only one proven talent—the
ability to know which behinds he must kiss and when to kiss them."

Nathan's words were so unexpected, Guy laughed despite himself.

"There that's better." Nathan reached up to drape his arm around
the younger man's shoulder in easy camaraderie. "If you have any
problems with Monsieur le Grand Idiot, let me know. My brother
may control the millions, but I am not without friends. Shall we join
the others?"

Guy did not want to appear rude, but he could not endure being in
the château any longer. "Please go on without me. The workers are
having their harvest festival tonight. I believe I'll join them."

"An eminently wise choice. It is certain to be far more stimulating
out there than the conversation of your father's guests, no insult
intended. I'd like to join you but I won't. One of the worst things
about growing older is the curse of having to maintain a certain
amount of dignity. Besides, the wine shall be better in here, and I am
looking forward to making the acquaintance of your lovely sister."

With a sweeping flourish, Nathan bowed and exited.

Guy felt curiously out of breath.

What a surprising and disarming man, he thought. I like him.

Chapter Thirteen

The heat of the bonfires leapt out and seared his face before he was even halfway across the field.

Shadow-figures, no longer recognizable as the people he had worked with for two weeks, swirled, eddied, swayed, and bobbed in a landscape out of Hieronymus Bosch.

Grabbing a glass of wine from a disembodied hand, Guy took a long, hard pull. For a second it burned his throat and then its fever coursed through him.

Suddenly two arms wrapped around his neck, and he was pulled down to a hard, demanding kiss. Just as abruptly, the arms and lips disappeared back into the night.

Without being fully conscious of it at first, Guy was searching for Marie-Odile. He moved from one fire to the next, away from the château and back towards it. He could not find her.

Not watching where he was going, he collided with someone.

"Jean-Gabriel," Guy shouted above the noise, "have you seen Marie-Odile?"

Bellay, as drunk as he had ever been, took a moment to focus and figure out who was talking to him. It took a great deal of effort. He was in a partially upright position only because sometime earlier he had maneuvered one arm around the substantial waist of a picker's wife and had anchored his hand on her enormous breast.

When he finally recognized Guy and collected some semblance of thought and coherence, he slurred, "Saw her...somewhere...someplace...there, no there...can't remember."

Guy went on with his search. Another glass of wine was thrust into his hand, and he finished it off with one swallow. Going back to the serving table for a refill, he finally saw Marie.

She was enveloped in the arms of a man, in the throes of some

80

frenzied love-making. Embarrassed, Guy was turning away when he caught a glimpse of her face. There was no passion there, only terror, and she was struggling to get free.

For a moment she pulled away and in that instant Guy saw the man. It was Mazet, Claude Mazet.

Mazet grabbed at Marie and caught the bodice of her dress. It gave and ripped. She stopped struggling, paralyzed by her exposure, naked to the waist, firelight shimmering over her white skin and tense, sharp nipples, accenting the fear and hatred combatting each other on the battleground of her face.

Then Claude recaptured her, one arm gripped around her body, the other thrust between her legs, lifting and then forcing her to the ground, his head rutting down her body, lips and teeth searching for her breast.

Two women were watching, too frightened to call out. Even if they had, their shouts would have been lost in the overwhelming cacophony of the night. Only those close by could see it was an assault. From the verandah, the men watching—the women making sure their attention was elsewhere—thought it a diverting orgiastic display.

Guy was close enough to see. He charged at Claude, grabbing his collar and wrenching him off the girl.

Claude growled with inhuman ferocity at the interruption and turned to beat off the trespasser. Guy gave him no opportunity. His fist smashed into Claude's face.

Claude went down, but was up again at once, charging, head lowered, an enraged bull ready to gore and mangle his challenger. Guy sidestepped, but took the full force of the charge on his hip. He collapsed and Claude seized the advantage and was on him, clawing at Guy's face, trying to gouge out his eyes.

The battle had caught the revelers' attention and the cry of "Fight!," "Fight!" went up, drawing a crowd around the combatants.

To the disappointment of many, the fight, although intense and bloody, did not last long. When it was over, Claude was on one knee, wiping a battered nose and wheezing with pain. Guy stood over him, eye blackened and shirt shredded.

"If you ever, ever touch her again, I'll kill you. I swear. I'll kill you. Now get up and be gone. And don't set foot on du Clocher again."

Guy then took the little that remained of his shirt and tenderly wrapped it around Marie who had lain motionless throughout the fight, not seeing, feeling, not moving. Guy led her away into the kindness of the sheltering night.

On the terrace, Nathan turned from the scene to find Jerome next to him. The banker clucked in mock-disapproval.

"The young Saint-Savin has a penchant," he observed, "for making enemies. It's a sign of weakness."

"Or youth," Nathan countered.

Chapter Fourteen

"Marie, are you all right?"

Guy had propelled her from the field, down the road, and toward the river. She had stumbled along, her body stiff and rigid, afraid that if she relaxed she would lose all control.

"Marie, are you all right?" Guy repeated. "Perhaps we should go to the château. Lise will get you something warm to drink, some clothes... Marie, my god, what is wrong?"

She was shaking her head, slowly then faster and faster, more violently, her whole body wracked with a shivering quake, forcing tears out from deep within her until she was sobbing.

Guy felt helpless. "Please don't cry, Marie. You don't need to be afraid anymore. I won't let anything happen to you. Come to the château. Come now."

When he tried to put his arms around her, she pulled away and let out an anguished "no" that added to Guy's overwhelming sense of inadequacy. He didn't know what he could do for her, and he wanted to do so much.

"Marie, I'll protect you from that animal. I meant what I said. Claude will never come back here. Never."

"Please, please...no," she moaned. "I can't think about him...what happened. I'm so ashamed."

Guy stepped back so he could see her better. She looked so anguished, so alone.

"Ashamed? Why? Why should you be ashamed? You did nothing."

She was still shaking. "It's what they'll think. Everyone will think that I led him on then changed my mind. They'll blame me. They always blame the woman. I can't face anyone now," she moaned. "Please leave me alone."

She was sobbing again. Guy gathered her to him, this time not letting her push him away.

83

"All right," he whispered through the dark tangle of her hair, "we won't go back now, but I won't leave you alone, either."

Arm firmly around her, he walked her down to the back of the Hotel du Port. The kitchen door was always open. Inside, Guy got three blankets from a storage chest, two small glasses, and a bottle of Jean-Gabriel Bellay's best marc de Bordeaux. He would replace it later with the best from du Clocher's cellar, a more than even trade.

At a tree near the water's edge, Guy wrapped one of the blankets around Marie and sat her down on the other. The third he draped over his own bare shoulders. Then he filled a glass with marc and held it to Marie's lips. She watched him over its rim as she downed the bracing drink.

They sat next to each other, almost touching, not speaking. Guy was beginning to fear that Marie had fallen back into her distressing trance when she broke the silence. It was with a quiet calm she said, "I don't want to go back."

"You don't have to. We'll stay here tonight. And when the sun rises, it will be easier to face things. If then you still don't want to see people, you'll stay in the château."

"I didn't mean that. I didn't mean back to my aunt's cottage. I don't want to go back to St. Emilion."

Guy was surprised. He knew how much Marie-Odile cared for her family. "Are you being mistreated there?"

"Oh no, it's not that." Marie was horrified Guy might think poorly of her parents, that they would be capable of hurting her. She regretted bringing up the subject, yet, at the same time, she knew she must, that she wanted to explain everything to Guy.

"I'm to be married."

Guy went cold. It was the same forlorn feeling he'd had when as a young child he'd been separated from his father during a visit to Paris. He had thought his father had abandoned him. He realized Marie was waiting for a response.

"I didn't...know. I wish you all the...all the..." He didn't know what he wanted to say or what he should say, so he settled for a lame "Congratulations."

"Oh no, don't congratulate me. I don't want to be married. I can't stand the thought of it. It's Father. He says it's time someone else paid for my food. That I'm a burden to the family. He's forcing me."

"He can't do that," Guy protested with righteous indignation. But within him, he realized Marie's father could indeed insist. Fathers did so all the time. It was an accepted, unquestioned practice.

He tried to mask his sadness.

"I thought I had no choice," Marie continued, ignoring his interruption. "But since I've been here I realized I do. I could work here. You would find a place for me, wouldn't you?" She moaned again. "Of course, that was before tonight. Now I can't stay here, either. It doesn't matter. It doesn't matter. I am not going back to St. Emilion. I'd rather die than marry someone I don't care for. Guy, what shall I do?"

Guy raised himself to his knees and looked down at Marie. He wanted her to look at him, so that she would know, so that she would see he meant what he was about to say. He needed to look at her so he would know she understood.

"Marie, I was allowed to hold you when you were a baby. You are my sister's best friend. You are good and wonderful and I won't let anything bad happen to you. You will stay here with us. You're part of our family from now on. And I will not allow anyone to so much as whisper a criticism of you. I won't." As he spoke, he wondered if he was capable of doing what he promised.

A tear formed at the corner of Marie's eye and started down her face. Guy reached over, without thought, to check it, to brush it away, as the first sign that he would take care of her. That was all. But when his fingers touched her soft, lovely face, they would not withdraw. Her forehead, cheeks, chin, her lips. They were so warm and alive beneath his touch. He traced her lips and they parted slightly. She was so lovely, eyes so large and dark, her neck so curved and sweet. Her lips...

He wanted to kiss her, only a gentle, reassuring kiss to erase her worries, but when he did, he was caught by them and couldn't break away. He didn't want to and the kiss stretched on longer and longer.

She was in his arms and he in hers and the kiss was no longer soft and tentative. It grew in strength, warmer and hotter with a fierceness that neither had ever felt before. He was kissing her hair, her ears, that curving neck. And Marie was pressing him closer, harder. Then she lay back, the blanket dropping open and his tattered shirt falling from her.

For a moment Guy could only stare, startled by her beauty. Then without willing it, his hand went to her breast. He caressed it, slowly, almost reverently, back and forth as her nipple hardened and she arched to meet his stroke. He cupped her breast then went down to it. He had to have it in his mouth, taste it, suckle it.

A loud deep groan startled him. He started to pull away from her, then he realized it had come from him. He had to have her. He went to her passionately, fiercely, with a desperate need. And she met him in kind.

Jerome ran his hand over the carriage's luxurious interior. It was a bit ostentatious, perhaps, but Jerome liked it. It was so, well, so reassuring.

"All in all, not an unenjoyable evening," he commented. "And there is certainly no question that du Clocher is a nice wine."

Nathan had been silent for the couple of miles they had traveled since leaving St. Julien, and that made Jerome feel uncomfortably like he wasn't in charge.

Nathan studied his brother, as if trying to remember who he was, then gave a small derisive laugh. "Calling du Clocher a 'nice' wine is like saying Michelangelo was an adequate ceiling painter."

"My, my, my," Jerome decided for the moment to overlook his brother's tone of ridicule, "you sound completely infatuated with the wine. Isn't that out of character for you, to be so head over heels?"

"I don't know if I can explain it so that you can understand this, Jerome. Du Clocher represents something one rarely, if ever, finds in life. Du Clocher is perfection, something worth expending your energies on, a perfection that comes partially from your own efforts. I would give anything to possess du Clocher."

"Well then, you shall," Jerome said smugly, control returning in a rush. "I'm glad we're having this chat, for from my vast experience as a banker and as a man of the world, I believe I can tell you exactly what you must do to possess your little obsession. You must pay money. Now, the most desirable course is to pay as little money as possible, but no matter what, money is the answer. Money is always the answer."

Nathan knew he should let this speech pass, but he couldn't, and against his better judgment he replied, "Yours is a profound-sounding piece of advice. Nonetheless, I must regretfully inform you flat out that you are wrong. Du Clocher is not for sale now. I doubt it will ever be for sale."

Jerome lit a small cheroot knowing his brother would find it noxious-smelling. "Such naivete, Nathan, even from you. Everything—and need I add, everyone?—has a price. Perhaps it was this lack of perception that led to your disgrace in Brazil. To this day, I cannot understand how in such a ripe area for the Banque Libermann, even you managed to fail."

Jerome never missed an opportunity to needle Nathan for what he called the "Brazilian Debacle," and Nathan always ignored the jibes. He didn't consider his years in Brazil poorly spent. Still Jerome continued to needle him, hoping to someday force a breach in his brother's composure.

"I believe you misjudge Edouard Saint-Savin," Nathan said. "Write him off as a pompous ass, but there is no denying his bond to du Clocher. I've watched him. It's his existence. Selling it would be tantamount to suicide. I hope that in my lifetime I feel as strongly about something as that."

Jerome had a remarkable memory for selective details. Usually these details concerned money and business. On one hand he could barely remember the order in which his children were born. On the other, he could recite almost verbatim what was said by whom in a public disagreement between co-owners of a foundry in Alsace. Unhappy partners might mean a dissolving partnership. A dissolving partnership could lead to a foundry on the selling block. A foundry on the block meant financing and borrowing—and Jerome Libermann always had money to lend. Nathan's last statement triggered something and Jerome dredged through the minutiae he'd stored and recalled the whispers he had heard about Edouard Saint-Savin.

"Would you be so certain that du Clocher could not be bought if I told you that dear Edouard is in serious financial trouble? That only a miracle can save the fellow, and that judging by his track record, Edouard is no maker of miracles."

"I hadn't heard. Still it makes no difference. Edouard will not give up du Clocher."

Jerome smiled, took a pull from his cigar, and slowly blew out a perfect circle of smoke. "Now this is lovely of you, Nathan. You've given me a challenge, though I'd wager it won't prove too much of a one. Tomorrow, dear brother, we will pay another visit to du Clocher, where I will enjoy having the opportunity of demonstrating to you how things are accomplished in the real world. I will make Edouard an offer. He may refuse at first, but in the end, I guarantee you, I will have du Clocher. And when I do, it will give me profound pleasure to present it to you, as a gift. Won't that be nice?"

Chapter Fifteen

Edouard was categorical in his refusal. He would listen to none of Jerome's offers, dismissing them, offended by them.

There were no spoken "I told you so's" from Nathan on the ride back to Paris, still Jerome was sure they were there, running gleefully through his brother's thoughts.

No matter. There were many ways to attain a property, and Jerome knew most of them. Edouard's adamance was a temporary roadblock, a minor impediment for Jerome. He would not be beaten. He would show Nathan, acquire that damned château, no matter what or how long it took.

The opera house, wedged into the tiny Rue Lepelletier, just off the Boulevard des Italiens, was filled with Paris's most fashionable people. It was a de rigueur event, no matter how one felt about Rossini.

That night, the great Massol was singing *Guillaume Tell,* a performance that promised to be of premier magnitude, one that would be mentioned in history books. Jerome Libermann would have attended for Massol alone, although the pomp and preening of the audience was a show well worth watching as well.

Intermission was a gaily colored tableau of swishing silks, matrons pecking each other on both cheeks and chattering as if they hadn't met in years; young officers peacock-strutting before demure young heiresses; men of affairs and office rumbling among themselves, seeking information, confirmation, and consideration. And in the middle of it all stood Jerome Libermann, unperturbed and untouched by bustle and only half-listening to the turgid critique his wife Rachel was offering on the opera. It was only when Charles de Morny spoke did Jerome realize that Louis-Napoleon's most trusted adviser was next to him.

"And is Rossini to your liking this evening?" Morny asked politely.

Jerome did not answer at first. He knew from experience that Morny's most innocent and forthright inquiries could be layered with subtleties and traps.

There was no question that Charles de Morny was a charming and engaging man. But he was also devious and self-serving, and his rapier wit had shredded quite a few egos around Paris. Jerome treated him with caution. He could never quite decide if he liked him. Besides, how was one to trust a man who boasted of his bastardy and used his happenstance of birth to advance his career?

Morny was, as he was happy to inform just about everyone, the son of Hortense de Beauharnais. Hortense's checkered history included being daughter of Napoleon's first wife Josephine as well as wife of his brother, Louis Bonaparte. Out of that marriage came a son, Louis-Napoleon. Out of an unsanctioned liaison issued Charles de Morny. Of course, there were some who believed the unsanctioned liaison was not with Monsieur Morny at all, but with her step-father-cum-brother-in-law, Napoleon Bonaparte. In any case, it was all too wonderful gossip and Morny did his best to fuel it.

Jerome carefully considered Morny's question. Was he really interested in the banker's opinion of the opera or was there more to his asking about a story in which an established government is openly defied by a Swiss archer?

"Massol," Jerome finally answered, "is in splendid form tonight. You are quite fortunate that the affairs of state did not keep you from enjoying it. I understand you and the president have been quite, shall we say, busy of late."

Morny glanced around to see who might be listening. Apparently satisfied that no one was paying attention, he said earnestly, "Yes, dear baron, controlling the beast of government, with that ugly Medusan Assembly goading it on, takes much time and effort. It is a near impossible task."

Jerome clucked sympathetically, sensing he need not fear Morny in this conversation. "If only there were a Perseus to smite off the Medusa's head, that would make governing so much easier, wouldn't it, Charles?"

Morny allowed himself a brief smile before dropping into the urgent tones of conspiracy. "A Perseus alone is not enough. Even he needed the help of the gods, someone to finance the sword, so to speak."

"A sword used in good cause by a hero would have no trouble receiving backing, I would judge."

Morny smiled again. He knew that Jerome Libermann would understand and could be counted on in what lay ahead.

Just then a glimpse of a copper-haired woman returning to her seat for the next act of the opera made Jerome think of something.

"Of course," he said with measured deliberation, "our hero would have to have a well-conceived plan of action if his would-be benefactor was to be reassured."

It was Morny's turn to be cautious. Libermann did not want to hear their plans—it was inconsequential to the banker what they did, as long as they came out on top—but he did want something. Morny relaxed slightly. And if there was something the head of the Banque Libermann wanted, the least that Morny and the president of the Republic could do was make sure he got it. Morny could only hope it wasn't something too outrageous.

"Baron Libermann, let me reassure you, should Perseus go after the Medusa, everything will be taken care of, according to a well-reasoned plan."

"Including the disposal of the Medusa's head? As the original Perseus discovered, even after death, the monster can do harm."

"Naturally, all precautions would be taken to dispose of the monster..."

"And all the vipers attached?"

Morny was beginning to understand. The esteemed banker had a particular viper in mind.

"Naturally, all the vipers. It would be a disastrous event if one escaped. Any assistance in identifying them would, naturally, be greatly welcomed."

The lobby was almost empty now and the need for caution lessened. Jerome wished to end the interview quickly so that he could return to the performance. "Well, if we were discussing the Assembly, a certain young Bordelaise aide has been writing highly inflammatory speeches for Monsieur de Pary. Now this aide might not seem much of a threat now, he has the potential of becoming a rabble-rousing enemy and should be dealt with as soon as possible."

Morny had no idea what this unfortunate Bordelaise had done to earn Jerome Libermann's displeasure, and Morny did not care. The banker was asking a small favor, and it would be granted.

"Do not worry," he said. "The young man's name has been added to the list of those enemies of the state who will soon be on their way to the penal colony in Cayenne. Thank you for alerting me to him and thank you for your upcoming support."

"And why do you thank me for support? The Banque Libermann always supports the government of France. Adieu," he called gaily and hurried off to join his wife.

Morny watched him go and then hurried off himself, not towards the opera but to history, which he would be making that very night.

Chapter Sixteen

Ten gendarmes slipped quietly through the claustrophobic mist of the early Parisian morning.

Many of the sounds of the city reluctantly coming to life in face of still-another drizzly gray day were absent. Grates being wound up at cafes. Hoofbeats of delivery horses on cobblestone. Barge bells clanging on the Seine. These were the sounds of morning. They had been replaced by hammering, of declarations being pounded onto posts and poles, echoing across the river, into the Marais, up to Montmartre, back across to the Luxembourg Gardens and the fashionable Faubourg, hammering that had the city in thrall, imprisoning its citizens within their apartments, houses, and rooms, longing for it to stop, fearing when it would.

The squad passed close to a soldier who was nailing up one such poster. The gendarmes didn't pause to read the proclamation with its still-wet ink. They had their orders and they hurried to carry them out.

"Halt," the leader said softly. He was a young sergeant filled with ambition. Nothing specifically had been said back in the station house about what was occurring that day. There was no need. All of France sensed it. Louis was making his bid, and this time it was no half-baked plan to sail across the Channel from England, expecting the French population to embrace him and, with cheers, make him king. No, from all the sergeant had heard—and he made it his business to listen—Louis had planned this day well, and the sergeant was determined to excel in his small part of the proceedings. Then who could tell? He didn't plan to be a sergeant forever.

He looked at his order and then glanced at the curiously narrow building before him. A number "12" had long before been chiseled into the stone face, and Number 12, rue Saint-Severin was the address on the paper in his hand.

The squad leader looked at the building with disgust. It had to be one of the narrowest in Paris and that did not bode well for the stairway. If there was any struggle, he wouldn't be able to deploy his men efficiently.

He looked down at the paper again and briefly wondered what the poor devil they'd been sent to arrest had done. The sergeant had been disappointed he wasn't assigned General Cavaignac or Changarnier or one of the Socialist leaders to round up. That would have been a real plum. Well, the sergeant would just make the most of the assignment he was given and hope for a better one next time.

The large oak door with its round iron knocker creaked open. A frizz of white hair over a furrowed, glaring face appeared around its edge.

"What's all this noise? What do you want this early in the morning?" the frizz demanded.

The sergeant knew this woman although he had never set eyes on her before. She was a Parisian concierge—distrustful, complaining, nagging, always angry with her tenants and yet always ready to shield them from outsiders, whom she hated even more. The sergeant would have to handle the situation carefully.

"Madame, I'm sorry to disturb you, but I have an arrest order for someone believed to live in this building. Would you care to take a look."

He held out the paper which she waved away disdainfully. "What do you take me for? I can't read. Tell me the name of the poor soul you vultures are looking for and I'll tell you if I know him."

"A Guy Saint-Savin," the sergeant answered, carefully rolling up his order and retying it with its ominous red ribbon.

"Guy! And what would you be doing with...!" The concierge tried to catch herself, but it was too late. The damage was done. There would be no denying she knew Guy now.

"Take me to his flat at once."

"He's not here," she said petulantly, but led them up the narrow winding staircase anyway.

She was not lying. Guy's one large room, with items strewn about as if the owner would soon get to putting them in their proper places, was empty.

The concierge immediately set to tidying the room. "Such a nice boy," she clucked, "messy but nice." And then with defiance added, "I told you he wasn't here."

The sergeant was seeing his hoped-for glory quickly fading away. "Then where?" he snapped. "You must know where he has gone."

"I don't spy on my tenants, you know. I'm not some busybody. All I know is he got a letter late yesterday or maybe it was the day before. Anyway, he left almost at once."

The sergeant quickly went to a desk near one of the room's two windows and saw the note, written in an exact and meticulous hand.

My dear brother Guy,

I know you are most busy with important matters in Paris, and I do not like bothering you. However, circumstances insist that I must. It is imperative you return home at once. I have urgent news that you must receive in person.
Come immediately. I implore you.
Your loving sister,

Solange.

The sergeant looked at the embossed crest of the paper. "Du Clocher," it read.

"What's this 'du Clocher'?" he demanded of the concierge.

"Shows your ignorance, not knowing what du Clocher is..." the woman began.

"Shut up, you old witch," the sergeant shouted with vehemence. "You answer my question or I'll throw you in jail too."

The mention of jail instilled the concierge with begrudging contriteness. "It's his vineyard, in Bordeaux, the village of St. Julien."

The sergeant left without another word and his squad followed dutifully. He would salvage this fiasco somehow. So the fox had escaped? The sergeant would return to the gendarmerie and report what had happened. No, that was no good. It would be remembered that he failed in a simple mission. And all that would happen is that one of the officers above him would notify Bordeaux and get credit for the capture. Why should the sergeant let someone else save the day and get the glory? He would show initiative that was sure to be appreciated. He would wire the prefect's office in Bordeaux and tell them of the warrant. With any luck, they would do the sergeant's work for him.

He smiled.

Chapter Seventeen

Baron Nathan Libermann was sipping expresso, contentedly reviewing his schedule for the day. New projects always delighted Nathan.
They were so fresh and unsullied by expectations colliding with
reality. Still he couldn't remember another project he looked forward
to more.

He had bought some land in the Medoc and was going to create a
vineyard through work and patience. Admittedly, it would never
produce the finest wine, but it would be the best the land could offer.
And should the day ever arrive that du Clocher... well, he would be
ready. He felt so at home in the Medoc, strangely a part of it, not an
outsider looking in. He didn't even miss Paris.

"Baron." The Marquise de Bougie's butler was standing behind his
chair.

Damn, thought the baron, I'm getting old. No one should be able
to sneak up on me that way.

Realizing he was scowling at the servant, Nathan smiled quickly. It
wasn't the butler's fault Nathan's reflexes weren't what they used to
be.

"Yes, Michel, what is it you want on such a fine day?"

It was a perfectly dreadful day, misty, cold, a Paris-like dreariness.
Michel was too well-trained to correct the baron, besides he wasn't
sure if there wasn't some impenetrable jest intended.

"There is a man who says he is a messenger, sir. He says it's most
urgent and most confidential."

"And what do you think, Michel? It is most urgent for him or for
me?"

Michel smoothed the front of his jacket. The Marquise de Bougie's
staff weren't sure how to treat Nathan, who had been a guest for the
past several weeks while supervising the construction of his own

château. He seemed to invite familiarity and did seem generally interested in the lives—tribulations and triumphs, no matter how small they might be—of the staff. Still, he was a baron and a friend of the marquise, and the marquise did not hold to the classes intermingling any more than they had to.

"I wouldn't know, sir, but I believe he has come from Baron Jerome."

"Then it is undoubtedly a matter of extreme importance—to Jerome. I suppose there is no avoiding it. Send in this messenger, please. And Michel, do tell the cook it was a perfectly delightful breakfast this morning. The croissants were as light as the clouds of heaven."

"As you wish."

The man Michel ushered in did not look like a messenger. He was elegantly dressed, well-manicured, and fastidiously mannered. Nathan recognized him as the Bordelaise agent for the Banque Libermann, a position of a certain amount of prominence.

"If you are here, Monsieur Bonchamps, I assume Jerome has news of catastrophic importance."

Bonchamps handed Nathan an envelope. Nathan could read nothing in the other man's expression, so he moved to the window, more for privacy than light.

One word had been written on the paper inside.

NAPOLEON

"So, he has done it at last," Nathan said quietly as the implications of that one word tumbled madly through his mind. "Thank you, monsieur, thank you for coming out," he said at last.

Not even waiting for the agent to take his leave, Nathan pulled the embroidered sash that hung along the wall. Michel was in the room before he had dropped the cord.

"Michel, have my horse saddled immediately. I must go to du Clocher. At once."

The horse's spittle lashed back across Guy's face. He was too preoccupied to notice or to wipe it away.

When he had received Solange's note, delivered by a friend of Jean-Gabriel Bellay returning from a visit to the Medoc, it was more curiosity than concern that gave rise to his fast departure from Paris. Furthermore, Solange's summons gave him an excuse to flee the miasma of intrigue and distrust smothering the capital. Guy had been waking up each morning with an undefined dread, the same dread he had as a young boy when he'd done something bad and was awaiting due punishment. He needed to leave.

The long trip to Bordeaux—taking trains as far as the lines ran, hiring horses to where the next train line began—had afforded Guy too much time to speculate over what was waiting for him in Bordeaux. The more he thought about it, the more strangely worded the note seemed.

He was almost home, almost there, with only one last curve in the road.

He didn't wait for the heaving horse to stop completely before he was out of the saddle and running, grime-streaked, sweating, into the château. Marcel had to jump aside to avoid being trampled.

"Monsieur Guy..." he called.

"Solange? Where is she?"

The cook and her helpers, washing and cutting leeks, dropped their knives when the desperate-eyed specter charged into the kitchen.

"Where's my sister? Where is she?"

Marcel had followed him through the house. "Sir, the salon...your..."

Guy was gone, back the way he'd come. He threw open the double doors and shot into the sitting room.

"All the world is a stage to my son, and every door an opportunity for a grand entrance."

Edouard's acidity made Guy stop short. His father and Nathan Libermann were sitting across from each other, each holding a flute of champagne. Guy looked from one to the other, and they looked back at him.

Finally he asked, "Is this some kind of celebration? Is there something I should know about?" Guy was puzzled. Perhaps he had completely misinterpreted Solange's message.

"Celebration? Did you hear that, my dear baron, celebration? Why Guy, all of France is celebrating today. Would you care for some champagne?

Edouard selected a glass from a butler's tray at his side and carefully filled it.

"Yes, the baron here was so kind to bring me the news so that I, too, could rejoice with the rest of the nation. He also came to assure me that your political peccadilloes are so insignificant that we need not fear any retribution from our new ruler." Edouard was speaking with unnatural deliberation, tasting the words, spitting them out, their bitterness too much to endure.

"What are you jabbering about, Father? What new ruler?"

Edouard arched an eyebrow in mock disbelief and went back to sipping his champagne.

Guy turned to Nathan. "Please, sir, what news is he talking about?"

"Then you left Paris before it happened?" Nathan asked, not sure if that was fortuitous or not.

"For god's sake! Before what happened?" Guy felt like screaming. His father and the baron were tossing something important back and forth between them and not giving Guy a chance to catch on.

"Before Louis-Napoleon dissolved the Assembly and took over the government," Edouard said angrily. "Did none of your highly placed cronies bother to tell you it was coming?"

Nathan had been glad he had changed his plans and stayed on after telling Edouard about the coup. Initially the count had appeared quite unmoved by the news, and Nathan saw no reason to stay. But something made him accept Edouard's calm offer of wine. When the count tried to open the bottle, he fumbled with the cork and almost dropped the bottle. Then Nathan saw his fear, fear of change, of recalcitrant corks, and a disintegrating, disordered world.

And it was good he had been there for the surprise arrival of the son, but now maybe it was time to leave, time the two settled their differences without the presence of an outsider. He stood to show his intention.

"I should be returning to the marquise, but before I go, Edouard, I must reassure you again. I know Louis and while he can be something of a scoundrel, he is basically fair. I'm not saying there will be no arrests. It's a fact of political life that some generals and influential politicians are going to be exiled or imprisoned in Algeria and Cayenne. Now no insult intended, Guy, but you just aren't important enough to be bothered with. You are safe and du Clocher is safe. And should by some inconceivable fluke, I am proved wrong, I will intercede. Do not worry."

Nathan was relieved to see that the flush was receding from Edouard's face and his hands had stopped trembling. And then as if there had been no outburst, Edouard said, "I am quite happy you have decided to come to Bordeaux, baron. I wish you hadn't settled for that hilltop parcel. It is so limiting. You'll never have anything better than a cru bourgeois."

Taking his cue from his host, Nathan replied with equal equanimity, "It's a beginning. I don't intend it to be the end. Now I must again thank you for your hospitality. As always it has been superb. Guy, if you wouldn't mind escorting me out. À *bientôt*, Edouard."

Guy was happy for the excuse to leave his father. Outside he cupped his hands to give Nathan a foot up onto his horse. Once settled in the saddle, the older man leaned down so his face was close to Guy's. "Be careful with your father," he said with gravity. "He is upset and very frightened."

"Frightened?"

"Terrified. He fears losing du Clocher more than anything else. And anything threatening that, real or imaginary, terrifies him. Send for me if you need me. I will always be at your service."

Guy was moved by Nathan's concern. He knew it was genuine.

"You are truly most kind, baron, but why?"

Nathan straightened up in the saddle, giving him time to adjust his thoughts. "I'm not entirely sure, Guy. Part of it is I've lived in so many places, known so many people, that now I want one place to be mine. I don't want to be the gypsy anymore. I want to see the same friends day after day, the same rooms, the same furniture. I want a home. You and your sister, your family, you belong here. I want to belong here as well. I'll help you because I like you for yourself and what you represent. Does any of this make sense? Well, listen, I will see you soon, under better circumstances, I hope. *Au revoir.*"

Nathan pulled back on the reins so hard, the horse reared. Unperturbed, the baron tipped his hat and galloped off.

Solange. And her message. Guy had forgotten all about it. Perhaps she was in her room. He was halfway back to the house when the sound of hoofbeats stopped him. Baron Nathan must have forgotten something, he thought. But no, there was more than one horse. And there was the crunch of wheels. Guy spun around in time to see Nathan coming around the bend riding beside a carriage. And behind him were five soldiers.

"Guy," Nathan called out, forcing a tight smile. "I saw you had visitors and thought I would return with them. Go ahead in and tell your father. I'll escort Monsieur Donnadieu into the salon for you."

Nathan dropped the smile and jerked his head toward the building. Guy took the warning and hurried away. Back in the parlor, he found his father sitting as he had left him, except there was nothing left in the champagne bottle and Edouard's glass was empty as well.

"Father," he said urgently, but Donnadieu sweeping into the room cut him off.

"My warmest greetings, Count Saint-Savin." The prefect had the smugness of someone who had at last attained what he desired and deserved. "I am so sorry I must be the bearer of such unfortunate tidings, but I am afraid it is my duty as prefect of Bordeaux to inform you that your son is under arrest by order of President Louis-Napoleon. I believe it's for deeds and actions that have proven contrary to the good of the country."

Donnadieu was clearly enjoying his moment. The young Saint-Savin would now learn he can't threaten a prefect.

"So Monsieur Guy," he continued, unable to show any grace in victory, "which do you prefer? Algeria or Cayenne? Personally I would select Algeria." Donnadieu had crossed the room, observed the empty champagne bottle, and was surveying the other bottles on the tray as he spoke. "The journey to North Africa is so less arduous than the Atlantic crossing. On the other hand, should you escape, who would bother looking for you in the jungles of South America? Of course, no one has escaped and lived to tell about it...well, no matter. You probably won't be given a choice anyway."

"Monsieur Donnadieu." Donnadieu almost dropped the cognac he had selected, Nathan's tone was so harsh. "This is the home of Count Saint-Savin, and you have come to it on a grave mission. Please conduct yourself properly."

The prefect was about to put Nathan in his place when he remembered what Nathan's place was and he recalled the rumor of who had financed Louis-Napoleon's escape from Ham and who was supposed to be Louis's dearest friend.

"Baron Nathan, I, of course, meant no disrespect." Donnadieu hoped he reached the proper degree of contrition. "This is indeed a grave mission, one I so wish had not fallen to me. But I must in all good consciousness carry out my duty and take this threat to our country into custody."

"Come now, Guy Saint-Savin is hardly a threat to anything except perhaps the fortunes of rival growers. There has been a mistake, and I shall rectify it by speaking directly to Louis. This is all too much nonsense."

"It is not nonsense at all. I have the order right here, from the duc de Morny himself."

Nathan was taken aback. "Why would Morny bother with Guy?" he wondered out loud. "This makes no sense at all. Again I say it is a mistake. I suggest you return to Bordeaux without Guy until I can straighten this out."

Donnadieu was losing his prey. He'd looked forward to teaching Guy some servility in the Bordeaux jail. Guy's affronts had gnawed away at him and now the hunger for revenge overrode his misgivings about offending Nathan Libermann.

"I tell you there is no mistake. My soldiers will take you into custody, Guy Saint-Savin, so come quietly. Unless, of course, you're planning to hide behind the baron's coattails? Or maybe it's your mother's skirts you'll be running behind. But why use her skirts for hiding you? Huh? Just let her raise them for the right men, the way she always has, and then maybe you'll be getting a cabinet post instead of a stinking jungle prison."

His words were so outrageous that even Donnadieu was stunned he had said them. Then startling everyone, Edouard screamed, "You low-based SCUM! How dare you?"

Donnadieu, now completely out of control and not caring what he said or whom he offended, answered back, "I dare easily. I dare because everyone in Paris knows that Fabienne Saint-Savin is a high-class whore who will sleep with anyone with a title, money, and stiff enough to push it into her. Which is why everyone says she wouldn't stay with you, that you weren't man enough to keep her."

What happened next lost all reality. It was a horrific nightmare in which legs won't move, screams can't be heard, and sense and reason no longer exist. Guy and Nathan stood motionless, unable to intervene, as Edouard lunged at the prefect, his hands seizing the other's throat. Donnadieu wrenched back, spun around, lost his balance, and slammed against a wall. A miracle hung before him, Guy's competition fencing swords. Donnadieu grabbed one from its hook and spun back around, meaning only to frighten off his attacker with the weapon.

That was no longer necessary. Edouard, going for the prefect again, caught the sword right below the Adam's apple, and it went clear through his neck. For an instant he still seemed to be lunging at Donnadieu. Then, as blood pumped out of his wound, pushed by the last brave efforts of his heart, Edouard folded to the floor, a marionette whose strings had been all cut at once and forever.

"I didn't mean..." Donnadieu stammered in horror, "...it was an accident...I was holding the sword..." He was still holding the hilt and to show he had meant no harm, to prove it had been a mistake, he pulled the gory weapon from the corpse.

Guy rushed for the other sword. "That was no accident, nor shall this be!"

The moment to talk, to explain was past. Now the two men—just a sword's length apart—moved around each other warily. And as the duelists circled in their dangerous minuet, so too did the points of their weapons.

Guy's focused gaze shifted back and forth between Donnadieu's eyes and his point. Guy sent an exploratory jab—a feint—toward the prefect's belly. Donnadieu blocked it with a firm and fast parry in what fencers call the fourth line.

With the quick, elegant movement of the thumb and index finger, Guy circled the point of his weapon away from the parry and into Donnadieu's sixth line near the prefect's shoulder. The response was a circling counter parry that was not nearly as fast or as solid as his opponent's fourth line defense. Here is his weakness, Guy thought.

Meanwhile, Donnadieu used the sword with the same lack of finesse and thought he displayed in everything else. He just poked again and again. Same place, same tempo, Guy told himself. Very well, the trap shall be set.

Donnadieu feinted ponderously. Guy duly parried. Feint. Parry. Feint. Parry. The duel was infused with the stately rhythm of a waltz, until suddenly Guy deftly swung his blade into Donnadieu's sixth with a blinding thrust.

Here comes the counter parry, Guy thought and he was not disappointed. Donnadieu made a desperate sweep. But Guy was ready. The two blades moved in a vortex of steel searching for steel. Donnadieu, however, could not catch the elusive blade and Guy sensing the tempo was his lunged with all his might.

He saw the point hit, the blade bow, and then felt the sword— always held tenderly in the hand—jump.

Then Donnadieu was down, the red blot on his shirt spreading into an ugly map across his chest. Guy and Nathan watched as it enlarged, reaching around his body, seeping obscenely down his trousers.

"Quickly, wrap him in my cloak." Guy dropped the sword and Nathan spun around, both shocked that Solange had been in the room and witnessed the fight.

"Please, my dear," Nathan entreated, going to her side, "leave the room. Don't see this. Don't look."

She brushed aside his plea. "I've already seen it all. Father is dead. This horrid man is dead. And now we must save Guy." She spoke with authority and decision, and Nathan who had never seen Solange in a crisis, could not have been more surprised. "Take my cloak. We don't want the blood to spread any more. Marie, come in here." Marie-Odile had been standing out in the hallway, too frightened to enter. "Marie," Solange continued, "go tell the soldiers outside that Monsieur Donnadieu has decided to dine here before returning to Bordeaux. Tell them you'll bring them their dinner shortly and then get the cook to prepare something. Be sure the soldiers get wine, plenty of wine."

Marie slipped out. She had been unable to look at Guy even once. And he had not looked at her. He was afraid of what he might see—disgust for killing a man, fear for his being able to do it, or worst of all, pity. It was then that Guy knew he had to face the consequences of his anger. He started to the door.

"Guy," Solange called sharply. "Where are you going?"

"To the soldiers," he answered dully. "To give myself up. I am not a murderer. I had no choice. Father... he killed my father... I will be freed when the facts are known..."

"No! You mustn't. They'll kill you."

"But I'm not a traitor and it was a fair fight."

More than the violence and blood, Solange's unexpected authority had dumbfounded Nathan. Now he spoke. "Hear me out, Guy. I think Solange may be right. There is something very wrong about all this. Why were you to be arrested in the first place? This makes no sense. I think until I can find out why, Solange is right. You must flee. Otherwise there is a good chance you'll be executed immediately. There will be no trial to prove your innocence."

"But I can't leave du Clocher. Where would I go? What would I do?"

Again it was Solange who took charge. "Father received a note the other day from that American, Captain Wethersby. He asked if you were here. He is sailing soon and wanted to see you before he left. Tonight. I am sure he said he was sailing tonight. He'll take you on."

The inevitability of the situation washed over Guy, and he could protest no more. Solange and Nathan were in charge of his destiny, and he would be carried along by their plans.

Marie had come back. The soldiers were totally engrossed in the cassoulet and wine she had taken them.

"It won't be safe for Guy to go to Bordeaux," Nathan pointed out. "We don't know if Donnadieu was the only one who knew about the arrest notice. Whom could we send with a message for this captain?"

"I'll go," Marie said firmly. "It will be me."

"Yes," agreed Solange, "you can wear one of my good dresses and take the carriage. No one would stop a lady."

"And then," said Marie in a rush, fearful of interruptions and losing her nerve, "I'll board the ship and leave with Guy."

"But that's idiocy," Guy objected. "I'll be a fugitive. I don't know where I'll be going or what I'll be."

"I know one thing you will be," Marie said softly with some shyness. "The father of my child. I'm going with you."

Solange rubbed her hand across her face, it seemed so long ago she had given that note to Jean-Gabriel's friend. "That's why I sent for you. I wanted you to be here, with Marie, when you found out. I wanted it to be happy...wonderful..." She looked around at the awful disarray and then down at her father's body. "Not like this...Marie, come quickly. We must get you a dress. And my jewelry. You can sell it when you reach America. It's not much, but it will have to do until I can send you more."

"Yes, go along. I'll write the note to Wethersby." Nathan was glad that there was something tangible he could do. "And, Guy, pour us some cognac."

Solange stood on the stone quay. Out in the water the sailing ship loomed large and forbidding. She strained for her last glimpse of Guy, swimming out to meet the dinghy, drawing further and further from her with each stroke. Suddenly he stopped and lifted one arm in a farewell salute. Then he once again plunged off into the rising mist and darkness until he was completely lost to her.

Solange shivered. She was alone. She turned back to the château where she must play hostess to Baron Nathan and two dead men.

Book Two

Chapter Eighteen

1853

Sea and sky met and were one. So still was the water, so calm and unmoving, the sky could have been reflecting the sea instead of the other way around. And with no cloud, bird, or ripple of wave, there was no horizon, only the unity of sky and sea.

The gallon-frigate sat stagnant, without a whiff of wind to fan any of the sails of its three masts. It floated and festered in the heat of sun; it floated and froze in the chill of moon. And sat as it had been sitting for weeks.

Most of the time the men lying on the decks were as still as the air and sea. They were too weak to complain, too thirsty to speak, too defeated to go below with the others. Time had stopped with the ship.

Guy would have been in the narrow, imprisoning cabin where Marie-Odile lay, sick and swollen with child, but she had finally gone to sleep, despite her hunger and pain. And he needed to breathe air not fouled with sweat, feces, and fear.

Solange would not have known him. His skin was raw and red from exposure, his lips black, almost charred from dehydration, and his body all bones and angles. Only his blue eyes, more prominent than ever in the gaunt, harsh face, were recognizable, although all their laughter and happiness had been replaced by despair.

"Four takes the three," croaked a figure, curled up like a newborn, to Guy's left. "Aceys over deuceys."

Guy glanced over. Sometimes he wished he could be like Carl there, mind deranged by heat and deprivation, and now happily playing imaginary card games with himself. If all that mattered were aceys and deuceys, then Guy could erase so much of what had happened since he dove into the cold Gironde.

He had made it easily to the *Mary-Bee* and into the warm, welcoming arms of Marie-Odile. Except for the worry that the ship might be intercepted by some French naval sloop, the crossing to New York had been pleasant, with even a measure of joy. He had convinced Marie they should be married. She had been against it at first.

"You'll regret it. I'm an uneducated peasant. You're an aristocrat, a count. We're from different stations. I will end up boring you and making you unhappy."

"That's ridiculous, you're more intelligent and have more sense than any duchess or countess I've ever met. And besides, we're going to a place where what you are when you're born isn't as important as what you make of yourself. Marie, I'd never be able to marry anyone else. I love you."

Captain Wethersby performed the ceremony in mid-Atlantic. The captain did so much for them. Once in New York, he arranged for the sale of Solange's jewels and would accept no payment for the passage.

"You'll pay it later, when this foolishness back in France is settled. I'll arrange it with the company. I'll go right to its owner, Mister Clay. He'll understand."

He had also arranged the next leg of their journey. Guy had decided that the East Coast was still dangerously close to Europe. Louis-Napoleon's agents could be anywhere. And he ruled out South America. He wanted to stay in the United States. He had studied its history and saw it as a great, if flawed, experiment. The question was where he could become successful, for the sake of his wife and child and du Clocher while at the same time not drawing attention to himself? There was only one answer.

California.

The tales spreading from John Augustus Sutter's mill were enough to exhilarate a Boston banker, enough to make the most cautious man pack his belongings, kiss his wife and children goodbye, and set off for the land of gold and promise. No matter how he struggled and failed elsewhere, a man, any man, it would seem, had a chance at riches in California. Guy desperately wanted that chance. He had to restore what Edouard had lost, and he had to be ready to return to du Clocher whenever Louis-Napoleon fell from power. And there was no predicting when that would be. It could come in two weeks or two years. Surely no longer.

Still, he hesitated. It was bound to be a rough life out there and the passage difficult. He didn't want to place Marie-Odile at risk. She had come to mean so much to him. He proposed that she stay behind, but Marie would not hear of it.

"I'm no pampered lady, Guy. I'm used to hard work. I'm strong, like my mother. Lord knows she never had problems having babies and I won't either. You'll see."

Finally Guy agreed, but only after Captain Wethersby promised to get them passage on a packet down to Panama captained by a friend of his. From there it would be overland at the Isthmus and then up the Pacific coast on one of the new, extraordinarily fast clipper ships that Wethersby's shipping line had taken off the China route to handle the hordes of people clamoring to get to San Francisco.

"Except for that little bit of a land trip in Panama, it'll be like you're with me all the way," Wethersby assured Guy. "My friends will treat you as I would. These men know their ships and they know the sea. Now I wouldn't recommend this unless I knew you were in safe hands."

Wethersby had frowned then. There was something else he should say, but he didn't want to worry his friends unduly. Still, it was his duty to caution them.

"I should tell you. There are some idiots and madmen on the sea. Men who should never have been given a ship. There are stories... I mean, you have so many people desperate to get to California and there's bound to be stories of greed and... and well, some men should never be given the honor of captaining a ship. But you're not to worry. The men you'll be sailing with are truly fine men. You'll see."

And Guy finally did "see." He and Marie soon left the cold New York Harbor for Panama.

It was there that the nightmare began. Muddy and foundering in a morass of desperate humanity, Cristobal was a shocking hell. Families slept in doorways, huddled under blankets, babies wailed with hunger, children begged for food, fathers clawed and raked for a way out, a way to reach sunshine and happiness.

Dirt, filth, and despair smothered the town. Guy and Marie could have left Cristobal immediately. The influence of Captain Wethersby and power of the Clay shipping line had insured that their places in the overland expedition had not been sold off to someone with more cash. But Guy let the expedition leave without them. He was frightened. There was too much talk and too much evidence of cholera, malaria, dysentery, and death going across the Isthmus. He would not chance the health of Marie and their unborn child. They would take the safer, slower route. They would book passage around Cape Horn and travel by sea all the way to California.

With no Captain Wethersby to make arrangements, finding a ship proved almost impossible. Shipping companies were sending anything that floated out to sea to cash in on the demand, and still there were not enough places.

After several weeks, Guy was able to book a cabin, through the sheer power of his personality and most of his money, on the *Bonnie Swift,* a dowdy cargo ship that had been hurriedly refitted to accommodate passengers.

As the anchor was about to be weighed, when Marie and Guy had settled into a tiny but adequate "cabin," separated from the next "cabin" by a makeshift partition, the captain took on more passengers. They had not gone through the shipping line's harried little agent as Guy had. The captain had sent out some of his crew to "book" them directly, finding most in Cristobal's fetid bars and squalid rooming houses.

So, moments before the *Bonnie Swift* was to set sail, an apologetic cabin boy informed Guy and Marie they would have to share their accommodations. Guy protested and then demanded his money be returned and they be allowed to disembark.

Marie had rested a pleading hand on his arm. "Please, I can't take another hour in that awful town. There's sickness and crime everywhere. We must leave. This will be all right."

Guy was to relive that scene over and over again, and hate himself for giving in. If only they had left the *Bonnie Swift,* if only...

But they did stay on and they did set sail and they got to know their cabinmates, as mismatched a couple as there ever was. The husband, George Washington Jones, was a short, plump butcher from the small Pennsylvania town of Solebury. He had liked his life there and enjoyed his good standing in the community. Then he met Elizabeth

McConnell, a quarry worker's daughter who saw George Washington as her chance at a better life. So she set out to snare him and snare him she did. She was handsome, talkative, and Jones fancied himself extremely lucky she had noticed him.

But marrying Jones wasn't enough for Elizabeth. She wanted more and that more was California.

It took months of whining and cajoling and bedroom blackmail before George Washington gave in. He finally reasoned that if there wasn't gold to be found, the West could always use a butcher.

Life on board the *Bonnie Swift* quickly fell into unrelieved tedium. The food was edible. The accommodations cramped but passably clean, and people found their friends. Some of the more disagreeable last-minute passengers took to playing cards and gambling wherever they found an empty spot. They were rowdy and rough but did take care to tone down their conversations and snarlings when one of the women was about.

There weren't many women on board, but the fact there were any at all made Guy feel somewhat better. There was even another woman expecting a child. Marie had taken to her immediately even though communicating was somewhat limited by Marie's sparse English. She and this woman, Fenella Delany, could often be found huddling and whispering. Fenella had been in the United States for two years, a refugee from the Irish potato blight. Her thin body still showed the hardships of her native country.

Fenella had married almost as soon as she got off the boat in New York. On her second day, at the corner grocery store, she had literally bumped into a sharp-featured, sharp-minded loner named Damon Delany. He had helped her pick up the vegetables that tumbled from her basket, insisted on carrying her groceries home, and proposed to her within the week. Delany was also an Irish immigrant, but he had been in the States for several years, working his way up from floorsweeper to warehouse manager in a New York importing firm. If he hadn't been Irish, he would have advanced much further and much faster. But he was a Mick and that only made him work all the harder, never wasting time on socializing and good times.

Delany did find there was one arena in which being a Mick wasn't such a handicap. And that was in politics. The big politicians needed ward leaders to get out the immigrant vote. Delany became a familiar figure, first in the ward halls, then even at City Hall. And he learned. He learned how deals were forged and money made and elections won. After much consideration, he decided this knowledge could best serve him in virgin territory, out in California.

Leaving New York wasn't hard for Delany. For while he had many acquaintances, he had no friends. His wife was all he needed. He trusted only her. Even on the *Bonnie Swift*, he had no time for the other men's planning and dreaming of the big strikes that awaited them. Delany had his own plans, and he was keeping them to himself. Guy's initial inclination was not to like the man, but after Marie chided him for this, he had to admit there was no specific reason for this dislike. So he set his misgivings aside.

The voyage south went quickly. There were a few times they hit spots where the wind died down to a whisper, but under the able direction of Jedediah Walton, the first mate, the sailors tacked and jibbed, caught whatever breeze there was, and got them out of the calm.

It was around Cape Horn that the *Bonnie Swift* ran into her first real trouble.

By all reckoning, it should have been too early in the southern winter for the savagery that overswept them, the unspeakable cold and gale. Still the ship would have pushed her way through, if it hadn't been for a miscalculation by Captain Spencer. He had set course a little too far south. Walton had tried to argue that judging by the weather they had already encountered, the wise course was to hug land and take the chance of hidden rocks and mean currents rather than swing away as was usually done. But the captain, who made few appearances on the bridge, became enraged that his authority was being questioned. He ordered Walton to swing south or march himself into the ship's brig.

They turned south and were set upon by wind and walls of furious water. The ship was hurled by waves and threatened by vast ice fields that suddenly seemed to materialize from nowhere.

It was only the crew that never stopped its frantic efforts and the quick-thinking of the first mate that got them through. There were casualties. The nine-year-old cabin boy was swept overboard, too sick from coast fever to hold onto a line. Another crew member did not get up from his hammock after the hour's rest Walton had ordered that he take.

At last, they were around the Horn, safe, they thought, on their way to Juan Fernandez, a tiny island off Chile. Here they could dock to take on supplies and feel solid land underneath their feet again. But some capricious, irritable god had decided to vent his ill-spirits on the *Bonnie Swift* and hurled one final storm at her. The livestock, miraculously still alive after the punishment of the Horn, had been brought on deck for relief, only to be washed overboard or drowned at their tethers in this new tempest.

When the storm had died, the passengers were assured that despite the loss of the animals there were enough provisions to see them to Juan Fernandez, that there would be landfall in a few days, and the rest of the journey would be smooth and easy. Landfall couldn't come too soon for Guy. While Marie-Odile and Fenella did not complain, the rough passage had been hard on them. They were both weak, and Guy was worried.

And then there was no wind. None whatsoever. And the *Bonnie Swift* did not move. Nothing moved and the sea turned to glass and the ship turned to hell.

Days passed. Weeks. The food dwindled until finally the ship's steward announced that nothing was left in the ship's store for passengers or crew except tainted meat, foul water, and wormy biscuits. They ate that, but even it was in short supply.

The cruel wretchedness affected different men in different ways. Some took to their bunks and gave up hope in the darkness. Others read the Bible and prayed for divine intervention. Others seized the remaining barrels of rum, drank, gambled, and forgot where they were. Grudges and slights were imagined and punished, fights broke out and men were lowered to a grave of water. There were those who seemed glued to the deck, eyes fixed on the sea and sky, waiting for the one wave, the one cloud that would herald the end of the ordeal.

Marie-Odile never left her bunk, too sick and too afraid she might steal strength from the tiny life that pitched within her. Her legs were swollen and her breathing labored. Guy suffered along with her.

"You pile of manure! You cheating son of a pig's ass. I'll kill you for this!"

Carl was suddenly screaming. It was so unexpected no one moved. He sprang up, still bellowing obscenities. Guy saw a knife in his hand.

"Watch out," he yelled. "Carl's gone mad."

A magic wand was waved over the deck bringing movement and activity everywhere as men dove for protection and Carl chased them around the ship with deranged fury, slashing at barrels, men, rigging, and anything else that was in his way.

Walton ran down the steps from the upper deck, shouting orders. "Jim, Adam, get that net. Dick run for a gun. You, lure him this way."

The crew had worked with their towering, powerful first mate long enough to know there was more danger in disobeying him than any armed lunatic could offer.

"You bastards," Carl was screaming, "you've stolen my deucey."

The crew was trying to get close enough to drop a net on Carl, but everytime they edged in, he lashed out again, forcing them back.

"Carl," Walton shouted with authority. Carl stopped, eyes narrowing, trying to focus and remember. "Carl," Walton said more quietly, "you will put down the knife. Now. Now, Carl."

"They cheated..."

"NOW."

Carl let the knife drop, whimpering. "It wasn't right, them cheating..."

Walton moved quickly, grabbed one of Carl's arms and motioned Guy to get the other. "Come then," he said, "this man's sick. The brig's no place for him. We'll lock him in the captain's storeroom. There's nothing in it now, anyway."

"Just one minute, mister." Captain Spencer was at the door leading to his quarters, his frilly white shirt only partially buttoned. Behind him, peering over his shoulder was Elizabeth Jones. "This man is to be punished, not coddled. I saw him running around, threatening everyone. I don't want him in my storeroom. Into the brig with him, I say."

"But, sir, the man is out of his head. There's no point punishing him," Walton protested.

"Are you questioning my orders again, mister? You're doing that a lot lately."

"No, of course not, sir. It's just that—"

"It's just nothing, Mister Walton. You tie this man to the mast until we reach California. There the Stockton Asylum can do what they want with the filth. And cut his rations in half. If he's so crazy, he won't notice." The captain, dismissing the matter, turned to go back to his quarters. Guy wasn't ready to let him go. Angrily, he put a rough hand on the captain's shoulder and spun him around.

"Who dares lay...?" The captain's dignity was offended.

"You can't do that." Guy matched his anger. "You'll kill the man on half rations. It's murder."

"Take your hand off me and don't you dare tell me what I can and cannot do. This is my ship and what I say is law. Mister Walton, have this man tied up as well."

A soft, cooing "sweetie" made the captain turn. It was Elizabeth. "Let him be," she whispered as she bent to Spencer and let her fingers run along her cleavage. "He didn't mean no harm. Be nice sweetie, for me."

The captain watched her fingers. Suddenly the little episode was getting tiresome. He had better things to do.

"Very well," he said, without turning back to the deck. "Just tie up the crazy one. But the other, if he cares so much for the loony, let him share his rations with him."

Elizabeth winked at Guy before following the captain into the dark corridor.

Damon Delany was at Guy's side.

"This voyage seems to be agreeing with the captain, wouldn't you say?" he asked. Delany sidled way before Guy could respond. Guy looked into the darkness into which the captain had receded. Yes, Spencer was looking remarkably fit, right down to his ironed shirt.

Chapter Nineteen

A fearful, pain-filled moan came deep from within Marie-Odile. She tried to turn in the narrow bunk, but couldn't find the strength.

Guy had fallen asleep on the floor beside her. He awoke with her movement and smoothed the hair from her forehead.

"Is there anything I can do?" he whispered, not wanting to waken George Washington Jones, who was lying on the other side of a sheet that divided the cabin.

Marie's eyelids fluttered open for a second. "No," was all she could rasp.

"There must be something. Here, a sip of water."

She shook her head "no." "Save... it."

"There's no good saving it if you die first. Oh please, Marie, drink something."

Guy heard George Washington stir. "She can have my ration, too."

Guy slipped past the sheet to George Washington's side. He didn't want Marie to hear.

"George, she needs more than water. Something is going wrong. I just know it. Do you think Elizabeth might take a look at her?"

"Elizabeth?" It sounded like a word in an unfamiliar language. "Elizabeth. I don't know. She's not here much. I'm not sure..."

Guy let him trail off. He wasn't going to press the subject. Elizabeth's blatant absences were being snickered about all over the ship. The card players made obscene comments about her whenever George Washington was in earshot. It had gotten so bad that the little butcher rarely left the cabin, as if not hearing about Elizabeth's infidelity would eliminate it from possibility.

Marie moaned again and George flinched. "Guy, I can't stand it. She's hurting so much. If only I could do something. Wait, wouldn't it be better for her if she had lady company? Wouldn't it be better if that

Missus Fenella lady shared the cabin with her instead of me? They could help each other." George Washington was elated. He had come up with a useful idea.

Guy wasn't sure Fenella was in any condition to help, still he didn't want to disappoint the little man, he was so eager to implement his plan. And who knew? The switch might be for the best. Surely it couldn't hurt. As it was, when Marie was awake, she was painfully conscious of disturbing George Washington. And she worried about him and how he was taking Elizabeth's absences.

"You wouldn't mind?"

"Oh no, not at all. Wish I could do more. All I know about, all I ever knew about's butchering. Fresh slaughter, clean slices, good meat. I know about that. Ladies, I don't know anything about. Nothing."

He looked pathetically bewildered, a simple man who should have been warned that there was more to life than keeping knives sharpened.

George Washington pulled on his salt-stained boots and clumped out into the passageway. Within minutes, Damon Delany had taken his place.

"It's all right with you, then?" he whispered to Guy.

"Of course. I think it would comfort the women to be together."

"Good. I do too. Please help me carry Fenella."

They had no sooner gotten Fenella settled into what had been Elizabeth's bunk than the former occupant was standing in the doorway.

"Out of sight, out of mind? And what exactly is happening here?" Elizabeth wasn't in the least put out, but thought it might be fun to tease the handsome count.

"Am I going to be cast overboard next?"

"I am sorry, Madam," Guy said courteously, cutting off any salvo Delany might have been about to discharge. "We really should have consulted you, but your husband..."

"That fart bag," Elizabeth snorted.

"... your husband offered your places so that the two women with child could be together."

"Oh, it's all right." Elizabeth actually looked concerned. "They're having a hard time, aren't they?"

"Do you think," Guy said hopefully, "you could help with them? I think there is something terribly wrong with Marie."

Elizabeth edged out of the cabin. "Oh no, no, no, no. I can't help.

No. No. Oh, my mother used to scream. She had so many babies, and she was always screaming. I never wanted any. Oh no. Please. I have to leave." She fled.

"The soul of womanly compassion, isn't she?" Damon observed dryly. "And such a picture of good health. She and the captain are such a fine couple, both pictures of good health."

Guy looked hard at Delany. Elizabeth hadn't collected her rations in days. She'd been eating in the captain's quarters. Guy's thoughts, leading him along disturbing paths, were interrupted by Jedediah Walton.

"Sirs, are the ladies all right?"

"And how do you expect them to be 'all right' on a garbage scow like this?" Delany's bitterness was an assault on the first mate.

Walton's face became a mask. "It's nature, sir, and bad luck. This crew is as good as any I've ever sailed with."

"And the captain, how would you measure the captain?"

Guy interrupted. The first mate was a good man and didn't deserve Delany's belligerence. "The ladies are as well as can be expected. They don't have enough food. There just isn't enough."

"I know, sir." Walton was a good man who took his responsibility seriously. "I've been giving you some of my rations. Some of the crew have offered theirs, but, well, look, I can't let them do that. They'll need all the strength they can muster when the wind comes up. A good wind, it has to come up soon. Well, anyway, here's the ration for today. What there is of it."

Walton apologetically handed them each a dented metal plate on which were leadened biscuits, a few shriveled, miserly beans, and a minuscule strand of jerky.

"I'm sorry, sirs, that's all there is. Cook's going to try for a broth for tomorrow, though what he'll make it with beats me." Walton left.

It was so mean a plate, so miserly, so inadequate. For a moment Guy was back at du Clocher, with Marcel at his elbow, offering him a platter mounded with roasted lamb, salsify, baby carrots, asking after the Leoville, was the wine to his liking, would he care for more?

More? He had to have more. He couldn't allow Marie and their baby to starve.

"Damon, I'm going to find food for Marie and Fenella."

Damon grabbed Guy. "Hold on there, fellow, where do you intend to find food?"

"I believe the captain knows where there's some. He is looking a little too fit. And so is Elizabeth Jones, for that matter."

"Don't do anything foolhardy," Damon said. He dropped his grip on Guy. Guy immediately rushed out.

For a second Delany allowed himself a small smile of satisfaction before replacing it with more appropriate somberness. He glanced at Fenella. She had seen nothing. She was still asleep.

Damon left to shadow Guy down the passageway. He reached the deck in time to see his new cabinmate disappear into the darkness towards the captain's quarters.

The plunge from darkness to light to darkness disoriented and blinded Guy, halting him. But the time it took him to see again did little to subdue the frustration and festering notion that an immense injustice was being done.

There were two doors to the left off the passageway and a third at the far end. One would be the captain's study, the second his living quarters, and the third, his storeroom.

Loud giggles from the door at the end identified it as the living quarters. One of the two side doors had to be the storeroom. Guy moved closer and saw a hasp and lock on one. That was it. Lacking any other tool, he took off his large belt buckle and with two blows broke the lock.

He pushed the door open slowly, not sure what he'd find, almost afraid of what he would. It was very dark, only one slice of light slanted in from a tiny porthole.

That was enough to see that the room was crammed with barrels of flour, great chunks of meat, whole smoked fish, dried beans and peas, and even some fresh limes. There was enough food to feed the entire ship for a week, more. It was there and it had been there all the time his Marie was delirious with hunger.

"YOU BASTARD!!! YOU THIEVING, MURDERING BASTARD!!"

Guy ran out to the deck. "There's food. FOOD. The captain's been stealing food from us."

A few men jumped to their feet and rushed Guy. The others stared stupidly.

"Food?" "Where's food?" "Who's stealing?" Questions jumbled out as more and more men tumbled onto the deck.

"Is he crazy?" "Where?" "What's going on?"

"Follow me," Guy motioned. "It's in there."

Turning around to head back down the passageway, Guy's path was blocked by Captain Spencer, scarlet-faced with outrage and aiming an enormous, cocked pistol.

"And where do you think you're going, you goddamned trouble-maker? This is my goddamned ship. My ship! And you don't go anywhere unless I permit it."

Ignoring the threatening gun, Guy turned back to the suddenly subdued crowd. "There's good food in there," he said. "Food, I tell you. We must have it. We'll take it now."

"MISTER WALTON!" the captain bellowed. Jedediah Walton stepped to the railing of the upper deck, rifle cradled across his arm.

"Aye, sir?"

"This piece of scum is daring to disobey your captain. He shall be punished."

"Sir, if you please, I think hunger has taken his senses."

The captain spoke slowly and ominously now. "I've been hearing too much lately what you think, Walton. Now you listen to me, mister. I am the captain and what I say goes. Question my orders and that's mutiny. You know the penalty for mutiny, mister? What about the rest of you? Well, it's death by hanging. That's what's the penalty for mutiny. Now move back, all of you, while I deal with Mister Troublemaker here."

A few hesitated, staring with uncertainty. They were desperate enough that with a leader they might risk the captain's gun and the hangman's noose. But they weren't sure and their potential leader was looking down a pistol barrel, so they too shuffled back. Delany had come back, watching from the stairs. Now he moved aside to let George Washington Jones up from below.

"What's happening?" the butcher whispered. "Is there food?"

"Shut up and watch."

Making sure the first mate had his rifle trained on the crowd, the captain got closer to Guy. "As for you, you make too much trouble. But don't worry, I'm not going to have you strung up on the spot. No, no, you're a fine gentleman. You deserve a fine trial when we get to Santa Barbara..."

"It's you who should be on trial, keeping food from..."

The captain crossed the remaining few steps between them and viciously backhanded Guy across the face.

"Shut up!" he yelled as he hit him again and again. "Shut up, I tell you." He paused to get his breath. "The whip, Walton, give it to me."

Head averted so the captain could not see his contempt, Walton muttered, "At once, sir." He came slowly down with an ugly-looking whip and some rope.

"And let me tell you something else, Mister Frenchman, no foreigner yet has ever been set free in Santa Barbara. You'll hang for sure. In the meantime, I'm going to make an example out of you. So everyone'll know you don't defy Captain John Spencer and get away with it. Walton, get a move on it and tie him next to his good friend, the loony. That way they can keep each other company, while I administer twenty lashes."

"You can't do this," Guy protested.

Walton was beside him, looping the heavy rope around his wrist. "I'm afraid he can, sir," he said quietly. "Don't make it worse for yourself."

The first mate tied Guy to the mast and moved to step aside.

"Grab his arms," the captain snarled, "and bring him up tight against the mast. We wouldn't want him to fall and hurt himself."

The whip flashed through the air.

Crack.

A fierce red line snaked across Guy's back.

Crack. A second. A third. Fourth. Fifth.

The captain was administering the punishment with unrelenting pleasure.

Crack.

Crack.

Crack.

Ten. Eleven.

There was silence except for the whip and the moans Guy could no longer hold back.

Crack. Twelve.

"John, honey, what are you doing?"

The whip went flaccid just as the captain was about to bring down thirteen.

Elizabeth had appeared with her hair disheveled and face flushed from awakening. She was wearing only a robe that one hand was making an ineffectual effort to keep closed.

"I'm teaching this French bastard a lesson. I'm teaching him who's in charge."

Elizabeth glanced at Guy's raw back and shuddered. "C'mon sweetie, you've taught him enough. Come on back and teach me some lessons now."

When the captain turned to her, she let her robe drop open more, exposing her breasts, the insides of her thighs, and a dark mound of pubic hair. The captain dropped the bloody whip to take her outstretched hand, and if she heard George Washington Jones's anguished cry of "Elizabeth," she made no sign that she did.

Walton gently lowered Guy to the deck. "We've got some salve. It'll help. I'll bring some—while the captain's otherwise busy."

Guy was too much in pain to even nod. Damon Delany was then squatting at his side. "I'll watch after Marie, don't worry. I'll do all there is to do." And he left.

Guy lowered his head to his chest and wept.

Chapter Twenty

A week. A full week. At first Guy slipped in and out of consciousness. Sometimes he was on the *Bonnie Swift*, the sounds of wood creaking, cards being angrily slapped on barrels, men snarling accusations of cheating, Carl mumbling gibberish, the smell of mast and sail and seawater, of sweat and fear and disaster all pounding at him, blowing up in his head until he mercifully passed out again.

Then he would be bending over, picking big, beautiful grapes, longing to pop one in his mouth, feel its juice and goodness filling him, soothing him. But then Edouard would appear, with Donnadieu behind him. Edouard would snatch the fruit from him and hand it to the prefect. And snap! Guy would be back on the *Bonnie Swift* with its horrors and reality once again strangling him, its vile smells smothering him until he could suffer no more and he lapsed back into coma.

Sometimes he would be in a cafe, the Relais on Rue de la Hachette, down from the Petit Pont. It would be bright and lively and he and his friend Jules would be arguing politics. As Guy reached for his glass of wine, a file of soldiers would march into the cafe, overturning tables and brutally pushing aside patrons. The captain would sweep aside Guy's glass and yell, "You'll see who's in charge here," as he drew a whip from his scabbard.

That ended on the third day, and Guy wasn't sure if it hadn't been preferable in his limbo of nightmare. As it was, he knew that the searing, cruel pain he felt was real and would not go away by closing his eyes and mind. Then there was Carl, who moaned and whimpered and once in a while would sidle over and lay his head in Guy's lap, a miserable, rank, and fetid cur looking for affection.

Guy smelled little better. There was no water with which to wash and during the three days he had lapsed in and out of consciousness,

121

he had soiled himself. When he returned to sanity, he prevailed on Delany, when the Irishman had come up to report no change in Marie's condition—her legs were still swelling and her color was bad—to bring him a change of clothes. Jedediah Walton, seeing Guy struggling to get out of his stinking, torn garments, had come over and without a word untied the knots. When Guy was finished, Walton retied the rope and returned to the bridge, not waiting for thanks.

There was even less to eat than before. Guy would take a small bite of his hardtack and put the rest away for Marie. He tried to get Carl to eat something of his rations, coaxing as a new mother would a colicky baby with little success.

Occasionally Carl would sit up straight, look around, and ask where he was.

"You're on the *Bonnie Swift*," Guy would answer. "Somewhere, nowhere in the Pacific."

"Still no wind then?" Carl would ask as if their predicament delighted him. And then with great optimism he would invariably add, "Well, soon."

These periods of sanity sometimes ended right there, with Carl lapsing into another of his garbled card games. A few times, he stayed in his right mind for longer. He asked Guy questions about France, about what he intended to do in California, about Marie and what they were going to name the baby. Carl would talk about himself, too, about his boyhood as a printer's apprentice and how he had saved his money and was ready when California beckoned. He got very reticent when Guy asked what he planned to do there. Carl would only wink slyly, and say one thing was sure, he wasn't wasting time looking for fool's gold.

Inevitably, the conversation would end. Sometimes abruptly with Carl lapsing into his gibberish. Sometimes with Carl falling into a childlike sleep only to awaken raving and drooling.

And still there was no wind.

On the sixth day, Carl had another period of lucidity. He was very weak, as weak as Guy had seen him.

As usual he asked where he was. The question was hardly more than a whisper.

"You're on the *Bonnie Swift*," Guy answered.

And as always, Carl asked, "Still no wind then?" This time he did not follow with his optimistic "soon," instead he dragged over as close to Guy's face as he could get, grasping Guy's shirt for support.

"I'm going to die soon, you know."

"No, Carl, no. The wind will come. Soon, like you always say."

"Oh yes, it's coming, but not soon enough, not for me. I'm gone. You're going to make it though. I know it. I feel it." Carl raised his voice, startling Guy. "First mate," he yelled. "I need you here. Bring witnesses."

Guy thought Carl had gone crazy again. But no, he was clear-eyed and sure.

"What's wrong with you?" Walton demanded, running over with two sailors in tow.

"I need witnesses for my last will and testament. You listen. I am Carl Wegge. I have no home now except this damned ship. I did come from Lowell, Massachusetts, the United States of America, and may god bless her for always. I will be dead soon, so before you all as witnesses, I want you to know that all my earthly goods, packed somewhere in the hold of this accursed ship, should be given to this man here. Guy—what's your name Guy, anyway?"

"Saint-Savin, Guy Saint-Savin."

Carl giggled. "Funny name. Well, no matter. I give my earthly goods to this fellow here, and let God punish any man who tries to keep it from him." His voice seemed to lose strength and he muttered, "That's all I wanted. Thank you. I'm tired. So tired..."

Carl put his head down onto Guy's lap. "Just let me rest here, for a second, out of the sun, for a second..."

Carl closed his eyes. One of the sailors crossed himself and they moved away. They were all going to die, Guy thought. Carl would be the lucky one if he died soon. Guy leaned his cheek against the mast, closed his eyes, and slept as well.

Guy opened his eyes. It was dark. Carl was a tiny, pitiful figure, curled up and wrapped in a shroud of cold moonlight. He was dead.

"Mister Walton!" Guy yelled. "Jedediah! Please! Someone, help!"

No one came. Guy called again only to realize something was going on. There was a scurrying all around him, having nothing to do with his cry. He forced his eyes to focus on the dancing visions and see the rush and movement for what it actually was—the crew. Rays of moonlight suddenly illuminated the deck. Sailors were climbing the rigging and lowering the sails. Guy squeezed his eyes shut and shook his head savagely, convinced he was dreaming again.

When he reopened his eyes, the sailors were still hurrying to their tasks. Then Guy realized Jedediah Walton was shouting orders, and he was shouting loud to be heard above...the wind! The wind, strong and insistent, a fast-rising wind, anxious to reassert its power. The wind had returned and the *Bonnie Swift* was snatched back from hell. Ahead was Juan Fernandez, land, food, water, and salvation.

Guy looked down at the little man at last at peace, in his lap. Poor Carl. He had come so close. Guy would mourn for him even if no one else would. Guy didn't call out again. There would be time enough later.

At dawn the next morning, with the prow of the *Bonnie Swift* shearing impatiently through the water, her sails billowing and straining with the wind, Carl's body, wrapped in dirty burlap, was dumped into the ocean. The captain kept to his cabin so the task of saying a few words fell to Jedediah Walton. He read haltingly but with feeling and grace from the well-worn Bible his mother had given him when he first set out to sea.

Guy was untied for the ceremony. At its end, he went back to the mast and waited. He didn't notice Delany come up on deck, say something to Walton, and return immediately below.

Walton was clearly bothered. He was in battle with himself over duties as a first mate and duties as a man. He looked towards the captain's quarters, shrugged, and went to Guy. Instead of picking up the ropes, he said, "Your wife is having her baby. Go to her. She needs you." Guy was already running.

Walton pushed hair off his face. "Probably could be flogged for this," he muttered. "Hell, if the captain hasn't left his whore yet, not likely he's going to before we reach Juan Fernandez. So let him be damned. WATCH those lines, Scotty, we've got some sailing to do."

There were people crowding every doorway as Guy pushed past them to get to his cabin. A few patted him as he went by, mumbled comforting words, and shook their head in pity. As he got closer, he heard the moans, low, keening moans, terrible sounds that filled him with fear. Then a scream, shrill and unbearable. And then another. Guy ran. He had to get to Marie. He had to stop her pain. At the entrance to his cabin, from where those terrible noises were coming, Guy collided with Delany.

Guy grabbed him and shook him. "WHAT'S GOING ON? What's happening in there?"

"It's over," Delany answered, his voice choked with unfallen tears. "She's dead."

"No!" Guy shoved him aside and rushed in. The sheet had been taken down and a Mrs. Callaghan, a New York farmer's wife who had taken no umbrage at being dragged halfway around the world by a husband who had been blinded by gold dust, was bending over one of the beds. She wheeled around with anger. "Shush now, we've got enough noise and trouble in here without some hysterical man adding to it. Make yourself useful. Wipe that one's forehead—hurry up now."

She motioned to the bed nearest the outside wall. Guy squeezed past Mrs. Callaghan, taking the cloth she held out. The screams had subsided to pitiful mews. Guy gently pulled back the cover. To his shock, elation, and dismay, it was Marie-Odile, her face stripped of color except for two brilliant spots of red heat on her cheeks. Guy touched her face, seeking reassurance that what he thought was not true.

"She's alive," he whispered hoarsely. He'd been so sure Delany had meant Marie was dead when he had said "she."

Mrs. Callaghan looked up to reprimand him then saw his expression and softened. "Take it easy, dearie. She's alive, but just barely. She needs a doctor, good food, water."

Mrs. Callaghan picked up a bundle from the next bed.

Guy then remembered the cabin's other occupant. "Oh God," he moaned, "it's Fenella then. Fenella has died."

"For goodness sake, hush up man. That poor missus is asleep. She had a rough time, as well. Who would have thought they'd both go into labor at the same time. And now she's asleep. And that's God's mercy. She'll need all her strength when she gets the news. All her strength." Mrs. Callaghan looked down at the bundle she was holding. Guy still did not understand.

"It's the baby," Mrs. Callaghan said. "Mrs. Delany's little one. It was born dead. Not a single breath did that little girl take, poor wee thing." Mrs. Callaghan moved to the door, shaking her head, but before she stepped out, she added, "Now tend to your wife, man. Your child is yet to come." And she bustled out of the cabin.

Guy gently dabbed at Marie-Odile's swollen, pain-seared face. Her eyes were open but unseeing.

"Marie, my love, my dearest, it's Guy. Please look at me. Please see that I'm here now. Everything will be all right."

With great effort, Marie blinked her eyes and managed a smile. "I love you," she whispered. The smile was lost. Marie bit her lip as she pulled for breath. The pain was coming back. The thin, hot needle pushing farther and farther into her stomach, agony radiating from it in all directions. If she could breathe, if she could only push it away. But it kept going in further. It hurt, oh, she couldn't stand the hurt. It wouldn't stop. It kept getting worse. Marie screamed and screamed and dug her fingernails into Guy's hands as he tried to keep her arching body on the bed.

"Marie, stop. You've got to stop."

Guy was being pulled gently away from the bed by Fenella Delany, who was bracing herself against the wall to stay up. "Mrs. Callaghan," she said, "get her, Guy. Marie's baby, it's coming." Then she slumped to the floor in a faint.

Guy was unable to think. Should he go for Mrs. Callaghan, or pick up Fenella, or stay with Marie? He was immobilized and beyond making a decision. Mrs. Callaghan saved him from further inaction by bursting back into the room.

"That fool girl," she yelled over Marie's screams. "Get Mrs. Delany back into her bed. Then hold your wife down. That baby's ready to come out. Lord it's going to be a big one."

Guy quickly picked up Fenella—she weighed next to nothing—placed her gently on the bed, and turned back to his wife.

The next two hours were a blurred horror for Guy, with Mrs. Callaghan exhorting Marie to push harder, to keep pushing, and Marie trying until exhaustion would force her to stop. She was alternately moaning and screaming and begging for respite, her efforts growing weaker and weaker.

The baby was coming out turned, making it worse for Marie and worse for the child. But finally, with one last exertion, the baby, an angry, squalling boy, was clear.

"Oooo, he's a fine one," Mrs. Callaghan crooned. "Big, fine one. Ooo, you did well, Marie, darling." She cut the umbilical cord with a small knife pulled from her apron pocket, cleaned off the screaming little creature, and bundled him up in one of Marie's soft wool shawls.

"Here you go, missus. Here's your fine little boy."

Marie tried to raise her arms to accept her baby, but couldn't. So Guy carefully laid him next to her and cradled her arm around him. The baby was so tiny, yet so alive and vibrant.

Marie felt his warmth and life and she was happy. She gazed at the dark peach fuzz that was sticking out of the shawl. "I love you, Guy. I love you both so much."

"And I love you." Guy leaned down and kissed her, a long, tender kiss. When he pulled back, her eyes were closed. And then he saw that the arm that had been around the baby had fallen loose.

"Mrs. Callaghan, quick there's something wrong with Marie."

Mrs. Callaghan was there at once. She picked up the baby and shoved him into Guy's arms. "Get out. I'll see what I can do."

Guy waited in the passageway, clutching the outraged infant. It continued its howling and no amount of patting or rocking would lessen his fury. Finally an exhausted Mrs. Callaghan came out.

"Give me the babe," she said. Guy followed her back into the cabin. Fenella was awake and propped against the wall. Mrs. Callaghan took the baby to her. Fenella untied the top of her nightdress. Guy was about to turn away in confused embarrassment when he understood her purpose. Fenealla was gently guiding the little head of the baby to her breast and the wails were giving way to loud suckling.

"That little one's going to make it, mark my words," Mrs. Callaghan said firmly and then left.

Guy watched the little head bobbing up and down, so full of life. He could not look at the other bed. He did not want to see what was there. If he didn't see it, then it wouldn't be true.

Fennella's sad, mourning, "I'm sorry, Guy," released him and he stumbled to Marie's bed. He dropped to his knees and gathered her still form into his arms. "Oh God," he keened, rocking back and forth. "Oh God." What had he done? Taking her away from France to be a fugitive. Taking her on this wretched ship where she would suffer and. . .

Guy lowered her gently and stood up. This wretched ship had killed Marie, this wretched ship and its murdering, thieving captain. Well, that bastard would know justice today. Captain John Spencer would pay for murdering Marie-Odile.

Guy raced from the cabin, up and across the heaving deck, and into the captain's passageway. Jedediah Walton saw him and went to get his rifle. He was sure he would be needing it.

Guy pounded on the door to the captain's cabin, screaming, "Let me in, you filth. I'm going to kill you. I'm going to kill you with my bare hands. LET ME IN!"

He put his shoulder to the door to force it open, but it gave easily. Guy stepped across the threshold, only to stop, dazed.

There was an eerie red haze in the room as two candles cast flickery, menacing fingers of light. There was red everywhere, on the four-postered bed, on the oriental rug, on the logbook and decanter and chair and clothes and on George Washington Jones, who sat cross-legged on the floor wearing a grin of great satisfaction.

"Oh, Guy, I'm so glad it's you. I'm so glad you're the first to hear the news."

"News?" Guy was gagging. There was a heavy, oppressive smell to the room that was cloying and suffocating. "What news?"

"Oh," said Jones with childlike delight, "your dear, sweet wife will have enough to eat now. Plenty to eat to make her strong, for her baby. Plenty for everyone. I don't know why I didn't think of this before. I'm a butcher, you see, and now there will be plenty of meat."

Guy didn't want to look to where George Washington Jones was pointing, but he couldn't stop himself. He was pointing to a mahogany desk next to which, neatly arranged, were lumps of meat, skinned, deboned, expertly carved and dripping with blood. And on the desk were the gape-mouthed heads of Captain John Spencer and Mistress Elizabeth Jones.

"Oh Jesus!" gasped Walton. He had just arrived. "Oh, my great God, what did you do, Jones?"

"Oh, it was nothing. A little tricky maybe, but I'm a good butcher. I'm especially good with swine. No one will be hungry now. No sirree, not with George Washington Jones around."

Walton pulled Guy out and closed the door behind him. Just then they heard an exultant, "Land ho!"

Book Three

Chapter Twenty-one

November, 1852

Solange propped her elbows on the rough-hewed table and wearily rested, head to hand. She closed her eyes and breathed deeply, savoring the familiar odor of oak barrels and musty fermenting wine. It was damp, dark, and cold in the chai. She would have been more comfortable in the château's library, but she rarely went into that room any more. There were any number of rooms in the château that would have been suitable for what she was doing. Solange was there because she felt reassured by the candlelight flickering on the enormous barrels, as if the nearness of the wine would inspire her and solve her problems.

Problems. She sighed and looked again at the vineyard's leather-bound ledger book. It was the current history of the château, the plantings, the crop, the fermentation, and most important to Solange at the moment, the money. Or rather, the money that was not there and would not be coming.

She shivered as a chill whisper of wind blew across her back. Someone had come into the chai. She didn't bother looking up. It could be only one person, and he was going to ask a question she didn't want to answer.

"Is it bad?" Jacques Mazet asked.

Solange bit the corner of her lip and blinked back tears she refused to shed. She nodded.

"Here's some soup. Eat it."

"Oh, Jacques," Solange said with dismay, "has the cook come back? I told her she mustn't. I have no money to pay her. I had only enough to pay the pickers. And you, you've taken nothing for six months…"

Solange broke off. If she continued, she would cry, and she hadn't cried once since that night a year before. She hadn't cried for her father or her brother and she wasn't going to cry for du Clocher. She would cry for no one and no thing.

It had been hard to walk back up the hill after watching Guy disappear into the mist. She and Nathan had decided they would wait as long as possible before raising the cry that Donnadieu and Edouard were fighting. Then the soldiers would come in, find the bodies, and assume they had killed each other.

It hadn't worked out that way. Solange had no sooner gotten back to the château when in stampeded the soldiers. They had been aroused from their stupor by Claude Mazet, a Claude Mazet who had been living quite comfortably in St. Julien since his banishment from du Clocher, on funds that no one could account for. And there he had been, on that night, to pay back a debt he owed, he'd explained, some money he'd borrowed from one of the maids. And they had been in the hallway when the commotion began. They'd seen it all, he said, seen Donnadieu set on by Edouard and then slain by Guy.

The soldiers searched for Guy, but at least in that, they were too late.

Solange had protested Claude Mazet's version. Later Nathan was to wonder about the coincidence of Claude being there and why Claude had not called the soldiers sooner, before Guy got away. The only logical conclusion he could find was Claude had not been there, that the maid had sent for him after the fact. That night all Nathan could do was quietly counsel Solange to say no more. The damage of Claude's statement had been done. They would have to see to undoing it later.

There had been a great uproar in Bordeaux over the "scandale du Clocher." There was much talk and speculation over what had actually occurred and to where the young Saint-Savin had made off. Solange was certain there was also speculation over her exact role in the tragedy—whether she had been having an affair with Donnadieu, and her father and brother had opposed it—violently.

She stopped going into Bordeaux and kept to the château, seeing only General Hopewell and occasionally Nathan.

Actually, there wasn't much time for anything else. The vineyard totally preoccupied her. It had been a year of disaster.

The powdery white oidium continued to spread, rotting stalks, wasting leaves, splitting fruit, ravaging three-quarters of the vines. What they had been able to save would make good wine, but there was precious little of it. Du Clocher was not alone in suffering devastation. Every château in the Medoc had been damaged terribly. There would be very little wine this year. Yet the other vineyards in the Medoc were not facing the same financial ruin as Solange.

The small cru meant prices would rise dramatically. While the quantity would not be there, most châteaux would still make a good deal of money because they would sell so high.

Most châteaux. Not du Clocher.

Solange looked down at the ledger. If Cornelius Schroeder held her to that ridiculous contract her father had signed, she would be ruined. He would get the wine at a laughably low price, and he would make all the profit from the sale. Solange would not get enough to keep the château running for another year.

"There's only one thing to be done, Jacques. I must renegotiate the contract with Monsieur Schroeder."

Jacques shook his head gravely, being a realist above all else. "Why should he change anything? It's better for him the way it is."

"That's true." Solange rubbed her brow. She had been thinking about this for some time. "But he has only this year left. Perhaps if he believes I will go to another negociant next year, he will reconsider. I'd also suggest favorable prices for him—not one price for a number of years as father agreed to, but a fair price that would be a bit below what other châteaux were getting, something, anything to give him extra profit, and let us save ourselves now."

Solange studied Jacques for a reaction and frowned. She wasn't even convincing her own maître, much less Schroeder.

"Well, if all else fails, I can ask for an advance on next year's cru if I sign with him now. He might consider that."

Jacques's "maybe" was not filled with much hope.

"We'll find out soon enough, won't we, Jacques? He'll be here tomorrow for the vat tasting. It's good, isn't it?"

"Excellent. If only there were more..."

"Don't worry. The honorable monsieur will acquiesce. I know he will. He must."

Chapter Twenty-two

While Solange and Jacques worried about money matters at du Clocher, Monsieur Cornelius Schroeder, all 247 well-fed pounds of him, was doing some worrying of his own.

Under other circumstances, Schroeder would have felt content and self-satisfied sitting in the luxurious dining room of Chapon Fin, one of Bordeaux's finest restaurants, avidly awaiting his order of feuilleté d'escargots, aiguillettes de caneton, accompanied by a Clos d'Estournel, and finished with a granite du Sauternes. He had never regretted leaving Holland with its dreary climate and drearier food. He might not have been the most successful wine merchant, still no one could claim to enjoy the benefits of the profession more.

At that particular moment, nervously nibbling on a roll, he never felt less successful. Things had not been going well for several years. It certainly wasn't his fault. It was circumstance. For Schroeder, it was always circumstance. The one thing that had kept the firm of Cornelius Schroeder & Cie, solvent was his contract with Edouard Saint-Savin, and that would expire this year. He knew he couldn't lose it and stay in business.

In the meantime, there was that day's luncheon. It was highly out of the ordinary, which worried Schroeder even more. For the fourteenth or fifteenth time, the wine merchant hefted his girth sideways to peer around the marble column separating his table from the reception area. Still no sign of his dining companion. Schroeder groaned softly, and then glanced around to make sure none of the other diners had noticed.

Since he had received the invitation—no, it was more like a summons, and why shouldn't it be?—the afternoon before, Schroeder had fretted and sweated. Why did Jerome Libermann wish to have lunch with him, a lowly, inconsequential Bordelaise wine merchant?

Admittedly Schroeder owed a great deal of money to the Banque Libermann. The year before when Schroeder suddenly found himself short of necessary cash to pay some vineyards, he had been delighted, if a bit surprised, that the Banque Libermann had given him a loan of all the money he'd petitioned for, and then some—and then some more. And truthfully, there was even more after that. No matter how much Schroeder asked for, the Banque Libermann gave him. It was Jerome Libermann's own secretary who handled the transactions. Schroeder had made all good effort to make payments on these loans, as the Dutchman had assured Monsieur Bonchamps, the bank's local agent, only two weeks earlier. Monsieur Bonchamps had not seen it in quite the same way and had added that the matter would be discussed in Paris.

That had worried Schroeder further. Paris? His paltry loan discussed in Paris?

And that was the last he had heard until yesterday, when a liveried coachman, not bothering to hide his disdain for the dusty cluttered offices of Cornelius Schroeder & Cie, had handed him an ornately penned message from the head of the Banque Libermann. The note requested the merchant's presence at the Chapon Fin the next day at 1:30. It was now 2:15 and Schroeder, famished and anxious, was wondering how he would support his new mistress—a delightful brunette who had been happy to take Mademoiselle Elise Deschamps's place—much less his family, if the bank took away his business. Oh God, he would kill himself before returning to Holland in disgrace. He reached for another roll and smothered it with good farm butter from Cahors.

It was then as Schroeder sat knife in hand, roll at mouth, butter sliding down his vest that Jerome Libermann made his entrance. The banker was not a physically imposing man, thin, with long bony fingers and a head that, like his brother's, was large and slightly out of proportion. What made him noticeable was his self-assured detachment and the assumption, always realized, that he would be deferred to and given his way. Conversations stopped and heads turned in the restaurant. Even those who did not know him sensed he was someone very important.

Schroeder sputtered, tried to stand and wipe his mouth at the same time. The result was an overturned wine glass and a flustered wine merchant who never got further than an inch off the banquette.

Jerome chose not to notice. He lowered himself with almost feminine grace onto the thick, upholstered chair that had been pulled out for him, carefully peeled off his gloves, finger by finger, and ordered his wine, a '36 Lafitte. He did all this without turning his head to see if anyone was behind him. There was, of course, and the maître d' glided away immediately to insure that the baron would be presented with the antique crystal saved for visits by kings and princes.

Jerome smiled, and Schroeder suddenly wished he were anywhere else, even Holland.

"It is a lovely restaurant," the banker said, "as my brother promised. I'm on my way back to the capital after visiting his new little purchase."

"Oh yes." Schroeder was immensely relieved the conversation was beginning so neutrally. "I have heard he is starting a vineyard. Very risky, very risky indeed. It is so much wiser to take an existing château. At least then you know what the soil is capable of producing."

"I am interested you say that, Monsieur Schroeder. That is one purpose of our little meeting today, to discuss the most efficacious ways of buying into this region. I have been contemplating some purchases of my own."

Before Schroeder could finish puffing up with the pride of being asked for advice by one such as Jerome Libermann, the wine steward arrived, carefully cradling a bottle. He bowed and although his sommelier cup swayed around his neck, he kept the bottle steady.

"Baron," the sommelier intoned deferentially, "your wine was decanted earlier according to the instructions your coachman brought yesterday. I will now decant the other two bottles he delivered, as you also requested."

Jerome nodded.

The sommelier raised a finger. Two young boys appeared carrying a small table covered with fine linen. On it was a simple silver candleholder in which stood one white candle, a bottle cradle with elaborately wrought vines and grapes snaking across the silver, a simple, clear decanter, and a corkscrew. Schroeder strained to see what the bottle was as the sommelier placed it on the table, but could not.

The sommelier surveyed the table carefully, moved the decanter towards the edge, and again motioned to the boys. One scurried away to return with a lit candle which he used to light the one in the holder.

In the meantime, the sommelier laid the bottle into its cradle and gently inserted the corkscrew, taking care not to disturb the wine. He then pulled out the cork, cleanly and with not so much as the slightest jerk or false move.

With equal caution, he picked up the cradle and moved it so that the bottle's neck was just over the candle. Seeing that the light came through clearly, the man began to slowly pour from the bottle into the decanter, watching the neck so that not one errant speck of sediment would find its way into the decanter.

When he was finished, he set the bottle down with a flourish and blew out the candle.

"Excellently done," Jerome congratulated him. "You certainly did not need any muslin to catch the stray sediment."

"Baron," the sommelier was offended, "only the most heavy-handed would need muslin for anything save a Port or a Hermitage."

"So true. You may pour the Lafitte." Jerome was impressed by the sommelier's skill. Perhaps he should add him to his staff in Paris. But who knew? So many of these provincials preferred to stay where they were.

Schroeder's jitters had returned. He couldn't help noticing that there was only one glass for the Lafitte, and he couldn't help wondering why the other two bottles were being decanted. Could Jerome Libermann possibly be planning to drink three bottles of Lafitte for lunch?

Jerome returned the conversation to the wine trade by asking Schroeder what his function was exactly.

Schroeder explained that the merchants were the most important element in the life of the wine, that they took the newly fermented wine, fermented it further, sold it, bottled it. "Without us," he said with little modesty, "no bottle would reach your table."

"Then you are counselling me to acquire a negociant's firm and not a château?"

Oh good lord no, that was not what Schroeder meant at all. Jerome was in too good a position to acquire the Dutchman's own company. Schroeder had never meant to suggest that, so he quickly conceded, "Well, perhaps I overstated our position slightly. I mean, truly, the winegrowers are first with the grape. If the growing and initial fermentation is not done properly, well, poof, bad wine. Besides it is so lovely in the Medoc. Such a nice setting to spend time away from the bustle of Paris. Bordeaux city would hardly be enough of a change for a man like yourself."

Schroeder was relieved when the conversation halted to allow the serving of the first course. Jerome's coachman had apparently pre-ordered the meal. A glorious-smelling plate of lamproie bordelaise was set ceremoniously in front of the baron. Schroeder hadn't even known the Chapon Fin prepared that dish and made a mental note to order it the next time he came—if he could afford a next time.

"Yes," Jerome said, resuming the conversation, "so I have noticed on my visits with my brother. It is lovely. By the way, you are the exclusive merchant for that château where the unfortunate murder occurred last year?"

"Du Clocher? Of course. Yes. Yes. For years, it has been all mine."

Jerome laid down his fork and stared at Schroeder, causing the large man to fidget and his neck fat roll.

"Sole negociant? Then perhaps you can explain something to me." Jerome took a sip of his Lafitte, and if Schroeder hadn't been so nervous, he would have been envious. However, the negociant surmised that the true purpose of the luncheon summons was about to be thrown down on the table.

"Perhaps," Jerome went on, "you can explain this odd thing I've come across."

"Concerning du Clocher?" Oh please, prayed Schroeder silently, let this be a simple question, something general and not criminal.

Jerome did not answer, instead he motioned to the sommelier. "The other wines, bring them and pour some of each for Monsieur Schroeder."

Again the boys were summoned. This time they arrived with two bottles and two glasses. The sommelier poured from each and left.

Schroeder stared at the glasses as if they contained poison. Jerome, although greatly enjoying the drama, gave no sign he was aware of the negociant's distress. Instead he said, with nonchalance, "Now, before you taste that, let me tell you about the odd thing I mentioned. I was a guest of Edouard Saint-Savin last year..."

"May he rest in peace," Schroeder muttered.

"...and he was kind enough to present me with several of his château's finest vintages. Quite lovely. I admired them and served them in my own home. An acquaintance, having sampled some I served, was delighted to run across more of the '39 in London. He bought many bottles and generously presented me with some."

Schroeder was sweating. He desperately wanted to wipe his face, but was too afraid to perform even that simple act.

"And that's when I noticed the peculiar thing." Jerome was unrelenting. Someone else might have delivered the coup de grâce out of compassion. Someone else was not Jerome Libermann. "There, Monsieur Schroeder, you have two glasses of '39 du Clocher, each from a different bottle. Would you be so kind as to taste them both?"

"I really don't see..." The last thing in the world Schroeder wanted to do was taste that wine.

"If you will," Jerome interrupted firmly, "taste them."

Schroeder took the first glass gingerly. He made a half-hearted attempt at proper form for smelling the bouquet and swishing the wine around on his palate before swallowing.

"Excellent example of the '39," he sighed, weak with relief.

"And now the other."

Schroeder took the smallest of sips and try as he might, could not keep his mouth from pursing with distaste. Jerome was the model of concern when he asked if there was anything wrong.

"It's a '39, you say? Obviously a bad bottle. Happens from time to time."

"From time to time? All the bottles, all forty of the bottles, purchased across the Channel taste like this one. And all tasted exactly the same. So different from those Edouard..."

"God rest his soul."

"...gave me."

Schroeder was practically drowning in sweat now, and Jerome at last tired of his agony. "Monsieur Schroeder, you and I both know that you have been adding cheaper wine to what you sold as du Clocher so that you would have more to sell."

"Oh no, baron, never. That's unethical..."

"Unethical and profitable. No, please be quiet until I am finished. I have no interest in ruining you, although we both know that with the knowledge I have that could be arranged easily."

"The loan... I'll be able to pay back the loan within..."

"Monsieur Schroeder, I told you to be quiet. It is du Clocher I am interested in, not you. It's too fine a vineyard to be destroyed by inexperienced management. While Edouard's daughter is a lovely girl, she is just that—a girl. I'm sure you agree."

While Schroeder did not agree at all—Solange had proved astute and quite capable—he hurriedly said, "Absolutely correct. You are absolutely correct, baron. The vineyards will be going to weed soon.

However, if you are thinking of buying du Clocher, I don't think the mademoiselle will sell. She is quite sure her brother will be returning soon."

"And I can assure you that will not be the case."

Jerome couldn't help but smile. Naturally he had regretted the unnecessary deaths of Saint-Savin and Donnadieu, still it couldn't have worked out better for his purposes. There had always been the distinct possibility that Nathan could have interceded on behalf of the young Saint-Savin and saved him from exile. But Louis-Napoleon couldn't overlook or pardon the murder of his prefect, not at that time, at least, not even for his friend Nathan Libermann.

Of course, Nathan had done some investigating and had discerned his brother's hand in the tragic events and had been infuriated—and powerless. "Amateurs shouldn't get involved in politics, at least not in France," was Jerome's only comment when confronted by his brother. However, the banker had been relieved when Nathan didn't discover that Claude Mazet had been added to the bank's payroll after being thrown out by Guy. That Mazet was there to forestall Nathan's covering up the events was merely another indication of Jerome's superior eye for details.

Yet for all these various successes, it rankled Jerome that du Clocher was still not his and that his brother was delighting in that fact. Well, he was close, very close to attaining it. A mere child, and a female at that, would not be able to withstand the manipulations of Jerome Libermann. But he had already spent more time on this matter than he had thought necessary and he wished to end it soon. Everything now seemed in place. Schroeder had been sucked in well over his head with debts, and the discovery of Schroeder's little practice of doctoring the wine had only iced the cake. Even Nature, in the guise of that plant disease, whatever it was called, had worked in Jerome's favor. Yes, he was close.

Jerome smiled. Schroeder did not care for that smile at all. "Yes, I am very interested in acquiring a property in the Medoc, and that property is du Clocher. Now you may be right, Mademoiselle Saint-Savin may not wish to sell. Then again, perhaps she will have no choice soon. One never knows. You will keep me apprised of developments at du Clocher, won't you, Monsieur Schroeder?"

"Of course, baron, you can rely on me for news of any new developments. Now, sir, as regards my indebtness to the Banque Libermann..."

"Oh that. I am sure you have a sound business. You are obviously a resourceful man of the world who knows when to seize opportunities that are laid before him and to whom he should give his loyalties. Consider that you now have an extension on your loan. It will, however, be reviewed monthly. Do we understand each other?"

Schroeder certainly did understand. He exited bowing and scraping. He had gotten a reprieve, but he would have to earn it. He would have to find some way to deliver du Clocher to Jerome.

Jerome watched him go with amusement, then requested a cognac. It was such a dreary trip back to Paris. He needed something to warm his way, although he was feeling quite pleased as it was without it.

Chapter Twenty-three

Cornelius Schroeder hefted his great weight off the seat, extended a pudgy hand to his assistant, Harry Busscher, who was standing outside, and once again engineered the miracle of extricating himself from his carriage.

On firm ground, he panted with relief. He really would have preferred to let Busscher suffer the indignities of travel and perform the tasting. His lunch at the Chapon Fin the day before had precluded that. He would suffer the pain of traveling to du Clocher and he would see what he could do for Jerome Libermann. Besides, he was sure to be fed well there.

After bowing over Solange's hand in greeting, Schroeder started for the château. Edouard had always provided a sumptuous feast on the rare occasions the negociant himself came out.

"Excuse me, sir, but the vats are this way," Solange said with polite firmness.

"Of course, yes," stammered a nonplussed Schroeder, who cast an unhappy eye at the château before regaining his composure. He asked coldly, "And how did *we* do this year?"

Solange frowned. They were certainly not starting out auspiciously. Perhaps she should have softened up Schroeder with wine and food before getting on with business. Her father always had. Then again, it had been her father who had gotten them into the predicament with Schroeder. Solange was instantly sorry for thinking unkindly of Edouard and she answered the negociant more meekly than she had intended, "Jacques and I agree the cru is excellent."

"Well, I'll be the judge of that," Schroeder said pompously, hoping that Solange's change in tone augured well for his being able to browbeat her. He felt uncomfortable dealing with this girl. The baron was right. It would be better to get such a complicated and delicate operation out of the hands of one so young.

Solange, Schroeder, and Busscher had reached the main chai. It was a long, low building, not much more than a shed, but inside were the implements and the heart of turning grapes into wine. There was the fouloir-égrappoir, into which the grapes were poured and crushed. There were oak fermenting vats and oak barriques that could hold up to sixty gallons of wine. These were the barrels that would be transported to Schroeder's warehouse on the Quai des Chartons for the second fermentation. Some would stay there for many years until sold. Some would be mixed with Spanish wine— Alicante or Benicarlo— to make it more acceptable to the English palate. It was a common practice to "work the bottle for the English"—*le travail à l'anglaise*—and all the negociants did it. What Jerome Libermann had discovered in the London bottles of du Clocher was that it was almost all Spanish wine containing little of the superior growth of the Medoc. No one would buy from Schroeder should that become public knowledge.

Jacques Mazet was at the door waiting with two candles. The overcast day would do little to lighten their way inside. He led them to a plain high table on which sat several glasses.

"Please, messieurs, take a glass," Solange directed, "and we will go right to the hogsheads."

At the far end of the chai, Mazet stopped at a hogshead which, if stood on its end, would have been as tall as he. From his pocket he took what looked like a combination of pliers and hammer. He used it to pull out a wooden peg that had been wedged into a hole at the top of the cane-wrapped barrique. He then lowered a glass pipette into the opening and withdrew a small sample of the immature wine. He squirted some into each glass and waited.

Busscher and Schroeder went through the ritual of tasting without swallowing and then spat the wine onto the dirt floor. Busscher smiled his congratulations at Solange. Schroeder bit his lip. Damn, it was good. He couldn't fault her.

"Excellent," Busscher said softly.

Schroeder threw a look of scathing displeasure at his assistant before conceding that it was indeed good.

They tasted several other vats. Schroeder asked when they would be ready for delivery, and Solange responded that it would probably be March at the earliest.

"So that's what your maître thinks?" It had occurred to the
negociant that perhaps Mazet was the girl's Achilles' heel, that she
might be relying totally on his expertise. Perhaps if the little man
could be hired away, why Solange would be helpless.

However, that hope was dashed when Mazet said, "The
mademoiselle tasted yesterday. I only agreed with her opinion."

Panic was creating a small swirl in Schroeder's stomach. The baron
was not a man to wait. Schroeder had to find some way, any way, to
dislodge this accursed girl.

They were back at the entrance to the chai. It was colder outside
than when they had gone in. Even Schroeder needed no urging to
walk briskly across to the proprietor's office, a small adjunct to the
chai. Hanging there was a detailed drawing of the vineyard, showing
every vine, and of the chai with the placement of every barrique and
vat and what was inside each.

Schroeder lowered himself into one of the small ladder-back chairs
and wished deeply he were in his mistress's apartment with a marc in
one hand and her in the other.

"So how much is there?" he asked peevishly. "Busscher, for God's
sake, get out your book and get this down."

There were twenty-three hogshead, minus one for the château.
There would be twenty-two. At first Schroeder didn't think he had
heard correctly. Then he motioned Busscher over and looked at what
had been written. Twenty-two. Only twenty-two. Schroeder did some
quick mental calculations. It was nothing. Solange would be getting
next to nothing. And he would make a killing. The news couldn't be
better. Then Schroeder remembered the Saint-Savin fortune. What
had he been thinking of? The poor returns on this harvest would
mean nothing to Solange overall, he realized. Therefore the girl's next
words were a delight and served to restore Schroeder's hopes.

"Monsieur, we must renegotiate the contract this year, not next.
We do not have enough money from this cru to survive with what you
have been paying my father."

"My lovely girl, a contract is a contract." Schroeder could afford to
be sweet and effusive now. She was obviously in grave trouble and
was turning to him for help. Him! How delicious. He had no idea
why the Saint-Savin money was not at her disposal. All the better that
it wasn't. But Solange was not to be put off.

"Monsieur, I realize that a contract must be honored. But what if I
were to offer to draw up another long-term contract with added

concessions to make it worth your while? Just as long as we do it this year, on this harvest, and not next."

"Oh no, no, really I can't. I'll be taking a beating on this meager cru as it is."

"No, you won't," interjected a confused Busscher. "No one had a large crop this year."

Schroeder's annoyed glare silenced his assistant, who couldn't fathom why it wouldn't be to his employer's advantage to renegotiate immediately.

"Well, then," Solange went on slowly as if speaking to an addled child, "perhaps you could advance us some money on next year's cru."

Oh, this was getting better and better, but Schroeder took care not to reveal his glee. He spoke with great solemnity. "You know for the sake of the very deep respect I had for your father..." Busscher looked with surprise at his employer. He had never heard Schroeder speak of Edouard in anything but the most disparaging terms. "...I would do everything in my power to help you out of your grave troubles—you are having grave troubles, you say?"

Solange bowed her head. The wind was picking up outside, drawing a chill from the Gironde, making the day increasingly somber and forbidding. "I didn't say, but we are." Solange was running out of options. Maybe the time had arrived to appeal to a gentleman's chivalrous nature, though she wasn't sure Schroeder was in possession of one.

"I need help," she said. "I had only enough to pay the pickers this year."

"That is most unfortunate, most unfortunate, indeed. Still if one is to survive, one must be strong."

Solange met his eyes with so much anger that the negociant flinched. So that was how he was going to play it. Well, Solange wasn't about to beg or grovel. "Very well, sir. I will be strong. I'll give you a choice. Either advance on next year's cru or change the terms of the present contract. Now. If you do neither, I will find another negociant after this cru."

For a second, Schroeder seriously considered acquiescing. Du Clocher was his best château, his company couldn't suffer losing it. Then his fear of Baron Libermann prevailed.

"Mademoiselle, I am deeply grieved by such threats after all my years of association with du Clocher." Schroeder did his best to sound deeply grieved. "Your father would be most shocked, I am sure. Still I must tell you, no matter what you say or how you say it, I am not in the position to give advances or make concessions. This is business, my young woman, and if you can't keep up your end of a bargain, then do something you're capable of. Get married! Have babies." He turned. "Busscher, make the necessary arrangements for transporting the wine while I wait in the carriage." Without looking at Solange, he said, "Good day, Mademoiselle Saint-Savin."

Schroeder lumbered from the room, quite pleased with what had transpired.

Solange chewed on a lock of her hair, a nervous habit left over from childhood. When she realized Busscher was staring, she stopped and looked back at him with the wide-eyed pained expression of a child who had been wrongly punished.

"Why?" she asked simply.

"I don't know, mademoiselle. I don't know."

"Has he become so successful that he can lose du Clocher?"

"On the contrary, without you, he is nothing. Are you really in such deep trouble?" Solange wasn't sure if she should answer, and yet, her brother had trusted this man, so why shouldn't she? When Solange nodded, Busscher offered that perhaps there might be friends to whom she could turn.

"I will try anything," she answered.

"Please, mademoiselle, don't lose hope. I will see what I can discover about my employer's behavior. Now to the arrangements for the transport."

Chapter Twenty-four

"Oh, my, my." General Hopewell was acutely embarrassed. It happened rarely. When it did, he was beside himself and his face colored to an agonized red.

He poured more port and walked to the window from which he could see one of his workers repairing pickets in the vineyard. Although his château was not as grand as du Clocher nor his wine so fine, they suited him.

"Oh, my," General Hopewell sighed again and turned back to Solange, who was sitting solemnly on his tufted leather couch, so sweet and feminine on something so masculine.

"I shouldn't have asked." She, too, was embarrassed. "I am sorry."

"Oh no, I would have been greatly pained if you hadn't." The general searched for words. "It's not your asking that has upset me. On the contrary, it's my not being able to help."

It had been a nice surprise when Solange's carriage had drawn up that late afternoon in front of Château Beausejour. General Hopewell, all smiles and hearty greetings, had gone out to greet her. His happiness became dismay when an exhausted, spirit-broken young woman stepped down from the carriage. He had bustled her inside and gotten her ensconced in the parlor with a cognac—knowing her disdain for port.

"Now, tell me what have you been doing?" he'd coaxed.

She obliged by launching into a full account of her day, starting with her appointment with the family's notaire, an aggressively prissy lawyer who since the scandal had wished he could find the nerve to strike the Saint-Savins from his client list. He didn't because one couldn't be too cautious. The family was, after all, aristocracy and the tides of fortune did ebb and flow. Monsieur Jacqueme did not wish to be left high and dry should the Saint-Savins regain their place in Bordelaise society.

Still, it was galling to have to deal with a girl. And even more galling when he heard why she was there. She wished him, a respected notaire, to arrange a loan for her, a mere child. Did she have a guardian? A trustee? Someone to take responsibility? No? Well, the best Monsieur Jacqueme could advise was she get married and let her husband handle her affairs. And so saying, he politely but firmly ushered her out.

Solange did not give up easily. She raised more than one eyebrow that day, advancing on more than one financial institution, demanding to see the manager or agent or whoever was in charge, and being turned down everywhere. With the same firmness of Monsieur Jacqueme and for the same reasons. A girl of sixteen was not fit to engage in such business transactions.

So she had gone to General Hopewell and apologetically asked for his aid.

"You must understand," he was saying, "I'm not saying 'no' to lending you money because I, too, believe you are incapable of handling it. I'm saying 'no' because, well, frankly, I have no money."

He returned to the window and raised his glass to his land. "I suppose this was an old man's folly. I could have sat in a cozy Sussex garden, with more than enough funds for my needs and comforts for as long as I lived. I couldn't, though. I loved it here, and I couldn't wait to retire and come back."

He crossed to his officer's table and poured more port.

"I'm afraid I've had too many years of overspending. There wasn't much here, you know, when I bought it. I've built, I've improved, experimented, expanded. A lot of money going out. Not that much coming in. And that blasted oidium has hit me, too. Worse than you."

As he spoke, the general saw Solange's shoulders sink further and further with defeat until he could stand no more. He sat beside her and wrapped her in his arms.

"Go ahead and cry. It's time you cried."

Solange lay still in his arms then shook her head and pulled away, dry-eyed.

"There must be a way," she said.

General Hopewell had already thought of one possibility but had rejected it. But the girl was so dejected and determined, perhaps he should go ahead and bring it up.

"You know," he began cautiously, "you do have family that might be able to help. You do have a mother."

Solange responded with undisguised bitterness. "Until last year I had no mother. She was dead. And then suddenly, I'm told she's alive. That she had abandoned us for Paris. That she was a *putain*..."

"Goodness, Solange, really. Where did you learn such a word?" The general reddened again. Where had she learned about whores?

"That's what that despicable man, Donnadieu, was saying. That she was an expensive *putain*. She deserted us. She's never cared. She never..." Solange could not finish until she took a deep gulp of fortifying air. "I still have no mother."

The usually outspoken General Hopewell was at a loss. Finally he said, "All right. Then she is not your mother. But in Paris, in a hotel *particulier*, a mansion of grand proportion, I am told, at the foot of the Champs Elysées, is a woman named Fabienne Saint-Savin. She is a woman who once carried you within her body, who once held you in her arms, and who might help you now."

Even as he spoke, based on what he had heard about Fabienne, the general had serious doubts that she would. Still, there was a chance and a chance was what Solange desperately needed.

The girl rose, walked carefully to the large globe on a pedestal next to the general's campaign desk. She twirled it slowly until it stopped. Her finger was touching the dot that was New York City. It was the last place she had had word from her brother.

"You're right, of course. I must try everything. Pride is nothing next to du Clocher. I shall go to Paris."

It was quite by coincidence that Nathan Libermann stopped at Château Beausejour the next day. He had heard the general was planning to experiment with sulfur in an effort to combat the oidium and was interested in how it was to be used. Nathan had stayed for dinner, although he despaired of the general's choice of menus. Over cigars and digestifs, General Hopewell mentioned what he had advised Solange to do.

"Oh, dear God," Nathan exclaimed. "She's gone to Fabienne? Why didn't she come to me?"

The general didn't know, in fact he had puzzled over that after Solange had left. Nathan could guess. He had seen little of the girl over the last year. She had distanced herself. Nathan wasn't sure if he reminded her too much of the tragedy or if she worried that he knew too much. He kept watch over her without imposing. After all, he was at least indirectly responsible for what had occurred.

And now she had gone to Fabienne. She was heading for still another disappointment. Nathan Libermann knew Fabienne Saint-

Savin. He knew her very well. She wouldn't even give her daughter an audience. Even if he was too late to stop the girl, he could insure one thing.

Nathan took his leave of General Hopewell and returned to his château. Not long afterward one of his servants was riding off at full gallop towards Bordeaux.

Chapter Twenty-five

It was a room of opulent proportions, of scrolls and curves, of elegant brocades patterned with pastel fawns and flowers. It was a room of stencilled medallions and architectural rosettes, of sweeping chandeliers and swooping, dipping rosewood chaises.

It was a room of dalliance and passion, one that disdained convention and the weak-of-will. At its heart was an extravagant, oversized mahogany bed crowned with a half tester and embraced by fringed silk lambrequin of the palest green and cossetted by side curtains of duchesse lace.

At that moment it was a room in repose. Thick, full drapes kept offensive rays of afternoon sun from penetrating and destroying the soothing, muted peace.

There was a slight stirring from beneath the lavender silk sheets. As if by signal, a time-worn woman crept into the room. She was carrying a silver tray laden with a fluted coffee urn, matching cup, and an amethyst vase with a rose of the same delicate color as the sheets. The woman silently set the tray on a dressing table adorned with a columned mirror reaching almost to the ceiling, seventeen feet above. The maid took from the table an ivory-handled comb and brush and a small mirror and placed them on the edge of the bed. Then she stole out to make sure the bath water was being heated to the temperature her mistress demanded.

Her mistress was awake. She never emerged from beneath the sheets until Inez left the room. Inez would not come back until after her mistress had rung the slender bell rope next to the bed, first having languorously stretched, sipped some coffee, and absently brushed her swirl of intense, fiery hair.

Fabienne Saint-Savin preferred entering gently into the day.

Once summoned, the gnarled maid picked up a filmy peignoir and draped it over Fabienne's shoulders. She followed her mistress into the salle de bain, assisting her into the over-sized talon-footed tub in which flower petals floated on the water's surface. Fabienne luxuriated for as long as the water stayed warm in the tub. Soft light from a stained-glass window high on the wall played across her soaring cheekbones, full mouth, highlighting her large lynx eyes, and erasing the small imperfections of age. Ingres could not have hoped to capture on canvas the lushness of Fabienne Saint-Savin.

Through with her ablutions, Fabienne sat before her dressing mirror, naked, appreciating the curve of her breasts and hip, as Inez skillfully applied the powder and color that only served to enhance a face already near perfection. As Fabienne studied the result of Inez's artistry, the maid disappeared into an adjoining dressing room, returning with the ensemble her mistress had chosen the night before.

Fabienne wasn't one for elaborate daytime costume. She saved her exotic plumage for the night. Dressing her then was not the two-hour ordeal it was with some women. After Inez had finished buttoning and smoothing and arranging the neckline so a teasing glimpse of decolletage was available for those who desired it, then and only then were the drapes drawn. If there was a possibility of visitors, then the sheer curtains behind the drapes remained closed, to mute the room.

Fabienne was reclining on a chaise with Inez brushing her hair when there was a tentative knock at the door leading to the hall.

"Yes?" Fabienne's voice was low and full. One of her admirers had proclaimed he would like to die with that voice close to his ear, whispering his name.

It was a chambermaid. She was young and pretty in an ordinary way. Fabienne reminded herself to have the girl fired. At one time it didn't bother her, now she disliked having young, attractive girls around. Fabienne was thirty-seven, and age, if anything, had only enhanced her beauty. But she didn't see that when she looked into the mirror. What she saw, mocking and taunting her, were the tiny lines that hadn't been there before, the slight sagging that refused to be camouflaged. She saw age and it angered her.

"What is it?" she snapped.

"Oh, I am sorry, my lady." The chambermaid was clearly terrified. "You have a visitor. She's been waiting for you ever so long."

"And why didn't Maurice come to tell me this? Has this household become so lax that a scullery maid announces my visitors?"

The girl tried to explain that Maurice was out on an errand Fabienne had given him, but her mistress was in no mood to hear excuses. With unsettling softness she cut her off. "Are you capable of telling me just who this visitor is or did you forget to inquire?"

"It's a girl, madam." The chambermaid was unable to decide whether she was embarrassed or confused, so ended up being both.

"And does this girl have a name?"

"Well, that's it, madam. She says her name is Solange . . . Saint-Savin."

Fabienne had forgotten—as she always did when there was something she wasn't looking forward to—the message from Nathan Libermann. She had no desire to receive her visitor and under other circumstances would have had no compunctions turning her away. However, she sighed inwardly, Nathan was a Libermann and Nathan was Nathan, so she would at least have to see this Solange.

"Inez, arrange my hair in that chignon you did last week, high at the back, drawn away from my face. And you, tell the girl I'll see her when I'm ready."

The chambermaid backed out of the room and went to give the girl the message. The servant felt sorry for her. If Fabienne was in usual form, it would be at least another hour before she had completed her toilette.

Solange had been sitting on the marble bench in the grand entrance foyer since nine that morning. She had left Lise, whom she had brought as a chaperone, back at the train station with their traveling bags and had taken a hansom cab straight to the address General Hopewell had found among her father's papers. Little did she know that the mere mention of Fabienne Saint-Savin's name would have been enough for the driver to deliver her where she wanted to go. The mansion was pointed out to foreigners and other visitors as one of the sights of the capital.

It was now after two. Solange regretted not registering first at a hotel, freshening up, and making herself more presentable before meeting her mother. So she waited. She had been offered a chair in one of the salons off the foyer, but declined. She didn't want to chance Fabienne leaving without seeing her.

So there she sat, somewhat dusty, a bit disheveled, anxious, bored, determined, and sensing the meeting would be a disaster. Under other circumstances, she would have left long before, insulted and rebuffed. Her journey's purpose, however, fixed her to that uncomfortable bench, staring up the curving onyx staircase.

At last, a small, bent woman came slowly down.

"The countess will see you now." Inez was studying Solange with obvious curiosity. Admittedly the daughter did not have the classic lines of her mother, but there was an intelligence that added to her beauty. Inez shook her head hard to rid her thoughts of such disloyalty and motioned for Solange to follow her upstairs and around a curving balustrade to a pair of imposing teak doors; in the center of each were medallions carved with the reposing naked figure of a woman. Solange wondered if the figures were supposed to be her mother, then dismissed the thought as ludicrous.

Inez shouldered a door open and announced, "She's here, mistress. The one who has been waiting."

Solange stepped in and gasped. She had never imagined that such a fabulous room existed, and she had never seen anyone as beautiful as Fabienne.

Fabienne, for her part, did not rise nor did she acknowledge the person before her was anything other than a perfect stranger.

"You may sit." She waved vaguely in the direction of a Louis XV fauteuil en cabriolet that an impulsive and hopeful duke had delivered to her after she had admired it at his mansion.

Solange did so, tucking her crossed feet well back under the chair.

"Good God! How old are you? You look like it's your first day in school, and the mother superior is visiting your classroom."

Solange blushed and answered sharply, "You, of all people, should know my age."

Fabienne looked her daughter over. Maybe the child had inherited her spirit. There was certainly none to get from Edouard.

"Mother, I have come..."

Fabienne cut her off. "I am the Countess Fabienne Saint-Savin to the world and to you. I am myself and no one's mother." She pronounced the last word with disdain.

"You don't need to remind me of that." Solange met Fabienne's sharpness with her own. "You never made any attempt to see me. You did not attend my father's funeral. You never even made inquiries after Guy."

"And who needed to make inquiries? His escapades were the topic of salon conversation throughout Paris for days. I found it not at all amusing and was quite happy when more stimulating subjects were found."

"Escapades? Amusing? Your husband is murdered. Your son flees for his life. And you are worried about being the object of gossip?"

To Solange's amazement, Fabienne laughed. "Me worry about gossip? Innocent child, I am, and have been for years, one of the primary objects of Parisian gossip. I enjoy it. I thrive on it. If people stopped talking about me, why, it would only mean my life had become boring. No, all the talk about Guy and du Clocher and asking what I knew—which, of course, was nothing—became tedious and I cannot tolerate tedium."

"Ready to face the consequences of perhaps boring you, I'll tell you I've received word that Guy did reach the United States."

"How nice." Fabienne was a virtuoso at conveying the advance stages of boredom in her low voice. "I do hope he plans to stay there. Returning to France at this time would be most unfortunate for him. Now is that all? Have you done your duty? Accomplished your mission?"

Solange wanted to say "yes" and leave. She wanted to banish this creature from her mind and memory. She wanted to go home where she was safe to curl up in her bed with a book and be a child again.

Solange went to the French doors that opened onto a small balcony overlooking the Rond Point and the Champs Elysées. She was pushing aside the curtains when Fabienne snapped, "Leave those alone," her hand already up to shield her face from the offending, revealing sunlight. "Are you quite finished? Inez...!"

"No, I am not finished," Solange said, dropping the curtain despite herself. "I haven't started."

"Well, I haven't all day. Say why you're here and then leave."

Solange sat down and took a deep breath. "There's trouble at du Clocher. A terrible blight has hit the vineyard. It destroyed much of this year's cru. I don't have money enough for next year's growth."

"Then sell it."

"But there'll be hardly any wine this year. I, I just said that. It won't bring me enough money."

"I didn't mean the wine. Sell the château. Sell du Clocher."

It seemed the simplest, most obvious solution to Fabienne. She was a pragmatist. One did what one had to to get money. Money was important. It allowed Fabienne to live as she pleased. Luckily, doing what she pleased was often her source of income. This was an attitude Solange would not be able to understand or accept. She cried, "You can't mean that! I could never sell du Clocher! It belongs to the Saint-Savins. It is the Saint-Savins."

The conversation was hitting new depths of dullness for Fabienne, and she turned her thoughts to something far more important—which of her many pieces of jewelry she would wear that night.

"You and Guy are the only Saint-Savins I know of," she said absently. "And Guy is no longer here. So get rid of it, if it's a nuisance."

"But I promised Guy, Mother..." Fabienne looked at her sharply. "...countess. Let me get to the point of my visit." With great effort, Solange was forcing herself to be calm. She must present her case with reason and dispassion. "I have a business proposition. I would like to borrow 100,000 francs, putting up du Clocher as collateral. The loan would be paid back, with interest, within five years."

Solange was interrupted by Fabienne's laughter. "And if you default?" Fabienne asked cheerily. "What happens then? I become a viniculteur, getting grape stains under my fingernails? Really, this is all too silly. Why in the world would you suppose I have that kind of money to lend? I have nothing. I'm practically a pauper."

Solange looked at the elegant room.

"Oh, this." Fabienne waved a dismissive hand. "This is nothing. Gifts. I receive many gifts. I have many admirers."

"Perhaps you have jewels you might..."

"Jewels! A woman must have jewels." It was now Fabienne's turn to respond with unchecked emotion. "Are you suggesting I give up the little I have to save something I have always detested? Look, it's time you leave. You have come on a fool's errand."

Still Solange would not give up. "Then your friends, perhaps you have influential friends who might help me."

"Bother my friends? Like some miserable hag in the street with her hand out? Out of the question. Why don't you go begging to your own influential friends? If Nathan Libermann cares enough to send me a message insisting I give you an audience, then Nathan Libermann surely cares enough to help you and your precious little château."

Solange couldn't believe Nathan had sent a message and that had been the only reason her mother had received her.

"Yes, the only reason. So why don't you trot off, like a nice child, and speak to Nathan?"

Solange nodded dumbly. She stood, let her gaze sweep the room and its occupant once more, and left.

Fabienne nodded. She would wear the emerald teardrop surrounded by rubies. It would show off her eyes.

Blindly Solange walked down the Champs Elysées, one minute blaming herself for mishandling the interview, the next raging against the uncaring monster who was supposed to be her mother. Before she realized it, she was at the Place de la Concorde. Edouard had taken her there many years before. She had loved the moat surrounding the Place. It had been filled with flowers and shrubs and was so beautiful it made her forget the horror that had taken place there. For it was at the Place de la Concorde, as drums rolled to drown out his words, that Louis XVI had cried, "My people, I die innocent of the crimes of which I am accused and I wish that my blood may consolidate the happiness of the French." A few moments later the executioner had held up Louis's severed head to the cheering crowd.

Solange had always shivered when she read about the guillotining at the Place, but that day with her father, a rare glorious, sunny day in Paris, the lovely moat had made her forget all horrors.

Now she stood looking across the plaza. The Chevaux de Marly, the magnificent horse statues, were standing guard at the entrance to the Champs Elysées and at the entrance to the Tuileries. And the obelisk that was brought all the way from Egypt was still stretching to the sky. But the flowers, the flowers were gone. The moat had been filled.

Nothing stays the same. Everything changes.

Solange made a decision. She would return to Bordeaux at once. And she would see Nathan Libermann.

Chapter Twenty-six

It was a room of modest proportions and little furniture. A narrow bed, a plain oak armoire, a time-faded but comfortable wing chair, a simple dressing table. Not much to notice and little to remember except for the two walls of books, hundreds and hundreds of books, all well worn and well read.

It was Solange's room. There were many larger and more elegant bedrooms at du Clocher. She had chosen this one when she was a tiny girl. It was secure and reassuring. On a cloudy, chilling day, she curled up in her chair with a book and was warmed by the tiny fireplace and what she read.

Solange was standing on tiptoes, trying to see in the dressing-table mirror how her dress was hanging. She was vaguely dissatisfied with her wardrobe. It seemed inadequate and certainly out-of-fashion judging by what she had seen in Paris. As it was, she had few "grown-up" outfits. There were mostly robes de jeunes hanging in her armoire, the shorter dresses that girls wore. The previous year would have been when she'd have tossed them out and gotten more sophisticated clothes. She had had neither the time nor the inclination to waste on shopping. So the plain green velvet she had on would have to do.

She'd lost weight and grown taller since Edouard had insisted she buy this dress. It just didn't look right. Maybe a ribbon around the waist, she thought. Solange had no ribbons, but then she remembered the many scarves her father had worn with his smoking jackets. She had gone into his bedroom suite only twice since his death, not getting much further than the doorway. Tonight was too important. She would have to go in and choose a scarf.

She found a satisfactory one almost immediately. It was jade and contrasted subtly with the dress. While searching for it, Solange came upon a small, delicate locket, nestled at the back of the drawer. There was a tiny catch on its side. Curious, she worked the catch until the locket snapped open. Inside were several strands of brilliant red hair. Solange stared at them, closed the locket, and put it back where she'd found it. She didn't want to think of her father treasuring it for all those years.

Just then came the sound of carriage wheels crunching on gravel. She pushed her chestnut hair off her face, hoping it looked present-able. She wasn't sure why it was so important to her that she look good for Nathan Libermann. She wasn't asking him for a loan. She wouldn't embarrass him the way she had General Hopewell. Solange knew from a conversation she had overheard that Nathan lived on the largesse of his father and probably only made do. No, from Nathan Libermann she did not want money. She wanted advice. She ran to greet him.

Nathan was already inside the entrance hall when she reached the top of the stairs. He looked up and saw her as he had the first time a year before. She was paler and had aged more than a year. Dark circles were under her eyes and she was enveloped by a proud sorrow. Damn Jerome, Nathan thought. Damn him and his stupid bets and machinations. He had done this to the poor girl. He had forced sadness and too much responsibility on her.

"Are you going to tumble into my arms again, Solange, or will your descent be a bit more sedate this time?"

"Oh, I had completely forgotten that."

"Not I. It was one of the most pleasurable introductions to a beautiful young woman I have ever experienced."

She's actually blushing, thought Nathan. I'd thought women had lost the ability.

"Are you coming down, mademoiselle? You have a guest who is looking forward to quenching his thirst and appetite at your always magnificent table." Nathan made a grand sweeping bow, filled with pomp and mischief.

Solange, in like spirit, gave him a sweet curtsy, descended with great caution, took the arm he offered, and silently congratulated herself for having the good sense to bring the cook back for the day, even if she could ill-afford the expense of doing so.

Nathan sat back in the brocaded dining chair. He raised the snifter filled with aromatic cognac to the light of the candelabra and smiled at his chestnut-haloed companion.

Baron Nathan Libermann was indeed a contented man.

The setting, the food, the wine, the woman left him in a mood to savor, to remember. It was odd. He wasn't sure at what point in the evening he had stopped thinking of Solange as a girl. He had been extremely impressed with the way she held her own in a spirited debate over who was more important to the romantic movement, Chateaubriand or Rousseau. He questioned her on other authors and found there were few she had not read and of the rest she had a passing knowledge. She had even read some of the authors from his own publishing house, books he knew had had a very limited circulation. Her scope of reading had been so extensive because Guy, knowing her voracious appetite for books, had constantly scoured Parisian shops and brought back what he found. It didn't matter if they were in French, English, German, Italian. Solange read them all.

It had been a very pleasant evening, and sitting there, reviewing it, quite a few minutes passed in silence without Nathan realizing it. He found Solange watching him intently, trying to make up her mind about something or perhaps searching for words. Nathan wasn't sure which.

"Tell me about it," he prodded gently. "I might be able to help."

Solange redirected her gaze to the napkin she had been scrunching in her lap. She smoothed it impatiently. "I want to thank you for sending the message to my moth... to Fabienne." Nathan didn't miss the correction and could guess how the interview went. Poor Solange. What a miserable way to meet one's mother for the first time since infancy.

"The meeting, it did no good then?"

"No, not directly. Fabienne did make a suggestion and... oh, never mind, I don't want to talk to you about it. You've been so kind. I don't want to impose further."

"My dear, I have never allowed people to impose on me. If I don't want to do something, I will let you know."

She smiled. "Yes, I believe you will. Well, I need advice. Actually, I need money. Fabienne said I should approach influential friends. I've tried all the banks. They have many reasons for turning me down."

I bet they do, Nathan thought, and all supplied by my brother.

"So I thought that you..."

"Of course, I can, I'll give you... name the amount."

"Oh no, no, no." Solange was flustered. "I wasn't asking you for

money. I know you can't afford to lend any. It's your brother. He's a
banker. I need advice on how to approach him for a loan. And perhaps
you might also be able to say something to him that would help."

The scowl that Nathan directed at her was so sudden that Solange
found herself shrinking into her chair. She hated having to ask for
help. For his part, Nathan was appalled by Solange's proposal. Ask
Jerome for a loan? She was a sheep leading herself to slaughter. Of
course Jerome could give her a loan. And he would make sure that it
couldn't be repaid. It would be so tidy. He could have du Clocher in a
year. Solange would be handing it to him.

"I think it would be a terrible mistake going to the Banque
Libermann," he said at last.

She rubbed her hands over her eyes. Some day she would get a
good night's sleep again. "That's all right. I understand. You can't help
me."

"I wasn't saying that at all. Forget Jerome. He won't be helpful.
Believe me. Besides, I have little influence with him. No, I was
going to suggest that if you won't take direct assistance from me, you
try a new bank, one that was just formed. It's less conservative, more
willing to take chances. It's called the Crédit Mobilier, and there I
might be able to help."

She shook her head wearily. Her spontaneity and vigor from earlier
in the evening was gone. She was about ready to admit defeat. "It's no
use. They'll say I'm too young. Too inexperienced. Too something.
There's only one other thing I can do."

"Solange, you do not have to sell. I . . ."

"It's not selling. There's no choice about that. No, I've made up my
mind. I'm getting married."

Nathan almost slid off his chair. As it was, he spilled cognac all over
the front of his shirt.

"You're going to do what? Or maybe more to the point, to whom?"

"I'm not exactly sure yet. I've only just made up my mind to marry.
But I'm sure there must be someone."

"Oh, my dear, my dear, my dear. Of course there is 'someone.'
There are many 'ones.' You're beautiful, lovely, desirable . . ." Oh no.
He was making her blush again. "But you are also quite young and
very innocent."

"Many women marry at my age and younger."

"Very true, but most of them have a specific man in mind before
they make that decision. Besides, have you thought about your
dowry? For all the barbarism of the practice, the *dot* is still very

important in France. What do you intend to offer? Du Clocher?"

He could see she was horrified by the idea. "So what do you intend to do?" he pressed, sounding harsher than he intended. He couldn't help it. Each of her ideas was more awful than the last. He had to do something to keep her from making a terrible mistake. And then, he had the solution and he was as sure of it as he had ever been sure of anything.

"You will marry me." Before she could protest, he went on. "I could try to become your guardian or trustee. That would take too long. I take it you need money desperately. You refuse to borrow from me. Still I can be of assistance. You will marry me. Now before you say anything, let me explain. It will be merely a marriage of convenience. It will not be consummated. It will be an arrangement. I can be your counselor, your friend. You will keep du Clocher and run it as you see fit. I will be here for help, signing papers, for whatever is needed. When you are older and no longer need me, when you find someone you truly want to marry, our arrangement will be dissolved."

"But why?"

"Why what?"

"Why would you do this for me? My family has already been such a burden on you, getting you involved in murder and inquiries and..."

He waved her quiet. "Solange, I have already told you. I do only what I want to do. And I want to do this very much. I'll continue my life much as I lived it before. I will have my interests and my companions. I'll also have this..." His gesture took in the room, the building, the land, the soul and substance of du Clocher and it took in her. "I assure you. I will get more out of this arrangement than I put in."

Nathan could have offered to lend her money. He could have convinced her he had it and she should take it. He didn't want to. As soon as he had gotten the idea of marrying her, he wanted it to happen.

Solange was weighing what Nathan had said. There were many objections, reasons why it would never work. She knew there were. But she was also tired and so much wanting someone else to take some of the weight from her, only for a little way, only for a little while.

"And what of your friends?" she asked. "What will Louis-Napoleon think of your marrying the sister of his enemy."

Nathan tried not to smile. "Oh dear one, I would be very surprised if our soon-to-be Emperor Napoleon II has ever heard of Guy Saint-Savin."

In two weeks, at the end of the required time for posting of banns, with Jacques Mazet and General Hopewell as witnesses, Solange Saint-Savin and Baron Nathan Libermann were married. Baron Jerome Libermann declined to attend.

Book Four

Chapter Twenty-seven

May, 1853

Nathan Libermann sat on the terrace of du Clocher making little headway with the account ledgers he was supposed to be reviewing. Some small movement, a fluffy cloud drifting overhead, a bee lighting on a flower, a worker stretching his muscles loose in the fields, anything and everything took his attention from the numbers in front of him.

It was a wonderful day, warm in the sun, smelling fresh and renewed. Nathan was wondering if his friend the emperor was finding married life as pleasurable as he was. What a funny prank of fate that the forever-bachelors had wed a couple of months apart.

Nathan caught sight of Solange. She was in a near field, bending over a vine with Mazet. When she stood, the sun filtered through her simple white dress, clearly outlining her long legs and slim body. Well, thought Nathan, there was one aspect of conjugal life of which Louis was partaking that he, Baron Libermann, was not. Then again, from all he'd heard of the exquisitely icy Eugenie, perhaps the emperor wasn't partaking either.

Nathan wasn't complaining. The marriage was his arrangement. Yet, he couldn't help imagining...

He had intended to be merely a visitor at du Clocher. He planned to continue living at his own château and once in a while visit with Solange. He'd be there if she needed him, but she would make her own decisions, her own mistakes and triumphs. Nathan deplored the attitude of the French male that women were amusing ornaments best kept in the house, nursery, and bed. While not setting out to play Pygmalion, he wanted to help Solange be strong and independent.

It wasn't long before Nathan was spending more time at du Clocher than at his own château. It began innocently enough. A few late dinners and Solange suggested he choose a bedroom suite and leave some clothes there so he wouldn't have to travel back until the next morning. He selected one in the opposite wing from her room. Then dinner at du Clocher was three times a week instead of two, then four, then five, and it seemed natural and logical that Nathan move in completely. He took over the entire wing and had his privacy when he wanted it and company when he didn't. Even his ageless Alsatian valet fell in quite easily with the household's routine. Oh yes, Nathan Libermann was a contented man.

One measure of this was that he barely left du Clocher in six months. There were two essential trips to Paris to secure the loan from Crédit Mobilier. As anticipated, this was no problem. The Pereire brothers, founders of the new bank, loved being able to boast that Jerome Libermann's brother had come to them. (If there had been any difficulties, Nathan had resolved to put up his own money and tell Solange it came from the bank.) Nathan hadn't even attended Louis's coronation, the only man in France who dared to turn down the invitation.

His thoughts were interrupted by Henri, who had been quite politic in usurping Marcel's duties as butler and was virtually running the household.

"Baron, letters for you." He held out a small tray on which were two envelopes. "And a Monsieur Busscher is here to see you."

"Busscher? Busscher?" Nathan was distracted by the envelopes. One was from his mother, the other from Jerome. "I know no... oh, wait, Henri, he must be here for the mademoiselle..." Henri raised his eyebrows slightly. Nathan did have a difficult time thinking of Solange as his wife. "Yes, yes," he continued, "he must be here for the baroness. I believe he works for that negociant of hers."

"Excuse me, baron. He specifically asked for you."

"All right, then. Show him in."

Nathan weighed both envelopes carefully and decided to defer unpleasantness. He opened the one from his mother. As always, it was written in the careful, tight hand of the neighborhood scribe. Having to dictate her letters inhibited his mother. Still her love and affection—affection that caused such jealousy in Jerome—came through anyway.

To my son Nathan [the letter read],

I write to you again to ask why you married and I wasn't there? You tell me nothing of this girl except she is beautiful. Of what importance is beauty? Is she a good wife? Does she care for you? Will she have many babies? Is she Jewish?

My son, I have not seen you for so long. I wish to pat your face and hold your hand before taking my last breath.

Your devoted mother

P.S. If you love the girl, then I am happy. But please arrange your life so that I may see your children before I die.

Nathan laughed. His mother was in her eighties and indefatigable. She still baked her own bread, prepared all the meals, and only in the past ten years allowed any servants in the house. And those she drove to near-suicide by inspecting every table they dusted and spoon they polished. Nathan shuddered to think what her reaction would be to the arrangement he had with Solange. One did not trifle with the institutions of marriage and family. They were too sacred. Yet even this she would forgive him. She always forgave Nathan. The other sons had better toe the line. For Nathan, she nudged the line over to where he was standing.

There was the other envelope. What would Jerome have to say? He had been curiously silent since the wedding. This was his first communication. There was no use postponing the inevitable any further. With annoyance Nathan ripped open the envelope.

My brother Nathan,

I suppose congratulations are in order. I extend them, if somewhat belatedly. However, I must tell you that nothing has changed concerning my promise to acquire du Clocher. You may have married the girl; I shall wait to see if you married the château. If indeed you have, then further congratulations will be forthcoming.

But I know you well, and I don't believe all is as it appears. If my suspicions are proved right, I advise you not to give up your Paris mansion or that little château you bought. I might change my mind about presenting you with du Clocher and you would need a place to live.

Jerome

Jerome's arrogant insight intrigued Nathan. He would have to make sure there was no way Jerome could learn the truth. He would assign Henri the task of ferreting out any disloyal members of the household staff and dismissing them. But now his valet was announcing the visitor.

Busscher was young and agreeable-looking, in clothes that were adequately cut if of second-rate material. Industrious, sincere, trustworthy was Nathan's immediate impression. Over the years he found his initial evaluations to be correct most of the time.

He asked Busscher to sit down and offered him refreshments. Busscher, ill at ease, declined.

"Henri said you wanted to see me? You are Monsieur Schroeder's assistant, are you not?" Busscher nodded. "Then it's my wife you should be seeing. This is her vineyard."

"Yes sir, but I thought that as you are her husband..."

Nathan tapped his fingers on his brother's letter, glad Jerome wasn't there to hear him say, "Nothing has changed. My wife is in charge, as before." The younger man was obviously pleased by the news. "Now, if you'd like to see her, I believe she is with Mazet. You may either go to her, or I will send someone to say you're here."

"Baron, if you please, what I have to say should be heard by you both. While the baroness is more than capable when it comes to the vineyard, she might need your counseling on this matter."

"Could you tell me what this matter concerns?"

"I think it better if I explained all at once."

"So be it." Nathan was sure Busscher was not bearing good news.

Solange rushed into the room, brushing perspiration from her forehead, flushed, hair helter-skelter. The baron is a lucky man, thought Busscher with a twinge of envy. I'm a lucky man, Nathan thought wistfully.

"Harry," Solange cried happily, arms outstretched in greeting. She dropped them immediately, troubled. "You have news? You've discovered something?"

Busscher glanced at Nathan. Solange assured him she had told the baron all about her disturbing last meeting with Cornelius Schroeder.

"Then I will get directly to the point. As you know, I was here several weeks ago reviewing the château's records. They confirmed some suspicions I've had. But I wanted to be sure. I had to wait until Monsieur Schroeder was away from Bordeaux and that was not until yesterday. Anyway, I compared your records with his."

Busscher couldn't have been more sure of his facts, still he was nervous. What if he were wrong. He was about to make a grave accusation. He went on. "According to the accounts, Schroeder & Cie sells more du Clocher overseas than you produce."

Solange interrupted, impatient. "I don't see what's wrong. All negociants add some Spanish to Bordeaux for the British market. It's common practice."

"I think Monsieur Busscher is saying something else," Nathan said slowly, having guessed what was coming next.

"That's right, baron. No more than thirty parts of Spanish, and perhaps a bit of brandy and some unfermented white should be added to a barrel of claret, at the most. It's hardly drinkable then, a bit heady, but that's how the English like it, and who's to account for their peculiar taste? Still, Schroeder's figures don't tally. The only way he could have sold as much as he did was to pass off wine as du Clocher that wasn't du Clocher at all. As a matter of fact, I'm sure I know what he's been selling. He acquired a vineyard in the Entre-Deux-Mers. It produces a minor though not disagreeable wine. I don't find any indication that he's sold any of that, although I know that the caves have been filled with it at times."

Busscher stopped for a reaction and got the opposite of what he expected. He was ready for an indignant, outraged Solange and had wanted the baron there to calm her. Instead it was Nathan who exploded. "This is an outrage! This Schroeder is a thief and a scoundrel! I should take a riding crop to him and make him pay for his crimes with the skin off his back."

Solange, on the other hand, took the news coolly. She thanked Busscher, saying she would consider what to do, gave a soothing pat to Nathan's arm, and left to find Mazet.

Her performance perplexed Nathan so much so that he asked Busscher what he made of it.

Busscher thought for a moment. "From what I had seen and heard of her brother, such calmness from him would be cause for concern. Solange? I'm not sure."

"But you've known her for a long time," Nathan pressed.

"Oh, no. We met shortly before her father's death. In the last year, however, I've had many dealings with her as Monsieur Schroeder's agent. I admire her very much."

Nathan wondered briefly if Busscher's feeling for Solange didn't extend beyond admiration. He immediately chided himself for being such a cliché, the jealous older husband with the beautiful young wife. In the past, it had been he who had caused the jealousy, he had been the "other man."

After Busscher left, Nathan thought a long time about the complex enigma his young wife was. He found it exciting.

Chapter Twenty-eight

Robed and hooded figures slipped through shadows and darkness, coming from side streets and alleys. They moved silently, an intermittent, eerie red procession, disappearing into a somber, stone building.

Solange watched them, hidden beneath the arches of a building across the street. Cornelius Schroeder had been evading her for days, not responding to letters, not appearing at his office, frustrating Solange's every attempt to contact and confront him.

Tonight there would be no room or time for evasions. Solange was meeting him where he least expected. Tonight was the monthly meeting of the Jurade.

Her father had been a member. As a child she had been frightened when he dressed for the society that was so filled with secrets and ceremony. The blood-red robe with its high, pointy hood had always transformed him, in her skittering mind, from man to creature, creature to demon. She would never kiss him goodbye on the night of a Jurade meeting.

The traditions and rites of the Jurade were closely guarded from outsiders, creating mystery where none existed. In truth the society was little more than a social club for the important winemen of the region. It was considered a high honor when one was asked to join. Women were strictly forbidden and never in the Jurade's two-hundred-year history had one so much as entered its vast meeting room, not even to serve dinner or clean up the next day.

Solange told Nathan nothing of her plan. That morning she had talked vaguely of business in the city and getting back late. She had to think quickly when Nathan offered to accompany her. She dissuaded him by claiming that what she had to do would bore him and that she would have no time to be with him anyway.

Nathan hadn't believed her completely. Still he wasn't going to insist and end up seeming as if he didn't trust her or that she needed a chaperon.

Solange had hidden a small traveling bag in her carriage the night before. She had her driver leave her near the Grande Cloche, instructing him to meet her there at ten that night. Then she took the traveling bag and checked into a small hotel where she didn't think she would meet anyone she knew.

She tried one last time to get Schroeder at his offices. She was told he was not there.

She returned to her room and waited until dark. When it was time, she took Edouard's Jurade robe from the bag, put it over her dress, and pulled the hood close to hide her face, and then hurried to the hiding spot across from the meeting hall.

It took almost an hour for members to stop arriving. Only then did Solange cautiously cross the street and enter as well. It was an august, imperious building with marbled floors and stone columns. There were many others like it in Bordeaux, of a scale meant to impress and diminish mere humans. The hooded figures had gone down a wide staircase and through a fortress-thick doors left slightly ajar.

The doors were still open when Solange arrived, indicating the meeting had yet to get underway. She slipped through into a room of white stone walls, dancing candlelight, and faceless figures.

There were small groups of red robes scattered around the immense room. Conversations, low-timbered and buzzing, echoed off the high ceilings. Solange glided from group to group. It was all but impossible to see who was under those robes without going right up and staring. She began to despair running down her quarry, when a fat, raucous laugh she had heard coming many times from her father's library after the negociant had finished feasting and tasting, rolled out from one corner. She had found Cornelius Schroeder.

He was with three other robed figures. It would have been better to confront him alone. It wasn't Solange's plan to create a scene, but her anger and frustration had built to an explosion point. To fatten his own pocket Schroeder had tarnished what had been entrusted to her. And he didn't have the courage to face her. Well, she would have her audience, and she didn't care where it was, when, or in front of whom. She would have her say and she would make him answer.

Solange pulled on Schroeder's sleeve.

"Yes, who is it?" Schroeder was miffed. He was talking to three of the most influential winemen in Bordeaux—Monsieur Larose, proprietor of Château Gruaud-Larose, Philippe Cottin, owner of the distinguished firm of Dubos Frères, and Julien Jugla, who had recently purchased Cheval d'Or in St. Emilion. He had never felt completely accepted by the other members of the Jurade and was constantly toadying up to whomever he thought most important.

Solange, as tall as the negociant, leaned close to his ear. "Monsieur Schroeder, I will speak to you now."

"What in the world...?" Schroeder was so flustered, he brushed his hood off. "It's you. It can't be. You've no right..."

"If you will come with me to the lobby, we can have our conversation, and you will be saved the embarrassment in front of your friends."

"Me, embarrassed?" Schroeder blustered. "It is you who should be embarrassed. See here, messieurs, look who has dared enter the Jurade." Schroeder grabbed Solange's hood and pulled it back. Her deep chestnut hair fell loose and streaming.

"Mademoiselle Saint-Savin, Baroness Libermann, this is outrageous. You know women are never allowed here." Solange recognized Cottin's voice. Guy used to mimic his pomposity so accurately that as a girl she would look forward to the merchant's visits so that her brother would have more grist for his performances. Now she couldn't care less about his outrage. She had quite enough outrage of her own.

"Monsieur Schroeder, if you won't come with me, I'll say what I have to right here." Anger or no anger, Solange was in control of herself. She was reasoned, temperate, firm. "I would like an explanation for the discrepancies between the amount of wine supplied to you from du Clocher and what your books show that you have sold."

"My books? My books?" Schroeder raised his palms to the ceiling in theatrical bewilderment. "What do you know about my books? Really, baroness, you have obviously taken leave of your senses coming here like this. Don't you agree, gentlemen? Now why don't you scurry on out like a good little girl, and I'm sure all will be forgiven."

Solange's glare made him squirm. "You've been avoiding me," she said. "And I know why. Your books show you sold far more wine from du Clocher than can be legitimately accounted for."

"Are you accusing me of something, young lady?" Schroeder would have sounded more menacing if his voice hadn't cracked just then.

"I make no accusations. I ask for explanations."

"How dare you?" Schroeder judged it was time to go on the offensive, if only to divert further talk and thought from his accounts. "How dare you besmirch my reputation before my esteemed colleagues? And what do you mean, I've been avoiding you? I don't know what you're talking about. You've either gone mad or you should be...you should be spanked."

Monsieur Larose, who had known Solange since she was a baby, tried to intervene on her behalf. "Schroeder, Schroeder, let's not get carried away. Granted, it is highly improper of Solange to be here..."

Solange did not have much left of whatever patience and prudence she started out with. "Improper? How can you speak of propriety when this thief, this disgrace to Bordeaux, has been dragging the name of du Clocher into the mud for years."

"Did you hear that? Did you hear what she said?" Schroeder's head shifted from side to side, eyes beseeching support. "She called me a thief, right here, at a hallowed meeting of the Jurade. A thief!"

All talk had ceased, and Schroeder was yelling to a rapt audience. Solange responded in kind. "I'm calling you a thief because you are one. As for calling the Jurade 'hallowed,' that's a blasphemy. The Jurade's just an excuse for old men to get together and drink too much."

"Solange." Larose threw his hood back, genuinely shocked. "That's enough. Whatever argument you have with Schroeder should be taken elsewhere. In the meantime, you apologize to everyone here. And unless you can provide proof immediately, I suggest you apologize to Monsieur Schroeder as well."

Larose disliked taking Schroeder's side, for he had long suspected the man was a scoundrel. Still Solange was out of line to cast aspersions on everyone and everything in her way.

"Proof. Of course, there's no proof," Schroeder went on, happy for the ally. "It's all raving poppycock. Listen to her. How would she know what is in my ledgers? Anyway, even if she had seen them, what would she understand? She's a woman."

Even as he spoke, the merchant knew who had betrayed him. He would take care of that traitor later. For now he had to walk a delicate line. He didn't want to get carried away berating the girl, knowing how little he was liked and not caring to tip sympathy to her side. On the other hand, he wanted the scene to end and Solange on her way in case she had evidence with her. He took a bold tack.

"My dear gentlemen, while not wishing to dignify the baroness's accusations, I will open my ledgers to any of you who would care to examine them. I have nothing to hide. I am a fair, honest man." When several of the men looked as if they were prepared to take him up on his proposal immediately, he added nervously, "Tomorrow. Come by tomorrow."

Solange recognized the trap. "No, now! Why not open them for inspection tonight?"

Much to Schroeder's relief, Cottin huffed, "Don't be absurd. I think it's quite admirable that Monsieur Schroeder makes such an offer without hauling him off like some criminal. You are out of line, young lady. And I, for one, would appreciate your leaving. At once."

Solange looked around in appeal. She sensed that given so much as an hour, Schroeder could make his accounts read any way he wanted. She found no support as the men turned back to their groups, whispering and speculating and more than one asking what did they expect? Edouard had been a fine man, but the children were obviously mad. Look at what the son had done, and so and so on, as gossip and rumors were dredged up and relished. Schroeder could have easily become a hero that night, if he weren't so disliked.

Larose took Solange, not ungently, by the elbow and led her through the crowd. "You should never have come," he said quietly. "No matter what your dispute with Schroeder, your appearance here is improper."

"Sorry if I embarrassed you," Solange said wearily, "but I had to come. Don't you see? I had to."

As she left, Solange could hear Schroeder expounding indignantly. "...another indication...what I've been saying all along...too young...incompetent...destroying a great vineyard...glad to be done with her and I caution anyone against taking her on."

Solange wondered if he could do it, stop any other merchant from handling du Clocher. At that moment she didn't care. She wanted to go home. She wanted Nathan.

Chapter Twenty-nine

Nathan couldn't help admiring Solange's escapade. It was impetuous, unwise, potentially disastrous, yet at the same time brave, admirable, and thoroughly audacious. How many women, or men for that matter, would have dared enter the lion's den like that? Quite amazing.

By the time Solange had returned from Bordeaux, it was past midnight. Nathan heard her come in and go straight to her room.

The next morning she joined him for breakfast. With no introduction or preliminaries, she launched into a monotonic account of the previous night's events.

Nathan tried to interrupt with questions. Solange would not have her purging interrupted and ignored them. She finally ended with the solemnity of a condemned person. "And that is that. Guy should have never entrusted the vineyard to me. I have failed. I have ruined du Clocher. Forever."

"One second, my dear. Granted, what you did was improvident..."

"You would have never done anything so stupid."

Nathan shook his head with amusement. "Rest assured. I've made my share of mistakes. Now as I was saying, what you did may have been improvident, but it is far too early to strike the death knell. Let's put aside the self-pity and examine your options."

Solange craved reassurances, yet knew they would be unrealistic. She had been such a fool. "Oh, Nathan, I can't think. Why did I do it? I couldn't stop myself. I had to go. Nathan, help me. Help me. I've failed. I know I have."

What a complex mix she is, thought Nathan, able to face a room of hostile men twice her age and still be such a young child. He went to her chair and motioned for her to stand so he could fold her to his

174

chest and stroke her hair. She welcomed the shelter of his shoulder and embrace. They stood, not wanting to move.

At last Nathan said, "Now, sit down, shake off your remorse, and let's talk seriously about what's to be done. We both agree that Schroeder is a complete ass. However, I'd venture to say he is not a complete idiot. So we'll need a plan to protect that Busscher."

Solange's face again creased into anguish. "You think Schroeder will guess..."

"Of course he will. Who else could have given you the information? If I don't miss my bet, your friend Busscher is out on the Quai des Chartons at this very moment, wondering what hit him."

"But that's awful. I didn't consider what might happen to Harry. I should have never asked for his help."

"If I recall correctly, he volunteered," Nathan corrected her. "And my respect goes out to him for doing so. He's a man of his word. You can trust him. So first there's Harry. Second, there's the wine. From what you say, no merchant would dare handle du Clocher right now."

Solange frowned. It was that worry that had kept her awake all night thinking.

"So," continued Nathan, "you and Jacques will have to make arrangements for storing the wine and handling the second fermentation yourself. I'm sure that in time, with enough suggestions whispered into the right ears and perhaps a little bit of arm-twisting, I shall be able to convince a negociant—a reputable one, this time— to take on the château. I mean, it will be to their advantage once the little furor you caused has subsided."

Solange rose and went to the window. Hazy light drifted around her. Nathan wanted to hold her again, yet knew it was out of the question. He would not be her father and could not be her lover.

Solange turned back to him with resolution. "I refuse to go grovelling to a bunch of *clochards*."

"Now, now, I don't think you can call them all drunken bums. True, it is a bit childish dressing up the way they do. I suppose that's enough to condemn them outright, still..."

"I've thought this over. I don't need them."

"What do you mean? How else do you propose to sell your wine?"

She had a plan, one that could work. She had spent the entire sleepless night going over it, working out details, searching for flaws. There had been one problem, and Nathan had just inadvertently solved it.

"We'll do it ourselves. We'll grow the grape, ferment it, ware-house, and we'll do our own bottling. We'll have control from start to finish."

"And the selling?" Nathan asked thoughtfully.

"Harry!" Solange was triumphant. The last piece had fallen into place. "Harry will sell it for us. I wasn't sure I could get him to leave Schroeder, and now I won't have to. He's honest. You said so yourself. And he did all Schroeder's work anyway. He's been making most of the trips to London. I think he's been wanting to start his own firm for a long time, but he didn't have the capital. Well, now he won't need money because he'll have du Clocher. Once we're established, he can take on other châteaux and have his own business outright. It will work. I know it will. Say you approve, Nathan, say you think it's a good idea."

Nathan searched her face for any doubts or misgivings. She was totally sure of her idea. What a change from only minutes before. What a testimony to the resiliency of youth and an exceptional mind!

"You don't need my approval. You know that. You do as you please."

"But it will be much easier with it." Solange was near pleading.

"You will always have my support. I just can't help being worried. You're taking on a formidable foe—the entire Bordeaux wine estab-lishment. Those merchants aren't going to be pleased with what you're planning."

Solange shook her head violently, sending combs and pins flying. "Their likes and dislikes mean nothing to me. I'm going to do what's best for du Clocher, and they can all be damned."

"Damned or not, I predict this will not end quietly. I'm afraid your former friends and colleagues will seek revenge somehow."

"I'll be ready for them."

"Oh, my dear, my dear," Nathan laughed with delight, "I am suddenly feeling very sorry for the wine merchants of Bordeaux."

Book Five

Chapter Thirty

San Francisco
18 September 1854

My beloved sister,

It is hard to believe it has been almost three years since I saw you last, and it is harder still to believe that two years have passed since the *Bonnie Swift*, that hellish ship that carried me from Panama, docked here.

So much has happened and I have changed so much. Not a day went by that I didn't think of you and worry about you. And not a day went by that I didn't want to write. I trust you received my last letter. I know how you must have grieved on learning of Marie-Odile's death. I will never stop grieving.

It has been a terrible two years. This land of golden opportunities has been only dross and misery for me. But, let me begin at the beginning.

On arriving in San Fransisco, I was given that poor mad Carl's possessions as he had willed. Damon Delany and I opened the

177

crates to find them filled with guns and pistols. It was a true windfall. I was almost out of money and had no way of supporting the baby. Fenella Delany had taken him over, thank God, like her own. She had even named him. She wanted to call him "Edouard," but I couldn't let her. It's not that I hate father anymore—no, perhaps in all honesty I still do. Anyway, she settled on Kyle. Funny sort of name, Kyle Saint-Savin, but I suppose the boy's a mixture now and his name should reflect that.

We decided that Kyle should stay with Fenella and Damon. Actually, it was Fenella who decided that. I think you would like her. When you first meet her, she seems a pale, quiet person. But she's really very strong and very good. Damon and I became partners on the guns. He stayed behind to sell them; I went to the fields to find gold. It seemed a good arrangement. I knew Kyle would be well cared for. And with me in the hills and Delany with money to invest from the gun sales—guns are in great demand out here—we were sure at least one of us would strike it rich. Damon never seemed terribly interested in mining, anyway. "The money is in selling to miners, not being one," he told me. I'm still not sure what type of man he is, but I'd trust Fenella with my life.

So off I went. The mountains were beautiful and mean. Men were everywhere, pushing and shoving and looking for the magic space and the right place. I never found it. I would be in one gulch when stories of a strike two valleys over would reach us. I'd be in a town that would empty overnight because someone heard that on the next hill, the next mountain, the next someplace else there was gold for everyone. Oh, once in a while I would find gold, nothing much, barely enough to buy food. Food was fiendishly expensive. A couple of pounds of flour cost $200! There was even one time I could not endure another night outside, in the rain. I took everything I had and hiked five miles to the nearest "de luxe" hotel. De luxe? It was a tent crammed with men, scratching, dirty, smelly men of all nationalities. I did not care. It was shelter. I was out of the rain. It did not matter that the dirt "floor" was actually a foot of mud. I was inside and that night I dreamt I was back at du Clocher and in the morning I would join Jacques in the fields, taste the grapes... When I awoke, it was still raining and cold and California. If it had not been for you and du Clocher, and yes, the baby as well, I would have taken a gun and put a bullet through my head that very day.

In some ways, I had it easier than many—thanks to that old terror, Miss Riddleysham. Bless her. Pounding a good English accent into us and erasing any trace of a French one when we spoke English has saved my life here—literally. Solange, you could not believe the prejudices and injustices that are directed at foreigners, anyone who looks different, sounds different, is different. I can close my eyes now and see a night last year in a makeshift town that was never given a name. There a vile and wretched incident took place. Two young Mexicans—they're called "spiks," anyone with an accent is called "spik"—were accused of raping a woman. She was a prostitute. The boys had never laid a hand on her; in fact, they had never seen her before she made her accusation. But she was an American, and it was her word that they had violated her. The boys were dragged, screaming their innocence, screaming for pity, to a tree, and hanged. I tried to go to their aid, but was held back. It was over quickly and brutally. I can hear the evil yells of triumph from the other miners as the young bodies flailed and jerked, and I swear that, above the din, I heard their necks crack. Several months later I was in another town, another place with no name. Two men in a saloon were bragging over their whiskeys, bragging they had paid the whore to lie. They had wanted to jump the claim of the two Mexican boys. And when they did, there was nothing there, no gold at all. The boys died for nothing, for greed unrewarded. Justice here is for the strong and those who can survive. I took my hatchet that night and went looking for those men. I wanted to hack them to pieces. I wanted to look for their souls. But they had disappeared and I was spared the hangman's noose myself.

Why did I stay? Because I could not go back. How was I to help you and du Clocher? How was I to provide for that small, tiny being I left with Fenella?

I was there two years. Two years watching men scraping for their futures with jackknives on stone. Then it began to change. No longer were the stories of strikes about men, alone and searching. Companies were coming in, laying claims, buying claims, and pushing the individual man farther and farther out. About then I met an old geezer named Gus. He had been there from the beginning, been working at Sutter's Mill when James Wilson Marshall first found gold. Gus had seen it all, and he had a plan. He said it was time to push further north and east, away from the hordes. He took me with him.

We passed through one dusty, grimy mining town after another, many with strange names as haphazard as the towns themselves— Rough and Ready, You Bet, Dutch Flat, Goodyear's Bar. We went until there were no more towns and we were alone, completely alone.

Then we had a strike, a lode that looked promising. But winter came early last year and the ground was too cold for digging and the streams froze over. We prepared to wait it out. We had no idea what was ahead. It was beyond imagination. The cabin we had built in the fall had seemed so sturdy and adequate. Then winter came and the wind whipped through it, blizzards pounded it, and it got cold beyond all endurance. Gus and I sat and stared at each other, hugging ourselves for warmth. We ran out of provisions. They had seemed so ample when we laid them in. We did not know we would be unable to hunt for weeks at a time, that we would be prisoners in that little cabin.

Gus caught cold. The cold became chills, the chills fever. I envied him his warmth, no matter the pain that accompanied it. I envied another man's illness! Gus died. One terrible last gasping cough and he died. I was too weak to drag his body out. I lay next to the body for days. Then I was finally able to get him outside. He was stiff and hard to move. I laid him under a tree. How I wish now I had left poor Gus in the cabin. The next time I went out, he was gone. Some animal had dragged him off. I was alone again.

Spring finally came and the cold slowly left my body. Though even now I imagine I feel the frostbite in my fingers and toes and the ice in my lungs. I could not go on any more. I was not going to find gold, to strike it rich in the hills. I had to admit defeat and return to Damon and Fenella and to the boy. It is hard for me to think of him as anything but a crying, fragile infant. But Kyle must be walking by now, talking. He must be a little man, one who has never known his father.

It took me weeks to reach San Francisco. I was in no hurry. Too much ahead, too many unknowns, frightened me. I never knew fear before I came here. I walked valley after valley, hill after hill, wondering what was before me, a man all alone, with a small child, no prospects back in what passes here for civilization.

I have been in San Francisco for only a day now. It is very different from what I left. It feels more permanent, even respectable. But I have to go on. Damon and Fenella have settled south of here, down the peninsula. I must go for my child, the only thing left to me of my beloved Marie-Odile, and I must see what I can make of myself.

I love you, my dear sister. And one day I will return. I promise.

Guy

Chapter Thirty-one

"Hey, there now. Hey, there now. Whoa." The stubble-faced be-hemoth next to Guy pulled back on the reins, forcing the two horses to a stop. He leaned over the side of the buckboard and spit into the dirt.

"There she be." The driver pointed at a rambling, vine-covered stone house, with the ocher-tiled roof of Spanish California, back about a quarter of a mile off the road. A slow moving creek meandered nearby and white corral fencing wandered away from the house and over a slight rise, adding perspective to the dusty pastoral.

"No, no." Guy was confused. "I'm looking for the house of Damon Delany. Surely you've made a mistake." The one before him, while certainly not grand, was too large and comfortable, had too much evidence of prosperity, to belong to Delany, a man who had little more than the shirt on his back two years before.

The driver snorted. "Ain't no mistake, mister. Nobody round here could mistake Mis-ter Da-mon De-lany."

Guy had arrived in San Pasqual that morning. It was a town being reborn and rebuilt. In '49 the men of San Pasqual had joined the rush to the gold hills, leaving their women to make do. Now many of the men, wearied by discouragement and overcome by defeat, were coming back, to make a new life and a new town.

In San Francisco Guy had sold the little he had left—prospecting pans, shovels, some gold—and bought a ticket on the stagecoach that went down the peninsula to San Jose. All the seats were already filled so he rode up top with one Charley Parkhurst, the most loquacious, outgoing, self-proclaimed "son-of-a-gun" Guy had yet to meet. It was difficult hearing anything above the roar of the wind and the pounding of the hoofbeats. That didn't stop Charley from giving a running commentary on all they passed. Most of the monologue

181

consisted of such and such a horse thief being strung up here, how he had outrun bandits there, and which old California family had lost the hacienda over there to Yankee taxes. It was all told with such high spirits and good humor, Guy wondered if he was missing the joke somewhere in the din.

"See you soon," Charley had called from his perch as Guy painfully let himself down. There were no cushions or other softening amenities riding shotgun, only hard, unforgiving wood. "I come through San Pasqual every few days. Real regular. Spend my spare time over there." Charley indicated a humble, one-story shack with a sign "saloon" tacked over its doorway. "You come by and old Charley'll buy you a drink and show you the ropes."

Just then Charley spotted the giant with the buckboard. "Hey, Clem there, Clem," he called. "You headed out past that Delany spread?"

Clem nodded, throwing a suspicious glance at Guy.

"Now listen here, Clem, this is my new friend, Guy San-somethinorother. Anyway, he's okay and he's looking for the Delany place. You take him out, okay?"

"Sure, Charley," Clem didn't look too happy. "Friend of yours is a friend of mine. I'll leave soon as I load up the buck."

"Please, let me lend you a hand," Guy offered quickly.

Clem let out a loud laugh. "Hey, Charley, this here's a gentleman. What the hell's he going to Delany for?"

"Ain't my business and it ain't yours, neither. Just give the man a lift." Charley, seeing his passengers were safely ensconced, cracked his whip, and the stagecoach lumbered off trailing great billows of dust that took many minutes to settle.

Guy estimated they had ridden several miles, the flat land gradually molding into hills on one side, stretching out to a choppy bay on the other. Then Clem stopped. In all that time, the big driver had said nothing. Now he was getting impatient, he had his woman, children, stock to get to and he wanted to get rid of his passenger.

"Well, mister, change your mind? Don't want to see Mister Delany, after all?"

Guy shook his head, still staring at the hacienda. "It's just that I never anticipated this. Wait a minute. Does Damon work here? Is that it?"

Clem snorted. "Damon Delany works everywhere. Now, if you mean, does he own this place, look around. That's it, all around.

Every tree, rock, blade of grass, bit of dirt's got Delany's brand on it. And there's more, a lot more, you don't see. Now if you're getting off, get off."

"Of course." Guy got down. "You were most kind. If I can ever repay you—"

Clem cut him off. "Buy me a drink sometime. But promise me one thing. Let's don't talk about no Damon Delany anymore. Okay?" He clicked to his horses and left before Guy could ask him what Damon had done to cause his dislike.

Guy trudged down the long dusty road toward the house. He saw no one and the only activity were some horses bending low to graze on scraggly grass waiting for the rainy season.

The hacienda was a big friendly-looking house. When he reached the front door, Guy lifted the heavy, horseshoe-shaped knocker, let it drop, and waited. Nothing happened. He tried again. Still nothing. He walked around the side of the house, looking for another door. In the back there was an open area bounded by the hacienda, a stable, a long white-washed bunkhouse, and a paddock. There was also an open door into the main house. Guy went to it and poked his head in, ready to call out, when he saw he was in a kitchen, a square, low-ceilinged room with one big table dominating its center. It was overspread with vegetables, pots, and spoons. Near a small window embraced with cheerful calico, a woman bent over a basin, her back to Guy. She was intent on what she was washing until her attention was distracted by a mischievous little giggle at her feet. She turned to look down and Guy realized the woman was Fenella Delany. But it was a Fenella he had never seen before. Fenella was a small woman, but good food and sunshine had filled her out and put some color into her angular face. She had her light brown hair pulled back, which served to accent her large perceptive eyes fringed by thick, black lashes. She was laughing as she bent over to scoop up a delighted toddler. Her laughter made her almost pretty.

"And what are you up to, my precious boy?" she asked teasingly, searching for an appropriate spot on the squirming youngster to tickle. "And what were you doing, sneaking up on your Fenella?" She stopped, tensed, and instinctively pushed the child behind her skirts and reached for a meat cleaver.

"You there? Who might you be?" she challenged.

Guy stepped further into the room, out of the blinding sunshine.

"Who are you? Tell me quickly," Fenella demanded again.

"Have I changed so? Don't you recognize me?"

For an instant, Fenella wasn't sure, then recognition came and she cried out with happiness. "Kyle, it's your daddy. Your daddy's back, Kyle." Fenella ran to Guy, arms outstretched to hug him, but she stopped short. "Oh, Guy, what happened to you? You're so thin, so..."

"...so beaten," Guy finished for her. Fenella shook her head to deny that was what she meant. She pulled up a high-backed chair and shoved Guy into it.

Guy laughed. "I see there are some things about you that haven't changed. For a little slip of a woman, you have more determination than any five miners I've met."

Fenella fluttered around him with concern. "You've been sick. You haven't been taking care of yourself at all."

"I don't think I've been truly well since the day I boarded the *Bonnie Swift*."

Fenella glanced at Kyle, who was sitting very still on the floor, a reassuring pinkie in his mouth, warily watching his father. "We don't speak of that ship here," Fenella whispered. "We don't think of it." Fenella was a small frail bird until she pursed her lips and showed her strength. "I don't allow it." Then she picked up Kyle and buried her face in his long, tousled, honey hair.

When she looked up, she was smiling again. "Oh Guy, it's been so long. You've missed so much. This wonderful boy's first step. His first words. How he can talk. He never stops." Realizing the boy hadn't said a word since Guy came in, she added hastily, "He's a bit shy now, you understand, but usually he goes on and on. Here, go to your daddy, Kyle. Give him your biggest hug and kiss."

She tried to lower the boy onto his father's lap, but Kyle clutched at her frantically. "My boy, this is your father. I've told you all about him. He's home now. Give him a kiss. Show him you love him."

Kyle thrust out his lower lip, reminding Guy of Solange at that age. "Daddy Damon's my daddy. I want Daddy Damon."

Fenella, embarrassed and flustered, explained that Kyle had started calling Damon that when he heard the ranchhands' children calling their fathers "daddy." She had tried to discourage it, but the boy persisted. "I hope you don't mind."

"How could I mind? The boy's only known Damon—and you. Fenella, you've been so good, so wonderful to take care of my son. How can I thank you?"

"You thank me? No, no, it's me that thanks you. I couldn't have lived without Kyle." She paused. "Speaking of Damon, he's gone to

San Francisco and won't be back tonight. But that won't stop us from celebrating. I'm going to take you to a room where you can wash up and rest a bit while I cook up the tastiest dinner you've had in a long time. Come, Kyle, let's show your daddy where he can sleep."

Guy thought he would lie down only for a minute or two. But this was the first comfortable, downy-soft and clean bed he'd been in since France, and when he woke up, three hours had passed. Even then it took the tantalizing aromas that were filling the house to wake him.

Fenella had used the time well. The dining-room table was ladened with meats and breads and vegetable puddings. She had let Kyle stay up although it was well past his bedtime.

And she had a surprise for Guy, one she produced with laughter and ceremony. First she made sure he was sitting at the head of the table with a reluctant Kyle next to him before disappearing into another room to return with a bundle wrapped in linen.

"Mister Saint-Savin," she said dramatically. "I have saved this for more than a year, guarded it with my life, waiting for you to return. What is it? Just this!" Fenella whipped aside the cloth to reveal a bottle cradled in her arm. When Guy made no response, she took it to him. "Take a look. Don't you see what it is?"

It was a bottle of claret, a bottle of du Clocher.

"I saw it in a shop in San Francisco. I made Damon buy it. I told him price didn't matter. We had to have it because it was a sign you would return safely. And here you are and here it is."

Fenella's eagerness was erased by dismay. Her surprise had obviously backfired. Instead of looking happy, Guy looked sick and pained. He had paled and was staring into his lap.

"Don't you want it?" Fenella asked concerned.

With great effort, Guy reached out for the bottle. He ran a hand up and down it, making sure it was real. Then he clutched it to his chest and sobbed.

Kyle yelped with fear and Fenella immediately pulled him onto her lap. "It's all right, my sweet. Your daddy is just remembering. That's all. It's all right. Soon you will give him happy memories, memories that will make him smile, just like you've given me. Guy, there's an opener next to your plate. Please, I've never tasted a wine like du Clocher."

The once-so-familiar task of opening a wine bottle calmed Guy. He poured some into his glass, swirled, and tasted. He would never find out how or why, but this was a French bottle, pure and unadulterated and wonderful. He poured some into Fenella's glass and raised his in toast.

"To my best friend, I give the best of myself." He drank.

Fenella sipped cautiously then sighed. "I never imagined... I don't know how to describe it. It's, it's..."

"It's drinking a dream. Oh God. I can't tell you what this means to me. When I was in the mountains, I was a failure and I despaired. Tasting this du Clocher has made me realize something, made things so clear. I know what I want to do now. I know what I am. I'm going to make wine again." Guy continued in a rush, as ideas burst forth that had been brewing within him. "I passed through valleys to the north, beautiful long valleys with good slopes and much sunshine. I felt the soil, checked the drainage. And it's perfect, perfect for grapes. I'm not one to grub the earth for specks of metal. I was a winemaker once and I will be a winemaker again."

"Well, that's settled then," Fenella said happily, looking down at Kyle who had fallen asleep in her lap after a few nibbles of bread. "That's what you should do. And already I can help. I've met a man, a count like you. Except he's Hungarian. He's also planting grapes north of San Francisco. He says he has European vines, from France and Italy and Germany. I'm sure he will help you. You can get started immediately."

Guy shook his head ruefully. "That sounds wonderful, Fenella, except for one detail. While I didn't discover gold in the Sierras, I did discover something else. You need money in America, lots and lots of money to do anything. I don't have the capital to get started, to buy land, hire men, get cuttings, buy barrels and bottles. It would take a small fortune, which I certainly do not possess."

"That you 'certainly do not possess.'" Fenella sounded thoughtful. "Guy, you haven't taken any food. Serve yourself. You have to get your strength back if you're going to be starting a new enterprise."

Guy realized he was very hungry and needed no further urging to pile his plate with the tempting foods before him. He devoured a good bit of it before stopping for a long sip of wine. It was so good. And he was beginning to feel good, as well, still he couldn't run away from reality.

"Thank you for your confidence, Fenella. However, there will be no 'enterprise' for a long time. I must talk with Damon. He may have ideas for what I can do until I get on my feet. Then maybe someday, maybe then I can start on my dream."

"Yes." Fenella said. "You do need to talk to Damon. But first, tell me, didn't you receive any of our letters?"

"Letters? No. I was never in one place long enough. Besides, there wasn't much in the way of a postal service." He laughed with little humor. "There wasn't much in the way of anything I want to remember."

Fenella nodded. "So you don't know. You don't know anything. Guy, for goodness sakes, look around you. Look at this house, the furniture, the wine glasses even. Don't you recognize the finest crystal? What did we have when you left us in that horrid, dirty boarding house in San Francisco? What did we have? Nothing— nothing except Carl's crates of guns. Where do you think all this came from, this and all the other hundreds and hundreds—oh, for all I know, it may be thousands—of acres of land?"

"Well, I was wondering. I thought maybe you were managing it for someone."

"Guy, don't you understand? We're the 'someone.' This all came from the guns. Carl's guns. Men were willing to pay almost any price for them, and Damon got as much as he could. Then he took that money and bought everything from food to those condor feathers that miners needed for storing gold in. He went into the hills and fields and sold the goods for prices that would make you gasp."

Guy thought about how he had gasped more than once buying supplies in the mountains.

"But Damon wasn't satisfied," Fenella continued in a rush. "He wouldn't stop there. He took the profits and bought land. He made loans. He got horses and livestock. Guy, he built a fortune—not a small one—an enormous fortune, all from Carl's guns. And half of everything is yours."

Chapter Thirty-two

Somewhere in that haze between dreams and consciousness Guy heard voices.

"Please let him sleep."

"Come on, woman, it's after noon."

"But he needs it."

It couldn't be past noon, Guy thought fuzzily. It would be light if it were past noon. He rolled over—and fell hard onto the floor. Then he remembered where he was—or more to the point, where he wasn't. He wasn't outside, lying on stones and dirt. He wasn't being abused by raw wind and fickle rain. He wasn't sleeping with ears cocked for marauder and thief ready to steal his wash pan and his life at the first sign of laxity. Instead he was in a bed with a blanket and soft mattress, with a solid roof above him and a floor, a floor of polished wood and cool tile, below him. He was near his son, friends, and he was once again Guy Saint-Savin and not some miserable, drudging forty-niner. He was a man with a purpose and means to fulfill it.

The door swung open.

"So where is he? I thought you said he was in this room."

"I'm down here, Damon," Guy called from beside the bed.

"And what are you doing on the floor? Living off the land change your taste in bedroom furniture? Here, take my hand. I'll help you up."

The smaller man leaned over, gave a good tug, and Guy was on his feet. He clasped his free hand over Damon's.

"Fenella told me what you've done. No man could ever give another more help than that. You've restored my life."

Damon shrugged off Guy's hand. "Let's not get carried away." He was somehow a larger man than when Guy had last seen him. There was no longer the furtive turning in of his shoulders. He was straight, erect, in command, and despite his words, taking Guy's thanks as his due.

"We had a deal, partner. And for what I hear, I got the better end of it. Couldn't understand why you didn't come out of the hills sooner. But Fenella tells me you never got her letters. Not surprised. Not surprised at all. Now come on. We got some clothes for you here. Maybe not what you were used to back in that castle of yours in France, but a sight better than what you must have been wearing in the fields. Come on, Fenella, hurry up and give the man his clothes."

Fenella hurried around her husband, clearly not comfortable being in Guy's bedroom. That didn't stop her from casting a warm, quick smile at him before exiting.

"Yes, you get dressed and then we'll have a nice long talk about what you're going to do."

Guy found himself obeying Damon without thinking.

"So there you have it," Damon was saying between puffs on a big cheroot. "You and I own most of the land between here and San Jose. We have holdings up in San Francisco, and we own land on the other side of the bay, too. I'm thinking of investing in the new paddle boatline that's going to run along the Sacramento River—lot of territory up there ready to be developed—and, hey, hell, I must be boring you. Fenella, bring that bottle of brandy in."

Fenella was there at once with a bottle and two snifters.

"Lunch was extraordinary. Thank you," Guy said to her retreating back.

Damon took another pull on his cigar as he watched his wife leave. Guy thought at least that hadn't changed about Damon. He was still watchful, weighing every word and movement while carefully calculating his own and observing their effect. Guy wondered if Damon ever relaxed.

"She's quite a cook, isn't she?" Damon said. "Drives me crazy though. We should have servants, cooks, maids. Fenella shouldn't be sweating like this." Guy thought Damon smiled despite himself. "But no, she says this is her home and she'll take care of it. Real Irish woman, she is. When she puts her foot down, that's that."

"I've noticed."

They each took long swallows of brandy.

"I'm thinking of going into politics," Damon said unexpectedly. Guy was surprised. Damon never struck him as someone with the diplomacy and tact needed for political life. But, of course, all Guy

knew of political life was in France. Maybe things were different in
the States.

"Which office will you be seeking?" Guy asked politely.

"Them all, of course!" When Damon saw Guy's confusion, he
laughed. "Good God, man. I'm not going to run for any office. I'm the
kingmaker, not the king. I'm going to place my men in key positions.
I'm going to win elections for them. One thing I learned in New
York, though, is the importance of appearances. People have to think
you're important for you to be important. They get impressed and
caught up in the trappings." Damon gestured at the comfortable
room. "Now this is okay for here. But up in San Francisco, it's
mansions and butlers and 'yes sirs' and 'no sirs.' Fenella can have her
way here. Up there it's strictly top drawer, first class. The only help
she'll agree to now is some spik woman named Maria who comes
once a week."

Guy almost let the slur pass. It was, after all, Damon's home and
he had done well by Guy—more than well. Then he realized saying
nothing made him a party to the prejudice.

"What kind of woman was that, Damon?"

"Spik, you know, spik—not an American." Damon stopped and
narrowed his eyes and then quickly recovered. "Oh wait. I'm sorry. I
didn't mean you. You're different. Hell, back East, I would have been
called a spik if they had used that word. My parents were fresh off the
boat. Potato eaters. They called us 'Micks' instead. We dressed
different. Talked different."

He smiled. "That's when I learned you got to be part of where you
are. You're in America? Be American. Think Yankee, talk Yankee, act
Yankee. Now you take these spiks out here, these 'Old Californians.'
Mostly Mexicans and Spanish. Been here for generations, getting
lazier and lazier and refusing to change. Proud of their goddamned
'heritage,' they say. Well, they can be proud all they want, but this is
America now and a ton of pride isn't worth the sweat on a gnat's
bellybutton. They deserve to be called spiks because they won't even
try being American."

Guy was taken aback by Damon's uncharacteristic show of bias. He
protested, "But it's only been four years since California became part
of the United States. Before that this was their land. All of it."

"Well, it isn't theirs any longer and they better get used to that.
Come on, let's kill this chatter. If you don't like that word, I won't use
it. All right? Besides, maybe you have a point. Some of those people
may be voting one day. When I worked for a ward boss in New York,

he told me, 'Be nice to everyone. You may need every one of those votes someday.' Then he gave me a pile of coins to hand out, to make sure the voters knew just how nice we were. But it's your plans we should be talking about."

Guy was happy to change the subject. He didn't want to be criticizing and correcting his friend, although Damon's style of politics was clearly not to his liking.

"Fenella tells me you want to start a vineyard. I've been talking to this Harazthy fellow, and from what he says, you're on to something. That land north of San Francisco, I've already had it scouted out. Know what the prices are, who to see about getting them lower. There's no time to lose. You can't imagine how fast things are selling. Tell you what. I'll give you a guide, outfit you, and you can head up there right away. Stop in and talk to this Harazthy. Then pick your place. We'll own it within a month."

Damon was moving so quickly, Guy was having trouble taking it all in. "But what can I afford? How many acres should I be looking for? And it's not only the land..."

"I know, I know, you need money for cuttings and labor and whatever. Don't worry about anything. You find what you want. I'll take care of the rest. When you get back, I'll count it all out for you, every penny, dime, and dollar you have. And believe me, it's going to take a lot of counting."

By late afternoon Guy was back on the road running north, the same one he had bumped along in Charley Parkhurst's stagecoach the day before. But this time his companion was no loquacious, good-natured sort. He was an intense, swarthy young Californian with probing dark eyes who had been introduced only as Miguel. All attempts at small talk proved fruitless, so they were riding for the most part in silence.

It gave Guy time to think and wonder if Damon hadn't rushed him on his way for reasons other than the ones he gave. Guy had had several questions and there had been no time to ask them. Questions about Clem the buckboard driver's dislike of Damon. And why Damon traveled with the large pack of armed men.

When he questioned Miguel about the latter, Guy's companion had replied laconically, "Can be a dangerous country for a man like Mister Delany." He refused to amplify.

There would be time for explanations, Guy finally decided, but for now he had to rely on Damon. He knew what was happening far better than Guy. If Damon said to buy fast, Guy would take his advice.

Surprisingly there was one topic Miguel was willing to discuss and in great detail—the life and times of their soon-to-be host, Anton Harazthy.

Harazthy (by his own account and who was to challenge him?) was the privileged scion of a very wealthy and well-placed aristocratic family in Hungary. Among its vast holdings were several vineyards where Harazthy got his early introduction to winemaking.

The young count's future was all but insured. He was to live the charmed, blessed life of the wealthy aristocrat. It was all charted and should have been highly predictable. As it turned out, it wasn't because Harazthy himself was unpredictable. He was restless and looking for challenges, so he turned to politics. Since Hungary was part of the Austro-Hungarian Empire, Harazthy's new patron was therefore the king, in Vienna. This did not sit well with Harazthy, who found deep patriotic feelings within him, and he became a not-too-subtle campaigner for Hungarian independence.

After fomenting one intrigue too many, Harazthy was forced to flee for his life. He found sanctuary in Washington, D.C., where he was befriended by an influential general. The general was able to pressure the Austrian government into allowing the emigration of Harazthy's family.

After a while life in Washington palled. The count pulled up stakes and moved to Wisconsin where he bought a great deal of land. He tried to grow grapes, but the climate and soil were not suited and he ended up growing hops instead. In a few short years Harazthy had established a new industry for Wisconsin—brewing beer. He was a leading man in the community and a very rich one.

All was well until the harsh winters took their toll on Harazthy's health. His doctor told him to leave or die. Given the choice, Harazthy opted for California. He left his property in the hands of a trusted lawyer, again packed up his family and chose, he felt wisely, a southern route to the coast. It was a perfectly uneventful trip for them—until they reached their destination—Los Angeles. There they got news of the worst kind. It seemed the trusted lawyer had been told Harazthy's wagon train was wiped out by Indians. The lawyer immediately liquidated the entire estate, at a fraction of its worth.

Harazthy may have suspected his lawyer was involved in criminal collusion, but there was no way he could prove it. So he took what was left of his fortune and cheerfully set out to acquire another. Initially he bought land in Los Angeles. Then on a trip north, he discovered exactly what he had been looking for—the Sonoma Valley. And that's where Guy and Miguel were headed.

There was a great din outside the window.

"Please forgive the noise," Count Anton Harazthy was saying. "I'm having the house enlarged. My poor family needed something to live in and this humble abode was thrown up quickly. Now we're adding graciousness to basics."

"Basics" was something of an understatement. What already existed was, in fact, a grand, stately mixture of stone and wood, nestled in among glorious, majestic redwoods.

"So, you're Damon Delany's partner. I can't say we haven't been curious about you." Guy didn't like the way the Hungarian was sizing him up—and apparently finding him lacking.

To Guy's surprise, Miguel, who was sitting with them in the solarium, reminded Harazthy that Guy had not been active in Damon's operations. Harazthy raised his eyebrows and shrugged, indicating he would pass judgment later on. Then he smiled warmly. "So I understand you know something about wine," he said.

Guy was going to demand an explanation from Miguel later. In the meantime he answered, "You might say that. My family has a château in Bordeaux."

"Oh!" Harazthy rolled his eyes. "There is a heaven on earth and it is called the Medoc. And which vineyard? I have had the pleasure of visiting Bordeaux many times, perhaps I've been to yours."

"Du Clocher."

"Of course!" Harazthy slapped his forehead three times. "What an idiot I am. Saint-Savin. Du Clocher. How did I miss connecting the names? Of course, I've been to du Clocher. It must have been your father—was your father Edouard Saint-Savin?—who entertained me." Harazthy was beside himself. "You don't know how long I've waited for your arrival."

"But I didn't know myself I was coming here before three days ago."

"No, no, you don't understand." Harazthy was up and gesticulating. "I've been like a missionary among the heathens. These damned Americans don't understand wine. Why they think this dreadful Mission grape juice is drinkable. They ferment it and they think it's wine. I've been trying to introduce the other growers—though they hardly deserve to be called that—to European varietals. But nothing. They're mostly failed miners who think all you have to do is stick a root in the ground, pick the fruit, and ferment it. And, of course, call the resulting liquid wine. Wine? It's pig's urine. How can I get them to listen when these fool Americans cheerfully pay a lot of money for pig's urine? Why should we change? these so-called growers, ask. We're doing fine as it is. Not you, though. You would never utter such blasphemy. You know wine."

"And from what I have seen here, so do you."

Harazthy was pleased. It was good to hear a compliment from a peer. It was good to have a peer. "Now before you tell me what I can do to help you, you must taste some of the fruits of my labor and tell me what you think."

Harazthy poured three glasses of wine from one of many bottles on a square side table. He gave two to his guests, and waited with almost gleeful expectation for Guy to take a taste. Guy took a sip and then another before nodding.

"It surprises me," he said.

"Of course it surprises you—it's good," Harazthy roared happily, "and it's Californian."

"What is the predominant grape?" Guy couldn't quite place it.

"Zinfandel. It's a Zinfandel. Before you ask what's a Zinfandel and where it comes from, I, damn it all to hell, have to plead ignorance. All I know is it came from Europe, but nobody bothered to keep records. That's all I know. I say this over and over again, Saint-Savin, California can be the greatest wine-growing region in the world, bar none. Bar none, I say, and that includes Bordeaux. But we can't do it without systematic experimentation. We have to gather cuttings from all over the world. We have to plant them, see what produces best where. We have to work. Does anyone listen to me? Does anyone care? No, they do not. They bring over cuttings like this Zinfandel, and they don't even know where it comes from. It is enough to tire a man out."

Harazthy looked anything but tired. He looked ready to take on the world and all those who didn't have a good palate and Guy admired him for that.

"Consider you have a new ally," Guy said. "And as for this becoming the greatest wine-growing area..."

"Really, I meant no slur on Bordeaux..." Harazthy interjected.

"...I think it has the potential of being the second-greatest region."

When Harazthy stopped laughing, he said good-naturedly, "Fair enough. The second-best region. We're going to get along, Guy Saint-Savin, we're going to get along."

And they did. Harazthy insisted they stay several days so he could show off to Guy everything he'd done, give him an explanation and the reasoning for every position of every vine, outline what he was doing next, what he hoped to accomplish and what he had already accomplished.

Miguel went along for everything and absorbed it all. Guy was impressed with his questions—Miguel had lost some of his reticence as if Guy had passed some sort of test—and with his quick grasp of what they were being shown. Guy was also impressed by what Harazthy had done in so little time.

Finally it was time to leave. Miguel and Guy's saddlebags were filled with food Guy had only dreamed of for so long—pâtés, egg glace, duck, meringues.

After Harazthy had supervised the strapping of the bags to the horses, he gave the Sonoma one last endorsement. "You will be buying that property I showed you," he urged. "At the northern tip of the valley. It will be perfect for you. You'd be a fool to pass it up, don't you agree?"

Guy was tempted. It would be nice to be the Hungarian's close neighbor, to be near someone of like wine sensibilities, a European who shared—Guy caught himself. Was he thinking it would be nice to be near an aristocrat, someone who had enjoyed the leisure of thought and intellectual stimulation, who had partaken in the subtler, finer pleasures of life and not been beaten into submission by its hardships? It was a snobbish, elitist thought and not to Guy's liking. Still, at that moment, Guy could have easily said that yes, he would be buying in Sonoma. Instead he said, "Count, you have been so very, very kind to a stranger who knocked at your door..."

"Rubbish, you're no stranger. You're a kindred spirit. We're both men of wine."

Beneath all his bonhomie, Harazthy was a very persuasive man. Guy realized he could not show the slightest sign of wavering in his decision, otherwise he would be swept along in the Hungarian's well-intentioned wake. So it was with great deliberation he said, "I value your judgment and my mind says I should follow your advice, that this valley is right. But my heart is an insistent meddler and my heart says 'no.' When I came out of the hills, down those unfriendly, rocky slopes after my years looking for gold, I passed through several valleys. I was a defeated man. And then one day, sitting for a rest, with the sun warming my face and renewing my spirit, I opened my eyes for the first time in months, years. I really looked at where I was. I was sitting on the slopes above a long, wide valley with the narrowest of rivers running through it. And when I looked north, the valley narrowed and the slopes came in closer to that river. It was nothing like the Gironde, not at all like the Medoc. But I suddenly saw it for what it was, a place with water, soil that would welcome the vine, where grapes could be planted on the flat or on the slope. I was excited, I wanted to think again, use myself and what I knew. I saw this valley and it was where I was to be."

"Ah!" Harazthy threw up his hands in defeat. "So you've already seen the Napa."

They rode east over the hills, down across Lovall and Carneros valleys, and up again, Guy's excitement increasing with each mile.

At sunset, they camped on a peak, sheltered by tall pines. Digging into the bounty provided by Harazthy, they enjoyed a long meal. The Hungarian's enthusiasm had further fueled Guy's and he wanted Miguel to share it as well. Guy rambled on about the subtleties of wine-making, the mixture of elements from man and Nature. He spoke of the joys and defeats and the constant fear. And he spoke of du Clocher so intensely that Miguel finally asked why he had left.

It took a while before Guy could answer. It was not easy to admit he'd been forced to leave because of his own impetuosity, his youth, his anger. That while it would be nice to say he fled because of injustice and tyranny, the truth was his exile was the outcome of his own failings.

He told Miguel his story.

It was quite late by the end of the recital. An owl, on its lonely nocturnal search for food, hooted somewhere off in the darkness. Red coals had replaced the campfire's flames.

"We are both exiles, then," Miguel said.

"I don't understand. I thought you were a native Californian."

"Yes, I was born here, but I, too, have been driven from my land by tyrants and thieves. You're the lucky one. Someday you will be able to return to your homeland. Mine is lost forever."

"Who are these tyrants, these thieves? Why don't you fight them?"

Miguel rolled over and went to sleep.

Pure, clean sunbeams were beginning to cut through trees on a facing ridge and light the valley below them. Surveying the panorama with proprietary pride, Guy commented, "It's good light. Very good light."

He dismounted and picked up a handful of soil. "Not bad. Further down the slope, closer to the river..." He pointed to the thin ribbon of water that moved indolently through the middle of the valley "...it's even better."

"What did Harazthy mean when he said the climate might be too good for the grape?" Miguel asked.

"Oh that. Some people believe the vine needs a little hardship if it's to be great, that it has to work against the elements. We'll see about that. Come, let's go down and find our vineyard."

"Don't you mean your vineyard?"

It was one of those odd moments when an idea had been gestating in the back of his mind and then burst forth full-grown. Guy hadn't consciously weighed what he was about to say, but it seemed right and he already accepted it as what he wanted and needed to do.

"Listen, Miguel, I gather you're not really happy working for Damon. So I have a proposition. Wine-making is not one man. It's the work of many. I need someone. Someone I can teach. Someone smart who wants to learn."

"I don't think you're going to find a Jacques Mazet here."

"No, but I have found a Miguel de Cordoba. Will you come to work with me? It'll be hard work and we may fail, but I can tell you have the interest and the intelligence that's needed, and I sense I can trust you. Will you—if it's agreeable with Damon?"

"And how do you know so much about me in so little time?" Miguel asked pointedly.

"I just do. In this country I've discovered you don't have time to test your instincts. You have to move on them quickly or you get passed by. So what do you say?"

The valley stretched out before Miguel, challenging him. He looked torn, trying to ignore the temptation.

"What do you say?" Guy pressed again.

In answer, Miguel held out his hand to seal the deal.

Chapter Thirty-three

The long ride back took them through little towns just being born, towns still unsure of themselves and what they were. These were filled with people starting out, at new beginnings. Once in a while they passed older, more established towns: villages with a history that had been part of Old California. Time had aged them and they had no future except to wait by the road for something to happen, not sure what.

It was near such a town that Guy and Miguel heard a woman's screams. They urged their horses toward the sound, through a clump of trees and into a clearing where they found a modest house with its front door open wide. Men were carrying out furniture and household goods and piling them into buckboards. Guy and Miguel observed a young woman, distraught beyond reasoning, pulling at the chaps of a man, who seemed in charge of the loading, looming above her on horseback. They were too far away to hear what was being said, but it was obvious the woman was pleading.

Two men came out of the house, struggling under the weight of a large portrait. Without warning a boy, no more than seven or eight years old, rushed at them and struggled to pull the picture from their hands.

What happened next was not intentional, but in trying to shake the boy loose from the picture, one of the men shoved him, and the child was flung to the ground. At once the woman had him in her lap, cradling and rocking him, her head thrown back, crying in grief.

"What's going on?" Guy yelled to Miguel and without waiting for an answer started his horse on. He was pulled short by Miguel grabbing the horse's halter.

"Leave it be. There's nothing you can do."

"What do you mean? That woman needs help until the law comes to stop this."

"No," Miguel snapped, then his tone changed to stone. "You don't understand. They are the law."

Guy sat back in his saddle in disbelief. "Those men? The law? You're correct. I don't understand."

"They're sheriff's men. They're evicting her."

Guy looked back at the woman, her long black hair undone now and cloaking her and the child. "What has she done?"

"Done? She's done nothing but be an Old Californian, a spik. That's all that matters. Some Yankee wanted her land. He gets the taxes raised so she can't pay them. Or he says the land grant that gave her family the ranch two hundred years ago is no good. Or the papers get lost. It happens all the time."

"But that's not fair," Guy protested and then added with disgust. "Is there no civilization, no law in this country? Is it all barbarism and greed?"

"And were you treated any better in France?" Miguel asked and then wheeled his horse around and galloped back up the way they came. Guy swiveled in his saddle to watch him. Then he turned back to the woman. She was no longer crying. She was no longer begging. She had lost. She was defeated.

Guy turned his horse and rode after Miguel.

It was years before Guy was to piece together Miguel's complete story. It came out a little at a time, often from unexpected sources and in casual conversations, but never from Miguel himself. About himself he would not talk.

What Guy was to learn was that the de Cordobas had been a proud family, proud of its land, heritage, position in society, and its erudition. They almost worshipped education. It was their tradition. Miguel had been to the best schools in Spain, as had all the de Cordoba men. They came from a long line of Spanish aristocrats who had counseled kings and queens, fought and died gloriously for their country and monarchs, and whose families had been rewarded with riches and land.

After completing his schooling, Miguel returned to California expecting to carry forward the name and the honor of the de Cordobas. But by that time the decline of his family had already begun and it was not the result of any gross stupidity or negligence on the part of his father.

Ricardo de Cordoba had long ago earned the respect of his neighbors, friends, and acquaintances. Many came to him for advice and counsel, knowing that what they would receive would be reasoned and sound. He was always intent in his desire to be fair-minded and far-sighted. So when his neighbors asked his opinion on whether California should join the union and become a state, he thought hard and finally came to the conclusion that California's future lay with the United States. He put his energies into the passage of the statehood vote. And by so doing, planted the seeds of his own disaster.

For Ricardo de Cordoba had been wrong. There was no future for his California in the union. When the Yankees came, they came like locusts, gobbling up all they could, enacting laws that by their very nature could not be followed by the Old Californians, passing taxes that couldn't be paid. The de Cordobas had hundreds of acres of good land, thousands of head of stock, and suddenly they were paupers. Ricardo de Cordoba was humiliated. This was not in his ken or character. Never before had he had to deal with such abasement. He became confused and desperate. He grasped at the chance to borrow money for the taxes, with no foresight about the effects of the two percent a month interest that was demanded.

The interest destroyed him. Soon the sheriff's men came, efficient, uncaring. They allowed the family to keep a meager pile of clothes, cooking pots, and a few horses from the vast stable.

Miguel's father could not watch. He took his favorite stallion and rode off. Miguel found his corpse in the hills two months later. Ricardo de Cordoba had shot his horse. Then he sat under a tree until he, too, died.

Miguel buried him there, under that tree. He wasn't sure how he would tell his mother. His parents had been as close as two people could be. He didn't know if the words were within him to tell her. As it turned out, he didn't have to. While he had been gone, Fenella Delany had swooped down like a guardian angel and scooped his mother out of the squalid shack they had moved to. She insisted Miguel's mother come home with her. She had bathed and fed the old woman and comforted her. And she had told Miguel's mother the tragic news. Miguel felt he would never be able to repay Fenella for her kindness.

But his mother needed more than even Fenella's gentle ministering. Months later, Miguel returned to bury his mother there as well. Miguel's sisters, except for the youngest, were already married and continued their lives as best they could. The youngest married a Yankee and Miguel never spoke to her again. He never spoke very much to anyone after that until he met Guy. Miguel de Cordoba had withdrawn into himself. He lived for one purpose, biding his time for when he could best carry it out. He was waiting, an angry, bitter man, waiting.

"GET OFF THE STREET!"
"THEY'RE ALMOST HERE!"
"IT'S GOING TO BE A CLOSE ONE!"
The main street was lined with men, shouting, shoving good-naturedly, in high spirits.

"What's going on?" Guy asked Miguel as they tied up their mounts out of harm's way.

"You're lucky. You're about to see the town's one social event. You may even have time to place a bet."

"On what?"

Miguel pointed to first one end of the broad street and then the other. "On them." Guy squinted off to the north. There was a huge swirl of dust. He looked south. Another cloud. He looked back to Miguel.

Miguel was almost smiling. "This is the cultural high point of our community. It's the stagecoach race. When Charley Parkhurst and Stan Cunningham are driving, men come from miles to bet on who will get here first. Today it's Charley coming from San Francisco and Cunningham from San Jose. Charley's a madman, hates losing. Let's go to the saloon, that's the race's end."

They shouldered their way through the crowd to the saloon. It had acquired a name in their absence. A newly painted sign hung over the door, proclaiming the establishment was now the Harlow House and no longer merely an ignominious "saloon." Within moments the ponderous coaches came careening into town, whips cracking, horses labored and lathering, terrified passengers holding on with any strength they had left.

Guy recognized Parkhurst, halfway off his seat, screaming obscenities laced with endearments at his team. The man should have, by all rights, fallen off and been crushed under the wheels. He didn't and wasn't. Instead he rose upright to give one last crack of his whip. His team pulled in one gasp before the other coach.

A throng of shouting and cheering spectators converged on the winning coach. They pulled Parkhurst from his perch and carried him triumphantly into the Harlow House.

"Let's go in," Miguel shouted. "I'll introduce you to one Yankee worth knowing."

"Parkhurst?"

Miguel nodded.

"We've met. Let's go in anyway. I'd like to congratulate him."

Parkhurst was at a table near a small window, magnanimously acknowledging the acclamation when he spotted Miguel. He waved away his admirers to make room for him.

Guy meanwhile was trying to reach the bar to place his order. He waited as the harried barkeep tried to fill it under a heavy barrage of other screamed demands.

"That was quite a show," Guy shouted over the din to no one in particular.

"Show, nothing," yelled an exultant, bearded man at his right who began clomping Guy on the back. "I just won twenty bucks. Twenty! Let me get you a drink, stranger."

"That man's no stranger." It was Clem, the buckboard driver, who had obviously started his celebrating before the stagecoaches had reached the finish line. "Why he practically owns all of these parts. Don't you know? He's Damon Delany's partner."

The generous winner pulled his hand off Guy faster than if he had discovered it was down a rattlesnake hole. The saloon was suddenly quieter as sullen men strained to get a look at Guy.

"That true, mister? You in with that son of a bitch?"

"If you're referring to Damon Delany, it is true I'm his partner."

"Then you get damned hell out of here! You've no right to mingle with decent folk!"

Without further warning, Guy was seized on either side by rough hands that propelled him toward the door. He was punched, pummeled, and kicked by every furious man he passed. Held so tightly, there was no defending himself. By the time he was at the door, Guy was bleeding and nearly unconscious. He would have been heaved out if Charley Parkhurst hadn't jumped from table to table and planted himself in the doorway.

He yelled. "You're making a godawful mistake."

"No mistake, Charley," said the big money winner. "This here is scum, and Harlow House is too clean a place for the likes of him."

"Hold on fellows—"

"Come off it, Charley." It was Clem. "Just 'cause some guy rides your stage, don't make him your friend. He's lucky we don't shoot him in the back. That's what his friend would do."

"Hush up, all of you!" Charley was at least a head shorter than everyone else in the room, but he had authority and they listened. "Miguel over there was just telling me. This guy doesn't know nothing about Delany. He's been prospecting for two years, just got back. Now take your hands off him."

"So how's he Delany's partner," someone from the back shouted.

Charley gave a brief history that mollified the crowd enough so that the men returned to the business of drinking, but the room had lost most of its exuberance. Parkhurst half-carried, half-dragged Guy back to the table and then went for the much-needed drinks. Guy was too dazed to speak until Charley forced a good belt of whiskey down his throat. It was rough and strong and Guy choked on it.

When he regained his voice, he asked, "Why do these men hate Damon? What has he done to them?"

"Hey," Charley said, his good nature restored, "it's not what he's done to these men. It's what he's done to everyone. Damon Delany is an out-and-out piece of cow dung, and I don't know why he was put on God's good earth. You tell him, Miguel."

Miguel shook his head. "Let him ask Delany."

Charley spit on the floor in disgust. "Sure, and Delany's just going to up and admit he cheated people out of their land by secretly paying their taxes and then demanding folks repay the 'loan' immediately."

"But isn't that illegal?" Guy asked. "Wouldn't they have been notified their taxes were being paid?"

"Who would tell them? Delany's been stuffing ballot boxes and getting his bully boys into office. Delany demands the taxes and his bought-and-paid-for sheriff is right there for immediate eviction."

"Anything becomes legal if you're the law," Miguel added.

"That sure is right," Charley agreed. "Why Delany wasn't even brought to trial when he shot that kid who was only trying to keep his mama from being thrown off their ranch. I say it's not right, and so do lots of other folks around here. And it ain't just the old rancheros he's doing it to, it's everyone, everyone weak and who don't know better."

Guy was more dazed now than he had been from the beating. "You mean this money he's going to give me for my vineyard, it's blood money, greed and killing money?"

The other two nodded in response.

Guy stood up but had to steady himself on the table. Miguel reached out a hand to help him, but Guy waved him off and lurched out of the tavern.

Parkhurst stopped Miguel from following him. "Let him go. He'll have to see Delany sometime, might as well be now."

Miguel nodded and sat back down. Guy would be able to take care of himself against Damon Delany. He didn't need Miguel.

Chapter Thirty-four

It was dark and well into the night when Guy galloped up the road to the Delany ranch. He tried to open the front door. Finding it bolted, he banged on it yelling, "Open this door! LET ME IN!"

He pounded until the rasping of the bolt being cautiously pulled back quieted him. Fenella, clutching a robe close around her, peered out from behind the door.

"Oh, it's you!" she said with relief.

"I want to see him."

"Quiet, quiet, please. He's asleep."

"Then wake him NOW!"

Fenella had been in bed. The candle she was holding in her free hand flickered on a sleep-flushed face. But she was not too tired to stand her ground. She said firmly, "Guy, I don't know what's gotten into you, but I'll not wake up Kyle. He needs sleep and besides, it would frighten him to see you in this state."

Guy realized then what a lunatic he must seem and became embarrassed and contrite. Fenella was not his enemy. "I'm sorry. I didn't mean to frighten you and it's not Kyle I'm here to see. I've got business with Damon."

He said the last word with such loathing, it wrenched a sign of despair from Fenella. "Come in," she said. "Sit over there by what's left of the fire." The walk-in fireplace had a few embers still glowing in it. Fenella's knitting was on a rocking chair that had been drawn close to the warmth. It was so tranquil and homey, it made Guy ache with longing.

"I must see Damon," he said.

"He's not here, but it's time we talked. Now sit."

She led him by the hand to the couch. When he was settled, she pushed her rocking chair over so that they faced each other.

"I guess you've heard some things about Damon."

"Some things? My God, Fenella, how can you be so calm? How can you accept his lying and cheating? The sorrow he's caused? The killing, stealing?"

"I accept nothing, except that he's my husband. I've heard things too. I don't know if they're true. I don't want them to be. But he is my husband and I have Kyle to think of—and so do you."

He responded, almost angrily, "Yes, I do have Kyle to think of and what he'll think of me. If I accept any of this blood money Damon's gotten, I'm as bad as he is and I won't be a man Kyle can look up to. So that's why I'm taking nothing from Damon except half of what he got from the gun sales. That's all. Otherwise, I won't be able to face my son for the rest of my life. How can I teach him principles if I have none myself?"

"Oh stop it," Fenella had to make Guy understand. "Look around you. Out here principles are a luxury. You have to take the money, for your sister, that château of yours, and most important, your son. You can't eat principles. Be practical."

"I was told that money was stolen from people. I take it and I'm a thief, too."

In the near darkness she could make out his anger. She detected uncertainty as well. It was that uncertainty, the wavering she would have to work on. She had to protect him from himself and thereby protect Kyle. "I knew we'd talk like this some day. I guessed what you would say. So I thought this through. Now listen to me. Damon may have gotten some of that money through lying and dirty deals. I don't want to know about that. But what I do know is the money from the guns and selling supplies to the miners is clean money, earned fair and square. And he's got some, too, by giving loans."

"But what kind of interest did he charge? Was it usury?"

"Look, if some man takes a loan, he knows the terms. It's up to him to turn it down. It's not your place to protect other people from themselves. You have to protect your own. I've gone through the books—Damon made sure I learned about numbers—and I know how much there is from the fair deals. You'll have enough for your vineyard—at least to get started. Now don't argue. If you won't accept your full share, then you take that."

Guy put his hands wearily over his face. "How can you live with him, Fenella? Why do you stay?"

How could she explain that to him when she didn't want to understand it herself. Fenella had always accepted life as a compromise. You do what you can and hope for the best. She never actually thought of her marriage to Damon as a compromise because she wouldn't allow herself to think about it at all. Damon was Damon. A man with many faults, a man she could have easily hated—if she had thought about it. She didn't because he was her husband and a wife accepted her husband in sickness and in health, as long as they both shall live. To do otherwise was a sin in the eyes of God. The Catholic Church in the guise of an ill-tempered priest had beaten that into her, and Fenella didn't question it.

But Fenella would compromise only so far. And if honoring and obeying Damon became unacceptable, Fenella would find a way to rationalize her way around him.

And there were reasons she stayed with Damon. One reason she could never bring herself to discuss with anyone, not even her husband, was that he had been her first lover, her first and her only. She had been as much surprised as he on their wedding night, for Fenella, on dropping her nightgown was transformed from a drab little sparrow into a magnificent bird of paradise whose lovemaking was filled with delight and ferocity. And it was that lovemaking that bound Damon and Fenella together stronger than anything else.

None of this she said to Guy, only a simple, "He is my husband" had to suffice. She did add, "There are times when I find out something that I step in and stop it. He'll listen to me. But I pick my battles carefully." She paused. "The dogs are barking. It's Damon. Now you think about what I said. And please, don't be foolish."

Fenella went to the door, opened it, and waited for her husband. Guy watching her, wondered about the prisons of compromise into which people locked themselves. Fenella was right about one thing though. Idealism was an expensive luxury. Hadn't he learned that in France?

"Fenella, you're up. What a pleasant surprise." Damon tried to kiss her, but she turned away.

"You have a visitor," she said.

When Damon made out who it was, he said jovially, "Guy's no visitor, woman. *Mi casa es su casa.*"

"I'm not sure he wants your house, Damon."

"What are you talking about?" The meager light from Fenella's candle and the embers made it hard for Damon to see Guy and his wife, so he went on with forced good-nature. "I get it. You've found your own house. In that perfect little Eden up north? Just tell me the location, and it's yours. Fenella, for God's sakes, where's the brandy?"

Damon sat down on the couch and threw his arm expansively across the back, just like two good friends ready to enjoy a nice quiet drink together. He withdrew the arm when he heard the harshness of Guy's next words. "I've been hearing about how you acquire things, Damon. About taking over the taxes, about the evictions."

Damon looked at him warily, then said, "Yeah, it's a great land, out here, isn't it? Real land of opportunity—for smart operators, like us, that is. Didn't take me long to figure the system. You know what the system is out here? It's whatever you make it."

"Don't call me one of your 'smart operators.' I don't approve of what you've done."

Damon jumped up, his anger showing. "Wait one minute! Money is what counts in this country. I've shown I'm no rube, no spik, no potato eater. I'm an American now. I've proved it. I worked hard. I paid attention in New York. I know who you have to pay and how much you have to pay them. I know how to get what I want. This place! It's nothing. I've taken all there is to be taken around here. I'm going to San Francisco, Sacramento. I'm taking California. And you've got nothing to complain about, anyway. I kept my end of the bargain."

"I guess I was naive. I didn't know what the bargain was and I didn't bother to ask. But if doing things the way you do them is the American way, then let me remain an ignorant spik. I might be ignorant, but at least I won't be despicable."

They were both on their feet, both bodies rigid with hatred, straining towards each other.

"Saint-Savin," Damon hissed, "you think you're something goddamned special with that title in front of your name. Well, you're not because you don't have any brains behind your forehead. I thrive on people like you, dumb jerks who put their version of right and wrong above all else, who will jump in and defy the captain to get the food."

The meaning of Damon's words hit Guy harder than the fists of his attackers at the Harlow House. He felt sick. The room was spinning and unfocussed. He had to will himself steady. "Damon, are you telling me you knew the captain had food? You knew all the time?"

"Of course I did." Damon smiled, revelling in his superiority. "I make it my business to know things."

"Then why did you wait? Why didn't you say something?"

"I was waiting for you to be smart enough to catch on. I was waiting for you to make a move."

"But your own wife was starving. Your child! You could have saved your child!"

"And what if it were me that got killed? Then my child would have been good as dead anyway. You don't survive out here on righteous thoughts, my friend. You survive by your wits. Because you're the smartest. And that makes you the strongest. Sure, I knew the captain was hoarding, and I did do something about it. I let you know."

"Marie could have been saved." Guy was filled with sorrow and threat. "She might be alive today. Oh God! You're not only a liar and thief, you're a murderer as well!"

"Me? A murderer?" Damon laughed. It was easy to get the best of Guy. "I never gutted some muckety-muck cause he called my mother a whore. You're the one who did that. Now get out of my house, you miserable son of a bitch. You've no right to look down your nose at me or to tell me about right or wrong, not when I've provided you with a goddamned future. I've worked so you can be a jack-assed, dandified farmer, tending your miserable little grapes. I'm no thief. I'll give you your money. Then I don't ever want to see your face again. Now get out!"

When Guy didn't move, Damon strode to the door and yanked it open. Still Guy remained motionless. He was a bigger man than Damon, and Damon would never be able to throw him out without help. So he grabbed a bullwhip that was hanging near the door and played it out across the floor. "I'm telling you again. Leave before I give you a taste of what you deserve, you holier-than-thou bastard."

Damon arched the whip back. Time for threats were over. So intent were the men on each other, they didn't hear Fenella enter the room until she screamed and rushed between them so suddenly that Damon was unable to stop the downward slash of the whip. It caught her viciously across her left shoulder. She fell to the floor, blood oozing from the long gash.

"Stop it," she gasped. "Both of you stop it."

Both men moved to help her, but she waved them off. "Don't touch me! I won't have you touching me until...until you hear me out." She was speaking, hardly above a whisper and with great difficulty. "Guy, you take your share of the money. Damon, give him what is his. You might have gotten where you are today, Damon, but not this fast, not without Guy's guns. And he got those guns because he was righteous and caring. You remember that. You two do what I say. Then you stay away from each other."

She took their silence for assent. She looked at her husband, thinking about their baby, then she added. "One more thing, Kyle stays with me."

Guy tried to object.

"No buts," Fenella said. "I won't have my boy in the wilderness...you and your grapes...paying him no attention. I'll care for him, 'til you can. Do you hear?" She fainted.

Damon reached her first and lifted her tenderly. When Guy went to help, he snarled, "Get out now, before I have my men kill you for trespassing. I'll do what Fenella said. See to it you do, too." He carried her off toward the bedroom.

A week later Miguel and Guy were again back in the saddle on their way north. Guy had wrestled with the decision to leave Kyle behind. In the end, he knew it was best, that Fenella would give him loving care. She had also been able to assuage his fear that Damon might take his anger out on the boy. Fenella had assured him, when she came to meet him in town, that Damon actually loved Kyle and not to worry.

Even Miguel had agreed. "He'll be okay, the boy. It's Fenella I would worry about."

"Fenella? Why Fenella? You don't think Damon—"

"No, Damon won't hurt her. It's when she has to give up the boy. She'll have to someday. And that will be the worst day of her life. I've watched them. Kyle is everything to her. She has little else, you know."

Book Six

Chapter Thirty-five

1855

Nathan! Nathan!

He was close to her, responding to her urgency. In one brief, agonizing moment, he'd be in her, he'd have her, feeling her warm, moist delight around him.

Nathan started up, awake and naked in his bed. The urgent cries were no dream. Solange had rushed into his room calling his name.

"Oh, my goodness...oh, I'm sorry...I didn't know," she flustered and then realized she was staring at him. Solange turned to flee, still apologizing.

"My dear," Nathan called after her, "calm down. You're acting as if you've never seen a naked man before." He stopped and berated himself. Of course, she had never seen a man naked. It was quite unlikely that Edouard had even let her see her brother without clothes when they were children.

He sighed. What was he doing to her? It had seemed like such a perfect solution when he'd proposed their "marriage." Now he wondered. Twenty years old and Nathan doubted she had ever been kissed with passion.

"Solange, come back. See. I'm perfectly respectable. Covered completely. I have my robe on. Solange, for God's sake, we're married."

She reentered his bedroom, her exciting news taking precedence over her embarrassment.

"We must go to Paris," she announced.

If she'd come in to say she'd overthrown the government of Brazil, he wouldn't have been more astonished. This was the woman who in three years had gone no further from the Medoc than Bordeaux city, who refused steadfastly to visit anyone except General Hopewell, who let Nathan go off all over the continent without her. If truth be told, he had no desire to travel, but how was he going to urge her to expand her horizons if he stayed fulltime at du Clocher as well?

And he could have easily stayed. He could have let all his friends in Paris wonder what had become of him. Of course, some trips from Bordeaux were necessary. Nathan had strong sexual needs and he had many lady friends eager to satisfy them. Still, every departure from du Clocher was increasingly difficult.

And now, with no warning, Solange had burst into his bedroom to say they must go to Paris. He would have laughed longer if she hadn't looked so confused and hurt.

"Ah, well, do tell me why we must go? What has managed to entice you out of your monasticism?"

"I'm not a monk. I'm only doing what I have to do. And I'm going to Paris because I have to do that, too. Louis-Napoleon..."

"Now this is too much to bear!" Nathan cried in mock distress. "I have tried for years to get you to travel, but now you leave du Clocher for Louis? I'm crushed."

Solange was appalled that Nathan would think she would do anything for the emperor. She blamed the man for all that had befallen du Clocher. Solange was not one to let time erode her hatred. She even showed her disrespect by always referring to the emperor by his given names, a point not taken by Nathan, for that's what he did anyway.

"I wouldn't cross the road for Louis...oh, Nathan, you're teasing me."

Nathan reached to the foot of the bed where she was sitting and pulled her up next to him, his arm around her shoulders. "Yes, my dear," he answered with great fondness, "I was teasing you. You must try not to take everything so seriously."

"But isn't everything serious?"

"Lord, no. Life is to be enjoyed and laughed at. It's over so quickly, you have to delight in it while you can. Now, I promise to stop interrupting."

"There's going to be an exposition," Solange said as if that statement should explain everything. When Nathan raised his eyebrows in question, Solange hurried to explain. "It's to show the world how modern France is and how advanced we are."

Nathan couldn't help snorting. "What a wonderful fiction this is going to be. I hope Louis is good at conjuring."

"What's important is that all French wine will be on exhibit as well. Harry's been telling me all about it."

"This has come on suddenly," Nathan observed.

"No, no, everyone has known about it forever. No one bothered to inform me, that's all. Further, the negociants are devising a classification for Medocain wines, premier through cinquième. Du Clocher will have to be a premier."

Nathan frowned. "You say the negociants are making this list?"

"Yes, and the Chamber of Commerce will sanction it. It will be so wonderful to see 'premier cru' after the name of du Clocher."

While happy to see her enthusiasm, Nathan felt compelled to damp it down with some realistic caution. "My dear, listen to what you've said—the negociants are making up the list. The very same negociants who have ostracized you and didn't even invite you to exhibit."

Solange was instantly concerned. "They can't stop me from exhibiting, can they?"

"That's not what you should worry about. A short note to Louis and you will be the only château with a personal invitation from the emperor. No, that's not your worry. Be prepared, however, to be slighted in the classification."

Solange was relieved and tried not to smile too smugly. "But they can't, you see. The classification is based on the price the wine fetched over the last one hundred years. There can be only three or four châteaux that sold higher than du Clocher. No, our place in the premier classification is guaranteed by all the wonderful rows of figures we amassed since great-great-great-great grandfather planted the first vine."

Well, thought Nathan, not very reassured at all, I've sounded the alarm, albeit on deaf ears. He would speak with Busscher, who had proven adroit at handling the business side of du Clocher. There had been no drop in sales at all with the departure of Schroeder. In fact, they had improved. Busscher also proved a shrewd conduit of Bordelaise information. He was good at assessing men and situations. Busscher would give Nathan a realistic appraisal of the château's chance at the premier classification. And if he thought Solange was to be robbed of the honor, Nathan might have time to head off the chicanery.

"When shall we be departing for Paris?" Nathan asked.

Chapter Thirty-six

Paris had decided to show her glory that summer. Warm, delicious days. Twilights that lingered until after ten. A summer for sitting and sipping, wandering and admiring. Paris was a city cleaned, gussied-up, and smug.

The exposition itself went far beyond Louis-Napoleon's expectations. It had been organized to imitate the London exposition of four years earlier. It became an event unto itself, exuding ambition and determination for economic prosperity. And, of course, self-congratulations on how far the nation had come. It gave Louis the opportunity to affirm his standing as the royal head of a great nation, accepted by the likes of Queen Victoria, who was to visit the show, and not merely some bourgeois upstart with pretensions and little else.

It was a heady summer to be in the city of lights, and Nathan took advantage of that. He swooped up Solange in a whirlwind of shopping, dining, exploring, looking, and learning. They stayed at his hotel de particulier off the place des Vosges. It was only one of Nathan's several domiciles in Paris. It delighted him that Jerome knew of none of the others. There was the apartment near the Luxembourg Gardens, comfortable and small, walls lined with books, where he met with his literary friends. There was the all black and satin set of rooms near Montparnasse, where many young ladies and women from the lower classes—shop girls, streetwalkers, seamstresses—happily shared their time and talents with Nathan. He also had a luxury suite near the Champs Elysées, where many ladies of fashion wrought memories. The place des Vosges mansion, however, had been Nathan's true home, and, before Solange, he had never taken a woman there.

For all its size and majesty—there were thirty-two rooms—Solange was most impressed by its comfort. Nathan had decorated without pretension. She was given a suite and was happy to retreat to it at the end of each day after Nathan had marched her through his exhausting itinerary. He wanted to miss nothing. He wanted her to see his Paris as he knew it.

The tour began the morning after they arrived.

"We will start with the Right Bank," he announced at breakfast, which was served in a gracious solarium overlooking an inner garden brightened by big, brilliant flowers. "And we will walk, whether it is fashionable or not. You have good sensible walking shoes?"

He peered under the table and lifted her dress slightly and then dropped it before she could object.

"They'll do for today, but we'll have to stop at the bootmaker near the Madeleine and have him start immediately on another pair. And we must also see Alexander on the rue de Rivoli. I understand he is the ultra-chic couturier now. If we're to spend three weeks in Paris, you must have some proper clothes. Finished? Come along then."

They walked over to the Rue St. Antoine with Nathan giving a running commentary on the buildings and events that had transpired within them. "St. Antoine was the largest boulevard in Paris. Until now that is. Baron Haussmann is intent on changing that. It was along St. Antoine with the requisite flags and banners flying that Charles V rode in the mid-sixteenth century to celebrate his victory over the Spanish rebels. The cannons at the Bastille fired an eight-hundred volley salute, if you can imagine the racket that made. You see that building over there? That's the hotel de Sully."

He was pointing at a graceful building with two pavilions and beautifully curved walls.

"Isn't that where Voltaire angered Rohan-Chabot and was imprisoned in the Bastille for doing so?"

"Your knowledge of history amazes me, Solange. You're absolutely right. Come now. Further up, St. Antoine becomes the rue de Rivoli. There, you can see the Hotel de Ville. Quite a wedding cake, isn't it?"

"But the plaza looks so different. What happened? When my father brought me..."

"Your father brought you before the grand hand of Haussmann went to work. The baron got rid of all those little streets that used to surround the plaza and now it's maybe four times as large. Do you like it?"

People hurried from one end of the square to the other. Carriages were in a terrific muddle trying to traverse it. It was a teeming sea of dizzying activity.

"I'm not sure," Solange admitted. "I may not be cosmopolitan enough for it. It overwhelms me."

"I know. It overwhelms me, too. This Great Empire mentality that Louis has brought to Paris is not to my liking at all. Are you tired? I had Henri follow with the carriage. See, he's right behind us."

Solange was touched by Nathan's consideration. Still she declined. "It's much more interesting walking. Don't you think?" she asked. "You're so much closer to everything and you can stop and look at it all. In the carriage, it's a blur."

"It is more exciting."

"Exciting? Yes, I suppose that's what I mean."

How strange, thought Nathan. Save that one night of tragedy, Solange knew little of excitement or thrill or exhilaration. All her emotions were welded to du Clocher. Such a waste and a pity. But what could he do about it?

"Here, we'll continue on the Rue de Rivoli, look in the windows, and end up—well, I do have a destination in mind."

The next couple of hours were filled with looking and laughing. Nathan insisted on buying baubles and books, marionettes and lace, anything that caught Solange's eye. Henri was at the door of each shop as they emerged to collect packages and deposit them in the carriage.

"But what am I to do with all this?" Solange asked, although she was long past fighting against Nathan's extravagances.

"Enjoy it, my dear. What else?"

It was well into the afternoon by the time they reached their mysterious destination. Nathan had thought a good deal about the perfect place, and always came back to his original thought.

"Turn right." He couldn't wait for Solange. He took her elbow and guided her through a long, tall archway. On the other side, they emerged into crystalline sunshine and greenery.

"Where are we?" It was an oasis, a beautiful garden surrounded by protective buildings, where hurrying and heartache were out of the question and worries strictly forbidden.

"This," Nathan proclaimed as if it were his proudest possession, "is the Palais Royal. As you know, it's had its good times and its bad. It has served as a playground for kings and a marketplace for whores. The arcades were conveniently dark trysting spots at one time in the palais's existence. Of course, they were also wonderful for thugs and thieves. But what am I thinking of, talking to you of prostitutes and blackguards?"

"Nathan, I am twenty years old. I am a married woman. And I know about the lower regions of life. You needn't censor yourself." Solange said this with amusement.

Nathan suppressed his smile. "Yes? Well, our luncheon destination is right over there. The Café de Chartres."

The restaurant was dark and cool. Solange and Nathan were escorted to a corner table at a window. They were afforded attention and service that only the emperor could have expected. The cafe was a great favorite of Nathan's, and Nathan was obviously a great favorite of the cafe's.

Solange was ravenous from the walking and sightseeing. Nathan decided he enjoyed watching her eat as much as he enjoyed the actual meal. They both had snail soufflés with a sauce Poulette. Nathan followed that with a pigeon stuffed with the most subtle of foie gras while Solange opted for an escalope de foie de canard in Calvados. The oranges orientales were too beautiful to pass up, so they both had portions of that. All was accompanied by bottles from the cafe's impressive cellar, which was dominated by the best Bordeaux vintages. Nathan ordered three different bottles. He refused to have less than the perfect wine with each course, and a good portion of each bottle was finished.

When Nathan suggested champagne with the oranges, Solange burst into laughter so loud that the few diners and waiters left in the cafe turned to look and then smile indulgently at the flushed, lovely young woman who was happily taking her companion's hand in hers.

"Oh Nathan, I couldn't. I just couldn't. I wouldn't be able to walk to the door, much less the carriage."

"Then I would carry you," Nathan said gallantly and leaned over to kiss her fingers. Had he seen the way she looked at his bent head, he would have been confused by the mixture of bewilderment and gentleness playing across her face. By the time he looked up, a mischievous glint had replaced them.

"And who would carry you?" Solange asked.

"Why you impertinent little wench. I have been indulging in leisurely lunches and managing to maneuver my way out, under my own sails for so much longer than you've been alive that I shudder to think how long. Now if you will stop giggling—my God, Solange, I didn't know you could giggle—we will make a supremely dignified exit and fervently hope that Henri has not deserted us."

Solange fell asleep, her chestnut mane splayed over Nathan's shoulder, her head turned to his cheek, her soft warm breath caressing his lips.

"Henri," Nathan called, little above a whisper.

"Yes, baron?" Henri slipped open a small window behind him and turned slightly so he could peer down into the car.

"We won't be going directly home. Take us along the Champs Elysées, along the Seine, anywhere. Just don't take us home."

"Yes, baron," Henri said with complete understanding.

Chapter Thirty-seven

Nathan would have gladly spent the rest of the month, the year or more introducing Solange to his Paris. She, not unpredictably, was impatient by the second week.

"This is not a holiday. I have work to do."

"But my dear," Nathan argued, "there's still so much to see. We spent hardly any time at all at the Jardin d'Acclimation. We only saw a few of the animals. We were going back to the Hippodrome circus. And that bookstore, the one I told you about on the Left Bank, near the Pont Neuf. What of that? The exposition isn't going anywhere. There'll be time enough for it."

"No, I want to go now."

They were drinking café au lait at the marble table in the garden. Solange showed her impatience by rapping a steady tattoo with her spoon on the coffee cup.

"I don't see why you must. Harry is handling everything. No one could better serve du Clocher than Busscher. You know that."

"Yes. Yes. But I want to watch people as they taste my wine. Hear what they say. Talk to them. Besides, I want the negociants to know I'm not afraid of them, that I'll meet them head-on."

"I assure you, they already know that."

"Besides, I don't know when they're going to announce the classification, and I want to be there when they do."

Nathan had been able to find out next to nothing about the classification, and that worried him. The damned Bordelaise Chamber of Commerce was treating the whole thing like a state secret, pompous asses. Oh well, he thought to himself, there would be no holding Solange back now that she'd made up her mind.

"All right, then, it is the Champs Elysées. And Solange, do wear one of your new frocks—the white with blue trim, I should think. You shall make all the wives of the negociants look like charwomen."

It took them much longer to get to the Champs Elysées than they had anticipated. The streets near the exposition were choked with carriages and horses. Visitors were coming from all parts of France and all corners of the world. Nathan and Solange played a game of guessing from which country the occupants in nearby carriages came, by their dress and gestures, then having Henri tell them which language they were speaking to verify the winner. Nathan was very good. Solange thought everyone was from the United States.

After a while Nathan tired of the game.

"At least Louis didn't stick this out in some godforsaken place like the Bois de Vincennes," he grumbled. "We'd never get *there* at this rate."

"Look, we've almost arrived." Solange motioned out the window. Ahead was an impressive collection of tents, immaculate new buildings, and a buzz of activity.

"This whole exposition is a ridiculous fiasco, a chance for Louis to show off as if he were a boy boasting 'his' is bigger than 'theirs.'"

"Nathan, aren't you being unfair? You haven't seen it yet. And besides, if it can help du Clocher, it's worth it. Why don't we get out and walk the rest of the way?"

It wasn't long before Nathan had to admit begrudgingly that the exposition was something special. The eating halls, science exhibits, even the industrial shows were interesting. Solange went to them all, hoping to turn Nathan's mood, and he let himself be dragged around since he couldn't stop fearing what they would find at the wine display.

That exhibit was in a great cavern of a building, and it was lucky Harry had sent them a map of the layout. Nathan could sense Solange's displeasure as they snaked their way through the crowds. It was increasingly obvious that du Clocher had been given a less-than-advantageous location for its booth. Lafitte and Latour were quite close to the entrance, and the lesser vineyards were farther in direct proportion to their quality. Du Clocher was the farthest of all.

Trying to make the best of it, Nathan pointed and said, "Look, how nice. You are so close to the cheeses. We'll be able to nibble on your neighbors."

As they drew nearer, Nathan greatly regretted his jest, since the odor of the nearby cheese was pungent and hardly conducive to tasting fine wine.

"I am sorry, Solange. It's unconscionable they should treat you this way."

"It doesn't matter. They can play all the little schoolboy tricks they wish. It won't mean anything in the long run."

Nathan wished he was as confident. Just then Solange stiffened. "What's wrong?"

She didn't answer. Instead she nodded her head in imperious greeting and continued toward the du Clocher table. Cornelius Schroeder and Philippe Cottin automatically nodded back before realizing whom they were greeting. On catching their mistake, their derisive laughter followed in Nathan and Solange's wake.

"He really is the most uncouth man," Nathan said angrily.

"Pay them no attention. I don't."

Harry greeted them warmly, happy they were there. Nathan could understand why. The table was in such a bad spot that virtually no one was stopping at it. If he hadn't had the map, Nathan didn't think even he, with all his motivation, would have found it.

A quarter of an hour passed. Nothing happened. Another and another. Solange would not leave, not even when Schroeder, whom she had not seen since that night at the Jurade, walked by with a gloating smirk. She stood taller and straighter and said nothing.

Finally it was Nathan who could take no more.

"It's time we leave. You can do nothing here."

"No, if I leave, it will look as if I'm running."

"No it won't. Harry's here and he has his assistant. There's no reason for you to stay. Look, it's time you stopped refusing my help. It's all very fine for you to insist on succeeding on your own without my money, but you can at least accept my help. I'll send a note to Louis. He's scheduled to visit the exposition next week with Queen Victoria. I'll ask him to bring her and that fop consort Albert here, to your du Clocher."

Solange lowered her head. She didn't want Nathan to see all her fears and terror. Then these emotions gave way to anger. "Louis? Louis who brought this all on me and my family? Am I to turn to my worst enemy?"

"I've had enough of this foolishness. For God's sake, Solange, look at me and stop talking like a heroine in some novel. I've told you before. Louis's only interest in you is as my wife. Now grow up. If you truly want to make a success of du Clocher, then do what is necessary."

The jut of Solange's chin suggested she was about to let loose with an angry reply. Before she could, Harry's assistant came running up.

"If you please, madame and monsieur, they're posting the classifications."

"Why now?" Nathan wondered out loud.

It was Harry who supplied the answer. "The queen's visit. The ministry of state requested the wine be rated before Queen Victoria arrived so she would know she was being served only the best."

Solange was already moving towards the front entrance, making her way to a crowd gathered near the main door. She pushed to the front, excusing herself by rote, her attention riveted on two men, one on a ladder, the other standing below with the proclamations to be posted high, written large, for all to see.

Nathan shouldered his way through as well and joined her.

"They're not putting them up in any order. The cinquième cru is up and the deuxième." Solange was past hiding her excitement—and her anxiety.

Nathan saw she was right and quickly scanned the lists.

5th: Pontet Cadet ... Batailley ... Haut Batailley ... Grand-Pu-Lacoste ... Grand-Puy-Ducasse ... Lynch-Bages ... Lynch-Moussas ... Dauzac ... Mouton ... La Tertre ... Haut-Bages-Liberal ... Pedesclaux ... Belgrave ... Camensac ... Cos-Labory ... Clerc-Milon ... Croizet-Bages ... Cantlemarle. All reasonable and no du Clocher.

The workers hadn't finished hanging the second poster.

2nd: Rausan-Segla ... Rauzan-Gassies ... Leoville-Las-Cases ... Leoville-Poyferre ... Leoville-Barton ... Durfort-Vivens ... Lascombes ... Gruaud-Larose ... Brane-Cantenac ... Pichon-Longueville ... Pichon-Longueville-Lalande ... Ducru-Beaucaillou ... Cos d'Estournel ... Montrose.

Solange was pushing her hair back with nervous impatience. The men were taking a very long time to get the posters up.

3rd: Kirwan ... Issan ... Lagrange ... Langoa ... Giscours ... Malescot-St. Exupéry ... Catenac-Brown ... Palmer ... La Lagune ... Dismirail ... Calon-Ségur ... Ferriere ... Marquis d'Alesme-Becker ... Boyd-Cantenac.

That left but two.

1st: Lafitte ... Latour ... Margaux ... Haut-Brion.

Lafitte. Latour. Margaux. Haut-Brion. That was all.

"No," Solange cried. "It can't be! Where is du Clocher?"

"Higher than it belongs." A gloating Cornelius Schroeder was behind them. "Right there," he pointed.

The words and letters melted in Solange's eyes. St. Pierre-Sevaistre ... St. Pierre-Bontemps ... Benaire-Ducru ... Talbot ... Duhart-Milon ... Pouget ... La Tour-Carnet ... Lafon-Rochet ... Beychevelle ... Le Prieure ... Marquis de Terme ... DU CLOCHER.

The words mocked Solange. "Not even first in the fourth cru," she whispered.

Nathan swung around angrily. "You bastard," he said loudly to Schroeder. "You did this. Did you change the records? How did you do it?"

Schroeder laughed nervously and looked around the crowd for support. "Making false accusations seems to run in the family. Really, what have I to do with the classification? You're lucky du Clocher was included at all."

"Keep out of my way, Schroeder. You've made a powerful enemy today. Remember that," Nathan said as he hurried after Solange who was walking straight, tall, and blindly through the bystanders, who parted to let her pass.

When he caught up with her, he gently looped her arm through his.

"Take me home, Nathan," she said. "Take me home to du Clocher."

They left the next afternoon, but not before Nathan had written two short notes. One was to Louis-Napoleon saying that Nathan had changed his mind and would accept the invitation to the country party at Compiègne the following month.

The second note read:

You shall, under no circumstances, be present at the Emperor's Compiègne affair. Under no circumstances. I shall countenance no games, no intrigues.

N.

He read it over, started to change a word, then crumpled the paper. This message was best delivered in person. It would not take long.

"Hello, Inez," Nathan was saying as he handed the maid his hat and cane.

"Oh, baron," she giggled. "I don't think the countess is expecting you. She is quite *deshabillé*. Still in bed."

"Inez, you spoil her. It is past one o'clock. If she is still in bed, it's time she got up." Nathan climbed the onyx staircase, thinking, as always, that it was opulence without purpose. He opened the boudoir door and walked in.

Fabienne Saint-Savin was indeed in bed, a tangle of red hair and airy lace.

Nathan crossed to the window and pulled back the drapes. Immediately he heard a cry of indignation from the bed.

"Inez! How dare you? Close the drapes at once. I allow no light in this room. You know that."

Fabienne was sitting up, breasts exposed, arms shielding her eyes.

"Come, come, Fabienne, it's time to face the day."

"You?" Fabienne splayed her fingers across her face to hide it, unperturbed by the rest of her nakedness. "Inez, where are you?" The small Spanish maid was already shutting out the threatening light to shield her mistress from its revelations. Still Fabienne burrowed into the covers, hiding herself further from Nathan.

"I hate the day," her voice came muffled through the blankets, "and I refuse to face it. I start when I want, and I certainly don't want to start now. So get out, Nathan. I thought you had more manners than to barge into a lady's bedroom."

"I do."

"I am unamused. Inez, my robe."

The maid held it up, and Fabienne gathered it around, bending over to tie the satin sash. Without looking up, she said, "I assume you have come to say something. I will take care of my toilette now and will receive you afterwards."

She was up and out of the room so fast, Nathan had only the briefest glimpse of her face.

She's gotten older, he thought, and even more beautiful.

After some time had passed and still no Fabienne, Nathan went impatiently to the door. "I really don't have much time," he called. "Surely you don't have to primp for me."

"I primp for everyone. What is your rush?"

"I must take..." he hesitated. It seemed improper to mention her name here. "I must take my...wife back to Bordeaux."

"Ah yes, your child bride. My, my, who would have thought the most notorious roué in France would have become so attached to an inexperienced girl. Though I suppose by now she's not all that inexperienced after three years with you."

"I wish that were true," Nathan muttered.

"What did you say?" She stared at him. "No, don't repeat it. I heard what you said." Fabienne had the maddening ability of always hearing what she wanted to hear and remaining deaf to all else. For once she didn't care that her makeup was not completed or that her hair was disarranged. Fabienne came out to face Nathan.

"How can she have been in your bed for three years and be inexperienced?"

"Is it any of your business, Fabienne?" Nathan turned his back, but she would have none of that and walked around and confronted him. She wanted to see his expression and gauge his truth.

"Of course, it is. I am her mother."

Nathan rose to her bait. "You're no more her mother than I'm her lover."

Fabienne searched his face, looking for a hint of mischief, sarcasm, anything to refute what he had said. Finding nothing she went to a settee and sat down, devoid of her customary grace and flair. "How could this have happened? Is there something wrong with her? With you? How could you allow this to happen? Was the marriage *never* consummated?"

With great deliberation, Nathan was preparing to light a cigar. He rarely smoked. He needed to now—he knew Fabienne didn't care for cigars. He wanted to distract her. He needed time to frame his answer.

"As I said, I don't think this is any of your business, but I suppose there's no harm in telling you. If nothing else, you're not a gossip. Ours is a marriage of convenience."

"How can marriage be convenient without lovemaking?" Fabienne snapped. If Nathan had said he beat Solange regularly or gave her food only twice a week, or just about anything else, Fabienne would have accepted it. But life without the boudoir? It was abhorrent and cruel.

"Solange is different from you..." Nathan began, sounding lame even to himself.

"Different? Different! How old is she? Nineteen? Twenty? At her age I..." Fabienne stopped. Yes, she probably was different from her daughter, at any age.

Fabienne was different from most women. And most men for that matter. She was a dedicated, devout sybarite who found nothing immoral in doing anything to fulfill her needs. If it hadn't been for her great beauty, she would have been forced to repress her sensualism, live the existence of making do as most everyone else did. As it was, deceptively angelic amethyst eyes and delicately perfect features allowed her from an early age to indulge her whims and desires.

Her middle-class, bourgeois family and her upbringing should have been unremarkably banal. However, even in the convent school, Fabienne Duhamel manipulated favors and concessions. By the time she was sixteen, she had had several affairs. Initially she bartered her favors only for the generous gifts her lovers lavished on her. The third man changed that. He had brought her out, taught her not only how to make love but to enjoy it as well. Her days were spent thinking of her nights, of his hands and mouth on and in her, of his abandoning himself to her and she to him. And she dreamed of new things to do together and fillips and nuances to what she could do to him. It was not long before her imagination surpassed his tutoring, and she dominated him. Her lover needed her, so she abandoned him.

She discovered that power over her lovers was as important as the lovemaking. She never stopped craving the act itself, but she found the true aphrodisiac was the man's need for her.

Life in Paris with her parents became intolerably restrictive. It was difficult being discreet, which she had to be to keep her parents from shipping her off to more celibate surroundings until a suitable marriage could be arranged. Fabienne despised having to hide her nature, not to mention all the jewels she was accumulating.

A visit to Bordeaux provided the answer. She and her father were visiting the prefect there when they received an invitation for a weekend at du Clocher.

Edouard, twenty years older than Fabienne, greeted her as he did all women—with polite indifference. It piqued and challenged her. She would seduce and discard him, to prove she could do it.

Her plan began to change over the long weekend. She was taken with du Clocher and what came with it. She could see herself there dressed in swirling silks, sweeping into the parlor, the object of every man's admiration and desire. She could see flirtation on the terrace and consummation in the garden. The château was her nature wrought in stone and wood and brocade and china.

And she would be a countess. Her father was wealthy from his manufacturing concern, still, he would always be bourgeois and merely tolerated in the best of salons, if invited at all. The Countess Saint-Savin, on the other hand, would be invited to the most spectacular balls and would be welcomed at the most fashionable soirees. Men of power would be available to her, to be reduced to beggars by her, as they grovelled for her favors.

Edouard was outmatched from the start. Fabienne overwhelmed him and a marriage was soon arranged, although both she and her parents were disappointed that Edouard insisted the wedding be held in the small church at St. Julien rather than a cathedral in Paris. It was one of the few times Fabienne did not get her way.

Married life was all Fabienne had imagined. On his part, Edouard had no concept of what marriage should be, his mother having died when he was a baby and his father never remarrying. Fabienne was a fine hostess and that was what really mattered to him. He was quite blind to her dalliances, which soon had the Maconais matrons twittering in dismay. The men, on the other hand, took no part in the gossip, hoping that they, too, might someday be the cause of it.

None of Fabienne's lovers lasted longer than a month. The excitement was in the conquest. She had Edouard to take care of her sexual needs on a regular basis, although he was not one for experimenting.

This idyll lasted for little more than a year. Then Fabienne became snappish and out of sorts and finally furious when she was told she was pregnant. Edouard thought the anger must be one of those strange female reactions; they could act so strangely even when they weren't with child. He would have never guessed Fabienne's anger came from the restrictions that carrying a baby put on her. How could she make conquests when she was fat, bloated, and vomiting?

Not even the sight of a sweet-faced baby boy changed her attitude toward motherhood. She quickly relegated all care of the baby to Gaston Mazet's wife and returned to her romantic intrigues once she was able to fit back into her clothes. But she found it wasn't the same. Being made love to by a hard-muscled general among the roses while her husband pontificated on the terrace above their heads about the merits of an 1824 versus an 1825 no longer aroused her. She was restless. Being countess had opened her life in some ways and limited her world in others.

So it was that one day she entered her husband's library dressed for travel.

"I've decided to live in Paris for part of the year," she announced matter-of-factly. "I will need money for suitable accommodations and servants. You wouldn't want the name of Saint-Savin besmirched by my living in squalor, would you?"

Edouard made a half-hearted effort at dissuading his wife, although he sensed that was futile from the beginning. Besides, Edouard was afraid to alienate her. He might not have been her best lover, she was far and away his. He did not want to lose her sexual ministrations. He knew that refusing her would mean that.

There was no mention of her taking the baby. Nor was his name— Guy—ever spoken.

Edouard was extremely generous, buying Fabienne a house in the most fashionable district of the capital, supplying her with a queenly monthly allowance, and, of course, keeping her cellar well-stocked with bottles from du Clocher and other Bordelaise vineyards. Fabienne would have been sought after by Parisian society for that cellar alone.

As much money as Edouard provided, she asked for more. He sold Saint-Savin property and holdings to keep up with her demands. And still it wasn't enough. A bedroom had to be converted to an enormous closet for her clothes, and soon even that was inadequate. She entertained frequently and lavishly, traveled extensively, and was always adorned with marvelous jewels, although never so marvelous that they diverted attention from her own beauty.

When Edouard couldn't keep up with her demands, Fabienne found her own ways to finance the extravagances. There was always some baron or banker, marquis or minister, eager to present her with little somethings—sapphires, diamonds, horses, laces—in hopes of gaining entrance to her favors. One old duke even left her a mansion at one end of the Champs Elysées in appreciation for her attention. She refurbished it to extraordinary if a bit overdone elegance through the generosity of one of King Louis-Philippe's most trusted advisers. In return she promised him he would be the first to visit the private chambers.

Those chambers, the bedroom in particular, were widely discussed in the parlors of Paris. It was said, and correctly so, that Fabienne had a bed constructed that was three times the size of an ordinary one. It sat on a raised platform that was slightly tilted so that she could, if she wished, observe what was happening on the street below.

Fabienne rarely went back to du Clocher. Her life in Paris was too full. She might have stopped going altogether except for one unfortunate miscalculation on her part. Fabienne had the temerity to seduce one of Louis-Philippe's sons, a married man. This so enraged the good Queen Marie-Amelie that Fabienne found it best to quit the capital and return to playing countess at du Clocher.

Edouard was delighted. On the other hand, Guy, a beanpole of a five-year-old, was bewildered and dismayed. The first time he was told to kiss the extravagant creature everyone said was his mother, he ran out of the room sobbing.

Fabienne had thought three, maybe four months in exile would be sufficient. Her stay stretched much further when she found she was again pregnant. It was a girl, this time, a girl in whom Fabienne took as much interest as she had the boy, a girl Edouard named Solange, after his mother.

Four months after the baby's birth, Fabienne said she had to attend to some business in Paris. Edouard accompanied her. Within a week Fabienne ascertained she was no longer persona non grata in the court, and Edouard went back to du Clocher, alone.

"I did not come here to discuss the state of Solange's virginity," Nathan was saying.

"Then what did you come for? To beg for my advice on how she can lose it? Has age robbed you of your powers of seduction? Are you impotent or senile?"

"That's enough, Fabienne." Fabienne knew that tone and knew it was enough. "I came with a request which I now change to an order. We will be attending Napoleon's next party at Compiègne. You are not to attend. Under no circumstances do I want you there. I don't trust what you will say or do with Solange."

Fabienne wanted to defy him, remind him that no man gave her orders. She didn't. For two reasons. One, she would have never attended anyway. She rarely went out in the daylight now. And in the evenings she only went places where the lighting was kind, where she could stage-direct her appearances, and never grow old. She dined only in dimly lit restaurants. She drove with her carriage curtains drawn. She arrived late at the opera, after the lights had dimmed, and left early before they were raised. No, a week of Compiègne's unflattering sun would not be acceptable to Fabienne.

And the second reason—she was afraid of Nathan, afraid that if it ever mattered enough to him, he could control her and not she him. Fabienne could not run that risk.

"Well," she said, "I can only guess at what intrigues you have planned for Compiègne, and, quite frankly, I'm happy to leave you to them. The thought of a week with that red-haired prig, our most exalted empress Eugenie, leaves me quite cold. However, as long as I'm going to bestow this favor of my absence on you, you might grant me a favor in return."

"And what would that be?" Nathan asked suspiciously.

"You must tell me if it's true, that Napoleon only married that Spanish social climber because she refused him before the vows were said."

"From what I understand, she's more or less refusing him still."

Fabienne favored him with her most fabulous smile. "You've made me very happy, Nathan. I've refrained from entertaining Louis since his wedding. Now I shan't. I've missed him. He's almost as good as you."

Chapter Thirty-eight

"Can't I interest you in a bit more wine?"

Nathan and Solange were on the terrace at du Clocher, finishing their lunch. Solange had said little during the meal, instead she stared out at the fields as if she were already there, walking the rows, consulting with Mazet. She had been like that since their return from Paris, intent on the grapes, ignoring all else.

"I really don't understand how anyone could eat a meal without some wine... yes, Henri?"

Nathan's valet had come out through the french doors. He bowed slightly, a mannerism he refused to give up although Nathan often asked him to stop.

"Baron, baroness, the fitters have arrived."

His announcement broke through Solange's concentration. "What fitters?" she asked. "Are you adding to your wardrobe, Nathan?"

"No, my dear. Yours."

Solange bristled with annoyance. "I don't need any clothes. I don't need any more than I have. They suit me fine and suit du Clocher fine. I've told you that."

Nathan frowned. It was time for him to own up to what he had been planning.

"True, no one is going to find it odd, your running around du Clocher in your robes de jeune. However, Louis's court at Compiégne will find it worthy of comment that the Baroness Libermann is dressed like a Marseilles fishmonger. Henri, escort the tailors to the baroness's chambers. We will be with them shortly."

Henri bowed and left. He had little doubt his master would win in the end, he only wondered how long the struggle would last.

"I believe I shall have some of that wine now," Solange said, snapping her words like shots from a pistol. "Thank you. Now please explain what you meant about Compiégne."

232

Solange, too, over the years had become aware of Nathan's power of persuasion although he did not usually turn it on her. She also knew that when she eventually gave in to her husband, it would be on her terms.

Nathan stood, glass in hand, and started to walk the length of the terrace. Halfway down, he stopped. "You know I admire you very much, my dear..."

Solange, in fact, knew that but blushed slightly at the revelation.

"...and in admiring you, I have made extreme efforts not to interfere with you. You have not allowed me to help you financially. You have asked me only for the most inconsequential bits of advice. You've even spurned my shoulder as a suitable place to cry on. I have accepted this. I can accept it no longer. I must interfere. I must use my influence to help you. And if I have to stand here talking until next week, I will make you see the wisdom of this."

"All right, I accept whatever help you can give me," Solange said simply.

Nathan was thrown off balance. He had a whole strategy planned and she was accepting his offer before he had a chance to implement it.

"You don't know what I'm proposing," he protested.

"Don't you want me to accept?" Solange asked mischievously. Before he could answer she continued in a more serious tone. "I'm willing to admit I have mishandled many things since...since my father died. I wanted to do everything myself, in my way." She reached into her pocket and pulled out an envelope. "I received this letter from Guy. He has a vineyard, in California. He's already planted. He thinks, given time, the wine will be good. He's found a market. He's succeeding. He, who had nothing, is succeeding. I had everything given to me, and what have I been doing? Destroying the best vineyard in Bordeaux."

Solange was as close to tears as Nathan had ever seen her. He rushed back, pulled her from her chair, and shook her.

"You are not a failure. Now listen. The wine is as good—better than ever. The château is running smoothly. You have, against all odds, defied everyone and established a successful way to market your wine. All that you lack is the guile and the ability to manipulate circumstances and people."

He dropped his hands, wishing to himself she could always be without those traits.

"And that's why," he continued, "it's time to let me help. You're going to meet Louis. You're going to meet Eugenie. And you're going to meet all those fashionable and influential people who carry more weight in this country than they should. You're going to charm them and you're going to win their admiration. And you're going to make sure these petty Bordelaise negociants will never try to trick you again lest they bring upon themselves the wrath of your friends."

She looked so forlorn, Nathan had to embrace her, wanting to give her strength, wanting her to believe, in the future, in him. They stood cheek to cheek, each in a confusion of thoughts and emotions. Solange turned her head slightly toward Nathan, her lips brushing gently across his face until they met his. Involuntarily Nathan held her closer and he was kissing her.

There was noise behind them. Solange pulled away, flustered.

Henri had stepped out onto the terrace without seeing them. When he realized what he had broken up, he could have kicked himself.

"Sir... madame... I'm so sorry... I didn't mean to interrupt...."

Solange retreated to the balustrade, her back to the men. Nathan looked at her with longing, then with a harshness he had not intended, he said, "There was nothing to interrupt. We were discussing an upcoming trip."

Once again, the perfect butler, Henri said, "Yes sir. Madame, the tailors are set up and ready." He exited at once.

Solange was at the table again, sipping her wine. Nathan joined her.

"I took the liberty of instructing Alexander to design a suitable wardrobe for Compiègne," Nathan said as if nothing had happened. "He had your measurements from our visit to Paris. I knew you would have no patience for going back there for fittings so I had him send his tailors here. Do you mind?"

"I trust you, Nathan."

Chapter Thirty-nine

If she had to be truthful, pushed to be under great duress, Solange might have admitted she enjoyed the activity in the days that followed. The hours were completely filled with fittings and packing and bustling back to Paris.

She'd been startled by what Nathan considered the bare necessities for the week in Compiègne. But when they arrived at the railway station to embark on Louis's private train, her four trunks, five boxes specially constructed for crinolines, seven portemanteaux, and half a dozen hatboxes were paltry next to what was arriving for the other ladies.

There seemed to be many people getting on the train, and Nathan seemed to know them all. Everyone stopped to greet him, most warmly, a few warily, and several of the women almost beyond the bounds of decency.

"Are these all guests for the week?" Solange whispered to Nathan when she had a chance.

He glanced around. "There'll be one or two more. It's to be a small gathering, I understand."

When they were escorted to their compartment, Solange was glad she had worn the narrowest of her dresses. Some of the women were so crinolined, Solange was not sure they would be able to get through the doorways.

Once seated, she asked Nathan, "Why do women wear these silly dresses? They stick out everywhere. How are we supposed to sit?"

"Solange, you'll never be a woman of fashion if you ask whys and hows. If it's fashion, you're supposed to wear it."

"But that's ridiculous!"

"Of course it's ridiculous. And these dresses are ridiculous. They hide a woman's form. And that's the very reason they exist. You may thank Eugenie, whom you will be meeting soon, for your discomfort. You see when the empress was with child the first time, she disliked losing her figure and seeing other women of the court showing off theirs. Having the supreme power over fashion as empress, Eugenie changed the fashion. She had her dresses designed to camouflage her form, and all other women, if they wished to be à la mode, had to follow suit."

"I guess I'm to be thankful Eugenie didn't fall in love with the costumes of the Hippodrome clowns."

The train's whistle blew and great clouds of steam billowed back from the engine as it strained fiercely to pull the many cars behind it.

Solange and Nathan were still alone in their compartment.

"Is there no one else coming in with us?" Solange asked.

"Louis knows I find traveling taxing enough without having to socialize as well, so I'm sure we will be left alone. I had Henri pack us a picnic. We can lunch quite undisturbed."

Solange slid her hand along the leather banquette to Nathan. He was bending over a large wicker basket the size of a small trunk and didn't see the movement. By the time he straightened up with a champagne bottle and two flutes, her hand was demurely back at her side. He set the glasses on his lap, and with great economy of movement, opened the champagne, careful to twist the bottle and not the cork. He filled a glass for Solange and handed it to her, then filled his, took a sip, and exhaled with appreciation.

"There is no replacing a fine Bordeaux, and yet champagne does have its place. Is there something wrong? Don't you want any?"

Solange hadn't taken a taste. Before this she hadn't allowed herself any time to doubt or worry. Now, with each turn of the train's wheels, she was closer to uncertainty.

"Nathan, I'm not sure I can do this."

"Do what? Drink champagne? I've seen you do it, and do it well, many times in the past."

"No, I mean this whole thing. This week with the court. I've never done anything like it before. I won't know what to talk about. The women, they're all so grand and elegant. I'll be out of place...I'll make a fool of myself."

She was agitated for admitting her fears and agitated for having them. Nathan could see that and he would have loved to have said, fine, let's not do it then, let's go back to du Clocher and forget all this nonsense. For her sake, he couldn't. She was filled with self-recriminations and doubts about du Clocher. She could banish them this week. And besides, she needed to get away from her cloister. Nathan had thought about his meeting with Fabienne and about the moment he had held Solange on the terrace. His wife needed a husband. She was ready. If matters continued between them as they were going, she might come to him by default. Nathan would never have that. Besides, he was an honorable man, and because of the terms under which he had entered into their marriage, his honor would not allow him to take advantage of her. Solange would meet men, other men, young men, this week. She needed that.

"Listen to me, my dear. You are incapable of making a fool of yourself. You'll be charming. You'll enchant all the men and make all the women jealous...."

"I wouldn't want to do that," Solange said quickly and then reddened. "Not that I could."

Nathan was always so amazed at how unaware she was of her beauty. It was an endearing quality.

"I know these people," he continued. "Most of them are stupid posturers, and not worthy of you. There are a few interesting ones. I will introduce you to them all, and save you from the worst. You'll gain support where it's important and get the injustice of that stupid classification undone."

There had been little talk of the classification before this.

"How could they do it?" Solange asked bitterly. "How could they justify putting du Clocher in the fourth cru?"

Nathan looked past Solange. The city was turning to country. Trees and cottages replaced streets and buildings. Curious peasants gawked and disappeared. The real world was in that compartment. All else was a remote, unimportant blur outside the window.

"Because you completely lack deviousness," Nathan said, "it's not surprising you didn't anticipate what happened or figured out what they did. I, on the other hand, have a fair measure of chicanery. It was simple. Schroeder changed his records for the last ten years and gave the classification committee false figures. Oh, of course, they knew they were false, but if challenged, they could point to the figures as their justification for the ranking."

Solange shook her head not in anger but with contempt for herself. "I am stupid. It was so easy for them. He probably changed the amount sold as well as the price. This made du Clocher look insignificant."

"What's done is done. Now we must work to rectify the wrong. And for that you'll need influential friends—whom you are about to meet.

Now come, have an oeuf gelée. Food will brighten your spirits and champagne will give you confidence."

An hour later, as she tried to navigate the narrow corridor to the conveniences, Solange was thinking it wasn't so much confidence she needed as a sharp secateur to prune off inches of material from her crinoline. If women were going to continue wearing these awful dresses, men would have to construct wider aisles and entrances.

As the train swayed, Solange was carried along with it, feeling like a bell ready to sound. One bend in the track caught her off guard, causing her to fall heavily against a compartment door.

It swung open. Trying to regain her balance, Solange teetered in the doorway. With her equilibrium back, she realized she wasn't alone.

"Oh, I am sorry..." she started to apologize but couldn't go on when what she was witnessing finally registered in her mind. Even then it wasn't as if she were seeing the entire tableau. She was picking out and focussing on sections of the canvas and not seeing the entire picture.

There was a woman's head, thrown back, face flushed, mouth agape. The back of a man's head, bent to the woman, now pulling away. The woman's breast, exposed, cupped by his hand. The man rising from his perch on the woman's lap. His turning to Solange, trousers open, his erect, engorged member pointing accusingly at her. And then there was nothing else, only that *thing* aiming at her.

"Come in and join us," the man invited politely.

Solange jerked her gaze upwards. He had a small pointy beard, a Van Dyke she thought it was called. He wasn't unhandsome in a satanic way. And, oh God, what was she doing standing there with an aroused man, a half-naked woman, and an invitation to an orgy or worse?

Solange tugged her dress back into the passageway and fled, only half aware of the titian-haired woman, in the adjoining compartment, sitting straight and prim and reading a book, quite oblivious of the carnality next door.

Solange lunged back into her own compartment, slammed the door shut, and leaned against it.

Nathan looked up from his book.

"Did you have trouble finding the conveniences? My goodness, what is wrong. You're trembling."

"Nathan, you've got to promise, you must promise..."

"Anything, of course."

"... you have to stay close to me this weekend. Right by my side."

The depot near Compiégne was a flurry of magnificent women being handed into carriages, servants frantically loading luggage onto wagons, polite chatting, raucous laughter, and charged expectation of the week to come.

When the long caravan left the station, it made its slow way through fields and woods until it finally stopped in front of a splendid palace. Then the process of the station was reversed, women alighting, valets and maids unloading, a gay chitter-chatter as palace servants escorted guests to their appointed suites and chambers.

Solange and Nathan were escorted to a suite of rooms in the west wing, elaborately decorated with spring-colored silks and brocades. The butler who escorted them excused himself to go help their servants.

"Damn," Nathan muttered. "I should have thought of this before." The "this" being that while their suite had four rooms—a bath room, a dressing room, a sitting room, and a bedroom—there was only one bed.

"Why didn't I request a suite with two sleeping chambers?" Nathan berated himself out loud, even though inwardly he realized the oversight had been intentional. It was stupid, he knew, but it would have pricked his pride if Louis had found out he and Solange slept separately. Many married couples did, of course, still it would appear Nathan had to make an appointment to have his wife. If only Louis knew the truth.

"It doesn't matter, Nathan. And trying to change our rooms now would be next to impossible. Arranging for this many people must have been like planning a major battle."

Nathan didn't argue, instead he inspected the suite, hands clasped behind his back. Louis had done well by them. There were only two other sets of rooms that equalled this in grandeur, and they belonged to Louis and Eugenie.

"My dear, our problem is solved," he called upon entering the dressing room. There was a leather couch with curved arms, not unlike a sleigh bed.

"I shall sleep on this."

Solange followed him in. "No, no. Let me. This is cozy like my room at home."

"There will be no argument. I insist, as a gentleman, and besides to do otherwise would make me feel like a decrepit old man who has to be treated like a baby."

"You, old? Never. You're ageless..." She stopped, afraid of overstepping her bounds. Nathan was laughing as he walked back to the sitting room and didn't hear her add "...and wonderful."

Solange had thought Nathan overly extravagant when he insisted on bringing Lise. After all, she had pointed out, Henri was coming and why did they need two servants along?

"Two is terribly inadequate," Nathan had tried to explain. "You should have at least two more besides Lise to help you with your toilette plus a hairdresser plus a seamstress for alterations, and a sixth for cleaning the wardrobe. But we will make do. Lise is quite handy, and if she can't do a proper hairstyle for you, I'll hire a hairdresser away from one of the other guests."

Now, having been at Compiegne for a mere two hours, it was time to prepare for the first night's festivities, and Solange had changed her opinion about how much help was needed. Getting ready for the ball—there would be one every night, plus hunts during the day—was turning into a monumental endeavor which Nathan was taking delight in supervising.

First there was her bath. Steaming hot water in a gleaming clawfoot tub. Lise had added perfumes and flower petals, and Nathan had ordered Solange to soak for a good half hour.

She refused to allow Lise to towel her off—saying she was quite capable of doing that alone—but was willing to leave the rest of the dressing to her servant after she saw what she was expected to wear. It was somewhat akin to reconstructing a Chinese puzzle, one layer on another on another starting with a pantaloonlike undergarment that was pegged and gathered under her knees. There were stockings and corset and shoes, three petticoats, two crinolines, and all this before Lise had taken the dress from the armoire.

It was a beautiful evening gown. Nathan had had a hand in its design. "You must shine, my dear, but you must not outshine our empress," he had said.

It was white organdy embroidered with bouquets of pale flowers and encrusted with jewels. It hugged her tightly at the waist before billowing into layers of draped skirt. It took Lise twenty minutes to do up the glittery buttons on the back. The hairdresser, whom Nathan merely had to borrow, arranged her hair in a classic Greek upsweep so Solange's long, curving neck was accented. The neckline curved downward revealing a hint of decolletage. Nathan kept having Lise pull it down more then back up. He couldn't be satisfied.

Finally he asked, "Why am I fussing? Your ensemble is not complete."

He went into the dressing room and rooted around in one of his valises. He returned carrying a long wooden box. He opened the top and held it out to Solange. Its contents made her gasp. "They're magnificent," was all she could manage. Before her, displayed on red velvet, was a glorious necklace of diamonds and sapphires with earrings to match.

"Put them on, put them on," Nathan urged. "I always thought sapphire would suit you."

"I couldn't. What if I lost them?"

"What if you did? I'd buy you another. Besides, they're yours now. If you want to throw them out the window, do so. I have others for you."

"But, Nathan, this is too expensive a gift..."

"There is no arguing this, my dear. You insist on upholding the name and reputation of du Clocher. Well, I have a certain responsibility to the name of Libermann. Why, if my wife wasn't wearing the finest jewels, the court might start wondering if some catastrophe had befallen the family. And if they start wondering that, they might start worrying about the solvency of poor Jerome's bank. Start that worry and you start a run. Start a run and the bank fails. The Banque Libermann fails and the entire nation is thrown into economic ruin— all because you refused to wear my present."

"All right, all right." Solange was weak from laughter and the tight corset. "I now see that it's my patriotic duty to wear these jewels. I only wish I could sit down in this dress."

"Ah ha! And it is also your duty to your sex to suffer for fashion and beauty. That's the curse of being a woman. There." He adjusted the necklace. "You're perfect. Poor Eugenie. She shall be eclipsed tonight."

Chapter Forty

Solange tightened her grip on Nathan's arm. She had never seen such magnificence. The ballroom, ten steps below them, could have held the entire main floor of du Clocher.

From their vantage point under the colonnaded balcony that ran around the ballroom on three sides, Solange watched the brilliantly colored and glittering spectacle, washed in the light of one thousand candles.

"You said this was to be a small party," she whispered to Nathan.

"What's that? I couldn't hear you."

The cacophony of baritone conversation and soprano twittering competing with the orchestra that was playing diagonally across from them made shouting a necessity.

"I said," Solange tried again, "I thought this was supposed to be a small party."

Nathan surveyed the scene, did a quick count, and answered, "But it is, my dear, there can't be more than one hundred here, at most."

And then Nathan proceeded to introduce her to everyone of them, or so it seemed to her. Nathan knew everyone, had a word for everyone, and was basking in the unabashed admiration the men showed for his wife. Solange was quite curious about some of the women's attitudes toward her husband. They were almost possessive, she thought.

When they weren't meeting people, they danced, took food from one of the eleven tables offering pheasant and beef, patés and crudités, fish and boar, chicken and ecrévisses. One sip from their wine glasses and a servant was refilling them. Then it was more dancing and greeting and the ball wore on.

It was well into the early hours of the morning when Solange begged for relief.

"I don't think I can dance one more step, smile at one more duke, or take one more sip. Please, I must retire before I drop."

"Then I will retire, as well. Wait here for twenty seconds. I promise to return immediately. I must have a word with Baroness Dupin."

The baroness had sent an insistent note to Nathan earlier. She had been desolate without him, the note read, and demanded he appear in her chamber that night, otherwise she would be forced to do something drastic. Nathan needed to charm her out of making a scene and certainly could not do so in front of Solange.

Solange didn't want to be left standing alone, but felt she would look like a child if she objected. So she stood at the edge of the dance floor, clutching her champagne flute, eyes stretched wide to ward off numbing fatigue. She could see Nathan was having an animated conversation. She really knew so little about Nathan. When she realized she wouldn't mind eavesdropping, she was annoyed with herself and turned away as if not seeing them would wipe away her curiosity. In doing so she saw she was being observed—by the man from the train. She had looked for him, hoping not to find him, all evening. And now, there he was, staring at her with obvious interest. Fearful he might think *she* was trying to catch *his* eye, she turned back to the dance floor. She did not see the bearded man motion to a captain of the palace guard. The man did nothing more than nod in Solange's direction, and the officer immediately started toward her.

She was drifting to the dancers, on one hand loathing to be farther from Nathan, on the other anxious to distance herself from the staring Satan.

The officer had almost reached her when he spotted a young lieutenant, also of the guard, who was watching the scene unfold with undisguised contempt. The captain scowled. Who did that puppy think he was, judging a captain like that? The scowl metamorphosed into a smirk. He would teach him a lesson.

"Lieutenant," the captain called across the din.

The younger man moved effortlessly through the crowd. "Sir?"

"That young woman—" The captain pointed at Solange. "You know what you're to do."

"I thought that was *your* duty, sir." He drawled the last word, leaving no doubt it was said as a formality and not as a sign of respect.

"I'm making it yours. Do you wish to argue?"

Arguing with a commanding officer, especially a dolt like this one, was futile, so the lieutenant shrugged and reluctantly approached Solange.

"Mademoiselle," he said stiffly, startling her. She spun around as fast as the crinolines and gravity allowed and faced a tall, dark-haired man who would have been extremely handsome if his dark eyes weren't so angry.

"Madame," she corrected automatically.

"Madame," he said, making it sound like an insult, "*He* will see you later in his chamber."

She was sure she had misheard over the noise. "I don't understand. Who are you talking about?"

"Come, madame, surely this needs no explanation. You have been beckoned. Like every other woman in France, it would seem, you will comply."

The lieutenant's stiff insolence overcame any fear Solange might have had of making some sort of irreversible faux pas.

"I repeat. I don't know what you're talking about. And unless this 'He' to whom you're referring is my husband, I would kindly request you to stop ordering me to his bedchamber."

The lieutenant stared over her head, his disgust for his assignment all too apparent. "I have no taste for playing the procurer," he said. "I have been ordered to do this by my superior. Why make things difficult for me? Your presence has been requested. If you're worried about your husband, I'm sure, like so many other husbands, it can be arranged for him to be sent out of the country on a delicate mission of national importance."

"You are rude, insufferable, boorish..." There were several more adjectives Solange wanted to include, but she was forestalled by a delighted cry behind her.

"Thierry! What a nice surprise. I see you've met my wife." It was Nathan and he was heartily thumping the lieutenant on the back. "We were about to leave the festivities. Why don't you join Solange and me in our suite? Have a cognac, a chance to talk. What am I saying? You undoubtedly have some beautiful young woman you're escorting and couldn't possibly tear yourself away from the dancing."

"No, Uncle Nathan..."

"Uncle?" Solange was looking from man to man hoping for an explanation, but both were too engrossed in each other to notice.

"...I'm on duty."

"Duty? I thought you were leading charges in the Crimea."

Thierry frowned. "My father thought it too risky for a Libermann to be so close to the front. He had me transferred to the emperor's guard."

"And let me guess. He did this without consulting you."

"And when has my father consulted me on anything? You know I entered the military to escape his influence..."

"And you discovered that directly or indirectly the Libermann name cannot be escaped. Be honest, though, would you have gone so far without it? Now wait, I don't mean to insult your abilities, but be realistic. The French military is less than hospitable towards someone of our..."

"I know what you're getting at." The lieutenant shrugged his defeat. "I may be naive, uncle, but it quite amazes me. I, who have never thought about religion, never felt I had one and didn't care for one, suddenly find that being a Jew is forced upon me. Yes, you're right. There is anti-Semitism in the army and it would have taken me longer—if ever—to get promotions if I hadn't been Thierry Libermann. But I'll tell you something. Those men I led in the Crimea, they didn't care if my family was Jewish, Buddhist, or Baalist. They respected me because I was a good officer. And then, it was gone. All that I worked for wasted because Father wanted once again to demonstrate his power. And now I wear a fancy uniform and stand around like a trained monkey at the emperor's beck and bidding."

Solange became increasingly uneasy with the conversation and wanted to leave. She had no desire to sympathize with the arrogant young man, even if he was Nathan's nephew. She gave a discreet squeeze to her husband's arm.

"Well, we must talk about this more," Nathan said, picking up Solange's signal. "For now, though, I must take my exhausted Solange upstairs."

Until that moment, Thierry had quite forgotten his mission. He glanced around and saw the captain still watching.

"Uncle Nathan." This was going to be very difficult for Thierry. He had no wish to insult his uncle. "This is quite awkward, but I was sent over to speak to this woman... your wife, I mean... without knowing who she was... your wife, I mean."

"Sent? By whom?"

"Well, indirectly... through a superior officer... by orders of..."

Nathan waved for him to stop his misery. "Yes, I understand. '*He* would like to see you in a half hour'? Something along that line? Solange, I'm afraid you've gotten a most unfortunate introduction, albeit indirect, to Louis. It was the emperor who originated the request, wasn't it?"

Thierry nodded glumly.

"And you must do something?"

Thierry nodded again.

"Stop your worrying. I'll take care of it. Here, dance with Solange. I'll be right back."

Solange started after him, then remembered the strange staring man, and decided the lesser of two undesirables was Thierry.

"Shall we?" he asked politely.

"Shall we what?" she snapped. "Insult me some more? Being Nathan's nephew does not absolve you from your rude behavior."

Thierry would have snapped back at her except for one thing—she was right.

"I apologize," he said instead. "I was taking my anger out on a stranger. I had no right to assume your reaction. But I've seen how most women behave, and I find it appalling." He held up his hands in invitation. It was not so much her changing her mind as the hypnotic pulse of the dancers around them that moved Solange into Thierry's arms. He gathered her up and took control. She didn't like it. She didn't like having to look up to him, feeling small in his arms, being carried along. She didn't like his strong chiseled features or his dark, expressive eyes. She didn't like him. Then the music took over and nothing else mattered as Solange was caught up in the flow and the delight of the dance.

Nathan made his way to the balcony trying not to be waylaid by friends at every step. Louis watched his progress and gave an almost imperceptible nod to the guards who were discreetly ringing him. They let Nathan through.

"So my friend," the emperor said with the slow German accent that many of his subjects ridiculed him for, "I see you at last. What witchcraft has this Bordelaise wench of yours woven? You've become a reformed man, I understand."

Nathan accepted a glass of champagne from a liveried servant. "Reformed? That would suggest there was something wrong with my previous behavior. Shall we instead say 'changed'? My life has *changed* somewhat. You, on the other hand, would seem to have changed little."

"Oh, no, Nathan." Louis was so slow-speaking that some people on first meeting him assumed he was likewise slow-witted. "The empire, the empress, they have made a difference. There is so little time for the flirtations and the chase anymore."

"But still time for the finale," Nathan observed dryly.

"There are certain things that never change."

"So, one of the fringe benefits of the imperial throne is you now send emissaries to the women of your fancy. And the mere thought of the emperor conveniently makes them swoon."

Louis focussed his deep-set eyes on his friend, searching for hidden meanings, then drawled, "We are discussing some one in particular, perhaps?"

Nathan laughed. "You know why we've gotten along so well over the oh-so-many years? I'll tell you why. We both jump over several steps in the thought process, dispense with beating around the bush, and come right to the point. Yes, my insatiable friend, there is a particular one."

Louis scanned the dance floor. "Not that delightful chestnut filly? You spotted her first? Your taste has run the gamut, but never to the cradle."

He looked back to the dance floor. "Isn't that your nephew she's dancing with? Now, Nathan, it's up to the young buck to keep her. If she wishes to come to me instead, so be it."

"Louis, send one of your minions to troll them in. Introductions are in order."

It took little time for Thierry and Solange to be summoned and escorted to the balcony. At the top of the stairs Solange suddenly grabbed Thierry's arm.

"I can't go over there." She was panicked.

"Why not?" Thierry was surprised by her loss of composure and courage.

"That man, the one with the pointy beard, I met him... I saw him on the train... he was on, with a woman and he wanted me... no, no, no, I won't go over there."

"But you must. That's the emperor. That's Louis-Napoleon." He extricated his arm and nudged her forward.

Nathan had seen Solange's reaction. "Louis, have you met the young woman before? Perhaps on the train?"

"Perhaps."

"This gets more convoluted," Nathan said. "Come here, my dear. Louis, I'm sure she can dispense with the curtseying. Solange let me introduce you to Louis-Napoleon, emperor. Louis, this is Solange, the Baroness Solange Libermann, née Saint-Savin."

Louis was obviously having trouble with the relationship as implied by the name. He looked questioningly at Thierry.

"No," Nathan said quickly, realizing the emperor's assumption.

"No, no, she is *my* wife. I'm the Libermann she's married to."

The emperor threw back his head and laughed, causing many heads to turn with curiosity, and making the foursome an object of much speculation.

"So this is the Bordelaise. Much becomes clear." Louis clicked his heels and bowed over the hand of an astonished Solange. "I am absolutely charmed and honored at last to meet the conqueror of my friend's heart and devotion. She is superb, Nathan, absolutely superb. I would have expected no less."

If the emperor chose to ignore their previous meeting in the train, so would Solange. And if he were going to overlook that she was a Saint-Savin, all the better. She would begin her mission at once. She would make the emperor aware of du Clocher.

"The honor is mine, your highness." She curtseyed prettily. "I have so longed to meet you." Nathan raised his eyebrows at the lie. Solange ignored him. "Of course, you've been so busy with affairs of state, and we've been so busy with the vineyard."

"Yes, that's right, you have a wine. Which is it?"

"Du Clocher," Solange was quick to answer. "It truly ranks with Lafitte and Latour for body and character. And you'll not find a more subtle and deep bouquet in any other Bordeaux. It is a wine of great distinction."

"And you, Nathan, do you agree? Is that a fair description of the wine?"

"I have never found my wife wrong when it comes to wine. Her palate is without equal."

"That is a tremendous testimonial. For Nathan is a great connoisseur of fine wines. We must discuss this further, at a quieter occasion."

Nathan knew that Louis, having lost his quarry in Solange, would want to aim his sights at some other entertainment to pass the rest of the night. He also knew that nothing more need be said between them about Solange. Louis would under no circumstances approach the wife of Nathan Libermann again. And Nathan Libermann was probably the only man in the empire with a beautiful wife who could say that. Noticing the whispered attention being concentrated on Solange, he wondered if anyone else in that vast ballroom was aware of that fact.

Louis dropped his robe—he was naked underneath it—and got into the bed beside his wife. She awoke at the movement and gave out a small cry of distress.

"Your highness, what are you doing here?"

Louis answered by running his hand over her breast. She pushed him away.

"Please, stop. You know I'm pregnant. You don't want to do anything to harm the baby?"

Louis sat up in disgust. "Eugenie, you know the doctors say that making love would not harm the child."

She sat up as well, hugging her blankets to use them as shields against further advances. "Oh, they don't know. Only I know. And besides, it's a blasphemy, it's against God to partake in carnality while I am the vessel carrying the future emperor of France. Would you incur the wrath of God with this child after I miscarried the last?"

Louis knew there was no use saying more. As he tied the belt of his robe, he wondered about all those stories of Eugenie, the sexual adventuress. He wondered if she had started them herself to pique his interest. He gave a deep sigh and let himself out of her room into the hallway.

Louis couldn't be angry at Eugenie. It was his own fault, marrying the temptress without sampling her first. He had found her refusal challenging and had dismissed her occasional religious prattle as part of her play-acting. He had been so sure that underneath the camouflage of the morally proper and religious woman was the wanton creature she was said to be.

After months of flirtation and courtship, Louis had wanted her more than any other woman in his life. Chancing upon her unexpectedly he would get so hard and erect he wanted to scream with pain. He had paid a king's ransom to her maid for a snip of her pubic hair. He carried it next to his heart, and in the privacy of his room sniffed it, imagining the intoxicating scent of her womanhood.

He hadn't been totally disappointed after their marriage. There were times, when she had too much wine, that she became insatiable. Those times were rare, even though Louis had ordered the servants to always keep her glass filled.

Louis-Napoleon pursed his lips and exhaled with disgust. Why had the glorious creature at the ball had to have been Nathan's wife? It was too late to get someone else, and he needed someone.

Louis walked down the corridor, not caring about the horror his guards, who were around the corner in front of his door, would have if they found him wandering about unprotected. Louis cared only for relief just then and would have gladly given his life for it.

The unmistakable sounds of love-making stayed his progress. Louis frowned, trying to remember who had been assigned the room whose door he was standing at. It was Carlotta, one of Eugenie's ladies of the court and her husband, Giscard Simon, one of Louis's ministers. Carlotta and Louis had had several mutually enjoyable encounters in recent months.

Quietly Louis slipped into the room. A lone candle on the mantle gave off enough light for Louis to see. The groans of excitement were coming from the minister. He was on his back with a pillow clutched over his face as he fought to prolong his pleasure. Between his legs, the lovely, naked Carlotta was kneeling, working him with her mouth, up and down, up and down. Her buttocks were raised and the invitation proved too much for Louis. He dropped his robe and was on the bed, thrusting himself into her. She gasped and came away from her husband far enough to see who had taken such wanton yet welcome advantage of her vulnerability. She laughed with delight.

A muffled, "What is it, darling?" came from under the pillow, but Carlotta's mouth had again engulfed the minister and he could think of nothing else. Then she and Louis began to rock in unison, she working her husband, Louis working her until a moment of crescendo and three ecstatic screams sounded at once.

Louis pulled himself free, got on his robe, and left.

The minister's face came out from under the pillow.

"Did you say something, Carlotta?"

Carlotta was incapable of saying anything.

Time passed quickly. The days were filled with stag hunts and shooting in the forest. At night, before the other festivities, there were torchlit *curées* when the dogs were allowed to tear at their share of the fallen deer while the guests cheered them on.

Nathan grumbled fiercely over the hunts. He found little enjoyment in them and greatly resented being made to wear—as all the gentlemen were—a green coat and silk stockings that came up over the knee.

"This is 1855 and the Second Empire, not 1655 and Louis XIV."

He put up with it all after receiving a personal note from the emperor. It was Eugenie's wish that the men dress so and seeing that the empress was with child, already having had that one miscarriage, would Nathan oblige the idiocy?

Solange found much of the week tedious and tiring. She longed for the times the emperor sought them out so that she could turn on her charm and extol the virtues of her wine. Nathan tried to include

Thierry in their party whenever possible, although the antipathy the two younger people felt for each other did not seem to abate.

An outing Solange did enjoy took place at midweek. An expedition was formed for a jaunt through the forest on *char-à-bancs* to visit the castle of Pierrefonds. The wagons, festooned with ribbons, carried them through the frosty air. Solange could have spent hours exploring the enormous fortress, built in 1400 by Louis of Orleans. She was sorry to get back into the wagon even though the ride coming out had been so enjoyable.

There were grogs and other refreshments waiting for them back at Compiègne. Solange excused herself briefly from Nathan to see about tidying her hair. It was when returning that she fell into step, unseen, several feet back from the Grandduchess Stephane of Baden and Regine Chassaing, an immensely wealthy heiress to a shipping firm.

The grandduchess was fairly sniffing with disdain. "No, I don't entirely approve of the empress," she was saying. "She's much too informal. I understand she even calls the emperor by his given name. Why the Empress Josephine would never have presumed calling the first emperor anything less than 'your majesty.' Still, I can't help feeling somewhat sorry for the empress with all these eager young things throwing themselves at her husband. Take that strumpet, you know who I mean. It's shameful the way she's always hovering around the emperor."

Her companion interrupted, "Really, grandduchess, I don't mean to defend the young woman. Still the emperor does have something of a reputation with the ladies."

"Granted, but it's tarts like that who tempt him. Well, she's made her intentions all too obvious. No matter how frivolous the empress might be, she won't stand for this type of blatant behavior. That young Bordelaise will soon find out how much influence the empress has, and I would be happy to be there when she does."

Solange stopped. They were talking about her. They thought she was trying to seduce the emperor. It was with great difficulty that she rejoined Nathan in the drawing room. She was sure everyone was staring at her and talking about her. She reluctantly accepted a mug of steaming grog from Nathan and finished it, scalding her mouth, in two enormous gulps.

"Is it the drink—which I must say, you finished quite quickly—or is it something else that has you so flushed?" Nathan asked her.

"We must talk. Not here."

"How would that bench do?" He led her to a corner, out of earshot of the others. "Now sit and tell me what is wrong. No one will hear."

Most of the party, almost all of the one hundred guests, were coming and going, circulating from the drawing room to another behind it to still a third across the hall. None seemed the least interested in interrupting Solange and Nathan.

"I want to leave." Solange was filled with intense urgency. "I've made a terrible mistake. I can't stay any longer."

"What have you done that's so terribly wrong?"

Solange groaned. "Oh, you don't know what they're saying about me. They're saying I'm a tart who threw herself at the emperor. Nathan, you know I was only trying to interest him in du Clocher, never in me."

"Perhaps it's time we discussed your tactics..."

"So you think I've erred—"

"—I think no such thing. I was going to make a suggestion at some point during the week. I think that time is now. It's a matter of a slight course adjustment. It's your aim to have du Clocher drunk at court, served to visiting dignitaries, in short, to be made fashionable?"

Of course that was her intent.

"Then I should point out that perhaps you're focussing your attention on the wrong person. It is the empress who makes the decisions for the household. I thought to let you practice your selling wiles on Louis. You'd ingratiate yourself with him, and then, when you were ready, have you turn to Eugenie. I should have realized that the gossiping old crones of the court, with no better way to spend their dried-up time would seize on your attention to Louis as proof of a dalliance. I've been away too long from these nasty little intrigues. I've forgotten what happens."

Solange couldn't look up to face even Nathan's sympathetic eyes. Her attention was riveted to her locked hands.

"I don't know how it happens. I always fail."

"Balderdash! This is no failure. I merely miscalculated. Listen, my dear, didn't we agree that you would take my counsel this once? It was I who made the mistake. I held back that counsel. But in my defense, I have already taken steps to rectify the blunder. I've arranged that we will join the empress and emperor for aperitifs. As a matter of fact, we have very little time to get dressed. So let us go."

Solange emitted a sigh of despair. She hated getting dressed each evening. Nathan ignored it and went on. "Louis and I will make it quite clear to Eugenie that you're not competition. As for you and Eugenie, I suggest you turn to her, a cosmopolitan woman of great fashion and taste—one is allowed to fib at times like this—a woman whose wise counsel you would humbly seek. And so forth. From what I've heard, she's not at all secure in her role as empress. The old-line aristocracy has not accepted her. I believe she'll warm up quickly if you approach her properly."

Nathan couldn't have been more accurate in his prediction, although Solange found it hard to believe the beautiful, red-haired empress could be insecure about anything.

The hour together went well. Nathan and Louis entertained the women with accounts—highly expurgated—of their travels together. And the emperor made a point of telling Nathan how happy he was with Nathan's marriage to Solange.

"I feel remiss not introducing you sooner to the baron and baroness," Louis said contritely to Eugenie, "but Nathan has rarely come to Paris since his marriage. I suspect he's too enamored with his bride, which could not make me more elated."

When the men engaged in a separate conversation, Solange followed Nathan's advice and presented herself to Eugenie as a wide-eyed girl, innocent in worldly ways, somewhat overwhelmed by the sophistication of the court, and hoping for counsel. After a few well-placed compliments, blushingly made, with Solange explaining she was not sure if the etiquette of the court allowed her to make them, Eugenie was entirely won over.

"Your excellency," she called to Louis.

Louis and Nathan hurried back to the women. "Please, in front of my friend Baron Libermann, we don't need formalities, do we?" the emperor asked.

"As you wish, Louis." Eugenie smiled. She liked this Libermann. He was not at all what she expected after the many stories she had heard. The empress allowed herself to pout for a second. And what of the stories that were told about her? Depending on who did the telling, she was anything from a wanton adventuress to a priggish nun. She must remember not to judge others by gossip. "I know that the guests have already been invited for our private party tonight, still I would like to make an addition."

"Dearest, may I remind you, you are the one who makes all guest lists. They are yours to revise."

All lists except for this particular week at Compiègne. It had been the one time Louis had insisted on including someone and that someone had been Baron Libermann. No wonder I became a bit suspicious of this engaging young girl, thought Eugenie. I suspected it was actually she that Louis wanted to include. Gossip. I'm letting nattering gossip affect my perspective.

"Well, then, it's settled," Eugenie said happily. "Several of us will be playing charades. I've had a stage especially prepared. We have no end of costumes to choose from. And you, Solange, you shall be on my team."

So it was that later that evening Solange found herself outfitted as one of the Muses along with Eugenie and a lady-in-waiting, acting out the first part of the word *musad*. And it was with great glee she later heard from Nathan that the Grandduchess Stephane of Baden had been thoroughly shocked by the entertainment.

Chapter Forty-one

Solange kept her eyes glued to the pages before her. She did not look up when the train stopped at stations. She did not acknowledge her traveling companion's leaving to pace the corridor outside the compartment. She resolutely read page after page and did her best to concentrate on the words before her.

She was seething.

By the end of the week in Compiègne, she had felt she'd accomplished much. The empress had been warm and indicated an invitation to the Tuileries would be forthcoming. Solange had not, for the good of the château, ever let slip her continued hatred towards the emperor—although she had finally admitted to Nathan that Louis was engaging and interesting, even if he was a tyrant. With all this done, Solange was anxious and eager to return to the harvest in Bordeaux.

And then Nathan had made his request. Would she mind if Thierry, who desperately needed to get away from his detested duties with the Palace Guard, accompanied her to du Clocher? She protested, vehemently. There would be no time for entertaining. She would be busy getting ready for the harvest. And she added to herself that nothing had changed her initial opinion of the nephew. He was arrogant, unpleasant, and too full of his own importance.

Nathan heard her out, then asked again. He cared very much for his nephew, and he knew Thierry needed to get away, away from Paris, away from the court, and away from Jerome's interference. In the end Solange could not say no, even after Nathan added it would be several days before he would be following them to Bordeaux.

So there she was, nose in a book, doing her best to ignore the oh-so-straight-and-tall, oh-so-immaculately-uniformed, oh-so-insufferably conceited scion to the richest banking family in Europe.

255

"Don't you find him slightly melodramatic?"

Solange dropped the book in surprise. She hadn't realized Thierry had come back. They both bent to pick up the book, hitting heads in the process, each getting a hand on the novel, leading to a near-comic tug-of-war. Solange let loose first, smoothed her dress, and tried to regain her dignity. She then held out her hand for the book. Instead of relinquishing it, Thierry leafed through the pages.

"Do you mean Dickens? Do I find Charles Dickens melodramatic?" Solange asked with what she hoped was adequate hauteur.

"That's who you're reading, isn't it? This is his new novel, *Bleak House*? Frankly, I found *The Old Curiosity Shop* one of the worst pieces of tear-jerking drivel ever written."

While Solange tended to agree with Thierry's appraisal of that particular book, she wasn't about to admit it.

"Perhaps you missed the nuances in the translation," she responded tartly.

"I didn't read a translation. I read it in English. And in any language I would find Dickens overdrawn, and, frankly, tremendously light fare. Is that your usual reading? Light fare? Perhaps you tend more to ladies' books?"

"I read everything," she flared. "Philosophy, poetry, politics, drama. Lightweight, heavyweight, dull, and turgid. I don't care. The written word is precious to me and ... Dickens isn't so bad," she finished lamely.

Thierry grinned. "You're right. *Nicholas Nickleby* was quite good. I deliberately picked Dickens's worst to provoke you."

Solange grabbed her book back, lowered her head, and resumed reading. Maybe Thierry would find Bordeaux extremely dull and go back to Paris and its parties and rouged women and leave her in peace. What was she going to do with him until Nathan arrived? She simply did not have time to entertain Lieutenant Thierry Libermann. What was she to do?

She would ignore him, that's what she would do.

She couldn't. Ignore him.

He was everywhere, shadowing, asking her questions. What was this for? Why did she do that? When would she know the grapes were ready? And when he wasn't with Solange, Thierry was after Jacques Mazet.

Nathan, quite deliberately, stayed away for several more days than he said he would. He continued to brood over his conversation with

Fabienne, over his selfishness in holding Solange in such an unnatural relationship. Then he came up with the idea of throwing her
and Thierry together if only to give Solange the experience of being
with a man closer to her own age. And if something did come of
it... he liked his nephew very much.

Day was reluctantly giving way to night when Nathan's carriage
pulled around the oval in front of du Clocher. Henri came out to meet
him.

"Is the baroness home?" Nathan asked, knowing full well that at
this time of year, Solange would not be away from the château.

"Yes, baron. She will be dining in another hour. Will you be
joining her?"

"Indeed, yes. That journey from Paris, with all the improvements
in the rail service, doesn't seem any less arduous. I'm so tired, I'm
going to dispense with changing. Open a bottle of the '48, if you
would, and bring it to the terrace. I think I'll sit and enjoy the last
smidgeon of daylight while I can."

Nathan found the doors leading to the terrace half opened. He was
stepping through them when he heard soft laughter. He almost called
out to Solange, but then he saw there were two silhouettes, seated
near the balustrade, heads almost touching as they leaned to each
other in animated conversation.

Nathan thought he might change for dinner after all, and headed
back to his room.

Two days later, at breakfast, Thierry announced he was returning to
Paris.

"I requested only a fortnight's leave," he explained.

"Ask for more," Nathan suggested, reaching for the thick local
honey with which he intended to drown his croissant.

"Under any other circumstances, I would do that, but it's not my
commanding officers I'm worried about. It's my mother, one of her
command performances. 'Family must get together every so often if
it's to remain a family.'"

Thierry's mimicry of his mother was good, Nathan could have
sworn she had slipped into the room.

"And how is dear Rachel? Still waiting for my beloved Mama to die
so that she can take her place as matriarch? No, you're right, if Rachel
summons, one must answer."

"But you'll miss the harvest." Solange sounded as if she regretted
that.

"It does seem a shame to waste everything you and Jacques have been teaching me. But why must I? With your permission, and yours, Uncle Nathan, I would like to return in a week."

Before Nathan could endorse the request, Solange beat him to it. "Yes, of course, that would be... wonderful."

So, thought Nathan, there seems to be more here than Solange merely being around a young man. There seems to be a lot more, indeed. Nathan wasn't sure why that thought saddened him. He just knew he would find some excuse not to be there when Thierry returned.

Thierry loathed the family get-togethers, primarily because he knew that sooner or later in the course of the evening his mother would parade over some eligible young woman—Rachel's concept of "family" extended well beyond her husband, children, and relatives—and later Thierry would be grilled on what he thought of the girl, what was it he didn't like, how could he not like her, she was from such a good family, and on and on. Rachel didn't wait for Thierry's answers. She little cared what her son thought or felt. She wanted results and grandchildren.

Thierry had no choice but to remain with the party through dinner, forty-seven people seated at one long table adorned with the finest silver, china, and glittering candelabras. Once the interminable meal was over, he made his escape. The one room he was sure no cousins, aunts, uncles, or guests—and especially his mother—would dare enter was his father's study. Though never specifically designated forbidden territory, the study was accepted as such.

Thierry moved down the hall of the exceedingly ornate Faubourg St. Honoré mansion, fearful that a lilting "Thierry" would halt his advance. Luckily he heard none.

Once in safety, he closed the double doors and leaned his head against them, marveling at the irony of his choosing the military. He had wanted to escape the proscriptions of being the good son, being the good Libermann son. How he pitied his cousins. Their lives were regimented and restrained by the demands of their parents—they lived as they were expected to live. So what had he done? To escape this yoke he had joined the army, where regimentation was written in stone. Yet, until the transfer to Paris, the army's regimentation and rules had been far more desirable than the Libermann discipline.

Something made Thierry turn. He was not alone.

Jerome Libermann was sitting behind his desk, his forefingers tapping on pursed lips.

Jerome should have been overwhelmed by the desk, for he was, in fact, a small-boned man, almost delicate, and very thin, and the black marble desk was massive and imposing. Yet he fit it and it fit him, the snarling griffins, twisting and complicated, that served as legs, being carved extensions of the man who sat behind them. They were poised, waiting for those who ventured before them to make a slip, the tiniest mistake. Then talons and beaks would tear into the unfortunate soul, shredding and destroying him.

"Don't you find the party interesting?" Jerome asked dryly.

"I could ask the same of you, Father."

Jerome sighed as if he'd lost all hope of reasonable behavior from his son.

"Are you enjoying your new assignment? I suppose it came as a welcome surprise to be given the esteemed duty of guarding the emperor."

"And how much of a surprise was it to you?" Thrust and parry. Games on top of games. Thierry wearied of dealing with his father's manipulations. "I didn't want to leave the Crimea. You had no right to arrange my promotion, if you wish to call it that."

"You wound me. Why do you accuse me of meddling in your affairs, something you expressly requested I not do?"

"I don't accuse. I state fact. I asked the emperor and he said it had been your wish."

Jerome was surprised, but he had long since learned not to show what he was thinking. "Thierry, how wonderful, you're on intimate terms with Louis-Napoleon, and you so young."

"No, Father, I am hardly one of the emperor's confidants. However, Uncle Nathan is. We were together in Compiègne, and I took the opportunity to inquire after who had arranged my fate."

Jerome was not happy with this new information. "Yes, of course, it would have been Nathan. Now, listen, when you become a father you'll understand why I couldn't stand by and allow you to serve as cannon fodder in some outrageous undertaking so that Louis can prove his manhood. You're obviously too young to take responsibility for your romantic notions, therefore I must do it for you."

Well, thought Thierry, at least he's taking a new tack—romantic notions, indeed.

"Cannons and danger have little to do with your objections to my joining the military. We both know that. You object to my moving from under your thumb. You don't want me to control my fate—you reserve that right for yourself."

"You wish to control your own fate? Face facts. You have no future in the French Army, whether you're mowed down by cannon fire or not. You're Jewish, albeit Libermann Jewish. And whatever advancement you make would be because you're my son, not because of what you accomplish. You say you took this foolish path so that you could succeed on your own merits. I trust you now realize that's impossible." He paused, "Thierry, sit down. Your pacing back and forth distracts me."

Thierry was not about to comply with his father's directive. He knew very well that Jerome's chair sat on a platform behind the desk. No matter how tall the visitor, he felt at a disadvantage before the imposing desk and the imposing owner who loomed so high above. Thierry would give his father no advantage especially when Jerome was correct in what he said about the military.

"Look, Father." He was still pacing. "If I fail, I want it to be my own failure. I don't want your hand in everything I do. I mean, Nathan says some of the greatest successes come from failure."

"And what does Nathan know of successes? What has he accomplished? Beyond marrying that insignificant little nothing—who is young enough to be his daughter—just so he could get his hands on her château?"

"You're quite wrong about that, Father. That was not Nathan's reason for marrying Solange."

Jerome's antenna went up. He sensed he was about to learn something very interesting.

"And how are you so sure about your uncle's motives?"

"Solange told me. The château was made a limited company. Solange owns stock and her brother owns stock. As part of Nathan's prenuptial agreement, Solange kept control of her shares."

"Funny, Nathan never mentioned this to me." Funny, indeed. So Nathan thought he could win their argument through subterfuge. Nathan had no concept of subterfuge, not Jerome's brand of it, at least. Jerome was struck with another thought.

"When exactly did you learn all this from the young baroness?"

"Just last week. While at Compiègne Nathan invited me to visit Bordeaux. It's wonderful. I've never been any place I found more agreeable. And it wasn't only because it gave me a chance to get away from the court. There's something extraordinary about the place. And another thing. You're mistaken about Solange. She's a remarkable woman. Level-headed. Intelligent. Extremely interesting. She's conversant on many subjects. And she is very beautiful." The last statement caught Thierry short. He didn't know why he said it.

"It would seem you have something in common with Nathan, at least as far as your tastes go." Jerome wondered if he could put this insight to his use somehow. "Now hadn't you better go back to your dear mother's little gathering. She'll be extremely disappointed if she has nothing to interrogate you about later."

After Thierry left, Jerome reviewed the conversation he'd had with his son. Obviously it was time to return his attention to du Clocher, and not only because of that bet with Nathan. Jerome didn't want Thierry to have a haven. He wanted his son to become completely disgusted with his present duties and resign the army. Once that was done, Jerome was sure he could manipulate him into joining the Banque Libermann.

He would have his secretary locate the du Clocher file in the morning. What was the name of that disgruntled employee he had used before? The one the young Saint-Savin had conveniently fought with and who then had been so useful as a spy? Jerome was sure Nathan was still wondering about the coincidence of that fellow's being at the château and all the carnage. What was his name? No need to worry. It would be in the file. Jerome kept everything. There was no telling when it might prove useful again.

Chapter Forty-two

After Thierry departed, Solange regretted her impulsive approval that he return for the harvest. She was unaccountably uneasy about his being there. She attributed this disquiet, despite all evidence to the contrary, to his probably getting in the way during that crucial time. This uneasiness translated into her offering him a less than warm reception on his return. He wasn't sure what he had done to deserve this new coolness, but was determined to ignore it. Solange's disquiet was further enhanced by Nathan's absence. He suddenly had some mysterious business to which he had to attend and was gone.

Jacques Mazet pealed the harvest bell the morning after Thierry came back. Solange didn't know Thierry was even awake when there he was before her, dressed in old clothes.

"What may I do to assist?" he asked with exaggerated but not mocking formality.

"You may have your breakfast on the terrace and watch."

Solange turned brusquely and left the château, already having dismissed her guest from her thoughts.

A little while later, while supervising the distribution of baskets and secateurs, there was Mazet and Thierry next to her.

"He'll pick," Mazet said.

"Him? What does he know about picking?"

"What I'm about to show him." Mazet took one of the secateurs, a basket, and set off to a row, Thierry on his heels with what Solange interpreted as a self-satisfied smile plastered on his face.

Fine, she thought, let him work out in the sun, pulling his muscles and sweating for a while. We'll see how long he lasts.

Solange worked through the day, not stopping for lunch, and was near exhaustion by the time picking was suspended. She hurried to the château where she knew a hot bath was waiting for her. It would have been nice to soak out her weariness. There was no time. The first night ceremony had to be performed. She wished Nathan could have been at her side.

A breeze was blowing cool when she came out onto the terrace. Workers were drifting into the garden, eager for the merrymaking to come. Someone was leaning on the balustrade, back to Solange, and in the distorting darkening of twilight, she thought it was Guy. When the figure pulled himself straight and turned, Solange sighed a tiny sigh of disappointment.

"Is there something wrong?" Thierry asked gently.

"No." She was sharp and unfriendly. "Did you enjoy your day? It must have been pleasant watching the work from here."

"And who was watching?"

Solange was confused. "Didn't you stop picking and come back here?"

"I did not," Thierry said with feigned indignation. "I was in the fields until a little less than an hour ago, along with everyone else. As a matter of fact, Jacques said I was the second fastest picker of the day."

Solange was saved from having to say more by Jacque Mazet's stepping forward with the traditional bouquet of sprigs, flowers, and grape bunches.

"Madame and Monsieur, this is for the baroness, and we all wish for a bountiful harvest."

Mazet was hoisted up and Solange took the offering.

"I accept this with great pleasure, for myself and for my brother. Let there be a good harvest."

The cheer went up and the workers dispersed, leaving Solange to her discomfort with Thierry.

It was he who broke the silence. "That's a nice ceremony."

"It started with the first Saint-Savin at du Clocher, and it's done every year."

"And does it always bring a good harvest?"

"We have our bad years, naturally. But who knows, they might be worse without it."

Thierry had been staring out at the Gironde as it faded into the night. Now he glanced back at the unpredictable woman next to him. "It's funny. I wouldn't have guessed you to be superstitious."

Solange laughed. "Oh, I'm not. But why take a chance? Are you ready for dinner?"

He reached out and took her hand to stop her from going. "Could we stay here for just a little while more? It's so peaceful, so beautiful."

"Of course." She moved closer to him. He didn't relinquish her hand.

The vendage went well. So much better than the previous year's. The oidium, though not eradicated, was under control. The grapes were good and there were many of them. Solange was pleased—and relieved.

Then it was over. Weary men and women had again foiled the caprices of Nature, and they were eager to celebrate.

"Aren't you going to the party?" Thierry asked Solange after the bell ending the harvest was rung.

"I don't think so. Not this year," she answered. "I'm very tired."

"No, no, I insist. You can't be any more tired than I am. This was the most grueling punishment my body has ever endured. Fighting the Russians wasn't as taxing."

"You were very good." Solange had continued to be impressed with Thierry's dedication and perseverance. She surmised that once he decided to do something, he completed it with similar determination and fervor. She wondered if he was like his father. She had no idea. Jerome was little discussed and she knew next to nothing about him.

Thierry was impatient for an answer, one that pleased him. "You must come out. You've described this night so vividly, I don't want to miss the dancing. Please, you must dance with me, as payment for my humble contribution to the harvest."

She laughed. "An argument I am unable to resist. Yes, I'll go out, but only for one dance."

It turned out to be five. Solange had never felt so excited and gay. Thierry was—well—he was exhilarating. And more. Solange didn't want to dwell on exactly what constituted that "more." She just let the night and the happiness engulf her.

When she was finally back in the safety of her room, she found her thoughts of Thierry disturbing. She wished Nathan were there. Nathan would have protected her. But protected her from what?

Thoughts and feelings kept jumbling and muddling around. Long after the workers had fallen into their drunken stupors, Solange fitfully sought the sanctuary of sleep.

At last she surrendered to her restlessness and drifted downstairs to the terrace.

The now-cold breeze of the Gironde caressed and quieted her. She looked to the sky and was glad the harvest was over. Huge clouds were rolling in and rain would follow shortly.

She tensed. There was something not right. Something not as it should be. And then she saw them. Fingers of flame clawing out of the chai.

"Oh dear god, *fire*," she screamed. *"Fire!"*

She had to rouse the workers. She had to get help. Solange raced to the belltower and up the steps, miraculously not stumbling. Searching for breath, she pulled on the massive ropes and the bell sounded her terror. She pulled and pulled until all strength left her arms. Then she ran back down the steps and out to the chai.

Smoke was dense and blinding and at first she could barely make out the phantasmic furied movement that had no substance or sense. Her eyes burned and her throat closed. She had to struggle against the urge to flee this horror. Instead she plunged into it and the dizzying chaos became shapes and the shapes people, people moving with direction and purpose.

She could hear yells and cries, and above it all she heard Thierry. He was shouting directions and giving orders. Workers were frantically complying, forming two parallel lines down to the river. Others were running from cabins and storehouse, carrying buckets, pots, pans, bottles. These were being passed down one of the lines to the river, filled, and sent back up the other line. Thierry had marshalled a brigade and buckets of sloshing water were already being dashed on the flames.

She heard her name. "Solange? Over there, fill in the line," Thierry yelled.

She obeyed at once. Mechanically, wiping out all thought and worry of what was happening further up the line, closer to the fire, Solange passed bucket after bucket, pot after pot. She had no idea of how long this went on or when her arms became numb. Once Thierry hurried down the line, reversing the direction so that those who had been passing the water-heavy containers were given the respite of passing the empties.

Solange was still trying to send a bucket to the woman next to her even after a triumphant cry went up around her.

"It's over," a jubilant voice said near her ear. "The fire is out."

Solange's knees buckled and she began to sink. Thierry caught her before she reached the ground.

"The chai... the wine? Did we lose...?"

"Hardly anything. It was quick thinking to ring the bell. If you hadn't..." Thierry shrugged his shoulders and let his words trail off.

Solange felt stronger, the incapacitating wave of fatigue and fear had passed. Still she didn't try to extricate herself from Thierry's arms. He had taken charge and she didn't want it back just yet.

"And Jacques, he'll be all right, too." Thierry added.

"Jacques? What's wrong with Jacques?"

Thierry tilted her face so that he could see her reaction. "He's all right. He was in the chai when the fire started. He said he thought he saw someone go in and went to investigate. Whoever it was jumped him. Jacques managed to grab a bottle and hit the intruder, but was knocked unconscious anyway. He came to with flames all around him, but he was able to drag himself out."

Solange shook her head in disbelief. "You're saying the fire was started deliberately? That's what you're saying?"

"It would appear so. Don't think about that now. Let's see about the damage."

They spent the next hour checking the chai. Incredibly, for all the smoke and flame, little damage was done to the wine and structure. It was Thierry who made the macabre discovery that he thought best to withhold from Solange for the moment. She had been through enough that night. It was best she not be told about the body Thierry had stumbled over deep within the chai.

It was obviously the arsonist. He must have been more hurt by Jacques' blow than he had realized. After setting the fire, the smoke was intense. He probably passed out.

Thierry didn't know the man, though he looked somehow familiar. His identity could be sorted out tomorrow. Now Thierry needed to get Solange out and away. Rejoining her, he insisted they return to the château. There was no argument from Solange. Nor was there any when he put his arm around her to help her up the stairs. At the door to her room she reluctantly pulled away. After passing her hand wearily across her eyes, she straightened up.

"Thank you, Thierry, for your help," she began with formality. "If it hadn't been for your efforts, for your...oh, Thierry." She couldn't continue. The enormity of what might have happened overcame her.

"Don't think about what didn't happen. It's all over now and all is well." He patted her back as he would a small child who had skinned her knee. "Please Solange, here, look at me. Let me see you smile. Smile, so I know you're all right."

She tried, but couldn't. He ran his fingers gently over her lips, as if he was going to help them fashion a smile. His fingers trailed down to her neck, her shoulders. Her robe had loosened. He gently caressed where it veed at the silky curve of her breasts.

They were both shocked by what they felt and what they wanted. Solange put her hand up in a protest that was lost when he bent to kiss each finger. And then their lips met and there was no protest or gentleness. They went to each other with need and desire—and a hunger that eradicated all else.

Solange's robe dropped to the floor and she would have followed it, pulling Thierry with her and into her, but he had her up, off the ground, in his arms. He carried her down the hall to his room, kicking the door shut behind them.

Neither heard Nathan's carriage pull up outside.

Book Seven

Chapter Forty-three

From a distance it was a startling sight. The wilderness of hills blanketed by pines and redwoods suddenly interrupted by the handiwork of man. There among the randomness of Nature, order and symmetry had been imposed. There on the curving slopes and in the valley flat was evidence of man's force of will—tilled soil planted with even rows of vines, houses yet to become homes, sheds, barns, corrals. If one drew close enough, a small, rude sign could be seen hanging, a bit lopsided, over the largest building. On it was the word "Belltower."

On the slopes, walking a path spaced wide enough so that the vines on either side had enough room to reach out and expand, Miguel de Cordoba and Guy Saint-Savin examined the results of two years of fifteen-hour-a-day labor.

Miguel watched Guy taste a grape.

"It's good for the first harvest," Guy pronounced. Miguel's expression did not change. Guy was used to that. Miguel rarely loosened the tight check he kept on himself. He always seemed to be waiting for something, biding his time. Even when Guy had revealed he'd made the Californian a co-owner of some of the land—not any of the vineyards, they belonged to Guy, Kyle, and Solange, but some of the other acres on which (it had been Miguel's idea) they had planted fruit trees and other cash crops as a hedge for when there was a bad grape crop—even then Miguel had not smiled. He had tipped his wide-brimmed straw hat and thanked Guy. Nothing more, only a solemn thank you.

Harazthy had accused Guy of impetuous generosity for giving Miguel some of the land. Guy disagreed, amused that he had to defend his action by calling it "calculated."

"I can't lose Miguel. He's invaluable. I need him. Now I know he'll stay." What Guy didn't add was he had a goal—he wanted Miguel to smile someday, really smile.

"And the wine?" Miguel was asking. "How will the wine be?"

Guy turned a full circle, surveying what they had accomplished in such a short time. "You can't hurry wine," he answered. "This will be drinkable; but good wine, that will take another ten years. The vines have to endure the seasons, relish the sunshine, get their roots deeper, then the grapes can be made into truly excellent wine."

"It will earn the name of Belltower, yes? Why didn't you name the vineyard 'du Clocher,' instead of translating it into English?"

"There's only one du Clocher and that's in Bordeaux. Du Clocher will always be the most important part of me, I think. Yet in the last two years, working all this, I've felt more and more that I belong here as well. With this first crop ready for harvest, I've realized the time has come to accept that here is my home. That it's time to get my son and bring him here, with me."

Miguel said nothing.

Damon Delany rarely rode his ranch. His time was taken with other properties and keeping people and events to his liking in Sacramento and San Francisco. Any little misstep by him would be jumped upon and exploited by his enemies, who were numerous. Still once in a while he had to check his holdings. Most men in his position relied on reports from foremen and managers. Delany relied on no man and on only one woman.

He never questioned his dependence and need for Fenella Mary Dougherty—it was too intuitive and primal. He would feel foolish if he tried to explain. But when he had helped pick up her groceries back in New York, looked into the clear brown eyes, Damon Delany saw her strength and an inner beauty. He had made an immediate leap to devotion. And she had never disappointed him.

Oh, she had infuriated him at times, but he always knew, always, that what she did and what she said was uncompromised and true.

And he knew that he could push her only so far. Fenella was willing to live by his wishes and for his needs, follow meekly down his path—to a point. Then she would go no further. She had always been that way, so much so that many people often took her for granted, she seemed such a nondescript, compliant little soul.

Her father had taken her for granted. She was the oldest of eleven children and took care of the whole family when her mother was pregnant—her mother was always pregnant. One of Fenella's regular duties was to fetch her father from the pub on Saturday nights where, without exception, he got rip-roaring, loud, and shouting drunk and would have slept on the saloon floor if his quiet little daughter didn't arrive at midnight to get him.

What happened that one Saturday night would not have taken place if Patrick Dougherty hadn't been drunk and if in the sixth month of her tenth pregnancy Mrs. Dougherty hadn't banned him from her bed and body. But all this was true, and Saturday night being the time Patrick was at his randiest, having had the walk to sober him up enough to perform, and it also being true that Fenella had always been a good, obedient girl, without malice and certainly without thought, Patrick had forced his daughter down into the bushes. He had her skirt up and his hands in her warmth before the girl knew what he was about.

"Be a good girl," he grunted. "Let your daddy in," he had ordered. But while Fenella would cook his meals, clean his dirty underwear, scrub his house, take care of his children, wipe up his vomit, she would not allow him this. She got her hand on a rock and brought it soundly down on her father's head. He fell off her, his face awash in flowing blood. Fenella calmly took her handkerchief from her pocket, wiped the blood away, and led her father home. After that she continued to cook his meals, clean his dirty underwear, scrub his house, take care of his children, wipe up his vomit, but she sent Matthew, the next oldest child, to fetch him on Saturday nights. No word ever passed between them about the incident. She had never told anyone, not even Damon, about it, but Damon wouldn't have been surprised. He knew the iron underneath that fragile exterior.

Damon pushed open the hacienda's front door, made a couple of brushes at the dust caked to his clothes and called out, "Fenella, where the hell are you?"

Damn it. She was the only reason he kept this spread. Fenella kept insisting it was the best place for Kyle. Maybe she was right. All the gaudiness and gilt that was San Francisco might not be a healthy atmosphere for the boy. God, he was a good little fellow. Damon forgot sometimes that Kyle wasn't his own son. Where was he, anyway? Usually he'd be waiting and eager with as big a hug as a four-year-old could muster. Those sturdy little arms around Damon's neck always made him feel good and complete.

Another reason Damon didn't make Fenella move to the city was his fear. They had never discussed the revelation that Damon had been aware of the captain's hoarding on the *Bonnie Swift* and had told no one. Damon was afraid Fenella blamed him for their baby's death. He wasn't about to interfere with what she felt best for Kyle.

"Kyle! Fenella!"

Just then Damon noticed a letter propped up on a table near the door. It was addressed to Fenella. He opened it without hesitation.

My dearest Fenella,
You have been the most wonderful of women taking care of Kyle as you have. I will never be able to repay you. It is now time for Kyle to be with his father. Once the harvest is finished, in another couple of weeks, a month, at the latest, I will be sending someone for the boy. Again, my deepest thanks.

Guy

Damon crumpled the letter, threw it to the floor, and ran to his bedroom.

"Fenella," he yelled. "Fenella, where are you? Where's Kyle?" She was in their room packing her modest wardrobe in the battered trunk they had brought from New York.

"Didn't you hear me? Didn't you hear me calling?"

"Yes." She didn't look up.

"What are you doing?"

"I'm sure you read Guy's note. I'm packing."

Damon slammed the trunk's top down as the only way of getting her attention. Fenella did not flinch.

"You're not going anywhere. You're my wife. You go where I go. You go where I tell you to go."

"I don't want to hurt you, Damon, but I have to do this. I have to be with Kyle. He needs me. I am the only mother he has."

Despite her passive expression and cool tone, Damon could feel her sorrow. He gently took the dress she was holding and tried to ease her onto the bed. She resisted and was immovable.

Damon tried to reason with her. "Look, I love that boy, too. I love him like a son. You know that. But that doesn't make him mine or yours. He's Guy's. We can fight Guy, we could probably win and keep the boy. But it won't change the fact that he's Guy's son."

"No, we won't fight him." Fenella was flat and final. "I promised Guy I would take care of Kyle until he could make a home for him. I won't break my promise. And I won't abandon Kyle. He needs me."

Damon was losing his temper and his reason. "And what about your promise to me? The promise to be my wife? Will you break that?" Damon was yelling. "You will abandon that?"

"I'll be your wife for as long as you want me, but you don't need me now. Not really. You should have a refined hostess, a lady, for that city mansion you want to build. Someone who knows what to serve at dinner parties and how to order servants around. I'm no use to you anymore."

Damon had to turn his back. He couldn't let her see his torment, his desperation. He couldn't lose Fenella. What she didn't understand was he did need her, and this power over him was infuriating. Why couldn't he control her as he did everyone else?

"Damn it! I won't let you go. I forbid it." But even as he spoke he sensed the impotence in his command.

Fenella put the dress into the trunk and firmly closed the lid. "I'll send someone for that. I'm taking the buckboard. Kyle'll be able to sleep in the back." It was as if she were telling him of some short trip into San Pasqual, some inconsequential errand. Her calmness fanned his mounting frustration. He, Damon Delany, who controlled most of Northern California, couldn't get this waif of a woman to stay where she belonged—with him. He, who could have almost any woman he wanted, was losing this one, the only one he wanted.

He grabbed her arms roughly and jerked her to him. "You're mine and you're not going anywhere."

He bent to kiss her. He would have her, he would take her now, on the floor, on the bed. He'd hammer her into submission, extract her whimpers of pleasure, make her realize she couldn't leave.

Fenella tried to pull away. Damon tightened his grip, tighter, tighter, until she gasped from pain. That was enough to restore Damon's sanity. He released her. He hadn't meant to harm her, not Fenella, never Fenella.

She stared at him for one long second, turned on her heel and left, not looking back, not wanting to see the dead-eyed Damon, slouched on the bed, drained.

He was still there, unmoving, when one of the ranch hands came for the trunk. The man wondered who had run roughshod over the boss. One frown from Damon sent him scurrying from the room, trunk on his back, to wonder someplace safer.

Damon heard the buckboard pulling away. He heard Fenella's soothing lilt and Kyle's excited chatter.

Then he heard nothing.

He cried.

Chapter Forty-four

Guy Saint-Savin was standing in a grape cart ready to address the twenty-three tired and grimy men who were bunched below him. He laughed, a little self-consciously, as he held up a big tin cooking pot.

"This isn't exactly how we did it in France, but here we make do with what we have." With that Guy banged on the pot with a ladle.

"There, let it be known that the first harvest of the Belltower vineyard is now officially over. Go clean up. By the time you're done, the feast will be laid and the party can begin."

That promise was enough to breathe energy into the crew. They clapped and whistled and made their way to bunkhouses and cottages.

"It certainly isn't like Bordeaux," Guy said to Miguel, thinking of the servants back in France who would have a hot bath waiting for him. Then Guy smiled. "It's different, but that doesn't mean it isn't good."

Miguel made no comment. Guy wearily climbed down from the cart. "You think I'm crazy, don't you? Trying to bring the traditions of du Clocher here." He didn't wait for an answer. He knew there would be none. "Well, I'm not crazy. The men need something to look forward to. They need this diversion. We all need it. Now, come on. Cheer up. Count Harazthy and his family will be here soon. Thank God for him. If he weren't bringing wine from his cellar, tonight would be a very subdued affair."

Harazthy brought five barrels and a dozen bottles. He also brought his daughters, sons, sons-in-law, wife Marika, and an effervescence that was matched by none. Marika supplied a wagonload of curtains, chairs, dishes, dressers, and various knick-knacks, explaining that as long as Guy was to have his son at last, it was time to make the house,

large as it was, a home. She and the daughters refused to take even a
single sip of wine until the house was prettified to their liking.

Makeshift tables had been set up outside for the hams, buttered
potatoes, cornbread, jellies, beans, chickens, and the side of beef that
was slowly being turned nearby on an open fire.

Guy and Harazthy sat on two rocking chairs on the wrap-around
porch the count insisted be added to the house. "You have to survey
your domain," he explained. "You have to keep your eye on what the
thieves are thieving."

"I am a truly happy man tonight," Harazthy was saying. "I see a
new vineyard taking root. I have my wonderful family. Only one more
daughter to marry off and ..." Harazthy paused dramatically, "... and
now I no longer need to worry about money, money for my family,
money for my Buena Vista vineyard. I can now do all I want."

Guy jumped from his chair and grabbed the older man's hand in
congratulations. "Then it came through! You got the appointment!" he
shouted.

"Yes, yes. That fine and wise gentleman, President Franklin
Pierce, found it in the best interest of the state and the nation that I, a
poor refugee from the chicanery of Europe, be named director of the
federal mint in San Francisco."

"I'm so glad for you. It's exactly what you wanted."

"How could I not want it? It's an important and very well-paying
position that allows me time for Buena Vista. God couldn't have
planned it better. Now, why don't we open that bottle of Lafitte I hid
among the others? Before some of those revelers stumble into the
house and steal it from us."

As Guy went to fetch the bottle, he was struck by how similar the
party before him was to those he'd seen in Bordeaux. There were
bonfires, music, some people were even dancing—not the dances of
his youth, something more structured with one person calling
instructions and the dancers changing steps and patterns accordingly.
Of course, there weren't as many revelers as there had been in
Bordeaux. But what they lacked in numbers, they made up for in
enthusiasm. The celebration would get bigger each year, thought
Guy. He would see to that.

When he emerged with the Lafitte, he found Harazthy had left the
porch. The count and his wife were next to a buckboard, and getting
down was Fenella Delany. Though obviously near exhaustion, she
was refusing all assistance. Instead she hurried around to the back of
the wagon, dropped the gate, and held her arms up to a sleepy little

boy who was wiping his eyes and seeking comfort. With Kyle safely in her arms, Fenella turned to the house and saw Guy.

"I've brought you your son." she said, showing concern at what his reaction would be.

Kyle peeked at Guy and not seeing whom he expected, buried his head back into Fenella's shoulder.

"Come, Kyle," Fenella cooed as she put him down. "Give your daddy a kiss."

Guy took an awkward step toward his son. Fenella nudged the boy to meet him, but Kyle would have none of it. He clung to Fenella, hiding his head in the folds of her skirt.

"It will take a little time," clucked Marika Harazthy. "Now don't you worry. The boy will come around. Fenella, look at you. It's been so long since we've seen each other. Does your husband keep you chained to that ranch in San Pasqual? Here, let me show you the house. We'll find a comfortable bed for that fine-looking boy."

Fenella followed her gratefully. The long trip with a confused child had not been easy. She would have liked nothing better than to have snuggled under a down-filled comforter with a warm cup of milk and not have to think anymore. But she knew she owed Guy some sort of explanation, and he wouldn't let her rest until he had it.

The men went back to their rocking chairs, but Guy couldn't stay seated. He kept going to the door, peering in, returning to the chair, and then back to the door. Harazthy let him walk out his concern.

Guy shook his head. "I don't understand this. I didn't know Fenella was bringing Kyle. I wrote saying I would send someone for him. What made her come now? Do you think something's wrong?"

"Oh, you know women," the count answered. "She was probably worried about the boy traveling with a stranger. Came along to help him adjust. Be happy. Your son is here."

Guy frowned. "My son? I don't think he even knows he is my son."

When a half-hour had passed and the women didn't reappear, Guy couldn't contain his anxiety. He went into the house only to meet Marika Harazthy coming down the long corridor that angled off to the right of the main room and along which were two of the house's bedrooms.

"The boy's almost asleep. He wouldn't leave Fenella's arms. Poor thing, I think he's a little bewildered and maybe a bit frightened. Fenella should be out in a minute." She left him to rejoin her husband.

It was dark in the main room. Guy went around moving up the

wicks in the lanterns. With the added light he could see all the improvements the Harazthy women had made. Bright throw rugs were scattered around. Big, colorful pillows were plumped up on what had previously been an uncomfortable wood-framed couch. There were paintings of European countrysides propped against the walls. The room still had a forlorn, lonely look, but at least it wouldn't echo anymore. In addition to the hallway to the right, another one veered off to the left. Along it were four additional bedrooms. In the middle, behind the main room, was the kitchen and eating area. Nothing grand, Guy thought, nothing formal, still a good home for him and his son.

Thinking of the boy, Guy frowned again. What had he expected? Kyle hardly knew him. He was a virtual stranger. Was it fair to expect the little fellow to run to him with open arms and all his affection.

"You're thinking of Kyle, aren't you?" Fenella asked.

Guy started. She was a silently moving ghost who could reach into the recesses of his mind. "Yes, I was. I've missed so many years with him. I'm glad he's finally home. I mean, I can't help being a little disappointed by his reaction to me. He'll get over it. It'll just take a little time, I know that. And he'll never forget you. I know that, too. There's no way I can repay you for all you've done. Fenella, it'll be hard on Kyle at first, but in time, he'll come to understand why you had to leave him."

Fenella turned her palms upward as if she were stating the most obvious truth and was surprised he didn't know it already. "But I'm not leaving," she said.

"Well, not tonight, of course not."

"I'm not leaving," she repeated.

"What do you mean? Of course, you're leaving. You must. You can't stay." Then fearing he was sounding ungrateful, Guy quickly added, "You're married. You have to go back to your husband, to Damon."

"I won't leave Kyle."

"Fenella, I don't like Damon, but it's your duty. Your duty is with your husband."

"My duty is to who needs me. My duty is to my son, to Kyle."

She was crying so softly, Guy wasn't aware of when the tears had begun. He wasn't sure what he should say or do, what he could say or do. She was in such pain. Yet as much as Guy despised Damon, Fenella's leaving him was not right. She would come to regret it, if for no other reason than her religion would condemn her. Guy knew Fenella was a practicing Catholic, practicing in that she attended mass and made confession. No priest would condone her leaving Damon. She would be made to feel her guilt by her church.

Guy reached for her, to give her solace and make her understand. She pulled back with an involuntary cry of pain.

"What's wrong with your arms?" Guy demanded. He had barely touched her. "You've been hurt. Roll up your sleeves and let me see."

"No, there's nothing wrong." Fenella tried to move out of Guy's reach, but could not escape him. He pushed up the sleeves and reached for a lantern so he could see better.

Fenella's upper arms were a map of cruel and dark bruises where Damon had grabbed her in his angry desperation. Guy touched one gingerly. Fenella moaned.

"What happened? Did Damon do this to you? Did he beat you? Did he?"

"It isn't what you think. It was an..." Fenella trailed off.

"My God! For all he's done, I never thought he'd hurt you again, not intentionally. Well, I'm not going to give him the chance to hurt you anymore. You'll stay here. I'll protect you. Damon Delany will never hurt you again."

Fenella started to protest, to explain that Guy had misunderstood. Instead she said nothing.

Book Eight

Chapter Forty-five

December, 1856

It was midmorning. Solange was taking the short walk from the château to the chai where Jacques Mazet was waiting for her to taste the fermenting juice that a couple of months earlier had still been locked in the grape.

She was moving slowly, as if being drawn reluctantly to her task.

Nathan watched from the small balcony outside his bedroom. There was something wrong with her, he thought. She refused to admit it, however, which only meant he would have to force the issue. But first he would take a nice long bath, put on fresh clothes, and tackle the subject of lunch.

Henri was arranging soaps and brushes for Nathan in the bathroom. "Is there anything else you would like, baron?" he asked.

Nathan was about to say no, then changed his mind. He was just back from a tiring trip, and what if it were still morning? He was tired and thirsty.

"Please, bring me a glass of red wine."

"And the vintage, sir?"

"It can be cooking wine for all I care."

Henri would have liked to know what was bothering Nathan. Probing, however, was not his place. Henri knew his place and kept to it with dedication and loyalty. He hurried away to get his master something more pleasing to the palate than the cook's store.

Nathan exhaled sharply as he eased into the steamy water. He didn't want to think about anything. He wanted to retire to this warmth and put everything else aside. Damn it! He was too old for these trips. For the past two years whenever Thierry visited, Nathan found a reason for absenting himself from the château, knowing his presence would inhibit Solange.

As long as he had to travel, he arranged an interesting itinerary. There was the raven-haired princess in Deauville, who may or may not have been the aunt of all the beautiful and accommodating young women living in her villa. ("Denise," Nathan had once asked her, "the negress, can't you at least say she's the daughter of a friend?" "No, I cannot," the princess replied firmly, "because she *is* my niece.") Then there was the lovely and wealthy widow of Dijon, who at thirty-two had already buried four husbands.

"Nathan, stay with me," she often pleaded. "The others meant nothing to me. Stay and marry me."

"Dear one, you are magnificent and the thought of spending the rest of my days with you is enticing. However, I would like the rest of my days to be a few more than your other husbands had."

And Sophie. She and Nathan were friends from his long-ago days in the Russian court. She had been imported to be the mistress of an influential general, a cousin of the czar's. Sophie had made the general very happy and the general had made Sophie very rich. His death grieved her terribly. But not so terribly that she didn't keep her wits about her. She knew that the general's widow would soon find a way to repossess all of Sophie's hard-earned baubles and property. She appealed to Nathan. He had her whisked out of the country, handled the fast—and profitable—sale of her holdings, and personally escorted the jewels to Sophie, who was happy to settle down in a smart section of Paris where she opened a dress shop with some of the finest designers and tailors. Sophie enjoyed her success and always loved to lavish her gratitude on Nathan.

There were others, others who delighted in the baron's arrival and regretted his departure.

Henri came back with a tray, carrying a bottle of Pomerol '51 and a suitable glass. He set the tray down within Nathan's easy reach, and paused for any additional requests. Getting none, he left.

Nathan took a long, gratifying sip. Yes, he was getting too old for this carousing. Still, there was little choice. He had thrown Solange and Thierry together, and now he must live with the consequences.

The three never discussed the peculiar arrangement. Thierry came to du Clocher once a month. Nathan left once a month. There was no tension between them if by poor timing their paths crossed. Only Jacques Mazet seemed disturbed, but he, of course, said nothing.

Nathan wanted only happiness for his wife and nephew and banished from his thoughts the price he was paying.

After getting dressed, Nathan went across to the chai to see how much longer Solange would be working. It would be nice to sit in the salon with the fire crackling—the day was bright with a chilling nip to it—her chair pulled close to his.

He was at the door when he heard an alarmed Solange calling Mazet. "Jacques, there's been a disaster. Come quickly and taste this."

Inside, Nathan saw Solange in terrified distress holding a glass out to Mazet.

"Here, taste this. It's what you drew from the vat. It's off. It's terribly off. There's something wrong with it."

Mazet took the glass and, dispensing with all preliminaries, lifted it to his mouth. He smacked his lips together, examined the wine carefully, took another sip. With a worried brow, he handed the glass to Nathan to taste as well.

Nathan's frown mirrored Mazet's.

"It's awful, isn't it?" moaned Solange, seeing a whole year's labor wasted. "What could have gone wrong?"

Each man took another sip.

"But there's nothing wrong." Nathan was puzzled and worried. "It tastes as it should taste."

Solange grabbed the glass and tasted more. "No, no, it's off. Tell him, Jacques."

"I can't tell him that. He's right. This is as it should be."

Solange leaned against the testing table. "I don't understand. What is wrong with me?"

Nathan seized the opening.

"Solange, I'm taking you to Doctor Bernard. Today. He's the best in Bordeaux and as good as any in Paris. There's been something wrong with you for weeks and it's time we found out what."

"But I'm never sick." Solange didn't want to be pampered. She was too busy.

"Well, you're sick now and we're going to get it taken care of. Have you lost your courage? Are you afraid of what you'll hear? It's probably minor. Let's find out. Now, no more arguments. We go this afternoon."

Nathan was taken to Doctor Bernard's library, and Solange bustled off to a room for examination. There was, naturally no question of Nathan's waiting with the other patients. He and the doctor were friendly rivals at a high-stakes card table and, besides, Libermanns were never shunted to common waiting rooms.

A half hour passed. Nathan paced the room, trying to concentrate on the titles of the books on the shelves. He would take a book down, flip it open, then replace it, his eyes always drawn back to the magnet of the door. What was taking so long?

An hour. Nathan snapped closed his gold pocket watch. Five more minutes. Five more and he would go...

A solemn Doctor Bernard came in. Suddenly Nathan didn't want to hear what the doctor had to say. If Solange were dying, Nathan was dying as well.

The doctor poured cognac from a cut-glass decanter. "Sit down and drink this. You'll be needing it."

Nathan obeyed.

"How shall I begin?"

"Tell me right out. Are you sure of your diagnosis?"

"Sure. Of course, there's no doubt. You mean you already knew? From the baroness's reaction, I thought it was a complete surprise. Growing up without a mother, she seems naive in these respects."

Nathan was ready to explode. "What does having a mother have to do with her diagnosis? Isn't Solange dying?"

The doctor had to put his glass down, he was laughing so hard. Nathan was outraged. Seeing his reaction, Doctor Bernard got his amusement under control and continued more seriously.

"My goodness, baron, you are as ignorant as your wife in these matters. Forgive me for keeping you in suspense, but no, your wife is not dying—though in a few months she may claim the pain is killing her. Solange is as healthy a young woman as I've ever examined. She is also as pregnant a young woman as I've ever examined. Here now, sit down. You've lost all color, and I won't have a Libermann dropping dead in my office."

On the way back from Bordeaux, each kept to their own corner and thoughts. Each wondered what the other was thinking and feeling. For her part, Solange was in turmoil. It always seemed before, when there was a problem, there was a goal. The goal being the solution. Now Solange was neither sure what she wanted or what she should want.

When the carriage stopped before the château, Nathan got out and held up his hand to help Solange. It was then they looked at each other closely for the first time since leaving the doctor's. Nathan saw sorrow and fear and he was frightened. Solange saw his dismay and couldn't understand. She ran from him to the safety of her room.

At the front door Henri had to jump aside to let her pass. He raised a questioning eyebrow as Nathan handed him his cloak.

Nathan shrugged sadly. "I thought there was reason to celebrate. Now I'm not so sure. Please let me know when the baroness comes down from her room."

Except she didn't come down. Nathan ate a lonely, melancholy dinner.

It was almost midnight when he finally went upstairs. He was turning to go to his wing when he thought he heard movement in Solange's room.

"Damn it," he said out loud, "this thing has got to be confronted. I'll wait no longer."

For all his resolve, his knock was timid.

"Who is it?"

"May I come in?" Nathan didn't wait for a reply.

Solange was sitting straight-backed on the bed, a child waiting for reprimand. Nathan sat beside her.

"It's an overwhelming thought, isn't it? The idea that within you now is a growing being, a little person that will laugh and cry and bring joy and sadness. It has already brought joy—to me. Solange, I'm so happy we're having a baby. Tell me, aren't you happy, too?"

She could no longer hold her head up, it had grown heavy with the weight of her thoughts. "I don't know. I really don't know." She glanced up to see his dismay. "No, I don't mean that I don't want the baby. But it changes everything. I don't know what it will mean... to us and to ..." It was hard even saying his name, Nathan and she had so effectively ignored the situation. "...Thierry."

Nathan left her and walked to the window, afraid to be too near her, afraid she would see too much.

"Isn't that odd? I haven't once thought about Thierry. Doctor Bernard said you were having a baby and I was ecstatic. Our child. I was going to be a father. You know I never felt any dynastic urge. Procreate. Recreate yourself. Perpetuate the line, the name. But hearing Doctor Bernard today, I was truly ecstatic as if I had been waiting to hear those words all my life."

"We can't ignore Thierry. Don't you see how this changes everything? He can't be a casual visitor anymore, not with a child here. Oh, Nathan, it's his child. Thierry's child."

When Nathan didn't respond, Solange continued in a rush. "He must be told. I just don't know what this will mean. He's been waiting so long for an overseas posting, to get out of that awful emperor's guard. What if this makes him feel trapped? What if he feels he has to give up all that he has worked for because of this child?"

Nathan was tired. He didn't want to know the answers to these questions. Still he asked, "When do you propose to tell him?"

Solange rubbed her eyes. She had no right to ask this of Nathan. She knew that. Yet she must, she couldn't help herself. "Would you tell him for me? I've thought and thought. If he doesn't hear it from me, if he doesn't have to make his decision facing me, well, then, maybe he won't rush, maybe it will give him time to make the right choice, what's best for him. I don't want him unhappy."

And what of us? Nathan thought bitterly. What of our happiness?

"Of course, I'll tell him, if that's what you want."

And let me be damned for it, he thought.

Chapter Forty-six

Nathan had elected to walk. The carriage left him off at the edge of the Bois de Bologne, and he was taking a leisurely, appreciative stroll around the Lac Inférieur. Nathan wanted to enjoy his surroundings before Thierry came cantering up and spoiled the serenity.

There was no faulting the emperor for this undertaking. The woods were magnificent. Paris before the Second Empire had been hardly more than a medieval city, streets mired in mud and reeking garbage, tiny stores, and filthy slums. And most distressingly, no parks save the bits of green along the Champs Elysées and the small patch of Nature at the Place des Vosges. Otherwise, the citizens of Paris had to rely on the beneficence of kings to once in a while open the gates of the Tuileries, the Luxembourg Gardens, the Palais Royal, and the Jardins des Plantes to enjoy flowers and open air.

And now there was the Bois de Bologne. Once only frequented by thugs and gypsies, it had been transformed into enticing, meandering streams, fields of flowers, and beckoning lawns. Nathan sighed. It truly was beautiful.

The sound of hoofbeats destroyed the peace.

Thierry reined in his horse and dismounted.

"Uncle," he cried, "your timing for a meeting is impeccable even if your choice of location a bit curious."

"And what is curious about wanting to spend time in Paris's most glorious and tranquil place?"

"I've never thought of you as the tranquil type. Still it is quiet and there will be no interruptions as I tell you my news."

The two fell into step and started slowly strolling, although every once in a while Thierry had to pull himself back as he unintentionally picked up the pace.

"I have news for you, as well, but out with yours first."

Thierry was grateful for the chance to explode with his tidings.

"I've taken it. I've got it. I'm going to Algeria with the Fourth, my own command. I could have had it sooner, but..." he hesitated, "...but I didn't want to leave Solange. Damn, Nathan, what a muddle this is. You know I never wanted to do anything to cause you unhappiness. You do know that. But I can't help loving Solange. You must have known how I felt about her, how I had to be with her. Now you must also understand that I have to leave and I must take her with me. This assignment is what I've wanted for so long, to be away from my father, to show what I can do. Well, I've gone ahead and accepted, and now I must ask you to give Solange the divorce you promised."

This was certainly not the direction Nathan had expected the conversation to go. He found his jaw was clenched and he had to force himself to relax before he could proceed cautiously.

"What of du Clocher?" he asked. "Do you think Solange will leave it?"

Thierry momentarily looked annoyed. A human rival would be easier to confront. "I know how she feels about it. And frankly I am afraid. She might very well refuse me for her vineyard. But if you talk to her, she respects your opinion more than anyone else's. You could make her see there are more important things in life than some land and vines. Tell her I must go and she must go with me. Will you? Promise you will?"

The boy has no idea how much he's asking, Nathan thought. No idea what this will do to me.

"Of course, I promise."

"Good, I knew you would. I have to return immediately. There's so much to be done and no time to do it. Thank you, Nathan, I've always been able to count on you."

Thierry gave Nathan a fast embrace and was gone, completely forgetting that his uncle had news as well.

I could call after him, Nathan thought. I should call after him. Tell him about the baby. God! What was I hoping for? That Thierry on hearing he was to be a father would say, how nice, but let's leave the arrangement as it has been. You be Solange's husband, I her lover, and the child will merely be a pleasant nuance. Yes, you fool, that's what you were hoping for—and now, now I am to lose what I cherish most. You're a stupid man, Nathan Libermann, a stupid, foolish *old* man.

The woods didn't seem so fresh and beautiful anymore.

Chapter Forty-seven

"So he's gone?" Solange had difficulty asking the question. The words got caught somewhere in her head and didn't want to come out.

Nathan was ashamed.

Back at his hotel particulier after the meeting with Thierry, he had decided he would see his nephew again and tell him about the baby. But Nathan had put it off, only for two days, still he had put it off. Then when he called on Jerome, intending to use the visit to speak to Thierry, he was told his nephew had already left for Algeria. Nathan returned immediately to Bordeaux.

Now he was being punished for his silence by the anguish in Solange's voice and eyes.

"I wouldn't have wanted him to give up his dream, you know," she was saying. "I'm glad he had the courage to... to not feel obliged to come to me... because of the baby. He loved me for a while. That was enough."

She's so unhappy, Nathan thought. She believes he fled after hearing about the child. She thinks I told Thierry. I must explain, make amends.

Instead he drew her to him and whispered into her dark hair, "You are my wife and my love. It is my baby that grows within you."

"Nathan." She interrupted him with sadness. "You know it can't be your..."

"No, this is my child—now and for always. And you are my wife— from this moment on—and for always."

Nathan kissed her, kissed her with the love and the passion that he had hidden for so long, and she kissed him back.

Book Nine

Chapter Forty-eight

1859

Guy was awakened by the gentle slapping of waves. He started up in panic. In a blurred nether world between consciousness and sleep, he was on the *Bonnie Swift*.

He lowered his head back to the downy pillow of his bunk. No, this was a far cry from the *Bonnie Swift,* and this docking in San Francisco would be so much different than the one he'd made before.

There was a small rustling above his head followed by a delicate sigh.

Much different, he thought with a smile.

They must be in port. The rocking and pitching of the ship was gone, but it would be hours before they were put ashore. Hours before the other passengers were up. Hours to think of all that had happened, all that he hadn't planned for.

Who could have planned for the end of the gold rush? Granted it had to end sometime. The earth couldn't be expected to forever give up the precious yellow ore. Still, when it was over, it came as a shock. No more miners with money to fling around on fancy clothes, expensive horseflesh, compliant womanflesh, or a fine wine to make what was passing for the good life even better.

All the winegrowers were suffering. It was Harazthy—suffering least because of his position at the mint—who took action. He brought them all together at Buena Vista, gave them a lavish dinner, then sat them down to tell them what must be done.

"It's time for unity," he proclaimed. Guy, inspecting his companions, couldn't imagine a more diverse group—former miners who thought that dirt-farming back in Iowa gave them credentials to be winemakers; a couple of retired gamblers who had worked the riverboats, mining camps, and any other place that foolish men with money might be tempted to part with it; a count from Hungary, another from France; and Madam Karine, whose suspected former occupation once caused some ribald snickers among the male winegrowers visiting the Belltower. A thin-lipped, unnaturally pale Fenella came out of the kitchen and quietly announced that any man making remarks about the madam might as well leave and never come back.

"It doesn't matter what she was. It's what she is that matters now."

How Madam Karine made her money was never questioned again. The madam was the first to back Harazthy's proposal.

"He's right, you know. Yes, yes, another glass, sweetie, but make it a nice Scotch this time...." she had said.

"Madam Karine," Harazthy interrupted with good nature, "how are we going to make you a true viniculteur if you insist on drinking that devil's brew?"

"There's a time and a place for everything, count. Wine's fine for pleasure but Scotch's the potable for business. So let's get down to it. As I was saying, you're right. Okay, we've lost a good part of our market out here because those good-for-nothing gold-diggers went and spent all they had. Well, then, it's time we look for some other suckers. Right? Right?"

"Dear lady," Harazthy bowed graciously, "however it is phrased, I do welcome your support. So what do you all say? We elect a representative to go east..."

"Look, count, I just don't see where it's going to do any good," objected Samuel Riley, one of the former gamblers. "You know as well as I do that the New York and Ohio growers have got everything sewed up back there. So what do you think we can do?"

"More than we're doing now," Harazthy retorted angrily. "What they have the audacity to call wine there, from that awful Catawba grape, isn't good enough to be used in stew. If we can get Easterners to taste our wine, just taste it, why, then we have a market. No doubt about it. Believe me."

Eventually they did believe him. Guy was voted the representative. There was to be an East Coast exhibition in New York that would feature wine, and it offered the perfect opportunity for him to introduce the California vineyards.

Surprisingly, it was Fenella who argued against the trip. Although she never told anyone, not a week went by when she didn't wake up shivering and in a sweat from a nightmare that always put her back on the *Bonnie Swift*. She was afraid for Guy, afraid the nightmare would again be reality. It took days to reassure her that travel had improved greatly, that the passage over the Isthmus was not as bad, and the ships much faster. He would have no trouble. And he didn't.

At least not on the passage.

The trouble came in New York after an uneventful beginning. Guy was met by a tentative young man named Jeremy Cahill, who had been sent up from Washington by Harazthy's good friend, Senator Gwim of California, to assist at the exhibition.

They had gotten Guy settled in his hotel and then spent the next two days setting up the tasting table, carefully arranging the bottles Guy had carried and kept in his cabin, not wishing to take the chance they would be mishandled.

The night before the opening of the exhibition, Guy and Cahill had gone to doublecheck that all was perfect at the table.

But nothing was perfect. The booth was a shambles. Every bottle had been smashed.

Guy spun around as if he were going to find the culprits still lurking about. There were several men at other tables, but none would meet his eye. Instead they turned their backs to him.

It was a horrific blow, but Guy refused to accept the defeat. He was there to exhibit and somehow he would. The next day Cahill and he scoured New York, going to wine shops and exhibitors in the hopes of securing some California wine. Guy knew that at least some bottles of Buena Vista had made their way east in the past two years.

Finally late in the afternoon, in a staid Chelsea store of polished and shining mahogany and brass, the proprietor admitted to having some bottles of Buena Vista—somewhere.

Guy couldn't believe his luck, but the proprietor wasn't so enthusiastic.

"I'm always ready to try a new product," he began in way of

explaining how he happened to have Buena Vista. "One of our best customers requested the wine. Said he had enjoyed it while in San Francisco. I want to please our patrons, although I told him I had no idea where I might get some."

The proprietor had asked his usual suppliers, but none had any. Then only a few weeks earlier, one said he could supply him after all. The Chelsea storeowner had bought two cases.

"And that certainly was not my lucky day. The wine was dreadful. Worse than dreadful. My patron wouldn't take a single bottle after he tried it."

"I beg to contradict you. Buena Vista is a good wine. Perhaps the bottle you tasted had gone bad."

"No, every bottle we tasted was the same. I don't want to talk myself out of a sale, mind you, but I wouldn't recommend your buying any."

"I'll buy a bottle and see for myself."

"Have it your way, but remember, I warned you."

The proprietor dispatched a clerk to behind a curtain that led to the back of the store. Ten minutes later, the clerk re-emerged, dusty for his efforts.

Guy examined the bottle he'd brought. It was the right label. Nothing appeared wrong with the bottle.

The proprietor opened it and poured some for Guy. Guy checked the color, the bouquet, and then he tasted it. His expression went from puzzlement to disgust.

"This is not Buena Vista wine."

"Sir, what are you saying? Please. Look at the label. It clearly says 'Buena Vista.'"

"Labels can lie. My palate does not. Taste it yourself. That's not a Zinfandel. It's a mixture of Concord and Catawba."

The proprietor poured some for himself, took a sip, then said, "I don't know what you say this wine *should* taste like. I only know what it *does* taste like, and that's terrible. Sir, all I can say is this, this is the Buena Vista I have. Would you like some or not?"

"No, I don't want this vinegar. However, I do want the name of this supplier, the one who gave you this abomination."

"That would be Wine Import-Export. The office is in their warehouse off Fulton Street."

Mr. Terence Malloy, owner of Wine Import-Export, received Guy in his grimy, paper-strewn office. Malloy, waistcoat more unbuttoned than buttoned, revealing a grease-stained shirt underneath, had his feet propped up on his desk.

"So what can I do for you, Mister Sayvine?"

"That's Saint-Savin, sir, and what you can do for me is tell me how this awful liquid got into this bottle labeled Buena Vista. The owner of the Chelsea Fine Wines and Liqueurs says he obtained it from your firm."

"Here, let me see that." Malloy put out his hand for the bottle Guy had brought from the wine shop. Since he made no move to get up from his chair, Cahill skittered over with the bottle. Malloy pulled the cork and took a swig. A thin line of wine dribbled from the corner of his mouth, down his chin, to add color to the stains of his shirt. He made an ineffectual swipe at cleaning his face.

"Nothing more than horse's you-rin, ain't it? Just goes to show, don't buy that California piss."

Guy put both fists down on Malloy's desk and leaned over close to him. "I happen to be a California winegrower, sir, and I happen to know this is not California wine."

Malloy guffawed, unperturbed by the threat in Guy's stance. "Then you must be that poor fellow that lost all his bottles over at the exhibition. What a shame. But goes to show, you shouldn't be coming around where you're not wanted."

"Not wanted by whom?"

Malloy gestured at a plaque hanging on the wall behind him. "New York Winegrowers' Association," it read.

"By us." Any pretense at cordiality was gone. "We don't want you moving in on our business. Got that? And we'll do what has to be done to make sure you don't."

"Such as substituting bad wine for good and destroying our booth?"

"You catch on fast, don't you, mister? So you be a good boy and you go back to your friends and tell them we ain't going to take no competition from the likes of you. Bad enough what we get from the fucking Frenchies and those other foreigners. We don't need any from you hicks out west."

Guy's left hand sprang out and grabbed Malloy's filthy collar, hoisting the paunchy man out of his chair. His right pulled back into a fist. Guy wanted to smash it into the middle of Malloy's repugnant face. He wanted to beat him bloody and beyond recognition. Guy felt his old rage rising. He wasn't holding Terence Malloy. He was looking into Donnadieu's eyes. He was holding Captain John Spencer of the *Bonnie Swift*. He was about to smash his father apart. Guy let his fist fall to his side.

"We'd better be getting along," Cahill squeaked meekly.

Guy held Malloy up for one more second then dropped him back into the chair.

"You're right. I wouldn't want to soil my hands on slime like this." Guy turned and left. Cahill couldn't resist one last glance at Malloy, who wouldn't be recovering his bluster for some time to come.

I wished he'd knocked him silly, Cahill thought. I wished he had.

He caught up with Guy in the street. "Where are we going now, sir?"

"Not back to the exhibition, that's for sure. I'm afraid there is nothing left for you to do here. I'm sorry, you'll have to return to Washington."

"Oh, that's all right, sir. Senator Gwim always has plenty for me to do—though, I can't say it's anywhere as interesting or exciting as this."

My goodness, thought Guy, I'm glad someone enjoyed all this. But he wouldn't think of chiding the young man. Rather he said, "I'll have a letter for you to take to Senator Gwim. Perhaps the federal government might help us with these, how shall I put it, slightly unfair trade practices of the East Coast growers."

Cahill smiled, "Sir, I would say that you were putting it very diplomatically. I'm sure the senator will do what he can, though his time is quite taken up with the slavery question."

Guy was uneasy with Gwim's involvement with the "slavery question." He knew the senator was whole-heartedly pro-slavery. Under other circumstances, Guy would not have had anything to do with the man. But he was learning the hard facts of compromise and, damn it, the winegrowers needed Gwim's support. If they didn't improve their markets somehow, all the California vineyards would fail.

"You know, Jeremy, this trip might not be a complete loss."

"How so, sir?"

"That scum Malloy has touched off a thought. The world doesn't end at the Atlantic. I have an idea."

The next day Guy set out to put his idea in motion. He began making the rounds of exporters, hoping to find a firm that might be interested in shipping California wine to Europe. Guy thought there was a chance it might be bought there first as a novelty and then later on its own merit.

There were several exporters who showed moderate interest, but no one was willing to talk seriously. The day was getting late and Guy was trying not to be discouraged. It was, therefore, with delight he met Captain Wethersby in the offices of Guy's last appointment. It was decided that they should meet later for dinner.

During the meal, Captain Wethersby insisted Guy tell him all about the past years. At the end of the recitation, Wethersby leaned back in his chair, shaking his head. "That is quite a story, my friend, enough for three lifetimes. I would say it is long past when you should have some good luck. And," here Wethersby smiled, "I might be able to supply you with just that."

Wethersby was sure that the owner of his line, Samuel Farragut Clay, would be interested in handling the shipping.

"He's got the biggest company in America now, and it's because he's got imagination. Always looking for new products that need shipping, new markets, better ships, and if, you don't mind my immodesty, the best captains. I've an appointment with him tomorrow. Come with me, I think you'll find him very open to you. But be careful. He's a shrewd one."

The next evening, in a Fifth Avenue mansion that rivalled any in the Faubourg St. Honoré, Samuel Clay was in the middle of saying he found Guy's proposal interesting, when he was interrupted by the only person who would dare do so.

Ardis Elizabeth Clay did not so much enter a room as float in on sweet perfume and promise. Her effect was startling, and Guy was not the first man who forgot to breathe on seeing her for the first time. Her skin was as pale and delicate as a lily, her hair a crown of silvery blond, her eyes hypnotic, magic, her lips a full angel's bow of delight.

Captain Wethersby was amused at his friend's reaction. He had seen many men respond to Ardis Clay that way. She passed them unseeing and made straight to her father's chair.

Kissing the top of his nearly bald head, she said, "Darling, you must tell Mother I may go to Lutecia Bohlen's party next week. Mother is being so stubborn about it."

Clay looked indulgently at the glorious creature that had somehow sprung from him and his wife. "Ardis, at eighteen I would expect you to have better manners."

"Manners have nothing to do with Lutecia Bohlen's party."

Clay stopped her short by motioning to Guy and Wethersby who had both stood on her entrance. She sent a vague glance in their direction, started to murmur, "What a pleasure," when her glance was stopped on Guy. Suddenly he found he was being bestowed with the most exhilarating smile.

"And where are your manners, Father dear? You must introduce me."

"Yes, well," Clay was always fascinated with Ardis's shifts—from coaxing little girl to low-timbre temptress, and the numerous variations in between. "Captain Wethersby, I know you've met." Ardis nodded to show she had, her gaze never leaving Guy. "And this gentleman is Mister Guy Saint-Savin of California and France. I guess that's actually Count Saint-Savin, is it not?"

Guy wrenched his eyes from the daughter to the father. "Sir, 'mister' is what I prefer. The title of 'count' was for Bordeaux, not here. Perhaps, sir, we've kept you long enough. If I may meet you at your offices, I would like to go over my proposal in more detail."

After the two men had taken their leave, Clay turned to his daughter, waiting for the questions he knew she would be asking. When none were immediately forthcoming—she sat in her chair, looking at the door out of which Guy had left—Clay supplied some answers anyway.

"He's from Bordeaux. His family owns a château."

"I know. It's called du Clocher. We rode past it when we visited the Medoc on my birthday tour of the continent."

Clay was flabbergasted. "How in the world did you associate this man's name with a house we drove past two years ago?"

She turned to her father, her lips turning up sweetly. "Because I wanted it and was told I couldn't have it. That it was owned by a family named Saint-Savin and even your money couldn't buy it for me."

"I never could understand your infatuation with France, Ardis. Do you realize your learning to speak French has been one of the only times you've applied yourself to anything in your life?"

She didn't attempt explain. How could she tell her father that France so excited her romantic and extravagant nature?

"Mother's party next week, you'll be sure she invites Count Saint-Savin, won't you?" was her only reply as she swept out of the room.

Clay tapped his lip, thinking. He would have to keep an eye on this. Ardis was so unpredictable.

Guy attended the party. He dined at the Clays'. Had lunch at the Clays'. Went riding with the Clays. Then he dined with Ardis. Had lunch with Ardis. Went riding with Ardis. And found himself thinking of little besides when he would be with her next.

Had they met in California, Guy would have been too wrapped up in his work to do more than admire her beauty in an abstract way. But in New York, there was only Ardis and her distracting teal-blue eyes. When she was in a room with him, Guy could focus on little else. He was too aware of her presence, her scent, and of his desire.

After a month, Guy could find no legitimate reason for postponing his departure any longer. Clay agreed to approach firms in England and the Low Countries to see if there was interest in importing the California wine. If there was any at all, he would handle the business. Guy made contact with every other exporter and did all there was to be done. Still he didn't want to leave.

One afternoon, alone with Ardis in the drawing room, Guy confessed it was long past time for him to go.

Ardis cocked her head. "Then why haven't you, sir?"

It seemed so natural for him to say, "Because I don't want to be without you."

"One thing need not preclude the other."

Guy didn't understand what she meant, and then, feeling like a dunce, it was very clear. "You're right. But I am afraid, afraid to ask, for fear you'll say no."

Leaning over to him, Ardis brought her lips to his. And then her arms, and her body. Guy lost all sense of time and place. When finally they pulled apart, he said, "Ardis, I have little to offer, and I have no right to ask but I can't stop myself. Marry me. Marry me now. Right away. Marry me and you'll never regret it."

"Darling, the only thing I'll regret is you took so long to propose."

Ardis's mother agreed with Guy—that he had no right to ask Ardis to marry him. And Mrs. Clay objected vehemently, in the privacy of their rooms, to Mister Clay. She did not like the haste of the proposed marriage. She didn't like her daughter being hauled off to the wilderness. And she didn't like Guy's Roman Catholic background.

"What I don't understand, don't understand at all, is why Ardis wants the match," Mrs. Clay had complained. "She is absolutely the crème of New York's eligible young women. She could have her choice of any man. Why this one? Why?"

Samuel Clay looked with little fondness at his much-younger wife. He had married late in life, spending his youth building his enormous shipping line, the import-export business, and accumulating more money than he could possibly spend. Missy Stanhope Johnson, who at twenty-five was facing spinsterhood, had been eager to accept his marriage proposal, even though he was thirty years her senior and did not come from one of the city's "good" families. She had rejected all her earlier beaux as not suitable and then suddenly found herself in competition with much younger women. Besides, Clay did have his advantages. *He* might not have known how to spend all those millions, but Missy surely did.

She threw parties and balls, held soirées and extravagant dinners— to fill her evenings. Her days were spent on wardrobe and toilette. This left little time for Samuel and, later, Ardis. Clay did not object. He attended her functions if he felt like it—which was rarely—and worked late or ate out with his own friends when he didn't. Missy had lost her appeal not long after they were married. Her single-minded rush to do nothing had soon bored Clay.

Ardis, on the other hand, had never lost favor with her father. He adored her from the very beginning. However, he was realistic enough to recognize that Ardis had her faults. She was spoiled and headstrong, and he worried over what would happen to her when he died. He couldn't rely on Missy to give their daughter any sound guidance. Missy needed guidance herself.

And then there was the worry of the eager men who were after Ardis's fortune. No, it would be best to get the girl married off quickly. And he liked Guy and what Captain Wethersby had told him only confirmed his impression of the Frenchman. Guy was not a cheat, he had convictions, and he assured Clay—who wasn't sure how much he cared either way—that like many Frenchmen, he was not a practicing Catholic. There would be no question of children being raised in that religion.

Clay did not relish the idea of Ardis going west. He even tried enticing Guy into staying in New York by offering him employment in Clay Shipping. Despite Guy's refusal, Clay gave his consent to the marriage. He knew Ardis was willful enough to reject every other man if she did not get her way with Guy.

So it was that Ardis Elizabeth Clay became Ardis Elizabeth Clay Saint-Savin, and she and Guy left immediately to live happily ever after in California—before Missy had time to organize some awful party.

Guy's thoughts were interrupted by more rustling, followed by a whisper. "Guy, come up here. I'm cold."

He smiled and needed no further urging to climb the ladder and become entwined in the long, soft legs and eager, demanding arms of his wife.

Yes, this had been a much different voyage than the one on the *Bonnie Swift*.

Chapter Forty-nine

With adroit pushing and tugging, coming with long practice, Ardis, with the help of Guy, was able to free herself and her yards and yards of crinoline and lace from the landau. She stepped delicately down to the wooden plank walkway in front of the hotel, and glanced back at the muddy street.

"There's something so primitive and exciting about this city," she observed.

"Now Ardis, the town fathers of San Francisco would be horrified to hear you say that."

"But that's the way it is. I mean, look, you don't even have real sidewalks, only these boards."

"Built especially to protect the dresses of our lovely ladies."

"It's wonderful. On one hand, you have all these people..." Ardis was gesturing with her parasol as if the particular people near them were the specific people to whom she was referring, "...trying so hard to be sophisticated and civilized, building beautiful mansions and wanting so much to be like New York society. And on the other hand, you have that dreadful waterfront with all those river rats. Oh, let's stay here forever."

As she spoke Guy was propelling her through the lobby of the Palace Hotel, an establishment of which San Francisco was rightfully proud, toward the curving marble staircase. In the three days of lunching, dining, driving, looking, Ardis had made her desire to stay increasingly clear. She liked San Francisco.

For all her poking fun at the city, it was actually a vibrant and growing community. It had more than 250 streets and alleys, two public squares, sixteen hotels, five public markets, twenty bath-houses, fifteen flour and saw mills, 63 bakeries, thirteen foundries and iron works, nineteen banking establishments, eighteen public

302

stables, ten public schools with 21 teachers and 1,259 scholars, eighteen churches with 8,000 members, six military companies with 350 members, three hospitals (one private and two public), an almshouse, twelve newspapers, five theaters, a Philharmonic society, several lecture halls, twelve wharves, 42 wholesale liquor houses, 537 saloons, and 200 lawyers.

Ardis loved San Francisco. There were people, things to do. She wanted to have fun, and didn't seem to care when Guy patiently explained he was needed back at the vineyard. Ardis never expressed any interest in getting to her new home or meeting her new son. She pouted when Guy didn't agree to stay. She always got what she wanted. That was how, she believed, love was expressed, by her being given what she wanted.

Guy at times felt he was dealing with a young child. Actually Kyle was, for the most part, more reasonable than Ardis.

"And besides, you haven't introduced me to your friends here," Ardis said, refusing to give up her argument. "I want to meet everyone there is to know."

"I know very few people in San Francisco."

They were walking slowly up the stairs, Ardis setting the pace so that she gained the attention of every man in the huge marble and chandeliered lobby, including that of one of the desk clerks. He was so mesmerized by her, he almost forgot to hurry after them.

"Mister Saint-Savin," he called, holding out an envelope. "You received this while you were out. I believe it's quite urgent."

Guy ripped the seal, read a few lines, then took Ardis firmly by the elbow. "I'll finish reading this in our room." He dismissed the clerk with a thank you and almost dragged Ardis up the stairs.

"What is going on?" she asked indignantly once their door was shut. "What a rude display. You fairly manhandled me."

Guy wasn't listening. He was reading the letter, which was from Miguel.

Dear Guy,
I am sorry to be sending you such disturbing news, however, you must return to the Belltower at once. There is trouble. I'll begin at the beginning.
Perhaps you have heard the unhappy news that Count Harazthy was accused of stealing from the mint. Many thousands of dollars worth of gold are missing and he cannot account for it. We who know him know this accusation is ridiculous, but he has resigned

and had to put up his land as security while he fights the charges in court.

Squatters have moved onto his land and now someone—and I have been told it is Jake Cartwell, one of Damon Delany's men—has spread the rumor the Belltower is not legally yours, that you are a foreigner who bought from someone without legal title.

A small army of these squatters started up here from San Francisco. I only learned this through Charley Parkhurst. Now that he's given up the stage run and opened that little inn, he knows everything that is happening in the Napa. I was able to keep the squatters out of the vineyard. They are now camped in the orchard.

You must return. We are at a stand-off and I fear there will be violence.

Miguel

"Well, what is it?" Ardis asked petulantly. "What could possibly be so urgent?"

"There's trouble at the vineyard. We leave tonight."

Ardis was wise enough not to argue.

The full moon made the trip easier. Guy drove the carriage horses hard. They were about a mile from the vineyard when a horse and rider came out of the shielding darkness of trees and onto the road. Guy pulled up hard and reached for his rifle.

"Hey there. That the way to greet a friend?" The slight figure pushed back his oversized hat, and Guy saw it was Charley Parkhurst.

The start woke up Ardis and she now whispered from the passengers' compartment, "Is it one of those banditos? Are we being robbed?"

"A robber? Charley a robber? He's one of the most honest men on the face of the earth."

"Now, don't go so far, friend." Charley was never comfortable with praise or thanks.

"Ardis, you've been wanting to meet my friends. Here's one of the best friends a person can have. Ardis, Charley Parkhurst. Charley, my wife."

Ardis's lips pursed into a pout. She wished Guy wouldn't tease her like this. Really, this grimy, uncouth-looking fellow couldn't possibly be his friend. But as the seconds passed, it became obvious Guy had intended no joke. Ardis was not at all sure she approved of her French count keeping such company. Striving to remember her manners and good breeding, she finally came out with an unconvincing, "It is a great pleasure."

Charley tipped his hat with all the gentility he could muster. "Nice to meet you, ma'am. Guy sure picked a pretty one, if you don't mind my saying. But listen, I come out to meet you 'cause them damned squatters are all over the place now. And I know I've seen some more of Delany's boys around, too. Thought you might need a little help. Come on, we better get to the house."

They met no one on the way, though Guy could see the lights of campfires among the trees. Fenella and Miguel were waiting for them.

As Guy was helping Ardis down, she whispered to him, "Am I to meet more of your friends now?" On solid ground, she smoothed and plumped her dress, which in that setting looked more impractical than it had in the city. Then she spotted Fenella. "Oh, you must be the housekeeper," she said, using the grande-dame voice her mother always used with the servants. "Would you please come and assist me."

Fenella blushed, not sure what she should do, but was saved by Guy. "She's no housekeeper," he corrected, although he was fairly sure Ardis knew who it was. "Let me introduce Fenella Delany. She's been the only mother Kyle has ever known and a saint to me."

Ardis was not thrilled with the warmth and tenderness she detected in Guy's voice. She looked at Fenella more closely. Mousy, little thing, she thought.

"And this is Miguel de Cordoba."

Ardis was all sweetness and graciousness when she turned to him. "I am so happy to meet you. Guy tells me you've been of great assistance."

Miguel showed no sign of being grateful for Ardis's kind words. In fact, his return stare was so hard and grim that Ardis had to force herself not to flinch. Had she been one to notice such details, she would have seen that this expression had appeared when she addressed Fenella in her lady-of-the-manor tone. Miguel had become increasingly protective of Fenella over the years. She had been nice to him when he'd started working for Damon, offering kindness and care, and which being unsolicited made her actions all the more precious to Miguel. He would have no one talking down to Fenella Delany.

Guy in his worry about the squatters totally overlooked the dynamics of the scene and was now anxious to get everyone inside to safety. "We shouldn't be out here," he said. "Ardis, go with Fenella. She'll show you your room. I need to talk with Miguel."

"Darling, you're not abandoning me so soon?" Ardis was exhausted and welcomed retiring to a soft bed; still, that wasn't going to stop her from complaining.

"This is important," Guy said as everyone went inside, Charley Parkhurt having long since slipped off into the night. "And besides, putting you in Fenella's care is hardly abandonment."

Ardis's expression clearly stated she was not in agreement, but followed Fenella to the bedroom corridor anyway.

"Has anything else happened?" Guy asked when the women were out of earshot and he and Miguel seated.

"Something's going to happen. These people have been told they're Americans and the land is theirs. I don't think they're bad people, they just want to believe what they're being told. Liquor is being brought in for them. Tempers are rising."

"Delany?"

Miguel shrugged. "It sounds like him."

Guy rubbed his hand over his eyes. He was very tired. Maybe he shouldn't have gone to New York. If he had stayed, perhaps he could have prevented all this. But then he wouldn't have met Ardis.

"I suppose we could take legal action, get the sheriff to throw them off," he said at last.

Miguel snorted. "Legal action? In California? How many politicians have you bought and paid for? How many bribes have you handed out? In California legal action can drag on for years. Look at Count Harazthy. His land should be protected by the court during the trial. Do you think any sheriff has gone out there?"

"So what's left for us to do?" Guy didn't need any answer. He knew it already. He would have to evict the squatters by force, run them off the land if they didn't go peacefully. Let them be the ones to summon the sheriff.

"Okay then. At sunup get all the men together and make sure they have plenty of ammunition. Maybe a few dozen guns and rifles will scare the squatters away."

"And if it doesn't?" Miguel asked.

Guy didn't have that answer.

Chapter Fifty

The false dawn was made murky by a shimmering mist as the thirty-five men and horses picked their way through the sparse underbrush.

Each man carried a sinister, long rifle in his arm and a dread of what was to come in his heart.

Quietly they encircled the squatters' camp, where fires had long since flickered out and the only sound was the occasional cry of a baby.

In place, the men waited for the sun to rise and the camp to come to life. It did when a scruffy-faced, heavy-jowled ex-miner came stumbling out of a tent, trying to rub the day into his eyes. When at last he could see, he didn't like what he saw. He took two careful steps backwards, trying to reach his tent and gun, before Guy called out with menacing authority, "I wouldn't move, friend, unless you're planning on pulling down your tent and getting out of here now."

Heads popped out of every tent, and men scrambled to get their trousers on.

"Come out, all of you," Guy called, "and don't bother bringing your weapons unless you're real intent on dying."

The handful of squatters who looked as if they might want to fight had their minds changed by the thirty-five long barrels staring down at them.

"Now, gentlemen," Guy continued conversationally, "I think you all have been getting some false information. I understand you've been told I don't have proper title to this land and that it's up for the taking. Wrong, gentlemen. Let me assure you, that's very wrong. I own it outright, fair and square, and there's no disputing that. With that in mind, I'm now asking you to pull up stakes and move on. No one wants any trouble, specially not with your women and children here. So go peacefully and there'll be no problem."

There was the dark, discontented rumbling of a mob's disappointment, but most of the squatters seemed willing to bend to the strength of Guy's argument. One, however, was not. Everything was enormous about the man, his size, his muscles, even his beard. He had no family with him. He knew better than to bring them—he knew peace would not prevail because he wouldn't let it. Miguel nudged Guy. He had recognized him, Jake Cartwell, Damon Delany's man.

Cartwell growled his defiance. "And why should we believe you? You're nothing but a lying, cheating spik. You'd say anything to steal what belongs to good honest Americans."

"Brave words for someone looking up the barrel of my rifle. But I suppose you're being paid enough to be brave."

"What the hell are you talking about?" yelled Cartwell raising his arm and bringing it down.

A shot rang out. It hung frozen for one terrible moment, and then before Guy could stop them, his men opened fire in return. The squatters dove back into their tents. Many came out armed.

Suddenly the air around Guy was filled with a shower of sharp, popping sounds that drowned out the orders he was vainly yelling. He wheeled in his saddle to see a man fall from a horse, another kneeling with a rifle from which came a seemingly silent puff of smoke. There were bodies cringing for cover, and wagons and tents on fire. Soon all was shrouded by the growing cloud of blue, sulfur-laden gunsmoke.

The battle seemed to go on forever, but only lasted five minutes. Then the squatters laid down their guns and the smoke slowly thinned to reveal a horror of fire, blood, pain, and anguish. Two of Guy's men had superficial wounds. The squatters hadn't been as lucky. Five men dead, a dozen wounded, and one small boy, too curious for his own good, lay in his mother's arms as his brief life left him. Cartwell and the men who had shared his tent were gone.

"Oh, my God, Miguel, what have we done?

"What we had to do," Miguel answered without hesitation.

Delany made sure the San Francisco headlines screamed daily with outrage at the Vineyard Massacre. Guy was vilified in editorials when the squatters claimed his men had fired on unarmed people. And the papers discounted no rumor or speculation on Guy's past in France and the reasons he left his home country. One even solemnly reported he'd fled after raping Hortense, Louis-Napoleon's mother.

"Good God," Guy murmured with disgust on reading that, "she was dead before I was born."

There was no let-up on the barrage until, in response, a committee for vigilance was formed. It was the third one San Francisco had seen. The others were a reaction to the unrestrained and murderous lawlessness that had come out of the Barbary Coast and had threatened to engulf the entire city. One gang, in particular, a group of ex-convicts from Australia with the whimsical sobriquet of the Sidney Ducks, had been a target of the committees. They had had a good number of the gang rounded up, tried quickly, and dispatched at the end of a rope even quicker.

The previous committees had been disbanded once it was decided that the clean-up had been adequate and the citizenry lost its taste for wholesale justice. Even with all the publicity and outrage, the Vineyard Massacre would not have been enough alone for a third committee to be formed. But the Sidney Ducks had regrouped and were showing strength.

Charley Parkhurst came tearing down the road one morning shouting that a posse from the committee was right behind him, on its way to arrest Guy.

Miguel was for holding the posse off by force. Fenella argued otherwise and prevailed. Guy must go, she'd said. He wouldn't be convicted. He was innocent. Even though Guy wasn't as confident in the system as she, he surrendered. Sooner or later he would be taken. He had already fled one country, where could he go next?

Fenella packed a few things for him to take. Kyle shook hands with his father. Ardis did nothing. She was infuriated that Guy had done this to her, brought her out west to witness her husband being led away like a common criminal. She turned her head when he tried to kiss her goodbye.

Guy was taken to a shabby room with a cot and a chipped basin for washing in one of the industrial sections of the city. His jailers spoke little to him, but he was told his trial would be soon. It seemed that two Sidney Ducks, who were to be tried at the same time, hadn't been as reasonable as Guy when the posse arrived for them. They were barricaded in a saloon on the Barbary Coast. The trials were postponed until the men could be flushed out.

As Guy paced the rotting floorboards of his strangling room, he wondered what Ardis and Fenella were doing about getting him a lawyer. He knew his men had volunteered to be witnesses, to swear that the first shot had come from the other side. But would that be enough? Taunts and stones had been hurled at him when he was brought into the city. To the good people of San Francisco, he was the villain and they wanted revenge not truth. Guy was afraid blood, his blood, was what they would get.

On the second day, two of his jailers came with leg shackles.

"You don't need those," Guy argued. "I came willingly to prove my innocence. You had no fight from me."

A grunt was his reply as the irons were fastened around his ankles, and he was led off, dirty, sweaty, unshaven, and bleary-eyed.

He rode in an open wagon a couple of blocks to a warehouse. Inside it was crowded with spectators, twenty armed guards, and the forty members of the committee who were seated at several tables arranged in a large "U." Guy was shoved into a chair in the center of the "U," surrounded on three sides by his judges and accusers. Two other chairs became the repositories for the two cursing and spitting Sydney Ducks, whose faces were covered with blood, a testament to their unwillingness to sanction the committee's authority.

Guy recognized several committee members. John Carlyle owned a fabric shop where Fenella bought her material. Sam Cramer, a lumber man from whom Guy purchased oak for barrels. Jefferson William Simpson, a lawyer. And there was Kincaid Johnson, one of Damon Delany's political cronies. With the exception of Johnson, an insufferable blowhard always trying to insure he remain in the good graces of Delany, the ones Guy knew were reasonable men. Under ordinary circumstances.

Their treatment of the Ducks showed, however, these were extraordinary times. Simpson read a list of their crimes and asked what they pleaded.

"Go fuck your grandmother's dog," one of them screamed, spittle flying in all directions.

"And what does the committee vote?" asked Simpson as if he had received a reasonable answer to his original question. "All those for guilty, raise hands."

Forty hands went up.

"All those for death."

Forty hands again.

"We hereby sentence you to death by hanging. Bailiffs, please remove the prisoners."

It took three guards for each man to get them out of the room, and even then one of the Ducks had to be knocked unconscious.

Simpson coolly picked up another piece of paper.

"We shall now hear the case of Guy Saint-Savin. Guy Saint-Savin is accused of willingly causing the murder of five unarmed men and one small boy. What do you plead?"

Guy searched the rows of spectators as he rose. Ardis, wearing the black of mourning, was with Miguel near the front. He could also pick out many of his men. He could not, however, find John Randolph, the lawyer he expected to be there in his defense.

"Your plea?" Simpson asked again.

"Gentlemen of the committee, I am completely innocent of the charges and hope that upon hearing the evidence, you will exonerate me."

His answer was greeted with guffaws and hoots from the crowd behind him. "Don't waste time, hang him now," someone yelled.

"We'll hear the first witness for the prosecution..."

"Mr. Simpson," Guy interrupted, "if you please. My counsel, John Randolph, does not seem to be present."

"No need for Randolph. We sent him away." It was Kincaid Johnson puffing the words out with his cigar smoke.

"But how can I present my case?"

"For glory's sake, Saint-Savin," Johnson waved his cigar indignantly. "We're going to hear what the folks have to say, we're going to vote, and what happens, happens. Don't need any danged-awful lawyers— begging your pardon, Jefferson—messing up the works. You got that? So sit down."

Simpson, looking greatly uncomfortable with his colleague's lack of respect for jurisprudence, stared down at his paper before calling out, "Mrs. Matthew Henderson, if you will."

A tiny woman in a patched checkered dress and a straw hat too old and tattered to add to her appearance came slowly up to the committee. She stood a few feet from Guy and nervously clutched her skirt with calloused and work-ploughed hands.

"Now Mrs. Henderson, tell us who you are and what you saw," Simpson directed gently.

"I'm...I'm..." she began.

"Louder," several spectators yelled.

"I'm Molly Henderson, Mrs. Matthew Henderson. It was my boy...my little Dickie that was shot...and it was *him*." She pointed at Guy. "*Him* that shot him. *Him* that killed my little boy."

Guy jumped up as best his leg irons would allow. "That's not true. I never fired my gun. Never. I shot no one."

Mrs. Henderson was clawing at the tears on her face. "You good as killed him. You and your men, shooting innocent folks, shooting my poor Dickie."

"That will be all, Mrs. Henderson. You may leave now," Simpson said kindly.

"But I haven't had a chance to question her."

"I told you, already, we make the rules," Johnson shouted. "Now sit down and shut up."

Guy looked around for support in this travesty. He found Miguel stone-faced and Ardis glacial, although in truth she was exhilarated by the proceedings. There was such drama and excitement. Those Duck men had been so raw, vibrant. Nothing like this ever happened in her father's world. Besides she had come to realize her standing was not suffering. She was perceived as a victim, the poor innocent bride of an evil pariah. She was glad she had come to the trial although it had taken a tongue-lashing from that awful Fenella to get her there.

The other men that Guy thought he could count on for support were so outnumbered there was not going to be much they could do. So the proceedings continued. Eight more squatters testified, all saying more or less the same, that they had come out of their tents without weapons and had been fired on by Guy's men. Guy was allowed no cross-examination, and the ugly rumblings of the crowd got meaner with each statement.

Jake Cartwell was at the back of the warehouse. After the fourth witness, he left grinning. He wasted no time getting to the Palace Hotel and to suite 406-08.

He knocked, happy to be the bearer of such good tidings.

"Who is it?" an annoyed voice called out.

"It's me, boss, Cartwell."

"Cartwell? Right. Wait a minute."

Damon Delany, clad only in a blue silk dressing robe, opened the door. He stepped back a couple of feet, allowing Cartwell only enough room to close the door behind him without advancing into the elegant sitting room.

"So what do you want?" Delany demanded unpleasantly.

Cartwell was puzzled by the reception. He'd thought Delany would be anxious to hear his news. Cartwell glanced at the bedroom door. Maybe he'd interrupted something.

"You told me to let you know about the trial. It's in the bag. The Frenchie's going to hang, sure as..."

Delany cut him off with a fierce, slashing wave. Cartwell realized the bedroom door had been opened a crack and nodded at Delany to show he understood.

"Yeah, well, uh, just was over there to see what was going on, you know. Everyone's saying the French guy's men, they were the ones who shot first and that the French guy was giving the orders. So it looks like a guilty vote and the...well, you know what happens then."

Delany was staring at the bedroom door. He made a decision.

"Well, it certainly sounds like a miscarriage of justice. Didn't you tell me you were there, Cartwell? Didn't you say you were sure the first shot came from one of the tents?"

Cartwell swayed from foot to foot, completely flabbergasted. The look on his boss's face told him he'd better agree, and quickly.

"Yeah, Mr. Delany, it was just like you said. No question. I was there and the shot came from the squatters. Couldn't say who pulled the trigger, mind you."

"Of course, not," Damon said soothingly. "No one could expect you to know that. Must have been confusing that morning. So much happening. So much tension."

"That's just how it was."

Initially Damon had been furious when he'd gotten the report of the Vineyard Massacre. He knew it was Cartwell or one of his other men who started it, thinking it an opportunity to get rid of Saint-Savin. But killing Guy had not been part of Damon's plan. He wanted to hurt Guy and destroy him, but he wanted it to be a long, drawn-out process. He knew full well Guy had bought the land legally. But he also knew the previous owner's family had gotten title to the property through a land grant seventy-five years before. These land grants were being challenged. Delany figured Guy could be tied up for years trying to prove title and would eventually have to give up and leave. Delany could beat him through attrition while at the same time not appearing part of the fight at all. It had been a lovely plan, and these blockheads had blasted it out of the water.

But when Guy was arrested, Delany thought he would let events take their course, though he hadn't stopped Cartwell from insuring certain squatters' memories were as they should be.

Delany looked at the bedroom door. Now he had no choice. He had to intervene.

"Cartwell, there's only one thing to do now. You've got to stop this terrible farce. Go back to the committee and tell them what you told me. Tell them about the shot you heard fired—*from a tent*. Now hurry, before it's too late. And Cartwell, be sure to tell the committee I sent you over to testify."

Cartwell rushed from the room. What was that all about? He wondered. Sure as hell wished I knew who was in that bedroom.

Cartwell's horse was frothing by the time he reached the warehouse. Cartwell reined him and ran in.

The warehouse was empty.

Cartwell ran back outside. Two old men were sitting on a crate nearby.

"Where'd they go?" Cartwell yelled to them. "Where'd everybody go?"

"That way." One of the men pointed down a side street. "Taking the French fellow for a hanging."

"Holy shit," Cartwell muttered, as he jumped back on his horse and rode for his life, which he knew he wouldn't have long if he didn't stop the execution.

The square, actually little more than an open space between buildings that boasted one good strong tree, was packed with a jostling, boisterous audience looking forward to a good show. Cartwell forced his horse through them, cursing those who were slow to move and threatening to trample anyone who stayed his way. He got to the tree as Guy, standing on a barrel was having a noose placed around his neck.

The committee for vigilance was all there although most looked as if they wished they were not. There was so much noise that Cartwell's yells at first went unheard. Finally, he took out his pistol and fired a shot into the air.

"Listen to me! You've got to listen." He brandished the pistol around to underline his command.

Kincaid Johnson realized it was Cartwell and knew it in his best interest to let Damon Delany's man speak.

"Now, now, let's hear the man. Let him say his piece," Johnson called.

When there was enough order for the committee members to hear him, Cartwell said, "I was there, too. I was with those squatters. And I tell you this fellow's men didn't shoot first. First shot came from the tents."

"Really!" Jefferson Simpson was outraged. He wasn't sure how many more of these gross irregularities he could take. He had never liked the concept of the committee to begin with and had only joined in hopes of checking any abuses. But this was too much. "We had ten witnesses who totally disagree with you and thirty more willing to say the same thing. So who are you to come forward now and why should we believe you?"

" 'Cause Damon Delany told me it was my duty to tell what happened, that's why."

Delany. The committee members looked at each other nervously. There was hardly one of them who didn't owe Delany in some way or another or who knew that one day they would be going to Delany for a favor.

Kincaid Johnson finally broke the silence. "I think we can all agree this changes everything."

Most of the committee nodded.

"Now wait a second," Simpson was beginning to wonder if he was being made the fool. "You say you were in the Napa Valley when the shooting occurred?"

"That's right," Cartwell answered. "I heard about some free land and went to see what it was all about—just like everyone else."

"And you say you're certain..."

Kincaid Johnson cut him off. "Listen, this testimony is good enough for me. How about the rest of you?"

The other committee members, with the exception of Simpson, nodded quickly.

"So what about you, Jefferson?" Johnson asked. "You for changing your vote and letting this innocent man free?"

Simpson was not at all sure what he was for. There was something very wrong. He wondered if all the other testimony hadn't been bought to convict Saint-Savin. But then why this reprieve? He sighed, a very distressed man who would never be coerced onto such a committee again, a man who would work to insure no more committees be formed in San Francisco.

"Yes, I change my vote. The man is not guilty," Simpson said at last.

The very crowd who minutes before had been howling for Guy's blood, now cheered his release, and cheered even louder when Ardis threw her arms around her husband's neck and kissed him, now the rapturous, relieved wife who had stood by him stoically, confident of his innocence.

Simpson approached them. "I cannot tell you how deeply grieved I am by my role in this terrible affair. Would you both, please, be my guests for dinner tonight? I have a house on Nob Hill. I would be delighted and grateful if you would."

"And we would be delighted to come," Ardis answered before Guy could refuse the invitation.

Chapter Fifty-one

Simpson's dinner party was one of the year's greatest social successes, with many of the city's "best" people vying to attend. They were all eager to make amends for what was now being categorized as the scandalous treatment afforded Guy.

There was dancing under crystal chandeliers, champagne, excellent food, and even Ardis was impressed by the mansion. And she was delighted by the invitations they received to other parties. Ardis accepted them all with delight. She and Guy were suddenly the most sought-after couple in the city.

They stayed a week, their suite at the Palace filled with flowers and delicacies sent by Ardis's new acquaintances. Guy put up with all the attention for Ardis's enjoyment. Besides, if any trouble did develop with his land title, these people might be able to help. And what's more, a person with such friends didn't get hauled in front of vigilance committees. Some of these people, he actually liked, Jefferson Simpson in particular.

Simpson had apologized to Guy again. He'd been cajoled onto the committee to give it respectability—he was one of the most respected lawyers in San Francisco and his name was often mentioned as a future senator. Simpson confessed to Guy that he would never go into politics, he didn't have the stomach for it. He couldn't curry favor as the present Senator Gwim did and he would never work with a Damon Delany, who now virtually controlled the state north of Salinas.

After a week, even with the pleasure of Simpson's company and Ardis's excitement, Guy was ready to quit the city. It was time to get back to the Belltower. Ardis was at her dressing table holding a diamond earring to one ear and a ruby to the other, trying to decide which she would wear to the Crockers' dinner.

317

Guy stood behind her, hands on her shoulders. Her image was so lovely in the mirror, he suddenly wanted to do nothing else except hold her and say to hell with the dinner. He leaned down and kissed the back of her neck.

"Please, darling, you'll mess my hair," Ardis said.

Guy pulled her up from the chair and turned her around. She was wearing a low-cut white gown. He bent to kiss the hollow between her breasts.

"But the Crockers..."

"It's not the Crockers I want, it's you."

Ardis laughed and went to him, pulling the pins from her hair as she went.

An hour later the room was dark and the two lay in each other's arms, spent and floating. Ardis's lovemaking was so different from Marie-Odile's, Guy was thinking. Ardis, for all of her appearance of the fine-featured patrician, was fire and earthiness in bed. Marie had been gentle and tender until passion overtook her. Guy was suddenly ashamed. He shouldn't be comparing the two women, his wives. At the same time, within him he knew that so much of the intensity he felt for Ardis was the heat of their lovemaking. It was hard to look at her and not want to lead her to the bedroom.

A whisper from the bedsheets made Guy open his eyes. Ardis was putting on her robe.

"Where're you going?" Guy asked, yawning.

"To get ready for the Crockers, of course. If we hurry, we'll still be only fashionably late. And I'll love making excuses while all the time thinking about the real reason we weren't on time."

Guy pushed himself up on his elbows. "Ardis, let's not go. We'll send regrets. It's time we went back to Napa, anyway."

Ardis was annoyed. "Go back? Why? It's wonderful here. This is almost as good as New York. I don't like it in Napa."

"But you've only been there a couple of nights. How could you possibly know you don't like it?"

Ardis didn't answer immediately, she was too intent on pushing a stray lock into place, curled just so against her cheek. "Oh, it didn't take long for me to know. It's so dreary there. What will I do? Who will I talk to?"

"There's me and Kyle, Miguel, and Fenella..."

Ardis heard her line of attack and seized it. "Fenella! Why she's terrible. She hates me. Do you know she yelled at me when I said I wouldn't come to your trial?"

Guy bolted upright. "You weren't coming to my trial?"

Ardis wasn't listening to what she was saying and paying no attention to its effect on her husband. "No, I wasn't going. It was too humiliating."

"Humiliating to stand by your husband when he was unjustly accused?"

"Darling, I didn't know that. But now I do and everything is all right. Come, let's hurry up and get dressed."

Guy lay back in the bed. He had to think. "I'm not going," he said coldly. "You go ahead if you want."

"For goodness sakes, a lady can't go unescorted..." Ardis finally turned her gaze from the mirror and saw Guy's expression. "Well, all right then. I'll go myself."

His staying might turn out to be more fun. Ardis was never allowed to go anywhere alone in New York.

She was awakened the next morning by a tapping at the door. She was very annoyed to be disturbed, having gotten in quite late from the Crockers'. She glanced over to Guy's side of the bed. It was empty. She would have to get up.

It was a maid. "I'm here, ma'am, to pack your bags," she explained.

"My bags? But I didn't send for you. We're not going anywhere."

"It was your husband, ma'am. Said I should be here first thing."

Ardis was about to dismiss her, then thought better of it. Guy had obviously made up his mind to go and that was that. Ardis set about to dressing in a sulk.

When Guy returned at noon she was waiting and still sulking. He ignored her mood, gave her a kiss on the cheek because she would allow no more, and said they would be leaving after lunch.

As the months passed, Ardis became no less disgruntled with Napa. There were no parties, no luxuries, it was all so grubby and mean to her. Her one source of enjoyment were the visits to and from the Harazthys.

Her relationship with Kyle did not help the situation either. She never took to him and the boy avoided her. And then, of course, there was Fenella. She was a source of constant annoyance to Ardis, who resented her very presence at the Belltower.

Had Fenella been a servant to be ordered about, there would have been no problem. Ardis tried doing just that at first, but she didn't get far. Fenella was too much a part of the household and Kyle more her child than Guy's. The men respected and liked her. And what Guy felt for Fenella... well, Ardis wouldn't lower herself by speculating. Not that she could consider Fenella any kind of rival. What man would choose that creature over her? Still she didn't like Fenella and made sure the other woman knew that.

The truth was Ardis had very little to do at the Belltower. Guy hadn't considered that. Fenella ran the house, and there was nothing for Ardis to do in the vineyard, or at least nothing she would do. The nearest neighbors were too busy themselves for much socializing. So day after day Ardis became more restless and resentful that Guy spent so little time with her.

She wrote long, complaining letters to her father. At first he dismissed them as the work of an over-indulged child. But after a time he began to worry that he had misjudged Guy, especially as Ardis became more and more creative with her embellishments. Perhaps he should have gone along with his wife and insisted Ardis marry a malleable banker he could keep under his thumb. No, that wouldn't have done. Clay wanted a strong man for his daughter, someone stronger than she. And he was sure that was what she had gotten. Still, the letters were worrisome.

Matters didn't improve when Guy became occupied in Sacramento with Harazthy lobbying for the formation of a committee "on the improvement of the grape vine in California." The Hungarian was unperturbed that he was fighting for his reputation and his property in court. He was sure in the end he would be exonerated. In the meantime, Harazthy was using his time and energy urging the legislature to send him to Europe. He maintained the trip would be to study the "technical and cultural practices" used abroad and more importantly to buy a variety of vines to be tested scientifically back in California soil.

This had been Harazthy's dream for years. After many trips he and Guy were able to convince Assemblyman Marcus Morrison to introduce a resolution calling for the appointment of three commissioners. Their duty would be to report on "the ways and means best adapted to promote improvement and growth of wine in California."

Not to anyone's great surprise, Harazthy was named a commissioner. But the lobbying wasn't over. He and Guy kept up their steady assault on Sacramento in an attempt to gain state funding of the European expedition. They needed those European vines, they argued, if they were to improve the local industry. The different varieties could be systematically test-planted to determine which were best for the soil and climate. They painted a picture of wine-making developing into a major money-making industry for California.

When they weren't pushing for that, Guy was promoting his idea for the establishment of a state agricultural college, which would include viniculture in its curriculum. One area that Guy left to Harazthy was the problem of the unfair competition and devious practices of the Ohio and New York growers. Guy couldn't bring himself to deal with the two United States senators from California. One was Damon Delany's man, and the other, Senator Gwim, a former southerner, was increasingly vocal in his advocacy of slavery.

All these efforts proved taxing and took up much time, but all in all they proved successful. Guy managed to both charm and overwhelm his opponents and many forgot allegiances in face of his arguments. Besides, what Guy was lobbying for would undoubtedly sit well with their constituents. It all sounded noncontroversial enough.

Despite the gains, the exercise was wearing on Guy. What he had seen in the French National Assembly had not prepared him for the simple, crude corruption that permeated California government. It was so pervasive that the bought votes, horse-trading, gifts and graft were taken for granted. He was relieved when Harazthy got the go-ahead on the European trip, although it did bother him that the count would be traveling on his own money and not the state's. True, Governor John G. Downey had promised Harazthy he would be reimbursed on his return. Still, there was nothing in writing.

"Don't worry," said an exuberant Harazthy, "there'll be no problem. The governor is a gentleman. He gave me his word."

Guy was more than ready to hang up his lobbyist's hat and return home with the news of the great triumph. Maybe the end of his frequent trips to Sacramento would calm the troubled waters back at the Belltower.

He saved revealing the good news for the dinner table when they were all together, Kyle, Fenella, Ardis, Miguel, and several of the men. (Ardis hated eating with the "help," as she put it, but Guy would not budge on the issue.)

"Is everyone's glass filled?" Guy asked. "Then a toast is in order. After all these trips to the capital, we have finally done it. Governor Downey has given his blessings to the European trip."

There were congratulations—everyone knew how hard Guy had worked—and the toast drunk.

"Oh darling!" Ardis was bubbling with pleasure. "That's wonderful. When do we leave? Will it be just France? Italy, too? Please, please, Spain as well. I didn't get there with Father. I imagine it's so exotic."

"What are you talking about?" The others at the table became very quiet. "I thought you understood, Ardis. Haven't you listened to anything I've said over the last months? Harazthy and his son, Antonin, are going. There was never any question of our going as well."

Ardis could only stare. Then she threw her napkin onto the table. "This isn't fair. You did as much work as he did. Why can't you go too? I know why. You don't want to go. You don't want me to have any fun. If you had your way I would rot and die from boredom in this hole." She looked defiantly at the others, daring them to disagree, and huffed from the room.

No one could look up from their plates. They didn't want to look at Guy, for they were sharing his embarrassment. Except for Miguel. He went on eating as if nothing had happened.

After the door to Ardis's room had closed with a resounding slam, Fenella lay her hand over Guy's. "Go to her," she urged softly. "Make her understand."

"She doesn't understand anything," Guy said bitterly, "nothing except her own pleasure."

"She's young. Give her time."

Guy stood up slowly. "Why are you always defending her? I know she's made your life miserable with her demands, her sarcasms, complaints. I'm not blind and I'm not deaf."

"No one can make my life miserable if I don't let them, so don't worry about me. She's your wife. Go to her and console her. She's very disappointed."

Guy wasn't sure if Fenella was right, but he went anyway. As he was walking down the corridor he heard Miguel say, "It's not that she's young. She's no good." Guy wasn't sure he could truthfully contradict him.

Ardis was at the Queen Anne desk she had brought with her from New York. The design, with its graceful legs and delicate lines, suited her. She was writing something and didn't turn around. Guy shrugged.

"Ardis, I am sorry you're upset," he began.

"No, you're not." Anger made her voice sharp and unattractive.

Guy felt chilled but continued anyway. "I thought I had explained."

"Explained? Explained what? You just don't want to go. The only thing important to you is this damned vineyard. Well, let me tell you, it's dirty and squalid and not worth anything. You're making me stay here because you're cruel and mean."

"For god's sake, look at me, Ardis." When she didn't, Guy swung her chair around. "You're talking like a child. If I go back to France, I'll be arrested and sent to jail. You know I was wrongly accused of murdering someone. You know that. It was political and I can't go back while Louis-Napoleon is in power."

"What made you so important that the emperor of France should care so much?"

Over the years Guy had asked that question over and over. "I'm not really sure myself. All I do know is my brother-in-law has written recently to say that it's still not safe for me there."

It had been an ambiguous letter from Nathan, and had made Guy wonder if he was being warned of enemies he didn't realize he had.

"Then what about the rest of Europe? Why can't we go to Germany or Italy or Spain? Tell me that."

"There are two reasons. One, we don't have the money. And two, the continent isn't like the United States. There are spies and agents everywhere. Being across the border wouldn't necessarily protect me if an order came out of France to have me kidnapped and returned for trial."

Ardis was intrigued. It sounded so foreign and dangerous. Then she looked around the room with distaste, thinking of Guy's first reason. Simple white curtains, polished wood floors, an unadorned bed—this was not the boudoir of an Ardis Elizabeth Clay, the belle of New York. This belonged to a Fenella Delany, the drudge of Shantytown.

Ardis went back to her letter.

Ardis took to her room. She refused to have dinner with the "hired help" and ate her meals at her desk. At first Guy had said she would go hungry if she didn't come out, that it was too much work for Fenella, but Fenella interceded. She didn't mind, if that's what Ardis preferred. So Ardis became a virtual recluse.

"If I'm to be bored to death, I'm not going to make any pretenses about enjoying it," she said.

"You don't have to be bored. There're many things to do."

"Such as?"

"You could help Fenella with the school she's running for the children of the valley. You could ride. Take up sewing, crocheting, whatever it is that women do."

Ardis didn't dignify Guy's suggestions with a reply.

They shared the same bed for several weeks, with Ardis shunning any lovemaking, until Guy could no longer stand the tension. He moved his things to another room.

The weeks passed and the only thaw of any kind came with a letter from Clay. He was coming out west for a visit. Although he didn't write this, his daughter's horrifying accounts of her existence—in her letters she made it seem she was a virtual prisoner at the vineyard—had made him want to see for himself. In the meantime, to take no chances, he had his will changed with the help of two of New York's shrewdest lawyers so that through trusts, foundations, and loopholes, Guy would have no access to Ardis's inheritance.

His daughter was looking forward to her father's arrival more than anything else she could remember in her life. At least then she would get to spend time in San Francisco. Her father and she would stay there a month, then travel south to Los Angeles. From there they would decide where else to go. Her father promised to bring trunks and trunks filled with the latest fashions from New York and Paris. It was shameful how depleted her wardrobe had become with him only sending her a new frock once a month.

Her excitement and expectation were such that she even relaxed her exile and began reading out on the porch, as long as Fenella and Kyle were not around. It was she, then, who first saw the horseman coming from the south. And it was she who saw it was the captain from the Clay Shipping Line and guessed at once he was not bearing good news.

He had come to tell her Samuel Farragut Clay, the day before he was to start his journey west, had slumped over his office desk and died immediately. The news left Ardis not only grief-stricken but furious. Her father was the only person she knew she could trust—he gave her what she wanted—and now he had deserted her.

Ardis spurned all Guy's efforts at consoling her. It was a month later when she found that, even in death, her father had given her what she wanted. This time it was her freedom. The terms of his will gave her the power to be her own woman, dependent on no one, not even Guy.

Guy and Ardis left Jefferson Simpson's office, after the lawyer had read the will sent from New York, with Ardis in deep thought. It made no difference to Guy that he had been excluded from the inheritance. He had never thought of Ardis in terms of her father's wealth.

Back at the Palace, Ardis arranged her skirts on the settee. She had a proclamation. "It's now time for you to send Fenella back to her husband."

Guy had sensed something serious had been occupying her thoughts coming back from Simpson's office, but he hadn't expected this.

"I'm not sending Fenella anywhere. Damon abused her. I've promised her my protection, and I'm not going back on that promise. She'll always be welcome and will leave only when she chooses." Guy was very close to losing all control of his temper.

"Well, darling, then I must explain something as simply to you as possible." Ardis smiled sweetly. "Either Fenella is gone or I am gone." She held the trump card, she was sure of that. Guy would never let her go. She hadn't tried this threat before—she lacked that one small bit of confidence to cross the line. Her father's money, her money, now gave her all the confidence she needed. She would get what she wanted. And the first thing she wanted was Fenella's eviction. Other changes would follow.

"What are you doing?" Ardis hadn't been paying attention and was startled to see Guy at the door, hat in hand.

"I'm going back to the Belltower. Come if you like or stay and be damned."

Book Ten

Chapter Fifty-two

1863

Ardis couldn't muster the strength to open her eyes. She felt as if several swords were impaled in her head, her tongue had turned to cotton, and if she moved, her stomach would protest with a wave of uncontrollable dry heaves.

Ardis had had too much wine the night before, too much whisky, and should never have ended the evening in that opium den. Thinking of the den almost made her forget her present misery. It was so dark and sinister there and smelled of debauchery. She wondered how she got home.

Well, the day was going to have to begin sometime. What was it she was scheduled to do? Oh yes, Mrs. Rogers Taylor III was having a recital in her salon followed by high tea.

Ardis opened her eyes at last and got them to slowly survey the room. She was pleased with it. In fact, she was very pleased with the whole mansion she had built on Nob Hill. In many ways it represented her life perfectly. On one hand there was this bedroom, exotic with silks, teak, and incense, her own vision of the secretive and forbidden East, a room that would make her mother's staid society friends blanch—and then blush—but that excited Ardis's

occasional, discreet lovers, whom she took as much for the audacity of
doing so as to guarantee she would not weaken and return to Guy—
though they never satisfied her as her husband did. Then there were
the public rooms, the downstairs drawing rooms filled with ped-
igreed Louis XVI divans and chairs, Sèvres clocks on marble mantles,
and Wedgewood blue jasper vases. Formal, sedate, proper, where
Mrs. Rogers Taylor III could feel right at home.

Ardis was somewhat smug in the way she could keep her lives
separate, the dens of iniquity from the salons of propriety. Occasionally there was cross-pollination when she ran into Samuel Clemens,
Ambrose Bierce, or some other literary refugee from the Civil War at
one of the proper functions and then later at a saloon. Ardis, though
not given to lengthy analysis, puzzled over the rigid stuffiness of San
Francisco society. It was as if they wanted to out-etiquette the East,
to prove that they weren't unsophisticated backwoods ruffians, all
parvenus, nouveau riche, and without breeding.

Later that day, in a virginal white dress with only a slight, enticing
dip at the neckline, Ardis wished her hangover had made more
progress towards disappearing so her endless demure smiling would
have been less painful. She should have known Mrs. Rogers Taylor
III's entertainment would prove to be most dreary. But suddenly
Ardis was glad she had come, for there in the oppressive mahogany-
lined salon was someone she had been wanting to meet. Damon
Delany.

Naturally she had heard about him. Everyone had an opinion and a
story about Delany, invariably told with a mixture of awe, admiration,
fear, and contempt in various proportions. The one trait always
mentioned was his ruthlessness, a man who took what he wanted, any
way he could. Was that how he was with his women? Would he seize
her, demand her, rip her clothes, and plunge himself so deeply into
her she would scream with pain and pleasure....

"Mrs. Saint-Savin, are you all right?" The subject of her fantasy was
standing next to her, his mocking smile making her feel he had read
her mind. She blushed.

"You are Mrs. Saint-Savin, are you not? I have seen you so many
places and at so many functions and have never had the opportunity
to introduce myself. Will you forgive my boorishness? Perhaps I
could make amends somehow?"

Ardis wasn't sure if the mocking smile didn't extend to his words as
well, but she didn't care. She had made up her mind and was
chagrined she hadn't thought of this earlier. It would be delicious

revenge on her husband—for not following her, not prostrating himself before her, and promising her anything as long as she returned—if she took Damon Delany as her lover. Not to mention serving Fenella right. Could Damon make amends?

"Yes, you could Mister Delany. You could make amends by rescuing me from this tedium and taking me to dinner."

"You're not fond of tedium, are you, Mrs. Saint-Savin?"

"Boredom was designed by Satan as hell on earth. If something bores me, I remove it from my life."

"Is that why you live apart from your husband?"

Damon took Ardis to the restaurant in the Palace Hotel, hardly the inconspicuous hideaway she had in mind. But the visibility did not stop Ardis from blatant coquetry which Delany gentlemanly brushed aside. He did, however, keep her wine glass filled and accepted an invitation to join her for cognac when he had escorted her back to Nob Hill.

Ardis's staff was trained not to be in evidence when she came back late at night. So it was she who poured the cognac for Damon, making sure their hands touched when she offered him his snifter. And after they were both seated on the divan, it was she who reached across him, giving him a clear view of her lovely bosom, to get the inlaid box in which she kept the fine cigars she had for gentlemen visitors.

And when the conversation unexpectedly turned to bronze figures—Damon had begun to collect them—she herself went to fetch a particularly interesting one she had from Siam, an elephant being attacked by tigers.

She could feel his unreadable eyes following her as she swayed gracefully from the room, adding as much provocative swing as she could to her skirt. All evening he had focussed that inscrutable stare on her. She was sure he was interested. Why would he be the first who wasn't?

Damon hadn't realized how long she'd been gone until he noticed his snifter was empty. He got up to pour more. When he turned back to the room, Ardis had returned, holding the statue. But it was no longer the Ardis safeguarded and protected by corsets, crinolines, and convention. She had returned with platinum hair undone and a flowing, shimmering silk chemise designed to reveal, not conceal, cut so low that the rosepinkness of her nipples could be seen.

The impact of her beauty was such that Damon was aroused and impassioned without thought of being so. He didn't want to look at her but couldn't look away. As she floated nearer, he could smell her deep, musky scent. Then she was in his arms, the brass elephant dropping to the floor, and he could feel her spellbinding softness and couldn't stop his hand from slipping under the silk of her gown to the satin of her breast. She pressed against him, insistent and in need and he wanted her. He wanted to lose himself in her and possess her completely.

Then he heard her murmur something deep in her throat. All he could make out was "better than Fenella." He pushed her away so roughly and so suddenly that she lost her balance and fell to the floor. He stared at her coldly, sprawled there, legs at unbecoming angles, chest heaving with shock and anger. Then he left.

Ardis bit her lip to keep from screaming with frustration. She was moist with expectation and for the moment Damon's desertion overrode his rejection. She needed a man, right now. She needed a man to exorcise her ache, to fondle her, tease, and rub her, to play and crescendo, she wanted satisfaction. Her hand found the elephant figurine. She mounted it, rocking and stroking with increasing intensity until a whimper of satisfaction escaped her and she rolled off and lay still.

I'll get even, she thought. I'm going to make him want me so much he will do anything to have me. Then we'll see who walks away.

Two weeks passed with no improvement in Ardis's disposition. Damon Delany had left for Sacramento the day after their dinner at the Palace. She paid the hotel clerk to let her know when he returned.

Finally one afternoon, she received a note. Damon was back. She might have gone over to the hotel immediately except for a previous engagement, one she looked forward to. Maxwell Roth, a painter Ardis had recently met, was taking her to a club he'd been told about on the Barbary Coast. Roth wouldn't tell her what made this club so special—thereby piquing her interest considerably—and only suggested she might want to wear an outfit that wouldn't draw too much attention. Delany would have to wait.

Ardis and Roth were given a booth in an alcove off to the side. It was dimly lit and a beaded curtain guarded the opening to the alcove. It would be almost impossible for anyone to identify them, and this added to the allure of the seedy establishment for Ardis. She guessed the booths were reserved for couples who wished to insure their anonymity and privacy.

Roth was sweating with anticipation and Ardis could not imagine what kind of show could engender such expectation. Just then the stage lights went up slightly and a divan was carried out by two husky men. Few eyes were on them, however; they were focussed on the reclining woman, clad only in baubles and veils. Slow, pulsating music came from somewhere offstage and the woman responded to its primitive eroticism, starting to remove the civilizing impediments of the veils. As each was discarded, more of her body could be seen. The divan carriers, took her down to the tables, and spectators helped her remove the cloths, one by one, the men's hands sliding between her legs, and over her breasts. She arched her back to them, breathing hard, asking for more.

Ardis was so fascinated by the spectacle that she didn't realize Roth had slipped off the bench and was under the table until she heard her pantaloons rip and felt his tongue on her. She arched like the performer. The very air was heavy with the intoxicating vapors of sex.

Then without warning, Ardis brought her knee up hard against Roth's jaw. He reemerged red-faced and begging for forgiveness. "Please, please, don't be angry. I was carried away. I can't believe what I just did. How you must be offended."

Roth was a desperate man, he would have done anything, said anything to have Ardis back at his studio, but he saw he had lost her. And took her home at once.

Back in her boudoir, Ardis washed off the scent of the saloon, put on a delicate lime-green evening dress, arranged her hair, and draped a diamond chain around her neck. She'd had two glasses of rough whisky at the club, so she took care to rinse her mouth.

Looking in the mirror, she smiled approval and went out into the night.

Ardis checked the number on the door, "406-08." The ride to the Palace made her realize how tipsy she was. The realization did not shake her resolve. She would see Damon Delany that night.

She knocked. And waited. She knocked again. No answer. From a small beaded purse, Ardis took a key, a key the clerk had given her in exchange for quite a few dollars. She inserted it in the lock and turned. Then she was inside.

The gaslights were lit, enabling her to see just how well Damon

Delany lived. Hotel furnishings, luxurious themselves, had been replaced by exquisite furniture, rugs, and pieces of art, including the bronzes of which he had spoken.

There were three doors besides the one leading to the hall. Ardis was sure the middle one was the bedroom's. She crossed the room, intent on proving herself right, when the middle door swung open. Ardis smiled in anticipation.

Her smiled disappeared when she saw Fenella framed in the doorway wearing a modest cotton nightgown.

"What are you doing here?" Ardis asked with indignant disappointment.

"Hush," Fenella whispered, softly closing the door behind her. "Damon's asleep."

The two women faced each other. "Well?" Ardis pressed.

"I think it's more for me to ask why you're here."

"Wait one second. You've been separated from Damon for years. Guy said you stayed at the Belltower because Damon hurt you, that Guy had to protect you. Does he know you're here?"

There was a small hesitation in Fenella's composure. Ardis saw it and seized it. "Ah ha! So you've lied to Guy for all these years. He doesn't know, does he? All your little trips to San Francisco make a lot more sense now."

Fenella hadn't been merely buying that dowdy gingham she favored so at John Carlyle's store. The absurdity of the situation almost made Ardis laugh. Only Fenella Delany would cheat on someone who wasn't her lover with her own husband.

Fenella was doing her best not to show fear to Ardis. She wasn't sure how Guy would react if he knew she saw Damon regularly. "Guy has never inquired about my relationship with my husband—at least not since I came to stay at the Belltower—and I saw no reason to tell him."

Ardis's smile was not attractive. "Maybe it's time Guy should know the kind of sneaky person he's been harboring."

"Ardis, I beg you, think of Kyle. I don't stay at the vineyard for myself or for Guy. It's the boy. He needs my love. Don't be vindictive and harm him. I've kept my two lives separate. I don't discuss Guy and his business with Damon and I don't talk about Damon to Guy."

"Must make for terribly stimulating conversations. But then again, you're such a stimulating creature."

Ardis's sarcasm stung. Fenella retaliated by asking pointedly, "Let's get back to the question of why exactly you are here tonight, Ardis. And, by the bye, how you got in?"

"None of your goddamned mousy business," she yelled and made sure to slam the door on her way out.

Fenella wondered if she had made a grave mistake never telling Guy. She had been afraid had he known, he might again insist she return to Damon. Kyle was now eleven, tall for his age. His size made it easy to forget he was still a little boy and in need of her. He needed her kisses and hugs and affectionate attention. No one else gave him any. Fenella knew that Guy loved his son, but he wasn't able to show it. They were so formal and polite with each other it pained Fenella.

She shivered. What would Ardis do with her newfound information? Fenella glanced at the bedroom door. And why had she been here?

Chapter Fifty-three

The following morning Ardis's staff was surprised to find her dressed and demanding breakfast at seven. She had devised a plan coming back from the hotel and wanted to implement it as soon as possible. Oh yes, she was going back to the Belltower. She couldn't wait to see Guy's expression when he learned of Fenella's disloyalty. If he wouldn't get rid of that mealy-mouthed dishrag when Ardis wanted him to, she would enjoy this little vindicating drama now.

It was a beautiful day, warm, bright, clear. Ardis ignored it all. She could have been sealed in a crate for all she noticed. The sun was just setting, casting pale rose fingers across the sky when the carriage stopped in front of the main house.

Why couldn't Guy do something about this house, Ardis thought, not for the first time. The best thing would be to tear it down and replace it with something more suitable. You'd think he was a pauper, which she knew he wasn't. She was almost embarrassed to have her driver stay in the workers' quarters, they were, in her opinion, so mean. Still she couldn't send the carriage back to San Francisco, having no idea how long she'd be staying.

The house was fading into the creeping shadow of twilight. Why were there no lights? Then Ardis remembered that Fenella was in San Francisco and laughed. She certainly was in San Francisco, which meant Kyle would probably be visiting one of his valley friends. Oh no, it never occurred to her that Guy might be away.

The long trip had dampened her anticipation somewhat, and now Ardis was feeling a bit of the fool on a fool's errand. She went into the house hoping only for a bed to lie down on and something to drink. A movement near the couch made her cry out in surprise.

"Ardis?" Guy knew he was dreaming. He must have fallen asleep lying in the darkness, thinking of her. They had seen so little of each

334

other since she had gone to San Francisco. When they did get together he felt nothing more than a guest in her house, a guest who wasn't sure how long he was welcome.

He stood and the apparition took form and reality. He had her in his arms, embracing and kissing her, making sure she was real and with him again.

Ardis allowed the gale force of his emotion to blow away her restraint. She savored his ardent whispers of "Oh darling, I've missed you, needed you" as he kissed her hair, eyes, lips, neck. His overpowering desire was taking the breath from her body and her response was fueled by the exultation of his needing her and having to have her.

Without being conscious of having moved, they were in the bedroom. Guy undressed her, ripping buttons and hooks in his urgency, taking off his clothes with even less restraint. He turned to carry her to the bed, but before he could, she sank to her knees and took him into her mouth. She caressed him with lips and tongue, slowly up and down his shaft, whispering her fingers across him, gradually building the tempo, faster, more insistent, and when he thought he could stand it no longer, she was off him, and splayed across the bed. They came together in a coupling of moans and muffled screams. When it was over, only fingertips touching as their bodies struggled for renewed equilibrium, Guy said, "You were magnificent." And Ardis knew she had been.

She fell asleep, Fenella far from her mind.

The next morning Guy was gone when she awoke. He didn't come back until evening and then went straight to their bedroom where she was brushing her hair. He took the brush, threw it into a corner, and pulled her to the bed, taking time to discard only those articles of clothing most in the way of their goal.

Later Guy produced a picnic basket packed for him by one of the workers' wives. First he opened a bottle of du Clocher he had been hoarding. When they finished that, they had some of the Belltower's first vintage.

They made love again before following into a deep sated sleep.

Two days later Fenella returned in midafternoon when Guy was out in the fields.

"I'm surprised you had the nerve to come back," was Ardis's greeting.

"Hello, Ardis, I didn't think you'd be here."

"As you can see, I am, and I might be staying for a lot longer."

Fenella nodded. That made up her mind. "Where's Guy, please?"

Ardis waved her hand vaguely. "Out there someplace, doing whatever it is he does."

She doesn't care at all, Fenella thought sadly. Poor Guy. She went looking for him.

Although Ardis's saying she might stay was a spur-of-the-moment attempt to upset Fenella, the fact was she had liked being at the Belltower those few last days. It felt almost like home. For the first time she didn't have to worry about coming on Fenella and Kyle laughing together and then having the boy suddenly become silent and withdrawn. It wasn't that he was rude. Ardis just always felt he was waiting for her to leave so he could resume his conversation. She had felt free to roam around, rearrange things, she wasn't under Fenella's observation. She had even lost sight of the purpose of her visit, and had yet to work her mischief by telling Guy about her discovery at the Palace.

When Fenella came back into the house, she disappeared into her room. Curious, Ardis looked in and found her packing.

"So you've given in at last, have you? It's about time. You had no right staying here, not after he married me. But I suppose you had always squirreled away a hope that eventually he'd give in and marry you. What a shock I must have been."

Fenella would not rise to her taunting. She continued packing, and said Guy would explain.

Fenella was gone before he came back in from the fields; boxes, trunks, even some household goods, had been piled into a wagon.

Ardis was in the bedroom, waiting for him, wearing only a clingy robe. Guy didn't notice.

"Gone," he said sadly.

"She really had no place here anymore, now that I'm back." Ardis was trying, with only partial success, not to sound peevish. She didn't want to destroy the mood of the past few days. "We'll get a housekeeper, my cook from San Francisco, whatever's needed. You'll see, I'm quite good at directing a household. At least my mother taught me that. Now come over, sir, and I'll give you a demonstration of some of my other talents."

"Kyle's gone," Guy said roughly. "It's Kyle who's gone. Who did you think I was talking about?"

"Fenella, of course. Weren't you telling me she's left? I just wanted to let you know we can manage without her."

Guy sat down heavily on the bed and stared blankly at the wall. "Fenella's left with Kyle. She's taking him to San Francisco to school. She's been saying for a long time he needs a better education than he can receive here, that he needs to be prepared for college. I don't know why, but today she put her foot down—and now they're gone."

Guy was struggling to understand the sadness that was engulfing him. He had never been close to Kyle and he had regretted that. He just didn't know how to show his love. He could only hope his son knew it was there. Had Edouard hoped the same thing?

For her part, Ardis was flabbergasted, her victory spurious. Fenella hadn't been cast out for her. She had left on her own free will and supposedly could return the same way. Well, let her try. Ardis still held the trump card. She would not tell Guy now about Fenella and Damon. She would play that card if Fenella threatened her again.

And now there was neither time nor inclination to think about Fenella. Guy was seeking solace in Ardis's arms, urgent to find release from his pain within her. Her robe was gone and they strained for each other on the bed. Fenella didn't matter. Ardis was with Guy, he needed her, and she wanted him. And Fenella had no way of coming between them now.

The departure of Fenella and Kyle brought changes to the Belltower. Guy gave in and let Ardis manage the household staff. He also spent more time with her and tried to draw her into the workings of the vineyard. While she'd been away, he'd analyzed what had gone wrong and finally had to concede there was a legitimate basis for her boredom. He couldn't expect a girl plucked from the cosmopolitan activity of New York to adjust immediately to the simpler life of his valley. He knew she had a sharp mind. He decided he would challenge it.

He started first by seeking her advice about the agricultural college. How she thought the administration should be set up. What she considered the best location. They discussed lobbying techniques in Sacramento. He encouraged her to accompany him, to make contributions. She became so involved she eagerly discussed the arrival of the cuttings Harazthy was sending back from Europe, which they should try, how much they should plant to create the wine they wanted. It was then that Ardis came up with her plan.

"Darling," she said one night after dinner, "no matter what we plant, and no matter what quality of wine we produce, we'll never measure up to the Bordeaux vineyards."

Guy was amused by her newfound expertise.

Ardis saw that and quickly admonished him. "No, this is quite serious, and I ask you to hear me out. Guy, I know you're fond of all this." She waved disdainfully at the comfortable living room in which they were seated. "But if we want our wine taken seriously, we must present it in a proper setting. It really is time to build a house where we can entertain properly—and that includes prospective buyers. My father made many a deal over the dinner table. And we need a tasting room that will impress buyers even before they've sampled the wine. This house makes us look like some kind of dirt-grubbers and sod-pushers. It's time for a change."

A year earlier, Guy bristled at similar urging and dismissed it as another one of her spoiled demands. Now he answered thoughtfully, "I think you're right."

She clapped her hands prettily. "Wonderful. Oh, I knew you'd see my way sooner or later. I really am right, you know. I've already started making plans."

Guy grabbed her hands to stem her enthusiasm. "Wait, wait, wait. Hear me out. I think you're right, only not now. I don't have the money for that kind of building. I need to use what I have to buy those vines from Count Harazthy, to put more land under cultivation, hire more workers, improve the wine cellar, buy more barrels. A new house on top of all that is too much. I can't overextend myself, not right now."

"You goose." Ardis's laugh was a caress on silk. She slipped onto his lap. As she stroked his hair, she bestowed tiny, teasing kisses all over his face, until stopping to linger on his lips. After a while, she pulled away far enough to say again, "You goose. I've got the money. I've got money enough for one hundred houses and still have a fortune left over."

She felt him tense and could almost feel his jaw clench. "You know I won't touch your money. I'm not a kept man or that opportunistic gigolo your father saw me as."

"Darling, of course you're not," Ardis said. "We needn't talk about this now." She began kissing him again. They would discuss it later when Ardis had prepared her ground better. She was discovering that pouts and demands were not the best way to get what she wanted. In fact, she had come to enjoy plotting and subterfuge and whispered requests as he lay next to her, limp, satisfied and willing to give her the world.

Harazthy's return forced Ardis to postpone her campaign for a new house. The ebullient count invited Guy and her to join him in his triumph in Sacramento.

They met in Vallejo where they picked up the steamer to the capital. Harazthy was unable to stop talking, he was so full of the vineyards he'd visited, the cuttings he'd bought, the new methods he'd seen, the plans he'd made. And he brought news of Solange.

"I paid my respects and your angel of a sister insisted we stay the week. Du Clocher is truly heaven. So beautiful. Such wonderful wine. I can understand your sorrow at not being able to return."

Ardis looked at her husband with curiosity. She'd never realized he felt such sorrow. She tried to remember if he'd ever said anything and she hadn't been listening. The drizzle outside forced them into the boat's stateroom. Ardis was glad the boat was not crowded. The room was close and uncomfortable as it was. Harazthy and Guy didn't notice, they were so wrapped up in the cheerful optimism of the Hungarian's account.

"And Solange, how is she?"

"Golden, glowing, beautiful. Any fool can see she adores her husband and that boy of hers. And Nathan, why I think he would lay down his life for them. It was good to see a father care so much for his son. He's wonderful with him. He can't hug and kiss him enough."

Guy had a twinge of envy, but it passed as the talk returned to prospects and triumphs to come.

It was a much different mood that hung over the two men only twenty-four hours later. The governor's office had sent word to their hotel that he'd see them at two p.m. They went to his chambers exuberant and confident and came out only ten minutes later completely changed men, incredulous and downcast.

It came as no surprise, naturally, when Downey was not the man who greeted them. Leland Stanford was now governor, but Guy and Harazthy had been assured that it was the office and not the man who had made the guarantees about financing the European mission.

The shock came from Stanford's glacial reception. He had stared at them with his piercing eyes and cut Harazthy's decription of the trip off at once.

"Sir, I suppose you have prepared a bill for your expenses."

"Well, yes, I have, naturally, but let me tell you more. As we told

Governor Downey, this will mean so much for California."

"May I see the bill." Harazthy handed him several sheets of paper. "It says here you bought 200,000 cuttings."

"Yes, that's right. Fourteen hundred different varieties from France, Germany, Italy, Spain, Portugal, and Hungary. They're very important for our research. To experiment. I spared no expense..."

"That is evident," Stanford said sourly.

"...to guarantee their safe arrival. A gardener took care of the cuttings and roots across the Atlantic. In New York, he examined and packed them and at this very moment a Wells Fargo steamer is bringing them to San Francisco. I guarantee you, we will have 200,000 rooted vines ready in no time." Somewhere during the recitation Harazthy had begun to sound like a prisoner pleading his case before a hostile judge.

"And this cost $12,000?"

"I realize that might seem a very large sum at first glance, but I assure you it will be nothing in the long run. Nor will be the cost of setting up an experimental garden by the state. Some of the vines can be tested there, and the rest distributed to the state's vineyards. It shall be a wonderful project. And really the cost, in the long run, is minimal when you consider the results."

Stanford rifled through the papers again, not really studying them, then placed them resolutely on his desk. "Gentlemen, while cost in the long run is what matters to you, I am afraid it's the short term that concerns me. I do not believe I would have sanctioned this endeavor had I occupied the office when you first approached. But here we have it..." he gestured at the papers "... all $12,000 of it and I'm not sure the legislature will pay for it. I'm told some legislators have said they wish to wait for the vines' arrival so that they might inspect them, before discussion of payment begins. But quite frankly, I don't believe even then funds will be allocated. Many feel the state shouldn't favor one industry in this manner."

"But Governor Stanford," Harazthy, though shocked almost to immobility, would not give up, "many European countries spend state money on agricultural experimentation. How can we expect to compete with them if we have this foolish laissez-faire attitude?"

Stanford had no wish to debate the count and rose to show the men out. Guy would not be so easily dismissed. "One minute, sir." He was seething over the obvious injury being perpetrated. "I beg to remind you that Count Harazthy made this trip with the clear understanding the state of California would pay for it. Not the state of California *might* pay for it. He would be paid. Period. Is the word of the man in this office worth nothing? What is this flim-flam you're talking today?"

Harazthy grabbed Guy's arm and shook it to quiet him. "Please, take no mind, governor. My friend is impetuous. I am confident you will personally do all that can be done for a reasonable conclusion to this matter."

Stanford nodded, but Guy felt no more reassured. He knew Harazthy needed the money immediately. While the count was in Europe, his name had been cleared in the matter of the mint discrepancy. He'd had the squatters driven from his land. This left him little money, and what he had, he had outlaid for the European trip. He needed that money for the ambitious rebuilding of Buena Vista he was already beginning.

Over dinner that night Guy and Harazthy rehashed the interview until even they were tired of discussing it. Ardis listened patiently. She was succinct in her appraisal. "You bet on the wrong side."

"What could you mean?" Harazthy asked. "We 'bet' on the side of California, on its growth, its prosperity. And now this so-called governor is proclaiming himself a veritable welcher."

Guy shook his head wearily and with a certain amount of self-disgust for having put aside his misgivings. "I don't think that's what Ardis meant. We banked too much on the influence of Senator Gwim. He was the wrong side."

The sad fact was that at the outset of the Civil War, Gwim had packed his bags, denounced the North, and moved to Richmond. Furthermore, his allies who were pro-Confederacy lost all influence in Sacramento.

"Oh dear God," Harazthy moaned. "And I suppose with this Republican Lincoln in the White House, my being chairman of the state Democratic committee will not help the cause much either."

Guy was furious with himself. "Damn. Why didn't I anticipate this? I could have looked for allies instead of assuming fair play. At least they're keeping the agricultural college a separate issue."

Guy didn't remind Harazthy he'd urged him to get the gentleman's agreement with Downey put into writing. The Hungarian had too much to worry about as it was.

The next months became a frenzy of trips to Sacramento and San Francisco trying to curry favors and votes. The best they could ultimately muster was the introduction of a bill that would have given Hararzthy $8,457 toward the purchase of the cuttings and $1,549 to Wells Fargo for the shipping costs.

The bill was shelved 20 to 9.

Then the cuttings arrived and Wells Fargo had to be paid. And Harazthy had to pay his workers as well.

"At least," he pointed out to Guy one day, "they're only coolies. Could you imagine where I'd be if I had to pay them an American wage? Eight dollars a month plus board is bad enough. If they were white I would be paying thirty dollars a month. You know, you should hire some of these Chinamen. They're reliable, so hard working it makes me tired just to think about it. All of them want to bring their families over, so they don't spend their money getting drunk and rowdy. It adds up to economic sense, economic dollars for that matter."

What didn't add up was how Harazthy was going to pay all that he owed. Guy offered to lend him some money. The Hungarian refused all "charity." Despite being aware of Harazthy's grave difficulties, his solution still came as a shock to Guy. The count began selling off the precious vines piecemeal to raise capital. Gone were the noble ideas of controlled testing. Left were debts and bitterness. The best Guy could do was buy as many of the choicer vines as he could afford and regret what might have been.

Chapter Fifty-four

Ardis was at her desk, impatiently tapping the quill pen to her lips. She still hadn't persuaded Guy to build the new house. She was still sitting in her inelegant room with its high windows and the disgustingly homey touches of Fenella Delany, resenting the fact she didn't have better. But that was all about to change. Ardis was about to get her way.

She was about to get her way, although it was not exactly through her plan of choice. She didn't dwell on that. What mattered was she got what she wanted.

Ardis went back to her papers. She worked with intense concentration. The finished product must be exactly right, exactly what she had been carrying around in her memory.

"And what has you so busy?" Guy had come in without her noticing. He took the advantage of her preoccupation to sneak up behind her and nuzzle her neck.

"Oh!" Ardis was both startled and dismayed. She quickly covered over what she was working on. It was not quite the time for Guy to see it. She stood up and hugged her husband.

"You're late," she pouted sweetly, "but that's all right. I'll forgive you, if cook will. Now into the living room. Sit down with some wine. I've already had a bottle opened. And when you're comfortable and relaxed and not thinking about the vineyard, I'll have some news for you."

Guy happily complied. He knew enough not to press Ardis for her news until she was ready to reveal it. She had been to San Francisco for a couple of weeks, and he was pleased she was obviously in a mood conducive to the homecoming he wished to give her.

When Ardis remained standing at the mantel, Guy's good spirits were dampened by concern.

"Aren't you going to sit next to me?" he asked. Perhaps these good spirits of hers weren't meant for him. He secretly feared she would tire of Napa and go back permanently to her mansion. This had been her first trip to San Francisco since she had come back to the Belltower. As nonchalantly as he could, he had asked after the purpose of her trip to the city. She had blithely told him it was only to check that everything was functioning properly. He had tended not to believe that reason, since she had left her full staff to run the mansion even though she was not there and they would have sent word if a problem had developed.

"I know you wondered why I made this trip," Ardis said, as though reading his mind. "Now I didn't lie in saying I wished to make sure all was well on Nob Hill. However, I do admit to not telling you the full reason for my going."

Ardis rather enjoyed Guy's torment. She would have liked to prolong her news, to play on his agony further, but she rejected doing so. Her strategy would be better served by getting immediately to her news.

"I went to see my doctor..."

Guy was off the couch and pressing her to him. "Oh my God! You're ill. Why didn't you tell me? Why did you keep it a secret?"

Ardis disengaged herself, laughing. "No, you goose. A woman doesn't always go to a doctor because she's sick. She goes to find out if she's *enceinte.*"

Guy wasn't sure what she'd said. It didn't register that her last word was in French.

"Guy Saint-Savin, have you've been in the United States so long you've forgotten your mother tongue? Listen to me. Je suis *enceinte.*"

Enceinte? No, he still couldn't have heard right. *Enceinte?*

"You're pregnant? You're going to have a child?"

"Yes," Ardis answered with great self-satisfaction. "Are you happy?" she asked although she already knew he was.

By way of answer, Guy picked her up and carried her to the bedroom, where he added, "I am overjoyed."

It wasn't until the next morning, after cook had served them breakfast on the lovely shaded patio Ardis had designed, that she finally broached her subject.

"You know a child is going to mean many changes in our lives."

"All for the good," Guy said happily. He was being given a second chance. He hadn't been able to sleep last night thinking of the baby. He resolved to be a different father to it than he had been to Kyle. He would give it time and love. And a baby meant that Ardis would stay.

"Naturally," Ardis said, "this baby will bring us happiness and joy, but, dear, you can't expect me to raise our child here."

Guy stopped chewing his bread. "Why not? Where would you?"

"In San Francisco. I know you love this house, but it will be too small and it's just too...too common. Our child deserves better."

Guy looked around. Why couldn't she see the warmth and beauty here? It had been Kyle's home and he...That brought Guy up short.

"Is that what you want to do? Live in San Francisco?" He could probably spend weekends with them there, and, during the winter, a few weeks at a stretch, without neglecting the vineyard too much.

"No, darling, no, not unless I absolutely must. No dear, it's the house that's unacceptable, not the Napa Valley. It's time you said yes to a new house. It's time we built."

"I can't. You know that, not without jeopardizing the vineyard."

Ardis put her fork down on the table with resolution. "We'll do it with *my* money. I will not let you say 'no' this time. It's our child, your child and mine. You wouldn't deprive it because of some sort of masculine pride about using your wife's money, would you? What good is the money to me if I can't spend it on my child?"

Guy didn't give in at once, but finally he buckled before Ardis's determination. And she was then free to work on her designs without hiding them whenever Guy came into the room.

She had been making drawings and plans ever since their reunion, confident that eventually she would get her way. Guy only looked at the plans once.

"Ardis, are you trying to copy du Clocher?"

"Of course not, though I suppose there are some similarities. I did so love du Clocher that time I saw it. I want to get some feel of it in our house."

"I appreciate what you're doing. I just think a French château will look out of place here. And that belltower, that really is overdoing it."

"Don't you worry. You'll see. I'm right. It will be absolutely perfect."

Chapter Fifty-five

The house, or château, as Ardis insisted it be called, was *not* perfect. It was a stage-set in the wrong play.

If she was disappointed, she never let on. Instead, as soon as it was completed and the furnishings in place, she had had the bell in the tower rung and her first invitations sent out. After that hardly a week went by that the house wasn't filled with guests enjoying dinners and balls. Ardis had insisted a guest house be built as well, since, naturally, most of their guests would be coming from San Francisco. The guest house rivalled most mansions.

It had been one of those unpredictably hot spring days, and Guy came in from the fields feeling unusually tired.

Robert, Ardis's excessively proper English butler—he had worked for her father in New York—took Guy's straw hat and Guy, once again, wondered just how much his wife was paying Robert to get him to stay in the Napa Valley.

"Is there anything I might get for you, sir?"

Guy despised the formality—it was out of place and unnecessary—and ordinarily would have declined and served himself. Tonight he was too tired.

"A large, large whisky," he answered.

"And where should I bring it, sir?" One day Guy was confident he would get Robert to drop the "sir," but he conceded that day was a long way off.

"I'll be joining Ardis."

"Very good, sir. The countess has been expecting you." With the "château" had come the "countess."

Guy frowned as he dragged himself up the curving marble staircase with its stern mahogany banister. He wondered what Ardis was expecting him about. She probably needed his mumbled

346

approval of her new list of luminaries who would descend on them, devour their food, swill their wine, and stay on far too long for Guy's liking. In spite of his grumblings, Guy had to admit, however, that Belltower wine was becoming widely known throughout the state and even the country through Ardis's efforts, be they dilettantish or not. The real question was whether there would be any wine to sell in years to come.

At the top of the stairs, Guy stopped and looked both ways down the long corridor traversing the two wings, and then went, with purpose, to the right, down to the last door. There he paused to listen to the gentle humming coming from behind it. He tiptoed in.

A rocking chair was at the far side of the room, turned to the window, so that the vestiges of daylight swathed the occupants.

It was a classical, beautiful scene of loving maternal tenderness. The quiet rocking, the soothing hum.

A floor board creaked almost imperceptibly under his weight, enough to make the woman in the chair look around, ready to defend her charge.

But it wasn't Ardis, it was Fenella.

Her eyes were weary and dark-circled, evidence that Hugh Saint-Savin was one of those little ones who woke every three hours every night and had to be lullabyed and loved back to sleep. Fenella would allow no one else to go to him—although there was no fear Ardis might. Fenella's room was next to Hugh's so that he needed little more than one indignant, demanding wail before she was with him.

It was Fenella who sang to him, comforted him, fed him, bathed him. It was Ardis who looked in on him occasionally, murmured he looked well, and fled.

Ardis had initially planned to import a real English nanny. And would have done so except she surmised, correctly, that Guy would have less objection to her spending so little time with the baby if it was Fenella who cared for him rather than a stranger. So she had not argued when Fenella and Kyle came back to the Belltower shortly after Hugh was born.

From Ardis's point of view, there was little wrong with the arrangement. Fenella kept to the children's wing and Ardis, now firmly established as the mistress of the house—and it was her house, designed by her, paid for by her—no longer felt like the intruder. She could give her full attention to hostessing.

Guy was in awe of the baby. The little fellow was incredibly active, eager, and curious, and he was getting so big so fast. Guy had been

deprived of Kyle's infancy, hadn't witnessed that first smile or the first
time he'd pushed himself up like a wobbly turtle and peered around
for approval. Guy had missed the agonies of the first teeth, the pride
of the first tentative crawling. He couldn't help but smile thinking of
all of Hugh's triumphs, his miraculous transformation from squalling
little bundle to a definite personality in his own right.

Fenella raised her eyebrows in question.

"I wanted to look at him, for a moment, that's all," he whispered.
Fenella smiled her understanding, closed her eyes, and resumed
rocking.

It was such a perfect scene, Guy thought. Except it should have
been Ardis there. He turned reluctantly and went to his wife's
boudoir.

"Darling, you're so late tonight," she complained at once.

"I stopped in to see Hugh."

"And how is he?" It was a perfunctory question.

Guy bit off what he wanted to say, that she shouldn't have to ask,
that she should put as much effort into her son's care as she did in her
party lists, that they should be sharing a bedroom and not an
adjoining door. Ardis had insisted on separate bedrooms as the more
civilized, convenient arrangement, pointing out he got up much
earlier than she and invariably woke her up. Guy now felt he had to
check her calendar before making love.

He said none of this. It would make little difference if he did and
would only lead to unpleasantness. Instead he answered, "He was
asleep. Did Robert bring up my drink?"

Ardis gestured to a silver serving tray next to her chaise. Guy took
a glass from it and fell gratefully into one of the fauteuils. Ardis began
prattling about the governor coming next week, and would it be
suitable to invite Count Harazthy, and there was a delightful couple
visiting from New York... Guy knew to nod at suitable moments.
Otherwise he was relieved from contributing.

Tonight he wasn't sure if he was up to making even that minor
contribution. His thoughts and energies were consumed with the
vineyard. He and Miguel had been trying in vain to come up with a
solution to their labor problems. It made no sense to Guy that despite
a grave shortage of jobs throughout the area, he couldn't get enough
men to work for him. It wasn't that he didn't pay well, he did. Men
didn't want to sweat anymore, that was all. They don't want to earn
their wages, Guy thought bitterly.

"You aren't listening." Ardis's annoyance cut through his worries. "You've been so inattentive lately. What is going on?"

"It's the same problem," Guy answered wearily. "What I talked about last month."

"Oh, for heaven's sakes, you already know what the solution is. Only you're too stubborn to do it. Even Count Harazthy says so. Sometimes I think you like wallowing in your little despairs rather than pulling yourself out of them."

"We've gone through this before, Ardis, and I still haven't changed my mind. I will not hire coolie labor. It's practically slavery, the way they're exploited."

"Why do *you* have to be so virtuous? It's up to the Chinese to take the jobs or not. They know what they're going to get."

Guy took a long swallow of the whisky and let its numbing smoothness wash through him. "It's not really up to them. They have no choice. No one will give them a job at a fair wage. If they're going to live, they have to take what they can get." He took another sip and added thoughtfully, "You know, Fenella did have a suggestion."

"Oh, I'm sure she did, but except for children, what does she know about anything?"

"Fenella might not be well-educated, but never underestimate her. She has more wisdom and sense than..."

"Than what?" Ardis's eyes were slits of animosity. She resented the way Guy jumped to the little mouse's defense.

"...than most people," Guy finished weakly, realizing his indiscretion. He was too tired for an argument with his wife. The only outcome would be her flouncing off to San Francisco so she could meet new "delightful" people visiting from New York, or London, or Timbuktu, and invite them out to the Belltower. No, the wisest course of action was to let Ardis return to her party talk while he considered Fenella's suggestion.

They had been in the kitchen. When Ardis's chef accompanied her to San Francisco, Fenella took over the cooking and the family had their dinner at the large oak pedestal table in the center of the kitchen. Meals were relaxed and friendly then, and it was the only time Miguel would come into the main house. Otherwise he ate by himself in what everyone called the Old House.

Kyle was helping Fenella chop onions and peppers. Guy, with Hugh snuggled onto his lap, was bemoaning the paucity of hired hands to Miguel and the impossibility of maintaining the vineyard without a larger work force.

"But I know there are many men looking for jobs," Fenella said between chops. "I know some of the Chinese ladies who work for Count Harazthy. They say they have brothers and cousins and uncles all desperate for anything."

"I know that." Guy was deeply frustrated. For him the coolies were forbidden fruit—and he refused to be corrupted. "But they're men and I won't pay them as if they were little better than hired beasts of burden. Do you realize they get a quarter less than what a white man gets?"

"They're good men, though," Fenella pressed. "They all work hard. They save their money so they can bring their families from China. They're desperate, Guy, and they'll do a good job."

"I know that. You don't have to tell me, but I'm still not going to pay them as poorly as everyone else."

"So don't. Pay them what you'd pay any man for a good day's work."

Miguel leaned across the table to play with Hugh, weaving his hand in front of the boy's face as little fingers tried to grab him. Not taking his eyes from the child, Miguel said, "I don't think your neighbors would like that."

The subject was dropped.

Now, weeks later, the number of men at the vineyard had dipped even more, and Guy was getting desperate.

"What the hell do I care what my neighbors think?" he muttered into his whisky glass.

"Well, it really depends on which neighbors you're talking about and what they're thinking, wouldn't you say, dear?" Ardis answered, although she didn't have the slightest idea what he was talking about.

Chapter Fifty-six

Rivulets of sweat coursed down Guy's back. They felt good. Guy felt good. Four months earlier he couldn't have imagined that he would be standing to stretch after hours of picking, sun beating down on him and the hundred other men fanned out through the fields. That Miguel would be in the pressing room with five helpers, squeezing juice from the best and biggest crop the Belltower had ever had. That next to the vineyard a virtual village, a town, had sprung up, through the unflagging efforts of the Chinese workers who had descended on the Belltower, all begging to work.

The village had been built in the extra hours, the hours after the day's work was done, and now stood for the few families that had arrived and those that would come some day. Guy had never seen men work so fiercely and with such purpose.

A bell sounded. Lunch. He wasn't sorry for the break. His muscles were taking longer to become inured to the grueling exertion than they had when he was a younger man in France, all those eternities ago.

He wiped his blades, then noticed the others around him were still bending and cutting, bending and snipping. He walked over to a small, dark man who must have been at least fifteen years older than Guy.

"Mister Louis," Guy called. "It's time for a break."

The man looked up, first apprehensive, then confused. "Lunch break, Mister Louis. Lunch." Guy made motions toward his mouth. Louis smiled, bowing a couple of times, and called out something to the other men in the clattery gibberish Guy was becoming accustomed to hearing.

The workers hurried over to where they knew Fenella would have something filling and good—if somewhat exotic for their taste— waiting.

351

Mister Louis had hung back with Guy and fell in beside him.

Guy recalled the confusion of those first days after he and Miguel had begun hiring. So many of the men spoke nothing except Chinese. It was only luck that Mister Louis had presented himself. He spoke several Chinese dialects and quite passable English, although idioms were not his strong point. For days Guy had called him Mister Chu, having had him introduced as Louis Chu. It took Fenella to correct him.

"Louis is his family name," she'd explained. "That's how the Chinese do it. Family name first, given name second."

"For God's sake, why didn't the man say something?"

"Out of respect. He didn't want to embarrass you."

Walking with Mister Louis, Guy remembered that Ardis was back from San Francisco. He supposed he should join her for lunch, but then again, why? Why subject himself to the biting criticism which was all she had for him lately?

She had made it very clear she was greatly put out by the presence of the new workers. Or, more precisely, she was greatly put out by the consequences of paying them the same as American laborers. First, the few white workers that were left at the Belltower quit en masse when the Chinese appeared. Then word of Guy's policy spread throughout the valley. Ardis's invitations were being pointedly turned down. She quickly filled the vacancies with others from outside Napa. Still, she was miffed.

"You shouldn't allow them to take jobs from good Americans," she complained, having heard this argument from someone else.

"They're not taking jobs from anyone," Guy explained patiently. "Your good Americans didn't want the jobs in the first place."

"Yes, but our neighbors feel that while *you* can afford to be magnanimous, *they* can't."

"And what is that supposed to mean? I can 'afford' it. Does everyone think I use your money. That I'm a wealthy man because I'm married to an heiress?"

"Don't be crass," was all that she'd say. But she emphasized her displeasure by limiting him access to her bedroom. But Guy refused to give in to her sexual coercion and took to avoiding her.

No, Guy had no desire to lunch with his wife. He, a wealthy man! He almost snorted. This was going to be a good year, and he would do well, but a great deal of money had gone to building that admirable little village. While the workers had provided the labor, Guy had paid for the material and he did not skimp on quality. He didn't want some squalid shanty town at the Belltower. He wanted houses of which he could be proud and to which the workers could bring their families. And besides, if he and Ardis didn't argue during the day, perhaps a truce could be arranged for the night.

Fenella was still supervising the serving. When she saw Guy, she smiled, gave her ladle to the young woman beside her, and hurried over.

"Have you eaten? You must be starving. I have Kyle watching Hugh over near the pine tree. Come on then. Get your plate. No, no, Mister Louis don't go. Please join us."

When the three had piled up four plates with food—"That Kyle probably forgot about eating, he was so excited to be allowed in the fields for part of the morning," Fenella explained as she took the extra dish—they went over to the welcome coolness of the tree's shade.

"And how do you feel, son, after this morning?" Guy asked Kyle.

"Fine, sir. Well, maybe a little sore. I picked a lot, though. I worked really hard. So maybe, instead of watching Hugh, I might do some more this afternoon?" Kyle asked politely and with no great hope.

Fenella immediately set to teasing him. "Well, so my big grown man has gotten too big to take care of his little brother, has he? Next thing, he'll be bringing home a bride and having young ones of his own. Is that right? Is that what you'll be doing?" She added tickling and teasing the very proper, almost-adult who was transformed into a giggling, squirming fifteen-year-old.

"Fenella," Guy chided, "I'm not sure Mister Louis has seen such undignified behavior before."

"Mothers and sons are always such," Louis responded solemnly.

Guy watched him eat, or rather, watched him tentatively poke at what was on his plate as if he were testing to see if it were still alive.

"Mister Louis, have you never had Irish stew before?"

Mister Louis shook his head apologetically.

"Would you and the men like it better if, maybe, one of you did the cooking?" Guy asked.

"Please, sir, we would not do the missus dishonor by refusing to eat..."

"Oh, for goodness sakes," Fenella cut in. "What dishonor? Here it's been three days of hard picking, and it never occurred to me you might prefer your own food. I'm sorry. Of course, I'll turn the kitchen over to you. But there is one condition."

"Yes, missus?"

"That you teach me to cook the Chinese way. It always smells so delicious."

Mister Louis graced them with one of his infrequent smiles. "Of course, missus. With great happiness. Please, now I beg to talk with Pong Fey."

After he left, Fenella shook her head sadly. "It's not fair. Not fair at all."

"What's that?" Guy asked between mouthfuls of the savory stew, which he fervently hoped Fenella would not give up making entirely.

"That poor Pong Fey. He was only just married when he came over. Had to leave his young bride, his mother, aunt, and four cousins in China. He's desperately lonely for them."

"So why doesn't he bring them over? I'll guarantee jobs, and you know I've promised interest-free loans for their families' passages, as long as I can afford it. Is he afraid I'll say no because they're all women and children? You know I welcome women as well as men. Some of our best pickers in France were women."

Fenella regretted bringing the subject up, but now that she had, there was no backing away. "It's the quota laws. People don't like Chinese, so they've made those laws to keep them out. It's dreadful, Guy, it really is. Separating families like this. Even Mister Louis can't get his wife and children in."

"I didn't realize it was that bad." Guy chewed thoughtfully. "Maybe I can do something in Sacramento."

Guy was stonewalled. Even those politicians he had considered close allies wouldn't listen to his appeal. No one wanted to take the chance of being considered pro-Chinese. Any kind of dispensation for Guy's workers would earn them that label.

"There doesn't seem to be anyone strong enough to tear down this damned barrier," Guy told Fenella after months of frustration.

There was one man, Fenella thought. And she would ask him.

Chapter Fifty-seven

Fenella was brushing her long hair, her one source of pride. Slow, even strokes from her crown to the very tips that reached down to her waist. Damon lay on the bed, under disarranged sheets, drawing on a cigar and admiring her. Every so often he reached for a snifter and took a sip. He thought about making love again and then laughed. They only saw each other once every two or three months, and when they were together it was like their wedding night.

"Damon," Fenella called quietly, still facing the mirror as she worked her hair. "Damon, I have a favor to ask. I don't think it's a very big one, but it's something only you can do."

Damon took another pull on the cigar, expelling the smoke slowly toward the ceiling. She sounded very serious, she wasn't one to beat about the bush. He had always liked that.

"You know I'll do anything for you, everything. Haven't I always? Even though you've refused to come back to our home."

"Please not that, not now." It was a subject that Damon brought up often, that they parried around until he conceded defeat.

"I know, I know," he said. "Another abandoned baby you have to take care of. I wished you'd had a baby of your own." He instantly regretted saying that.

"You know what the doctors said. No more. Only that one."

She still grieves for her lost child, Damon thought. What would have happened to us if the baby had lived?

"What is it you want?" he asked tenderly.

"It's the Chinese workers at the Belltower, Damon."

Although thrown off balance by that topic, he came back lightly with, "You mean the wonderful Saint-Savin is mistreating our good Asian friends? You've shown good judgment coming to me, Fenella. I can certainly see a stop is put to that."

She did not respond to his teasing, instead responded seriously, "It's not that at all. You know Guy is good to them. It's their families. They can't bring them over because of the quota laws. Guy's tried, but only you can get them some special allowance. I know you could."

If she hadn't been facing away from him, she would have seen his clenched anger as his knuckles went white around the glass. No man had endured what he had, being deprived of his wife as he had. Their relationship was what she allowed, its perimeters the lines she drew. And he had put up with this because he feared losing her completely.

His anger towards her dissipated, he could never stay angry with Fenella. She was not his enemy. Guy Saint-Savin was his enemy. And that was what this request was about—it was about rescuing Guy Saint-Savin from his own disgusting altruism.

"Still something else for Saint-Savin, is it?" Damon's customary control had gotten lost in all the wine he had for dinner. He was filled with outrage. He should have killed that bastard years ago, with his hands around Saint-Savin's neck, squeezing the life from him. He drank more cognac and its heat further fired his anger.

"Something else for Saint-Savin? You want me to get more Chinks for that son-of-a-bitch, that's it? More Chinks? Do you know I've had to keep vigilantes from killing the Chinks he already has? I've had to keep them from tearing down his fancy house and pulling up his precious grapes? There're people who want to kill Saint-Savin for hiring those Asians. But I've stopped them. For Saint-Savin? Hell no. For you, Fenella, for you and Kyle. You appreciate that, Fenella? Hell no. You want more for Guy Saint-Savin. Well, I'm tired of helping him. I mean, for all I know you've been whoring with him for years. Is that what you've been doing, Fenella? Playing me for the goddamned fool? IS IT?"

He hurled his snifter across the room, away from her. It shattered with terrifying force. Damon stared at the rivers of brandy running to the floor, then he said, "Well, you can be damned, Fenella Delany. I'm not going to be your cuckold anymore."

Damon slammed the door to his dressing room. Fenella knew he wouldn't be back, not that night. She bowed her head and wept.

As Damon walked rapidly through the Palace lobby, he had little thought of where he was going. He was overcome by anger and self-pity. It had galled him that time after time he had been Saint-Savin's secret benefactor. It had always been that whatever plan he had for

ruining that damned French sodbuster, somehow Fenella had interceded in time. Now again she was asking, in her quiet, madonna
voice. And now he was again supposed to eagerly cry, "Yes, yes,
anything," to prove that he loved her, to atone for letting their child
die. Well, damn it, he wasn't doing it, not this time.

Damon, unseeing, collided with someone and would have pushed
past, if a silk-covered hand hadn't halted his progress.

"Why, if it isn't Mister Delany. And how are you, Mister Delany?
It's been such a long time." Ardis Saint-Savin was mockingly pointing
her evening purse at him.

Damon did not answer. He studied her coldly.

"Well, I hope you don't mind my saying you don't look very well.
No, not all. You seem so...so agitated. Perhaps you've had a little
argument, though I can't believe anyone would argue with a woman
as gracious and well-mannered as you." Ardis was not one to forget
Damon's humiliating departure from her embrace, and she hoped to
make him uncomfortable as well.

When he still said nothing, Ardis, getting somewhat nervous, said,
"It's been just charming running into you, but my carriage is outside
and I'll be going home now."

Before she could move on, Damon grabbed her upper arm and
pulled her out of the lobby.

An hour later, Damon was absolutely, totally drunk, a state he had
not been in since he was thirteen years old, after which he had vowed
never to lose control of himself like that again. He was drunk but the
alcohol had not softened his anger.

Getting over her initial fright, Ardis had spent the time playing the
flirt, something that, Damon uncharitably thought, she wouldn't
have many more years to do without appearing ridiculous.

They were sitting close to each other, almost touching, on the
divan. Ardis had teased on while Damon had drunk, almost in
silence. Now he was tired of her talk and her game. He seized her
behind the neck and kissed her roughly.

Ardis allowed the kiss to linger then indignantly pushed him away.
"Really, Mister Delany, why would you think you could take such
license with a respectably married woman, such as I?"

"Because, because I can remember that silk nothing you put on two
years ago. I remember how your breasts looked, how your nipples
felt, how you wanted me."

"Really sir, I must beg you to stop." Ardis was thoroughly enjoying the scene. She fluttered her hand over her decolletage as if the thought of his improper advances were about to give her the vapors. Let him wait, she thought, let him beg for it.

But Ardis had severely misjudged Damon and his mood. He wasn't about to wait. He could take no more frustrations, no more delays. He would have what he wanted, when he wanted.

He took the front of her dress and yanked her up off the divan. He pulled her head back by the hair with one hand and ripped away her dress with the other. His lips went to her breasts where they grasped her and fed on her.

She helped him tear off the rest of her clothes, and, naked, she dropped to the rug. Then he was on her, naked as well, and theirs was a melding of hate and desire. Each went to the other for their own fulfillment.

In the aftermath, they lay panting in their sweat. Then he rose, dressed, and downed the last of his drink.

Ardis stayed on the floor. She could still feel his imprint, on her, in her, and she knew he would be back.

The long walk off Nob Hill to his offices at the waterfront did little to sober or soothe Damon. Rutting with Ardis, instead of serving as revenge on Guy, only infuriated him further. Intellectually, he knew Fenella and Guy had never been lovers—at that moment, though, emotionally, he couldn't be sure of anything. If he had Saint-Savin's wife, whore that she was, why couldn't Guy have Damon's? It was enough. He would take no more.

Jake Cartwell was sprawled across two chairs, asleep. Damon kicked one away, so the unsuspecting man woke up as his rump hit the floor.

"Cartwell, the fellow in the Napa Valley who's all worked up about Saint-Savin's Chinks, what's his name?"

Cartwell was trying to rub some sense and coherency into his eyes. The boss didn't like to be kept waiting. "It's, uh, West, Lawrence West. Owns a little place up the road. Worked the last election for us up there."

"Fine. It's about time we repaid this Lawrence West for the work he did. Take some men and gather up whoever this West's got with him. It's time for some coolie thrashing. What do you think? Time for Guy Saint-Savin to know he's in the goddamned U. S. of A. now? That he's no fucking count over here. That he plays by our rules?"

It was an order that Cartwell was all too happy to carry out. He was hurrying to comply, but was caught short at the door by Damon calling out, "One thing. The boy, Kyle, you make sure nothing happens to him."

"Right boss, but you know it's been a helluva long time. I might not recognize him. Uh, one other thing, boss." Cartwell didn't like bringing this up, but on the other hand, he wouldn't have wanted to make a mistake. "What about the missus, boss? What about Missus Delany?"

"Don't worry. She's here, in San Francisco. Any other woman out there with that Guy Saint-Savin now deserves what she gets. Now move it."

When the crying had stopped, Fenella sat slumped at her dressing table, staring at herself in the mirror. Had she been wrong all these years? Had she been wrong to believe Damon was strong and didn't really need her? It was the boys, first Kyle then Hugh, who had needed her, demanded and deserved her attention. Denying them would have been a sin. But maybe her sin was one of selfishness. Maybe she had used them to fill the gap of her own lost child, thereby cruelly abandoning Damon.

She knew Damon didn't really believe she'd been unfaithful with Guy. Damon was hurt and angry. But Fenella had to admit, if she really searched through her feelings, that she was attracted to Guy as more than a friend. But there was nothing deeper than that and she would have never acted on that feeling.

All at once she began pinning up her hair. A person being wrong in the past didn't mean a person had to be wrong in the future. She felt bad for little Hugh, he was so tiny and needed a mother, a real mother, not Ardis. Still it was time she, Fenella Delany, faced the truth. Hugh was not her child and neither was Kyle, no matter how much she loved them. She had a husband and he was Damon. Her duty was to him.

Fenella pulled her small carpetbag from a closet and filled it with the few toiletries she'd brought. She would go back to the Belltower that night, before she changed her mind. She would tell Guy it was time she returned to her husband, that was where she belonged. And she would say goodbye.

Chapter Fifty-eight

The dark coolness of the cellar, filled with its musky reminder of what was stored in the oak hogsheads, was a pleasant relief from the harshness of the midday sun.

Fenella had slept little on the trip back. She always felt more secure, awake and watching the road along with the driver handling the reins. The bright light outside had been stinging her eyes.

"Guy," she called. The great house had been empty except for one of the maids. Old House, which Guy and the boys sometimes moved into when Ardis was away, was deserted. She couldn't make them out in any of the fields.

"Guy," she called again.

"He's gone to Napa with the boys. For supplies." Fenella jumped, Miguel was like an apparition, appearing out of nowhere. "You're back early, aren't you?" he asked.

"Miguel, I'm glad at least you're here. I've made a decision and I must tell someone." She sat down wearily on a barrel. "Oh, it's such a difficult thing to do, but I know I'm right. I should have done it a long time ago."

Miguel sat next to her, glad for all the times she had offered him warmth and comfort that, at last, he might be able to do the same for her. "You look as if you haven't slept."

"What you see isn't my being tired. It's knowing something must be done, knowing I have to do it, and still not wanting to."

Fenella wasn't talking wildly or ranting, still Miguel knew she was profoundly upset. She was usually one to address a subject directly, with thoughtful consideration. Not like this. Her stability had proved his touchstone, his anchor through the years. He had maintained his equilibrium, kept himself from going crazy with waiting, because she had been there.

360

The only thing he could think to ask was, "Is anyone sick? Has there been an accident?" although she had given him no reason to think there had been one.

Fenella folded her hands on her lap as if to keep her resolve from falling apart.

"I'm going back to live with my husband. I'm going back to Damon."

Miguel blinked hard several times. He didn't want to believe he had heard her declaration. He didn't want it to be true—that she was going to Damon Delany. Not back to Damon Delany.

Without thinking, he blurted, "You can't. You mustn't. You're an angel. He's the devil and he will be punished one day."

"Oh no, Miguel. He has done unkind things, even bad things, but Damon's not evil."

Miguel was up, arms slashing the air. "Not evil? Not evil? You're so good you're unable to imagine the evil he's done, the thieving, the murdering. He's a murderer, I say. You can't go to a murderer?"

Fenella put her hands out to him in supplication, begging Miguel for a return to calm and sanity. "Miguel, please, I know Damon. He's not what you say."

"Not what I say? Not what I say?" Miguel shook his head savagely, stunned by such innocence, even from Fenella. "He's worse than anything I could say. Oh, Damon Delany doesn't pull the trigger. He doesn't have to. He pays others to do it for him. Who do you think put those squatters up to coming here? Whose man pulled the trigger first? What about Judge Carl Miller, gunned down by a highway robber, was he? Funny how he just happened to be hearing a voting fraud case against Damon Delany. And what of John Redding, who decided to run against Delany's stooge in Sacramento? Falling out in a poker game, wasn't it? And that legislator who was holding up the money for the road near San Rafael? Whose company was building that road? Why Damon Delany's. Poor legislator, must have had too much to drink on the ferry, falling overboard like that. And what about my father? What about him?"

Fenella had been so astonished by Miguel's knowledge of Damon's history that she almost didn't hear the last two questions. "What are you saying" she whispered, afraid of the answer. "What about your father?"

"You never guessed then? I didn't think so. It was Damon Delany who stole my family's ranch, who sent my father into disgrace and caused his death. It was Damon Delany, Fenella, Damon Delany."

"Oh, my God, Miguel. You're wrong. You don't know what you're saying. But if you believe that I can understand how you must hate him."

"Hate? I have wanted to cut his beating heart from his body since the day I found my father. I've wanted to rip him open, tear out his guts, and make him eat them."

"Why didn't you?" she asked weakly.

Miguel slumped onto the barrel, head in hands. Fenella could barely make out his muffled answer. "Because I met you. Because of what you did for my poor mother. Because I could not harm an angel. I could never do anything, anything, that would cause you pain." He looked up and added fiercely, "Even if it were for your own good, like ridding the world of carrion like Delany."

Fenella stood and put her hands on Miguel's heaving shoulders. He didn't know what he was saying. She knew Damon better than anyone, and he couldn't have done what Miguel had said. No, no, Miguel, poor Miguel, must be mad. That must be it. After all these years, the pain of his parents' death had finally become too much for him. Fenella studied him carefully. Yes, that was what she had to believe. Miguel had to be wrong, otherwise there were too many sordid other things Fenella might have to concede her husband had engineered.

"Miguel," she said gently. "You are a Catholic. You know it has been a sin for me to be away from my husband. Perhaps if I had been with him, he might not have done... I don't think he's done anything. In any case, all I know is it is my duty to be with him. I have hurt him far too much already and I must atone for that."

"And what of us? The boys? Guy? Me? What of the hurt you'll do us?"

Fenella had thought about that for hours, and she had found no answer.

"I will always love you. Always."

She left to pack her things.

Guy and the boys returned in the early evening. What with the rush of dinner and getting Hugh to bed, there was no time for talk. Miguel had not come in for the meal. Except for noting this in passing, Guy and Kyle were so filled with talk of the long-hoped-for agricultural college at Davis that Miguel's absence wasn't questioned.

Fenella felt relieved. She wanted Guy alone and without interruption when she tried to explain her leaving. The moment never came that night. She would tell him in the morning.

A horse snorted among the trees. In nervous response, three, then four and five answered. Jake Cartwell adjusted the black cloth hood over his face. The ten men he'd pulled from stinkholes and bars on the waterfront were doing the same, he was glad to see.

Couldn't be too careful, Cartwell thought. Wasn't a fuck's chance in a nunnery they'd be recognized around here. Still the boss wouldn't be happy if they were. Let the dumb locals take the blame. Lawrence West had been overjoyed to get his men together with others from the valley. They'd been stoked with liquor and inflammatory talk throughout the night and now Cartwell could hardly restrain them from immediately teaching those "little slant-eyes they shouldn't be stealing jobs from us Americans."

Cartwell checked around. A little ways off in the clearing were the tidy houses of the vineyard workers, unprotected and unsuspecting. Easy targets. He could feel the restless tension of his men. No point in waiting any longer. He reached for his pistol and fired a shot skyward. Screeches and hollers mauled the night's air and the carnage began.

A frightened face appeared at a window and instantly disintegrated into a horror of blood, splintered bone, and the dangling, oozing remains of an eyeball.

Terrified men and women lost reason and ran from the protection of their homes looking for sanctuary outside. Men on horseback clubbed them from behind, shot them as they fell, and rode over their bodies. Men were grabbed by their pigtails, dangled aloft until daggers sliced and slashed through their hair and they fell, stripped of their pride, to the ground.

Guy and Miguel came running from opposite directions, both with rifles firing. They were quickly forced back.

"Get to the weapons!" Guy screamed at the Chinese. There was a store in a shed near Old House. Then Guy remembered the shed was locked. He was about to dash back, to shoot the lock off, when Kyle ran up to him.

"I've got the key, Father. I'll get the guns."

"No," Guy shouted, but too late. Kyle was already gone. Guy turned back to the fighting in time to see attackers hurling burning branches onto houses and through windows. Roofs shot up in flames.

Fenella came stumbling out of Old House into the smoke and mayhem. She could see the attack, the fleeing Chinese, the demoniac horsemen. She could hear the tortured screams.

Then she saw Kyle.

Coming from the shed, arms filled with rifles, he was near Louis Chu when the Chinaman was knocked flat by a horseman, who then jumped down, knife in hand, to capture his prize.

With a scream of outrage, Kyle dropped all but one of the rifles and ran swinging it at the man's head. The attacker went down, unconscious, and Kyle reached out his hand to pull up Mister Louis.

It was all happening so slowly and so fast, Fenella wasn't aware she was running, but when she saw the man in the black hood several yards away take a steady aim at Kyle's head, she ran faster.

"Oh God! No! Kyle!" She threw herself across him, knocking him down as the shot got off. "Oh. Kyle," she moaned and crumpled, blood soaking the back of her dress.

"Shit!" the gunman muttered, lifting his hood to get a better look. "The boss's missus. She wasn't supposed to be here."

Cartwell fired four shots in quick succession, wheeled his horse around, and galloped away down the road. Ten riders fell in behind him. The rest of the attackers seeing they were being deserted, scattered.

Guy fired several ineffectual shots of frustration in their direction. He had no idea what made them leave so suddenly, but it was none too soon. Screams of pain and keens of anguish wracked the air, mixing with the haze of gunsmoke and burning houses. Some of the men were already running with water to douse the fires.

Over the horrific din, he heard Kyle calling.

"Father! Help! Over here. Near the shed."

Guy found Kyle on his knees, cradling and frantically rocking Fenella, trying to shake life back into her.

"She's been shot," Kyle sobbed. "She's going to die. She's going to die."

Guy watched in paralyzed horror as blood pooled around Fenella. He didn't notice Miguel behind him, Miguel staring down at the still, chalky face of Fenella.

He didn't see Miguel turn away, stand for a minute, head down, fists clenched. And he didn't see Miguel rush to the stable.

Chapter Fifty-nine

He'd been there several times, usually with a message from Guy. He'd always been sent to the servants' entrance. That's how she treated him when Guy wasn't around. Like a servant. Not worth anything. That's how she treated most everyone she could.

He knew his way around. He climbed over the tall iron fence and crept up through the garden, to the side French windows. They led to the library, he knew.

The windows weren't even latched. He went in. There were a few lights casting shadows in the hallway.

He silently climbed the stairs, the thick Persian runner masking any noise from his movement.

He knew the room. He'd seen the maid take a note up to her on one of those silly little trays. The door handle turned without a sound. He stepped into the room.

Moonlight through an open window played across the two naked bodies, sleeping the deadened sleep of those just finished with lovemaking.

The clerk at the hotel had been right. He was here.

Miguel stood over them. Her silvery hair, tangled and messed, was covering his face. Miguel wanted to see it. He wanted to see the eyes flash with recognition. He carefully pushed the strands aside and put the gun to the man's temple.

Damon Delany opened his eyes. Miguel pulled the trigger. Ardis screamed. Miguel pulled the trigger again.

Book Eleven

Chapter Sixty

1870

Without opening her eyes, Solange stretched her arms over her head, brushing the long hair away from her face. Her hair was always loose and flowing the morning after she and Nathan made love. As they were preparing for bed, he would come up behind her and loosen it. Or they might be on the terrace or in the study.

Solange suppressed a giggle and rolled over to help her husband greet the day.

Nathan wasn't there. That was strange, Solange thought, he believed that the early side of noon was only suitable for sleeping or breakfast in bed.

Who knew what he was up to? Nathan always had some project or other, or he would be off with David, their now-tall, gangly adolescent who would not have believed anyone with the temerity to suggest Nathan wasn't his natural father.

Solange reached over for Nathan's pillow and buried her face in it. His scent was there. It made her smile.

Solange shook off her reverie, got up and quickly dressed. It was a lovely, bright July day. Perhaps Nathan had decided to breakfast on the terrace.

He wasn't there either. Nor was he with David and Jacques Mazet, who were walking back from Jean Bellay's inn, where Mazet took most of his meals now that his mother was dead.

Back inside the château, Solange began to fret. This wasn't like Nathan, to leave without a word. She rang for Lise.

"Lise, do you know where the baron is? I've looked everywhere for him. Perhaps Henri could tell us."

"I'm sorry, baroness, but Henri's not here."

"Well, where is he?"

"With the baron, of course."

Solange was losing her patience; still, with Lise, one had to take one's time. "And where would that be?"

"I don't know, baroness, but I think the baron left a letter."

"Would you get it for me, please? Thank you." If Lise hadn't been there since Edouard's days, Solange might have considered sending her away long ago. When Lise returned with the note, an ill-defined uneasiness stopped Solange from opening it right away. She couldn't imagine anything that might have come up this morning. So why hadn't Nathan told her he was leaving last night?

There was no use putting it off. Solange opened the letter.

My dearest beautiful one,

I have waited until now to tell you my plans because I knew you would protest and at worse, I might give in completely for I find denying you anything beyond my ability, or at best I might be delayed. Time right now is extremely valuable.

Though we have not been at the court much lately, you know that occasionally I've performed small services for the emperor. That trade mission to London last year, for one. And you know that Louis, foolishly perhaps, has called on me for my opinions which he has, foolishly perhaps, taken to heart.

I'm afraid France is about to embark on the most foolhardy and reckless undertaking. Those in the court who have noticed my influence have asked me to caution Louis against it.

It may be already too late. Nationalistic nonsense is running high both here and in Prussia. The *Ems* telegram which was supposed to be an account of our emissary's meeting with the king of Prussia has conveniently—for Bismarck, I feel—managed to inflame both sides. And now, that nitwit, the duc de Gramont, whom Bismarck has rightfully called the stupidest man in Europe, is saying French troops will be crossing the Rhine in a fortnight.

I know Louis is against this militaristic idiocy. But his illness,
those accursed gallstones, have weakened him so dreadfully that I
fear Eugenie has virtually taken the reins of state. She would like to
dispel all the talk that, being Spanish, her loyalties have never
actually lain with la Belle France, so she is fanning the mood for
marching on the Prussians.

France is not prepared for this adventure. Louis has told me of his
ill-fated attempts to modernize the army, give it an efficient chain of
command as the Prussians have. But the military will not be
budged. Why don't we have any reserves? Every able-bodied man
who can, now buys his way out of service. The officers we have are
little more than resplendent fops. And we are intending to face
Prussia? Prussia which is not a country with an army, but an army
with a country. If it hadn't been for Louis insisting, we wouldn't
even have that new breech-loading rifle, the *chassepot*, to answer
the Prussian's needle-gun.

It is folly and madness, and it must be stopped. I know it is
absurd that the fate of France should fall to such a ne'er-do-well as I,
still, I must do what I can. And besides, it is a friend who needs my
help. From what I have heard, Louis can hardly stand from pain, but
Eugenie would have him ride at the front of the attacking columns.

I should be home within the week. You know I shall miss you
greatly. I miss you already.

With all my love,

Nathan

"Lise!" Solange called sharply. "Lise, have my carriage readied
immediately."

"What is it, Mama?" David, freckled and sun-tanned, came in after
the flustered Lise had bustled out.

Solange waved the letter at him. "It's your Father. He's run off on
some fool's mission. I'm going after him."

David took the letter and read it.

"Why? Why are you going after him? You know once Father puts
his mind to something, he won't be deterred until it's finished. Do
you really think he can stop the war?" David asked, although he was
sure his father could.

"Quite possibly. Nathan is capable of anything. It's just that he's not
as young as he once was, and he won't admit it. He does nothing to
slow down. I'm afraid he'll overtax himself...."

"And you won't be there to take care of him," David teased.

Solange laughed in defeat. "All right. Nathan can certainly take care of himself. Still, I'll be glad when he gets home. Now, my wise son, isn't it time we went to see how our grapes are doing?"

Weeks passed and France was never to be the same again. With a speed that startled even the most ardent pessimist, the French army collapsed, and on September 1, Louis Napoleon sent a message to the King of Prussia.

My brother, not having been able to die with my soldiers, I have no alternative but to turn my sword over to Your Majesty. I am Your Majesty's devoted brother. Napoleon.

And so the white flag of surrender was raised and the Second Empire collapsed.

And still no word from Nathan.

Solange tried not to worry. She couldn't believe Nathan would have gone to the front. He had to be in Paris. Or he might be in Tours, where what was left of the French government had gathered to regroup. Everything was disrupted. Armies marched back and forth across the country. Eugenie was secreted out of Paris by an American dentist, of all people. It was beyond comprehension and completely disordered. Even the harvest was early that year.

And still no Nathan.

A sharp rapping at her door roused Solange from a troubled sleep.

"Yes, one minute," she called, disoriented and groping for her robe. "Who is it?"

"Jacques."

Jacques Mazet pounding on her bedroom door in the middle of the night? Jacques rarely came into the château at all. Oh no, Solange thought wildly, it must be Nathan. He must have bad news about Nathan.

Solange frantically threw open the door and started to demand she be told what Jacques had found out about Nathan when she saw Mazet was not alone. A disheveled David, nervously studying his shoes, was with him.

"He was in the stable," Mazet said with no preliminaries. "Saddling a horse. Going to slip away. I'm sorry. He wouldn't listen. I had to cuff him to make him stay."

"There's no need to be sorry for anything, Jacques. Thank you for intercepting him. And now, David, explain yourself. Just where did you think you were going?" Solange was so angry with her son, she could have cuffed him as well. There were too many other worries without David adding to them.

"Nobody's doing anything," David responded with anger of his own. "Nobody's looking for Father. I was going to find him."

"Find him! And where did you propose to look? And what were you going to do if some gang of conscripters found you and oh so politely suggested you join the army? For God's sake, David, use your head. You're needed here. Nathan would want you here. And besides, wasn't it you who said he could take care of himself?"

"I know." David was fighting back tears. "Except it's been so long, Mama, it's been so long."

And it had been.

Finally, in November, weeks after the harvest—a good harvest, but one in which Solange could take little joy—a note did arrive. Nathan was in Paris. Solange shouldn't worry despite what she may have heard. It was true the Prussians were closing their circle around the capital after unexpected resistance had arisen. Even though the Empire had surrendered, Paris had not. Parisians did not accept the defeat and were holding out. The Prussians were putting the city under siege. There didn't seem any way for Nathan to escape just then. Henri was with him, however, and they would be fine. Nathan missed her and loved her and would be with her as soon as possible.

More time passed and still Nathan remained in Paris. The news from there was evermore frightening. The efficient Prussians had efficiently sealed off the city. No food was getting in to feed the hungry Parisians. Winter had come and was uncommonly bitter. The beautiful trees along the Champs Elysées were cut down, and there was a riot over who would get the wood. The Seine iced over and along its banks the tattered remnants of the French army froze to death.

Solange read the latest grim dispatch. She would wait no longer. If Nathan couldn't find a way out, she would find a way in.

Chapter Sixty-one

"Halt! Who goes there?"

The four words paralyzed her. She thought she had made it. She couldn't be caught now, not so close, not now. Not after the two weeks, the two nerve-wracking, exhausting, terror-filled weeks that started in a rowboat across the Gironde, then riding hard north through Charente, Vienne, Indre, the Loire Valley, and at last the outskirts of Paris, skirting military camps, haggling for horses, bribing pickets.

For more than a day, she had cautiously searched for a breach in the German lines. An old fishmonger, sitting outside his shuttered store, told her to try Montrouge. Not even the Prussians were too eager to stand guard near the Catacombes, recipient of the bones of Paris. Hundreds of thousands of bodies were disposed there, in those stone subterranean caverns, and even the bravest of soldiers didn't like to be reminded he might be next.

She had long since abandoned her horse, and had waited until nightfall to sidle along the ancient Barrière d'Enfer—Highway of Hell, as it was appropriately named.

And then she thought she was through the lines. She knew the old walls of the city were yet to come; still, she never thought the Prussians would be so close to them.

She stood very still, praying that the darkness shielded her.

"What was it?" another voice asked.

Silence. Then the crunching of boots on pebbles. Silence.

"Must have been a rat," the first voice finally answered.

"There's enough of those around here." Solange could hear their laughter drifting away from her, and then she started breathing again.

Solange had entered hell.

Paris was a wretched, desperate city where young girls called to men from doorways, "Monsieur, I'll go upstairs with you for a morsel of bread, only a morsel." It was a city where dirty, drawn people roamed the streets scrounging for any bit of food they could find, which the rich had long since abandoned to its despair, taking with them all the dazzle and light.

Dawn was breaking, throwing a dull, dispirited cast on the Seine, when Solange finally reached the Pont de la Tournelle that went across to the Ile St. Louis. Her footsteps echoed with eerie persistence. On the island, where there should have been the sounds of shutters clanking open, deliveries being made, and the day coming to life, there were only the sounds of Solange's wary progress, over Pont Marie, through the Marais, and at last to the Place des Vosges. She took the last several yards across the square to Nathan's pavilion running and sobbing. She pounded the high brass knocker, not caring whom she awoke with her screams demanding she be let in. Then it struck her, Nathan might not be there, and she pounded all the harder.

The imposing door swung open.

"We weren't expecting you, madame," Henri said with even more than his usual formality.

"You're here. Thank God. Everything's all right, then. Where is he?" Solange, not standing on formalities, pushed her way past the butler and ran into the grand entrance hall—only to stop as if she'd run into a wall.

If it hadn't been for the ceilings painted with clouds and cherubs, she would have thought she was in the wrong house. She couldn't believe what she saw. She rushed, stunned, from room to room. There were no lights, no fires to lessen the frigid cold. There were great empty places where chairs, divans, tables, vases, paintings, ornaments that Nathan had lovingly collected in his travels were supposed to be.

"What has happened here?" Solange gasped to Henri when she finally stopped. "I thought the Prussians hadn't gotten past the city walls. Who did this?"

"I did, madame."

"You? No, not you. Why would you do this to Nathan, this outrage?"

Henri bowed his head, and Solange realized he was weeping.

"I had no choice, madame. There was nothing else I could do." He leaned, almost collapsed, against a wall, seeking some relief and any solace. "I had to let the other servants go. There's been no money. No money for them. No money for us. I've been burning furniture to keep the baron's room warm. As for food, I've done what I could with what I could get. You can't imagine how it has been."

But Solange could. The desperation and desolation was staring back at her from all over the room. She shivered. She was so cold. She had never experienced such complete, penetrating iciness. Then she thought of something that chilled her more.

"Why were you handling all this, Henri? Where is Nathan? Surely he has access to money somewhere. Why were you selling his things for food?"

Henri wouldn't look up. "I chose items of small value, madame. None of the really precious items. I wouldn't take those without the baron's approval."

"Henri, why aren't you answering my question?" Solange screamed. "Why couldn't you get Nathan's approval? Tell me! Where is he?"

Henri rubbed his hands over his ears, to wipe away Solange's questions, to erase the last months.

"It started at the front. He went to the front. He desperately wanted to stop the 'folly,' as he called it. But the battle had already started and he was shot."

Solange went so pale that Henri put a hand out to catch her, he was sure she was about to faint. She motioned him off and he continued.

"It was a minor wound, madame, nothing really. But after we returned to Paris, it became infected. Nothing would make it better. The baron was so ill. Often he was only half-awake, screaming to people who have been dead for years, talking to them as if they were right there with him. And then I couldn't find a doctor. They all left. There's nobody in Paris now except those too poor to go, those rich enough not to have to, and us. And us, madame."

Solange ran up the stairs, two at a time, and into Nathan's room. The contrast between the cold of the hallway and the warmth on the other side of the door was startling. His room, at least, looked as it should, untouched and bold. She was afraid to look at the massive four-postered bed. But she knew she had to. She walked closer.

Nathan was covered to the chin with thick woolen blankets. Henri had kept his hair neatly combed. He had been able to do nothing else, however, to disguise the ravages of the illness. Nathan's face had sunk into great hollows. His lips were thinned and tight, his complexion sickly and pasty. Solange touched his forehead, only to yank her hand back. He was smoldering, as hot as the coals in the fireplace.

"Does he ever wake up?"Solange whispered to Henri, who had followed her into the room.

"Not really. And you don't have to whisper, madame. He doesn't hear us. He hears only his memories."

Chapter Sixty-two

The only way of surviving the next days was not to think about them. Years later Solange could not describe or even remember much of what happened then. Minutes, hours, days, weeks spun into a horrific nightmare from which she could not wake up.

When she wasn't sitting with Nathan, wiping his brow, willing him to get better, she was scouring the house for jewelry and other expensive items to sell. Finding someone to buy them was next to impossible. Still she tried. She roamed through all sections of Paris, looking for anyone with money and the willingness to part with it for her exquisite offerings. There were some, some who seized the opportunity to make fortunes by paying a hundredth or a thousandth of the value of the items for sale, knowing that sooner or later Paris would be Paris, and they would never have to work again.

Solange got so little and what little food there was left in the city cost so much. There was still a meager amount of foodstuffs in the cavernous storerooms of Nathan's mansion. But these were dwindling at such a rate, Solange all but stopped eating herself. Nathan couldn't get better if he didn't have enough food. She could at least do that for him.

She had been wandering aimlessly through deserted streets and alleys. She had a diamond brooch Nathan had given her on what he called their fifth anniversary, the fifth anniversary of when they'd first made love—"That's when our marriage began," he had explained. She was going to sell it if she could.

She stopped to get her bearings when she saw she was at the foot of the Champs Elysées, across from a familiar spot. She knew it was hopeless, but Solange would abase herself in any way if it might help Nathan.

She crossed the boulevard and knocked on the door of Fabienne's mansion.

A young maid answered and when Solange asked to see Fabienne, she said, "Oh, you've just missed her."

"Then I'll wait for her," Solange said firmly and pushed by the girl. She went up the stairs and flung open the door to her mother's boudoir, fully expecting to find Fabienne there.

And she wasn't disappointed. Her mother, perfectly made up, beautifully combed, clad in white silk, was lying on the bed, her arms folded across her chest. At her feet sat two perfectly still fluffy white dogs.

Solange turned in confusion to the maid who had followed her up.

"It's been a day now, ma'am, since she died, ma'am. Been waiting for the men to come and take her away."

Solange stared at the girl with uncomprehending disbelief. Then she looked back at the macabre scene on the bed. "But the dogs?" she finally managed to ask.

"Oh, them," the girl answered nonchalantly. "She got them right after Inez, her old servant, died. That must have been ten years ago, I guess. Well, the countess, she always said that those dogs and Inez were the only living things she'd ever been able to trust. When the dogs passed on, first one and then the other, last year, why the countess went and had them stuffed. She's going to be buried with them, imagine that. Begging your pardon, ma'am, but the countess was a strange one, wasn't she? Did you know her well?"

"I didn't know her at all."

The gray drizzle of the winter morning cut through Solange's cloak. She was walking along the quai of the Left Bank. The Seine's water lapping at the retaining wall gave cadence to her step. She had been totally unsuccessful that morning. She had nothing to take back to the Place des Vosges, only her exhaustion and increasing desperation.

She paused and looked across the river. Notre Dame towered nearby, majestic and impervious to the degradation that surrounded it.

Something flicked across Solange's foot. Her first instinct was to jump back. She didn't. It had been something alive, something that could be eaten. Solange threw herself flat across the cobblestones and grabbed at the creature. She got its tail. It was an enormous, fat rat, teeth bared and gnashing in fright and anger.

Solange knelt and beat it against the stones, again and again, until it no longer breathed and she was panting. It was meat, something to eat. She would run home and give it to Henri and... Solange looked up. A semi-circle of hollow-eyed, wretched men, women, and listless children were watching her, staring at her prize.

Solange looked down at the battered, dirty mat of bloody vermin in her hand. She looked back at the crowd, then heaved the rat at them and fled, fighting back the nausea that washed over her.

When she finally could get herself to stop running, she was on rue St. Antoine, where, under ordinary circumstances, in normal times, she would be pushing her way through a bustle of determined shoppers, women demanding the plumpest chicken, the freshest eggs, the tenderest veal. Instead St. Antoine was empty and waiting.

Solange shook her head savagely. She would not cry. She would not.

That night Solange mixed some of the precious flour that remained with a bit of water. She took it to Nathan's room.

It looked so meager, a lump of mush in such a beautiful china bowl, someone's idea of a cruel practical joke. For a second she was tempted to eat it herself. She was very hungry. She lifted the spoon to her mouth, then replaced it quickly. She was strong. She didn't need nourishment, not yet. Besides, her hunger had reached the point where she no longer felt it.

"No wonder you're so thin. Stop dawdling with your food and eat it."

Solange was so startled, she jumped up from the chair, at the same time miraculously managing to save the bowl from crashing to the floor.

"Nathan, you're awake. You're talking. How do you feel?"

"A bit light-headed. When did you get here, my dear?"

"Eight weeks ago."

Nathan tried to sit up. The exertion was too much and that surprised him as much as Solange's answer.

"But that can't be. How long have I been asleep?"

It took quite some time for Solange to convince Nathan he had been sick for so long. Then he insisted she fill him in on what had befallen France and Paris.

"This is so hard to believe. Then what day is today? What's the date?"

Solange had to think, dates had so little importance recently. "It's December 31st," she said at last. "It's Reveillon. New Year's Eve."

Nathan smiled broadly for the first time. "Reveillon in Paris. I've always wanted to spend New Year's Eve with you here. There's something magical, special. You'll love it. It's a bit late for reservations, but don't worry. Monsieur Bernard at Chez Voisin will have a table for us. Imagine, being brought back to life on New Year's Eve."

Solange was flabbergasted and worried that Nathan was again hallucinating. "What are you talking about? Didn't you hear anything I said?"

"Of course, I heard," he responded with equanimity. "Now, isn't that white dress, the one you wore to Compiègne, at Louis's party so long ago, isn't that one here? I want you to wear it. It's always been my favorite. I don't care if it's out of fashion or not."

Solange took Nathan's hands to stop him. "I will wear anything you wish. But I will wear it here. Not Chez Voisin or anywhere else. Here. Don't you understand? Even if the restaurant is open, we have no money to pay for dinner."

"No money? What are you talking about? There's nothing left in the false bottom of the Ming? Or in the vault behind the panel in the library? And what about the loose brick in the wine cellar? And the jewels I saved for emergencies when currency wouldn't do? They're in the bedroom...."

"We didn't know, Nathan. Henri and I looked everywhere. We found nothing. Everything I brought from Bordeaux, I used to get here."

"Then why didn't you go to Jerome? We've had our differences, still he handles some of my finances."

"But the banks were all boarded up."

"There is absolutely no possibility that Jerome Libermann would leave Paris for anything as trivial as a siege, nor would he be caught short of money or supplies."

There was no dissuading Nathan. He had decided they were going to Chez Voisin and so they were going. Henri was dispatched to make the arrangements. No amount of argument from Solange that he was too weak, that the outing would overtax him, could change Nathan's mind. As far as he was concerned, he had awoken from a sleep that had been somewhat longer than he had expected.

As Solange dressed, Nathan began planning their departure from Paris. He'd been too long away from David, too long away from du

Clocher. Let someone else worry about affairs of state. He wanted to go home.

"I do, too," Solange said as she struggled with the formidable rows of buttons. "We're going to have to wait, though. It took several miracles and many bribes for me to get in. I don't know what it'll take to get out."

"A balloon," Nathan answered simply. "We won't go through the lines, we'll go over them. They've been floating messages in and out. Gambetta came in on one to reach the provisional government. We'll go out on one. There won't be a problem."

When Henri returned, with assurances from Monsieur Bernard that Nathan's favorite table would be ready for him, Solange was beginning to believe Nathan truly could accomplish anything. Her concern quickly returned, however, when it came time to dress him. He was far too weak to do it himself. Complaining loudly, he allowed Henri to bathe him. Then it took both Solange and the valet to get him in his clothes. He was so gaunt, so wasted, his pants had to be pinned to keep them on. Solange didn't think he would be able to sit up for an entire meal.

When it was time to leave, Henri announced he had hired two men to carry Nathan to the restaurant. Taking a carriage was out of the question. A hungry mob would rip the horses apart and carry off the carcasses. But Nathan would have none of the litter. He would walk, although he did have to accept the support of Solange and Henri's arms.

When they finally arrived at Chez Voisin and stepped into its romantically lit, warm interior, Solange felt they had been transported to a faraway dreamland where want and desperation were excluded. The fragrant smells that teased her nose almost made her faint with expectation.

"Baron Libermann, I am honored you could make it." Monsieur Bernard himself, probably the most renowned restaurateur in Paris and therefore the world, came hurrying up. Nathan had been one of his first customers and Bernard had never forgotten how the baron had brought his friends, sent others, thereby insuring that Chez Voisin became a success.

"Baroness, if you please, I will take your cloak." Solange held her wrap tightly, then smiled, abashed. Monsieur Bernard wasn't going to steal her cloak, and besides, it was warm here. She needn't be afraid. The restaurateur took the wrap as if he hadn't noticed the lapse and handed it to the maître d'. "Please, let me show you to your table."

It was by a large window from which the Seine and its idle barges could be seen.

"It's beautiful," Solange said solemnly to her husband.

"And it's Reveillon, so let's smile. This will mark the beginning of our best year, though every year with you has been wonderfully better than the last." Nathan picked up the glass of champagne that had miraculously materialized and saluted his wife. "And I love you more than I thought humanly possible. Now where is that menu?"

It was quite a different list than what usually appeared at Chez Voisin. Instead of wild boar, turkey, and duck, there was stewed kangaroo, camel roasted in the English style, and bear chops. The Jardin d'Acclimatation had no longer been able to feed the exotic animals. So they were slaughtered and their meat sold to exclusive restaurants.

Solange glanced around the room. It was as if she were the only sane person there, that she was the only one who realized what was happening outside the door and everyone else was intent on denying reality. But then, what was sanity? All she really knew was that this was the first time she had been truly warm in weeks.

Nathan seemed to know almost everyone in the restaurant, and they insisted on coming to the table to greet him. Their chit-chat never touched on the siege or the war. Far more important was speculation on which horse would win at Longchamp, asking after the Bordeaux vintage, when his next trip to Biarritz was planned, and on and on. Nathan, throughout it all, was outgoing and witty. To anyone else, he looked the picture of good health and spirits. Solange, however, could see he was tiring. After they'd finished dessert, she asked to go home.

"Impossible. It's not midnight yet."

"But I'm tired. I'd like to go."

"And we shall, my dear, we shall. As soon as midnight arrives and I greet the New Year in the appropriate way—kissing you."

When the hour was announced, a great clamor of joy and optimism rose throughout the restaurant. Nathan leaned across the table. Clasping Solange's hands, he kissed her with great love and tenderness. When he pulled back, he couldn't help wearily passing a hand over his eyes. "And now, my dear, I think it's time to go."

There was no question of the hired men carrying Nathan home. He was too weak to say "no" even if he had wanted to do so. Henri was sent to Jerome. Solange was sure the banker would know where to find a doctor.

Only an hour passed before Henri returned with the doctor. By then Nathan was in a profound, motionless sleep.

The doctor's examination was brief. Afterwards he led Solange a few steps from the bed.

"Madame, it is never easy for a doctor to say this..." he began.

"Please, tell me quickly and simply."

The doctor bowed his head. "Your husband will not live through the night. There is nothing I can do for him."

Solange nodded, tried to speak, but couldn't. The doctor left. When she turned back to the bed, Nathan was awake, his eyes so sunken and deep, watching her kindly.

She was horrified. "Did you hear?"

"Yes I did. But I didn't need a doctor to tell me I'm dying." Nathan spoke slowly and with difficulty. "I've lived a full life and these years with you have been happier than I could have dreamed of. My only regret in dying now is that I will be deprived of being with you longer."

"Please, don't speak. Save your strength. The doctor's wrong. He's got to be. You're going to get better."

"Come here, dear one. Sit by me." Solange did as he asked. "I am going to die, but before I do, there are things I must tell you, things you must know." Nathan closed his eyes. Solange hoped he might have fallen asleep. But with effort, he opened them again, determined to say what he must.

"These are things I should have told you long ago. But I was afraid. Afraid I might lose you. No, no, hear me out."

And so without looking at Solange, Nathan told of Jerome's boast he would get du Clocher, how Jerome had Guy's name included on the enemies' list. He told of his suspicions that Claude Mazet, burned to death in the chai fire that he had set, had been on Jerome's payroll, that Jerome had had Solange blacklisted for a loan.

"I had no way of stopping him. When he decides to do something, he will do it, no matter how long it takes or how many people he hurts. But when all his machinations and deceits led to our marrying, I couldn't help but rejoice. I loved you from the moment you fell down the stairs into my arms and, in a way, I loved you before that.

"There has been only one other woman in my life for whom I had feelings that even remotely came close to what I feel for you. It was not the same, though. There was no love or tenderness between us. It was need and blinding desire. Then Jerome put his mind to having her. Jerome used his money, his power, what she craved above all else. She left me for him. It was your mother. It was Fabienne."

"I always wondered how well you knew her. She's dead now. She died not long ago. I went to her to beg for money, and she denied me again, denied me by dying."

"Oh Solange, don't hate her. Pity her instead. She ended up a lonely, forgotten woman who snuck out at night to peer into the windows of property she owned."

Solange ran her hand over his brow. He was so hot. "All right, now you've told me," she said. "Now you rest. No more talking."

"No! No!" Nathan would not be stopped. "There's something else, more, the worst of all. The one thing in my life I've done that I'm truly ashamed of." He stopped to take deep, fortifying breaths of air. "You once asked me to do something for you, something you couldn't do yourself. You asked me to tell Thierry about the baby. I promised I would, I promised. But I never told him, Solange. He'd just gotten word about going abroad. He was happy. He was leaving. He wanted you to go with him. If I'd told him, I would have lost you. I would never have had David. I couldn't do it. Thierry left France never knowing. And now he's back. Maybe you two can be together at last—as you should have been."

Solange bit her lip. She would not—but she couldn't help it. Tears rolled from her eyes, tears held in for so many years, tears she had refused to shed so many times.

Seeing them, Nathan said, tortured, "I am so sorry, Solange. I am a selfish, miserable man who kept you from happiness."

"No, no, you're not selfish, not miserable. What you are, Nathan Libermann, is foolish. I never thought it possible I'd say that to you, ever. Still it's true. You are a fool. Why have you kept this to yourself all these years? Why have you tormented yourself with guilt? Don't you know, if given the choice, even back then, I would have stayed with you? It was you and always you. I thought you stayed with me out of pity and concern. I always worried about you sacrificing your life to help me. But I didn't release you, send you away. I loved you too much. And I love you so much now."

She kissed him, her tears mingling with his.

"You're right. I am a fool." They kissed again.

When at last they pulled apart, Nathan was visibly weakened by the ordeal of confession. Solange brushed damp strands of hair from his forehead. "Rest, dearest, rest," she pleaded. "You must get well."

"I am tired. But you must promise...promise me two things before I sleep."

"Of course, anything."

"First. You must go to Jerome for help. He's never hated you. It's been...between us, between brothers."

"But how can I? After what you've told me?"

"Hush, hush. You can. You will. I have a letter I wrote this evening, before we went out. It's in the drawer next to the bed. Give it to him. Do you promise?"

"Yes."

"Second, and more important, you must promise something for David. You must send him to university, make him travel...experience life. Then let him decide about du Clocher. I don't want it to be a burden, an obligation for my son as it was for you."

Solange knew he was right. Du Clocher had been her obsession and her cross. It shouldn't be their son's. She nodded her assent.

Nathan smiled. "I knew you'd understand. Now put on your nightclothes, then come back and lie with me. I want my arms around you, your sweet body close."

Solange awoke as the gray light of dawn pushed its way into the room. She turned to kiss Nathan.

Nathan was dead.

Chapter Sixty-three

Jerome Libermann received Solange in his library, seated behind his intimidating desk.

His household carried on quite untouched by the siege outside, and except for the absence of Rachel, who had decided an excursion to England was in order, it was life as usual.

Jerome studied Solange with undisguised curiosity. He had seen little of this woman with whom both his son and brother had been so enamored. She was very beautiful; still, Jerome sensed her attraction was far more than physical.

He broke off his thoughts to ask, "You have a purpose for this visit, baroness?"

Solange returned his stare coldly. "Your brother is dead. He asked me to give you this." She took out the letter from her beaded handbag and held it out to Jerome, who walked slowly around his desk to receive it.

He read it silently, displaying nothing. Without looking up, he said quietly, "So he told you, told you about my role at du Clocher. Well, I give you no apology or justification. It was between us, it was between brothers."

"That's what Nathan said, as well. But why did you stop? Why did you not continue to try and take it from me."

"Because of my son. He loved you, and he would have hated me if he'd found out. My son's feeling toward me took precedence over my feeling toward Nathan. Now what is it you need?"

Solange knew that was all the explanation she would ever get from Jerome Libermann and did not press for more. Instead she said, "I need to get Nathan's body out of Paris, back to Bordeaux. I will bury him there with his son's help."

Jerome started, momentarily puzzled, then he nodded. "Of course. His son. Nathan's son."

So he guessed about David, Solange thought. And Thierry.

As if reading her mind, Jerome added, "I will pass this letter to my son, as Nathan requested. And now, if you'll excuse me, I have some arrangements to make."

It was a lonely darkness into which the balloon rose the next morning, the loud swishing of its fire blotting out all other sounds, even the wind. Aloft, fires off, Solange held Nathan's swaddled body to hers, as they drifted away from Paris. A shot, and then another and another rang out far below them. The balloonist turned around, grinning. Those bastard Prussians couldn't hurt them, then he remembered what Solange was holding, and went back to his duties.

"You're going home, Nathan," she whispered. "You're coming home with me."

Epilogue

Chapter Sixty-four

1878

The tall, muscular man, with steel-gray streaking his hair, stared out beyond the fields below him. He didn't want to think about the devastation that was there.

It was not the charred remains of the once stately mansion and the regal belltower that he didn't want to see. They had burned down that terrible morning of the raid years before, burned down when a vindictive wind had suddenly blasted up and pushed the flames from the workers' cabins toward the main house and tower.

When Old House had been threatened, Guy Saint-Savin had put all efforts toward saving it. He let Ardis's follies be destroyed, and he had left them to rot and return to earth.

No, evidence of that devastation he no longer noticed. It was what he could see in the fields that he couldn't stand. So he looked out over the valley, waiting for a rider to come galloping into sight.

He was waiting for Kyle to get back from the agricultural college at Davis, where Hugh was now studying. But Guy's excitement at Kyle's return was not to receive news about his youngest son. Kyle was bringing back first word of experiments Davis scientists were conducting, experiments that might possibly save the whole valley below him.

Guy frowned. He hated waiting. And there was still no sign of
Kyle, so he forced himself to go to the vines and once again look at
the disheartening destruction there.

A terrible plague had hit California, plague in the form of a louse, a
miserable little bug that lived on the roots and sometimes the leaves
of the vine and was ravishing the vineyards.

Guy bent down to examine one of the infected plants. The grapes
were small and colorless. The leaves were already turning yellow, far
earlier than they should have. Guy shook his head in disgust. There
had better be good news from Davis or there would be no more wine
in the Napa Valley.

He stood up and looked at the sun. It was time for lunch. He
walked to Old House and into its kitchen. A woman was bending over
the stove. He tiptoed up behind her and kissed the nape of her neck.
She spun around laughing, and returned his kiss.

"Now, why don't you sit down and behave yourself?" asked Fenella.
"I'll bring your lunch in a second."

Guy was happy to establish himself at the large scarred, wooden
table, and to watch Fenella bustle about. She still walked stiffly as a
result of the bullet that tore through her the morning of the raid. But
that slight limp was the only evidence that remained of her wound,
although it had taken her months to recover.

During that time, Miguel had been brought to trial for the murder
of Damon and Ardis. He had waited patiently in the bedroom until a
maid, the next morning, found him there with the bodies, and ran
screaming for help. There had been much gossip and head-shaking
when Guy had hired Jefferson Simpson to defend Miguel, the
accused murderer of his wife. But not even the skilled Simpson could
save Miguel. It was impossible when the defendant would not defend
himself. He was indifferent to whether he lived or died. On the night
before his execution, Miguel had confided in Guy that he had only
been living for his father's revenge, and once Damon was dead, there
was no further purpose for existence.

Miguel added he regretted not living a little longer for only one
reason.

"What was that?" Guy had asked.

"I would have liked to have seen it when you and Fenella marry."
When Guy looked stunned, Miguel said, "You love each other,
though you don't know it. It's time you were together. You're both
good people and you'll make each other happy. Except for that, I'm
ready to die."

After Fenella recovered, Guy had related this conversation to her.

"I guess Miguel had some funny ideas at the end," Guy said when he was finished. Fenella made no response and the subject was dropped.

One night, not long afterwards, Fenella was on the porch, leaning against a column. Her back was hurting her. She was looking at the stars, trying to take her mind off the pain, when she lost her balance and fell. Guy heard her and rushed out of the house.

"Are you all right?" he asked frantically. "What happened?" Not waiting for an answer, he picked her up and carried her to her bed.

"Should I get a doctor?" he asked anxiously after carefully putting her down. Then he looked at her. Her hair was fanned across the pillow, her eyes were so dark and vulnerable. She stretched her arms to him, and he reached out to her.

The next morning Guy crept from Fenella's bedroom so the boys would not find where he had spent the night. He dressed and rode into Napa. By lunch he was back—with a ring.

Two days later Guy and Fenella were married with two ecstatic boys in attendance.

As Guy watched his wife bring the food to the table—she would never let him help—he thought, for all that had happened, how lucky he had been. He and Fenella had entwined and become one, sharing and trusting and loving. His life had been charmed and right after marrying Fenella.

He sighed. Well, they would ride this new calamity out as well. They would not give into this phylloxera, they would do whatever they had to beat it back.

Damn! He wished Kyle would return with news from Davis. And it had better be good.

Chapter Sixty-five

The tall woman stared out at the fields below her searching for some sign of hope. The devastated vines offered her none.

Solange knew that sooner or later she would have to make a decision, and there seemed little doubt what that would be. The phylloxera louse, that miserable little bug, had spread through du Clocher and the rest of the Medoc and there was no checking it. In one respect she was glad Jacques Mazet had not lived to see this. And she was glad that Harry Busscher had accumulated enough money over the years that he no longer had to depend on wine to live.

Oh, she knew she should sell the château. She really had little alternative—and truthfully, she had little reason to keep it.

Solange had kept her promise to Nathan about David. She gave the boy a world beyond du Clocher. Now that he was an adult, she feared the château had lost him forever. And Guy? Guy had a life and a world in California. What was du Clocher to him anymore?

So why was she holding on? Thierry Libermann had asked her the same question several weeks ago. Thierry had been visiting with his wife and children. Despite Nathan's hopes, they had never been reunited as lovers. She hadn't wanted that—she had never wanted another man after Nathan. She and Thierry did become friends; good enough friends that he, despite his suspicions, never questioned her about David. He accepted that David was his uncle's son and he wished to know no more.

Solange hadn't been able to answer Thierry when he asked her why she didn't sell. It hadn't only been David who had found there was more than du Clocher in life. She had traveled with him, met new friends, and had kept Nathan's mansion in Paris, which she visited frequently. So why did she keep du Clocher? For all the old reasons—for tradition, family, memories, to keep a promise? The old reasons didn't seem so important anymore. And frankly, she was tired. Maybe it was time for someone else to take over, someone with the energy for the triumphs and the heartbreaks. Maybe it was time to sell.

She was so preoccupied that she was unaware someone had joined her on the hill.

"You've been hard hit, haven't you."

She froze. That voice was so familiar and yet so foreign. No, it couldn't be, she had to be dreaming. She was afraid to turn around, but when she did, she didn't see the gray hair or the lines on the face or the slight stoop of age. All she could see was her brother, her brother just as he was twenty-eight years before, her brother whom she thought she would never again see this side of the grave.

"*Guy!*" She was in his arms and sobbing.

"It's all right, Solange, it's all right. I'm back and I've brought you something, something to save du Clocher. Please, Solange, stop crying. Please. Oh, I know I should have written, but I wanted to surprise you. Now, come on. Come back to the château, my wife is waiting for us. I'll show you what I've brought. They're cuttings, Solange, they're cuttings. We've discovered that if you graft European vines onto native American roots, the Catawba, the Concord, you can beat the phylloxera. Come, I'll show you."

Solange was too stunned to speak. She followed him silently up the hill, pausing once to look back over the fields.

She didn't feel so tired anymore.

She once again had hope.